Praise for

MAGGIE
STIEFVATER

Best Book to Curl Up With

Glamour

"If you are a fan of *Twilight*,
then you will love *Shiver*"

Waterstone's Books Quarterly

"A magnificent and haunting love story"

Youngscot.org

"Literary methadone ... all-consuming"

Sunday Telegraph

"This bittersweet tale had the publishing
world buzzing"

Glamour

"Full of deliciously illicit, star-crossed love"

Financial Times

Also by Maggie Stiefvater

The Raven Boys
The Dream Thieves
Blue Lily, Lily Blue

The Scorpio Races

Shiver
Linger
For ever
Sinner

Lament: The Faerie Queen's Deception
Ballad: A Gathering of Faerie

THE RAVEN KING

MAGGIE STIEFVATER

SCHOLASTIC

For Sarah, who gallantly took the Seat Perilous

Scholastic Children's Books
An imprint of Scholastic Ltd
Euston House, 24 Eversholt Street, London, NW1 1DB, UK
Registered office: Westfield Road, Southam, Warwickshire, CV47 0RA
SCHOLASTIC and associated logos are trademarks and/or
registered trademarks of Scholastic Inc.

First published in the US by Scholastic Inc., 2016
First published in the UK by Scholastic Ltd, 2016

ISBN 978 1407 13664 6

A CIP catalogue record for this book
is available from the British Library.

Printed by CPI Group (UK) Ltd, Croydon, CR0 4YY
Papers used by Scholastic Children's Books are made
from wood grown in sustainable forests.

3 5 7 9 10 8 6 4 2

www.scholastic.co.uk

www.maggiestiefvater.com

To sleep, to swim, and to dream, for ever

— ALGERNON CHARLES SWINBURNE,
"A SWIMMERS DREAM"

These signs have mark'd me extraordinary;
and all the courses of my life do show
I am not in the roll of common men

— WILLIAM SHAKESPEARE,
HENRY IV

Darling, the composer has stepped into fire.

— ANNE SEXTON,
"THE KISS"

PROLOGUE

Richard Gansey III had forgotten how many times he had been told he was destined for greatness.

He was bred for it; nobility and purpose coded in both sides of his pedigree. His mother's father had been a diplomat, an architect of fortunes; his father's father had been an architect, a diplomat of styles. His mother's mother had tutored the children of European princesses. His father's mother had built a girls' school with her own inheritance. The Ganseys were courtiers and kings, and when there was no castle to invite them, they built one.

He was a king.

Once upon a time, the youngest Gansey had been stung to death by hornets. In all things, he had been given every advantage, and mortality was no different. A voice had whispered in his ear: *You will live because of Glendower. Someone else on the ley line is dying when they should not, and so you will live when you should not.*

He'd died, but failed to stay dead.

He was a king.

His mother, royalty herself, tossed her hat into the Virginia congressional ring, and unsurprisingly she'd ascended elegantly to the top of the polls. Onward and upward. Had there ever been any doubt? Yes, actually, always, ever, because the Ganseys did not demand favours. Often they didn't even ask. They did unto others and silently hoped others would rise to do it unto them.

Doubt – all a Gansey did was doubt. A Gansey reached bravely into the night-blind water, fate uncertain until the hilt of a sword pressed into a hopeful palm.

Except – only a few months before, this Gansey had reached into the dark uncertainty of the future, stretching for the promise of a sword, and had instead pulled out a mirror.

Justice – in an inside-out way, it felt fair.

It was April 25, St. Mark's Eve. Years before, Gansey had read *The Grand Mystery: Ley Lines of the World* by Roger Malory. In it, Malory explained ponderously that a St. Mark's Eve vigil on the ley line would reveal the spirits of those who were to die within the next year. By this point, Gansey had seen all sorts of wonders performed near or on the ley lines – a girl who could read a book in full dark so long as she was on the line, an old woman who could lift a crate of fruit with only her mind, a trio of dusky-skinned triplets born on the line who cried tears of blood and bled salt water – but none of it had involved him. Required him. Explained him.

He didn't know why he'd been saved.

He needed to know why he'd been saved.

So he held a nightlong vigil on the ley line that had become his maze, shivering alone in the parking lot of the Holy Redeemer. He saw nothing, heard nothing. The following morning he crouched beside his Camaro, tired to the point of nonsense, and played back the night's audio.

On the recording, his own voice whispered, "Gansey." A pause. "That's all there is."

2

Finally, it was happening. He was no longer merely an observer in this world; he was a participant.

Even then, a small part of Gansey suspected what hearing his own name really meant. He knew it, probably, by the time his friends came to his car's rescue an hour later. He knew it, probably, when the psychics at 300 Fox Way read a tarot card for him. He knew it, probably, when he retold the entire story to Roger Malory in person.

Gansey knew whose voices whispered along the ley line on St. Mark's Eve. But he had spent several years chaining his fears and wasn't ready to unhook their leashes just yet.

It wasn't until one of the psychics at 300 Fox Way died, until death became a real thing once more, that Gansey couldn't deny the truth any longer.

The hounds of the Aglionby Hunt Club howled it that fall: *away, away, away.*

He was a king.

This was the year he was going to die.

ONE

Depending on where you began the story, it was a story about the women of 300 Fox Way.

Stories stretch in all ways. Once upon a time, there was a girl who was very good at playing with time. Step sideways: Once upon a time, there was a daughter of a girl who was very good at playing with time. Now skip back: Once upon a time, there was a king's daughter who was very good at playing with time.

Beginnings and endings as far as the eye could see.

With the notable exception of Blue Sargent, all of the women at 300 Fox Way were psychic. This might have suggested that the house's occupants had much in common, but practically, they had as much in common as a group of musicians, or doctors, or morticians. *Psychic* was not so much a personality type as a skill set. A belief system. A general agreement that time, like a story, was not a line; it was an ocean. If you couldn't find the precise moment you were looking for, it was possible you hadn't swum far enough. It was possible that you simply weren't a good enough swimmer yet. It was also possible, the women grudgingly agreed, that some moments were hidden far enough in time that they really should be left to deep-sea creatures. Like those anglerfish with all the teeth bits and the lanterns hanging off their faces. Or like Persephone Poldma. She was dead now, though, so perhaps she was a poor example.

It was a Monday when the still-living women of 300 Fox Way decided to finally assess Richard Gansey's impending doom, the disintegration of their lives as they knew them, and what those two things had to do with each other, if anything. Also, Jimi had done a chakra cleansing in exchange for a nice bottle of hot, peaty whiskey and was jonesing to finish it with company.

Calla stepped into the biting October day to turn the sign beside the letter box to read CLOSED COME BACK SOON! Inside, Jimi, a big believer in herb magick, brought out several small pillows stuffed with mugwort (to enhance the projection of the soul into other planes) and set rosemary to burn over charcoal (for memory and clairvoyance, which are the same thing in two different directions). Orla shook a smouldering bundle of sage over the tarot decks. Maura filled a black-glass scrying bowl. Gwenllian sang a gleeful, nasty little song as she lit a circle of candles and let the blinds down. Calla returned to the reading room with three statues cradled in the crook of her arm.

"It smells like a goddamn Italian restaurant in here," she told Jimi, who did not pause in her humming as she fanned the smoke and wiggled her large bottom. Calla placed the ferocious statue of Oya by her own chair and the dancing statue of Oshun next to Maura's. She gripped the third statue: Yemaya, a watery Yoruban goddess who had always stood beside Persephone's place when she wasn't standing, on Calla's bedroom dresser. "Maura, I don't know where to put Yemaya."

Maura pointed to Gwenllian, who pointed back. "You said you didn't want to do this with Adam, so it goes by her."

"I never said that," Calla said. "I said he was too close to all this."

The fact of the matter was that they were all too close to the situation. They'd been too close to the situation for months. They were so close to the situation that it was difficult to tell whether or not they were the situation.

Orla stopped chomping her gum for a moment long enough to ask, "Are we ready?"

"MmmmhmmmhmmmmissBluethoughmmmmhmmmm," offered Jimi, still humming and swaying.

It was true that Blue's absence was notable. As a powerful psychic amplifier, she would've been useful in a case like this, but they'd agreed in whispers the night before that it was cruel to discuss Gansey's fate in front of her any more than was strictly necessary. They'd make do with Gwenllian, even though she was half as powerful and twice as difficult.

"We'll tell her the upshot later," Maura said. "I think I had better get Artemus out of the pantry."

Artemus: Maura's ex-lover, Blue's biological father, Glendower's adviser, 300 Fox Way's closet dweller. He had been retrieved from a magical cave just a little over a week before and in that time had managed to contribute absolutely nothing to their emotional or intellectual resources. Calla found him spineless (she was not wrong). Maura thought him misunderstood (she was not wrong). Jimi reckoned he had the longest nose of any man she'd ever seen (she was not wrong). Orla didn't believe barricading oneself in a supply closet was a sufficient protection against a psychic who hated you (she was not wrong). Gwenllian was, in fact, the psychic who hated him (she was not wrong).

It took Maura quite a bit of doing to persuade him to leave the pantry, and even after he'd joined them at the table, he did not look at all like he belonged. Some of that was because he was a man, and some of it was because he was much taller than everyone else. But most of it was because he had dark, permanently worried eyes that indicated he had seen the world and it was too much for him. That earnest fear was entirely at odds with the varying degrees of self-confidence carried by the psychics in the room.

Maura and Calla had known him before Blue had been born and both were thinking that Artemus was ever so much less than he had been then. Well, Maura thought *ever so much less*. Calla merely thought *less*, as she hadn't had a very high opinion of him to begin with. But then, lanky men who appeared out of mystical groves had never been her type.

Jimi poured the whiskey.

Orla closed the doors to the reading room.

The women sat.

"What a cluster," Calla said, by way of opening (she was not wrong).

"He can't be saved, can he?" Jimi asked. She meant Gansey. She was a little misty-eyed. It was not that she was intensely fond of Gansey, but she was a very sentimental person, and the idea of any young man being cut down in his youth troubled her.

"Mm," said Maura.

The women all took a drink. Artemus did not. He shot a nervous look at Gwenllian. Gwenllian, always imposing with a nest of towering hair full of pencils and flowers, glared back at him. The heat in her expression should have ignited any alcohol remaining in her shot glass.

Maura asked, "Do we need to stop it, then?"

Orla, the youngest and loudest in the room, laughed in a youthful and loud way. "How exactly would you stop him?"

"I said *it*, not *him*," Maura replied, rather snottily. "I would not pretend to imagine I have any power to stop that boy from searching Virginia for his own grave. But the others."

Calla put her glass down with force. "Oh, I could stop him. But that's not the point. It's everything already in place."

(Everything already in place: the retired hit man currently sleeping with Maura; his supernatural-obsessed ex-boss currently sleeping in Boston; the creepy entity buried in rocks beneath the ley line; the unfamiliar creatures crawling out of a cave mouth behind an abandoned farmhouse; the ley line's growing power; the magical sentient forest on the ley line; one boy's bargain with the magical forest; one boy's ability to dream things to life; one dead boy who refused to be laid to rest; one girl who supernaturally amplified 90 per cent of the aforementioned list.)

The women took another drink.

"Should they keep going to that crazy forest?" Orla asked. She did not care for Cabeswater. She had gone with the group once before and had come close enough to the forest to . . . feel it. Her sort of clairvoyance was best over telephone lines or email; faces only got in the way of the truth. Cabeswater had no face, and the ley line was basically the world's best telephone line. She had been able to feel it asking her for things. She couldn't tell what they were, exactly. And she didn't necessarily think they were bad things. She could just sense the enormity of its requests, the weight of its promises. Life-changing. Orla was just fine with her life, thanks very much, so she'd tipped her hat and got out of there.

"The forest is fine," Artemus said.

All of the women looked at him.

"Describe 'fine,'" Maura said.

"Cabeswater loves them." Artemus folded his enormous hands in his lap and pointed his enormous nose at them. His gaze kept jerking back to Gwenllian, as if he feared she might leap at him. Gwenllian meaningfully snuffed one of the candles with her shot glass; the reading room got one tiny fire darker.

"Care to elaborate?" Calla asked.

Artemus did not.

Maura said, "We'll take that opinion under advisement."

The women took a drink.

"Is any of us in this room going to die?" Jimi asked. "Did anyone else we know appear at the church watch?"

"Doesn't apply to any of us," Maura said. The church watch generally only predicted the deaths of those who had been born in the town or directly on the spirit road (or, in Gansey's case, *re*born), and everyone currently at the table was an import.

"Applies to Blue, though," Orla pointed out.

Maura aggressively stacked and restacked her cards. "But it's not a guarantee of safety. There are fates worse than death."

"Let's shuffle, then," said Jimi.

Each woman held her tarot deck to her heart, shuffled, and then selected a single card at random. They placed the cards faceup on the table.

Tarot is a very personal thing, and as such, the art on each deck reflected the woman who owned it. Maura's was all dark lines and simple colours, at once perfunctory and childlike. Calla's was lush and oversaturated, the cards overflowing with detail. Every card in Orla's deck featured a couple kissing or making love, whether or not the card's meaning was about kissing or making love. Gwenllian had fashioned her own by scratching dark, frantic symbols on a deck of ordinary playing cards. Jimi stuck by the Sacred Cats and Holy Women deck that she'd found in a thrift store in 1992.

All of the women had turned over five different versions of the Tower. Calla's version of the Tower perhaps best depicted the card's meaning: A castle labelled STABILITY was in the process of being struck by lightning, burning down, and being attacked by what looked like garter snakes. A woman in a window was experiencing the full effects of the lightning bolt. At the top of the tower, a man had been thrown from the ramparts – or possibly he had jumped. In any case, he was on fire as well, and a snake flew after him.

"So we're all going to die unless we do something," Calla said.

Gwenllian sang, "*Owynus dei gratia Princeps Waliae*, ha la la, *Princeps Waliae*, ha la la—"

With a whimper, Artemus made as if to stand. Maura placed a steadying hand on his.

"We're all going to die," Maura said. "At some point. Let's not panic."

Calla's eyes were on Artemus. "Only one of us is panicking."

Jimi passed around the whiskey bottle. "Time to find some solutions, darlings. How are we looking for them?"

All of the women looked at the dark scrying bowl. There was nothing inherently remarkable about it: it was an $11 glass display bowl from one of those stores full of cat food, mulch and discount electronics. The cran-grape juice that filled it had no mystical powers. But still, there was something ominous about it, about how the fluid seemed a little restless. It reflected only the dark ceiling, but it looked like it wanted to show more. The scrying bowl contemplated possibilities, not all of them good.

(One of the possibilities: using the reflection to separate your soul from your body and ending up dead.)

Although Maura was the one who had brought the bowl out, she pushed it away now.

"Let's do a whole-life reading," Orla said. She popped her gum.

"Ugh, no," Calla said.

"For all of us?" Maura asked, as if Calla hadn't protested. "Our life as a group?"

Orla waved an arm to indicate all of the decks; her enormous wooden bangles clicked against each other with satisfaction.

"I like it," Maura said. Calla and Jimi sighed.

Ordinarily, a reading used only a portion of the seventy-eight cards in a deck. Three, or ten. Maybe one or two more, if clarification was needed. Each card's position asked a question: What is the state of your unconscious? What are you afraid of? What do you need? Each card placed in that position provided the answer.

Seventy-eight cards was a lot of Q&A.

Especially times five.

Calla and Jimi sighed again, but began to shuffle. Because it was true: They had a lot of questions. And they needed a lot of answers.

As one, the women stopped shuffling, closed their eyes, and held their decks to their hearts, focusing only on each other and the way that their lives were twined together. The candles flickered. Long and short and then long shadows played behind the goddess sculptures. Gwenllian hummed, and after a moment, Jimi did as well.

Only Artemus sat apart, brows furrowed.

But the women included him when they began to lay out the cards. First they braided a row of cards into a solid trunk, whispering positions and meanings to each other as they did. Then they laid out cards in branches that pointed to Artemus, to Jimi, to Orla. And they laid out cards in roots that pointed to Calla, to Maura, to Gwenllian. They knocked heads and laid cards over the top of each other and laughed over their bumbles and gasped over the order of the cards.

Eventually a story appeared. It was about the people they had changed, and the people who'd changed them. The reading included all the juicy bits: when Maura had fallen in love with Artemus; when Jimi had punched Calla; when Orla had secretly drained the common bank account for a business website that had yet to make money; when Blue had run away from home and been dragged home by the cops; when Persephone had died.

The branch that led to Artemus was grim and rotten, littered with swords and fear. The darkness in it led back to the trunk, joining up with something sinister mouldering in the root that belonged to Gwenllian. It was obvious that this darkness would be what killed them all if they did nothing, though it was impossible to tell what precisely it was. The women's clairvoyance had never been able to penetrate the area directly over the ley line, and this darkness was centred there.

The solution to the darkness, however, existed outside of the ley line. It was multifaceted, uncertain and difficult. The upshot was straightforward, though.

"They're supposed to work together?" Calla said with disbelief.

"That's what it says," Maura said.

Jimi reached for the whiskey bottle, but it was empty. "Can't we just take care of it ourselves?"

"We're just people," Maura replied. "Just ordinary people. They're special. Adam's tied to the ley line. Ronan's a dreamer. Blue amplifies all of that."

"Richie Rich is just a person," Orla said.

"Yes, and he's going to die."

The women contemplated the spread again.

"Does this mean she's still alive?" Maura asked, tapping on a card in one of the branches — the Queen of Swords.

"Probably," Calla grunted.

"Does this mean she's going to leave?" Orla asked, tapping on another card and referring to a different she.

"Probably," Maura sighed.

"Does this mean she's coming back?" Calla demanded, pointing to a third card and meaning a third she.

"Probably," shrieked Gwenllian, leaping up from the table. She began to spin with her arms in the air.

None of them could sit still any longer. Calla pushed back her chair. "I'm getting another drink."

Jimi clucked in agreement. "If it's the end of the world, I might as well, too."

As the others left the table, Maura remained, looking at Artemus's poisoned branch of cards and at Artemus himself, hunched behind it. Random men from mystical groves were no longer her type. But still, she remembered loving Artemus, and this Artemus was greatly diminished.

"Artemus?" she asked gently.

He didn't lift his head.

She touched his chin with a finger; he flinched. She tilted his face up so that they were eye to eye. He had never rushed to fill spaces with words, and he still didn't. He looked as if he might never speak again, if he could help it.

Since they had both climbed out of the cave, Maura had not asked him about anything that had happened in the years since she'd seen him last. But now she asked, "What happened to you to make you like this?"

He closed his eyes.

TWO

"Where the hell is Ronan?" Gansey asked, echoing the words that thousands of humans had uttered since mankind developed speech. As he stepped out of the science building, he tipped his head backwards, as if Ronan Lynch — dreamer of dreams, fighter of men, skipper of classes — might somehow be flying overhead. He was not. There was only a plane tracing silently through the deep blue above the Aglionby campus. On the other side of the iron fence beside them, the town of Henrietta made productive afternoon business noises. On this side, the students of Aglionby made unproductive afternoon teenage noises. "Was he in Technology?"

Adam Parrish — magician and puzzle, student and logician, man and boy — shuffled his ambitiously laden messenger bag on to his other shoulder. He saw no reason why Gansey would believe Ronan had been anywhere near the campus. It was taking all of Adam's willpower to focus on Aglionby after the week of magical caves and mysterious sleepers they'd just had, and Adam was the most motivated student there. Ronan, on the other hand, had only shown up to Latin with any regularity, and now that every Latin student had been ignominiously shunted into an extra section of French, what was left for him?

"Was he?" repeated Gansey.

"I thought it was a rhetorical question."

Gansey looked angry for approximately the length of time it took for a late butterfly to bluster by them in the autumn breeze. "He's not even trying."

It had been over one week since they'd retrieved Maura — Blue's mother — and Artemus — Blue's . . . father? — from the cave system. Three days since they had put Roger Malory — Gansey's ancient British friend — on a plane back to the UK. Two days back at school this week.

Zero days of Ronan attendance.

Was it a foul waste? Yes. Was it entirely Ronan Lynch's responsibility? Yes.

Behind them, the bell rang noisily in the science building, two minutes after the period had actually ended. It was a proper bell with a proper rope, and it was supposed to be rung properly at the end of the period by a proper student. The two-minute disparity prematurely aged Adam Parrish. He liked it when people knew how to do their jobs.

"Say something," Gansey said.

"That bell."

"Everything is terrible," agreed Gansey.

The two friends stepped off the walk to make the trek across the sports fields. It was a gift, this commute from the science building to Gruber Hall, ten luxurious minutes gulping air and sunshine between classes. Being on campus in general comforted Adam; the predictable routine cradled him. Study hard. Go to class. Hold up your hand. Answer the question. March towards graduation. Other classmates complained about the work. Work! Work was the island Adam swam to in a stormy sea.

And the sea was very stormy. Monsters churned in the ley line beneath them. A forest grew through the hands and eyes Adam had bargained away to Cabeswater. And Gansey was supposed to die before April. That was the troubled ocean – Glendower was the island. To wake him was to get a favour, and that favour *would* be to save Gansey's life. This enchanted country needed an enchanted king.

That weekend, Adam had dreamt twice that they had already found Glendower and were now seeking him again. The first night he'd had the dream, it had been a nightmare. The second time, a relief.

He asked carefully, "What's next for the Glendower search?"

"The Dittley cave," Gansey said.

This answer startled Adam. Ordinarily Gansey favoured the cautious approach, and the Dittley cave was the opposite. For starters, after they pulled Glendower's daughter Gwenllian out of it, strange animals had begun crawling from the mouth every so often. And for finishers, Piper Greenmantle had shot Jesse Dittley dead at its entrance. Everything about the cave reeked of past and future death. "You don't think Gwenllian would've told us if she thought her father was further down in that cave, instead of having us wander the cave of bones?"

"I think Gwenllian serves her own purpose," Gansey replied. "And I have yet to figure out what it might be."

"I just don't think it's a reasonable risk. Plus, it's a crime scene."

If Ronan had been there, he would have said, *Everywhere's a crime scene.*

Gansey said, "Does this mean you have different ideas?"

Ideas, plural? Adam would have been happy to have a single idea. The most promising way forward, a cave in Cabeswater, had collapsed during their last excursion, and no new opportunities had appeared to replace it. Gansey had observed that it felt like a test of worthiness, and Adam couldn't help but agree. Cabeswater had assigned them a trial, they'd set themselves at it, and somehow they'd been found wanting. It had felt so *right*, though. He and Ronan had worked together to clear the cave of hazards, and then the entire group had pooled their talents to briefly revive the skeletons of an ancient herd that had led Ronan and Blue to Maura. Every night since then, Adam had relived that memory before he went to sleep. Ronan's dreams, Adam focusing the ley line, Blue amplifying, Gansey speaking the entire plan into motion. Adam had never felt so . . . *intrinsic* before. They had been a fine machine.

But it hadn't taken them to Glendower.

Adam suggested, "Talk more to Artemus?"

Gansey made a *hm* sound. It would have been pessimistic coming from anyone but was doubly so coming from him. "I don't think we'll have a problem talking *to* Artemus. It's getting him to talk back I'm worried about."

"I thought you always said you were persuasive," Adam said.

"Experience has not proven this to be the case."

"Gansey Boy!" shouted a voice across the fields. Whitman, one of Gansey's old rowing teammates, lifted three fingers in salute. Gansey didn't respond until Adam lightly touched his shoulder with the back of his hand. Gansey blinked up, and then his face transformed into his Richard Campbell Gansey III smile. What a treasure that smile was, passed down through the ages from father to son, tucked away in hope chests during son-less generations, buffed and displayed proudly whenever company was over.

"Sitwhit," Gansey called back, his old Southern accent rolling generously through the vowels. "You left your keys in the door!"

Laughing, Whitman zipped up his fly. He loped up beside them, and he and Gansey fell into some effortless conversation. A moment later, two more boys had joined them, then two more again. They bantered lightly back and forth, buoyant and youthful and convivial, advertisements for clean living and good education.

This was a master class that Adam had never got good at, although he'd spent months in dedicated study. He analysed Gansey's mannerisms, dissected the other boys' reactions, and catalogued dialogue patterns. He watched how an easy gesture unfolded a bouquet of mannish conversation, elegant as a magic trick. He took careful note of the behind-the-scenes footage: how a miserable Gansey could become a hospitable one in just a moment. But he could never work out the practicum. Warm greetings iced in his mouth. Casual gestures became dismissive. A steady eye contact turned into an unnerving stare.

He'd retaken the class each quarter, but he thought, incred-ibly, maybe there were some skills even Adam Parrish couldn't pick up.

"Where's Parrish?" asked Engle.

"He's right there," Gansey replied.

"Don't know how I missed the wind off the glacier," Engle said. "What's up, man?"

It was a rhetorical question, answerable by a lightly painted smile. The boys were here for Gansey. Where's Parrish? In a place too far away to hike to in a day.

Once upon a time, this dynamic would have unsettled Adam. Threatened him. But now he was certain in his place as one of Gansey's two favourites, so he merely put his hands in his pockets and walked quietly alongside the rest.

Suddenly, Adam *felt* Gansey tense beside him. The others were still hooting and laughing, but Gansey's expression had gone pensive. Adam followed his gaze to the great columns that held up the roof of Gruber Hall. Headmaster Child stood at the top of the stairs between them, a textbook or something similar in hand. He was a leathery bird of a man, a hearty recommendation for sunscreen and broad-brimmed hats.

"All right, gentlemen," he called. "I could hear you from my office. Are we conducting ourselves like ravens? Class awaits."

Fist bumps were exchanged; hair was scrubbed; shoulders were knocked. The other boys dispersed; Gansey and Adam remained. Child lifted a hand to Gansey in a sort of wave before ducking into the offices of Gruber Hall.

Again Gansey looked angry, and then he looked nothing at all. He resumed his walk to class.

"What was that?" Adam asked.

Gansey pretended not to have heard as they climbed the stairs Child had just stood on.

"Gansey. What was that about?"

"What?"

"The hand. Child."

"It's friendly."

It was not unlike the world to be friendlier to Gansey than to Adam, but it was unlike Headmaster Child. "Tell me you won't tell me, but don't tell me a lie."

Gansey made a big fuss over tucking in his uniform shirt and pulling down his sweater. He didn't look at Adam. "I don't want to fight."

Adam made an educated guess. "Ronan."

Gansey's eyes went to him furtively and back to his sweater.

"No way," Adam said. "What. No. You didn't."

He didn't know exactly what he was accusing Gansey of. Just – he knew what Gansey wanted for Ronan, and he knew how Gansey got things.

"I don't want to fight," Gansey repeated.

He reached for the door; Adam put his hand on it, preventing him.

"Look around you. Do you see Ronan? He doesn't care. You stuffing it down his throat isn't going to make him hungry."

"I don't want to fight."

Gansey was saved by a buzzing from his person; his phone was ringing. Technically they were not meant to take calls during the school day, but he retrieved the phone and twisted the face so that Adam could see it. Two things struck Adam: First of all, the call said it was from Gansey's mother, which it probably was, and secondly, Gansey's phone said it was 6:21, which it definitely wasn't.

Adam's position changed subtly, no longer blocking Gansey from entering Gruber but rather pressing a hand to the door to act as a lookout.

Gansey put the phone to his ear. "Hello? Oh. Mom, I'm in

school. No, the weekend was yesterday. No. Of course. No, just go quickly."

As Gansey spoke to the phone, Cabeswater beckoned to Adam, offering to support his tired form, and for just a minute, he allowed it. For a few effortless breaths, everything was leaves and water, trunks and roots, rocks and moss. The ley line hummed inside him, waxing and waning with his pulse, or vice versa. Adam could tell that the forest needed to tell him something, but he couldn't quite work out what it was. He needed to scry after school or find the time to actually go to the forest.

The phone was hung up, put away. Gansey said, "She wanted to know if I liked the idea of holding a last-minute campaign thing here on campus this weekend. If Raven Day would conflict, if it would be OK to run it by Child. I said that — well, you heard what I said."

Actually, Adam had not. He had been listening to Cabeswater. In fact, he was still listening to it so intently that when it suddenly and unexpectedly swayed, he swayed, too. Unnerved, he snatched at the doorknob to ground himself.

The hum of the energy had vanished inside him.

Adam barely had time to wonder what had happened and whether the energy would return when the ley line mumbled to life inside him again. Leaves unfurled in the back of his mind. He released the doorknob.

"What was that?" Gansey asked.

"What?" Adam, a little breathless, nonetheless mimicked Gansey's earlier tone almost precisely.

"Don't be an ass. What happened?"

What had happened was someone had just docked an enormous amount of power from the ley line. Enough that it had made even Cabeswater catch its breath. In Adam's limited experience, there were only a few things that could make that happen.

As the energy slowly clocked back up to speed, he told Gansey, "I'm pretty sure I know what Ronan's doing."

THREE

That morning, Ronan Lynch had woken early, without any alarm, thinking *home, home, home.*

He'd left Gansey still sleeping — his phone clutched in a hand and his wireframes folded in slumber a few inches away on the mattress — and crept down the stairs with his raven pressed against his chest to keep her quiet. Outside, overgrown grass lapped dew on Ronan's boots, and mist curled around the tyres of the charcoal BMW. The sky over Monmouth Manufacturing was the colour of a muddy lake. It was cold, but Ronan's gasoline heart was firing. He settled into the car, letting it become his skin. The night air was still coiled beneath the seats and lurking in the door pockets; he shivered as he tethered his raven to the seat belt fastener in the passenger seat. Not the fanciest setup, but effective for keeping a corvid from flapping around one's sports car. Chainsaw bit him, but not as hard as the early morning cold.

"Hand me my jacket, turd?" he told the bird. She just pecked experimentally at the window controls, so he got it himself. His Aglionby jacket was back there, too, hopelessly crumpled beneath the language puzzle box, a dream object that translated several languages, including an imaginary one, into English. When was he going to school again? Ever? He thought he might officially quit tomorrow. This week. Next week. What was stopping him? Gansey. Declan. His father's memory.

It was a twenty-five-minute drive to Singer's Falls even at this hour of the morning, but it was still well before dawn when he passed through the nonexistent town and finally arrived at the Barns. Briars and branches and trees closed around the car as it tunneled down the half-mile drive. Carved out of wooded foothills, accessible only by the winding drive through the tangled forest, the property was alive with the sounds of the surrounding messy Virginia woods: oak leaves stuttering against each other, coyotes or deer crunching through the undergrowth, dry grass whispering, owls querying owls, everything breathing and shifting out of sight. It was too cold for fireflies, but a multitude of them glistened in and out of being above the fields nonetheless.

Those were his. Fanciful, purposeless, but lovely.

Ronan Lynch loved to dream about light.

There had been a time when the Barns was Ronan's entire ecosystem. The Lynches rarely left it when he was young, because they didn't need to, because it was a lot of work, because Niall Lynch didn't trust many people to take care of it in their absence.

It was better to meet friends at their houses, their mother, Aurora, explained, because Dad had a lot of breakable things around the farm.

One of the breakable things: Aurora Lynch. Golden-haired Aurora was the obvious queen of a place like the Barns, a gentle and joyous ruler of a peaceful and secret country. She was a patron of her sons' fanciful arts (although Declan, the eldest, was rarely fanciful), and she was a tireless playmate in her sons' games of make-believe (although Declan, the eldest, was rarely playful). She loved Niall, of course — everyone loved larger-than-life

Niall, the braggart poet, the musician king — but unlike everyone else, she preferred him in his silent moods. She loved the truth, and it was difficult to love both the truth and Niall Lynch when the latter was speaking.

She was the only person who he could not dazzle, and he loved her for it.

It was not until many years later that Ronan learned that the king had dreamt up his queen. But in retrospect, it made sense. His father loved to dream of light, too.

Inside the farmhouse, Ronan switched on a few lamps to push the darkness outside. A few minutes' search turned up a bucket of alphabet blocks, which he overturned for Chainsaw to sort through. Then he put on one of his father's Bothy Band records, and as the fiddle and pipes crackled and fuzzed through the narrow hallways, he wiped dust off the shelves and repaired a broken cabinet hinge in the kitchen. As the morning sun finally spilled golden into the protected glen, he continued the process of restaining the worn wood staircase up to his parents' old room.

He breathed in. He breathed out.

He forgot how to exhale when he wasn't at home.

Time kept its own clock here. A day at Aglionby was a smash-cut slideshow of images that didn't matter and conversations that didn't stick. But the same day, spent at the Barns, proceeded with lazy aplomb, full of four times as many things. Reading in the window seat, old movies in the living room, lazy repairing of a slamming barn door. Hours took as long as they needed.

Slowly his memories of *before* – everything this place had been to him when it had held the entire Lynch family – were being overlapped with memories and hopes of *after* – every minute that the Barns had been *his*, all of the time he'd spent here alone or with Adam, dreaming and scheming.

Home, home, home.

It was time to sleep. To dream. Ronan had a specific object he was trying to create, and he wasn't stupid enough to think he'd be able to get it on the first try.

Rules for dreams, intoned Jonah Milo.

Ronan was in English class. Milo, the English teacher, stood before a glowing Smart Board, dressed in plaid. His fingers were a metronome on the board, clicking with his words: *Rules for dreamers. Rules for the dreamt.*

Cabeswater? Ronan asked the classroom. Hatred glazed his thoughts. He would never forget the smell of this place: rubber and industrial cleaner, mildew and cafeteria teriyaki.

Mr Lynch, do you have something you want to share?

Sure: I'm not staying in this goddamn class a second longer –

No one's keeping you here, Mr Lynch. Aglionby is a choice. Milo looked disappointed. *Let's focus. Rules for dreams. Read it out loud, Mr Lynch.*

Ronan didn't. They couldn't make him.

Dreams are easily broken, Milo sang. His words were a laundry detergent advertising jingle. *It's difficult to maintain the necessary balance between subconscious and conscious. There's a chart on page four of your text.*

Page three was black. Page four was gone. There was no chart.

Rules for the dreamt. Mr Lynch, maybe sit up a bit, tuck in that shirt, and show me some Aglionby focus? A psychopomp could help you keep your waking thoughts. Everyone check to see if their dream buddy is here.

Ronan's dream buddy was not there.

Adam was, though, in the very back row of chairs. Attentive. Engaged. This Aglionby Student Represents America's Legacy. His textbook was visible in the thought bubble above his head, dense with writing and diagrams.

Milo's beard was longer than it had been at the beginning of class. *Rules for dreamers. Really this is about arrogance, isn't it? Mr Lynch, do you want to talk about how God is dead?*

This is bullshit, Ronan said.

If you know better, you can come up and teach this class yourself. I'm just trying to understand why you think you're not going to end up dead like your father. Mr Parrish, rules for the dreamer?

Adam replied with textbook precision. *Heaney states clearly on page twenty that dreamers are to be classified as weapons. We see in peer studies how this is borne out in reality. Example A: Ronan's father is dead. Example B: K is dead. Example C: Gansey is dead. Example D: I am also dead. Example E: God is dead, as you mentioned. I would add Matthew and Aurora Lynch to the list, but they are not human as per Glasser's 2012 study. I have diagrams here.*

Fuck you, Ronan said.

Adam looked withering. He was no longer Adam, but Declan. *Do your homework, Ronan, for once in your goddamn life. Don't you even know what you are?*

Ronan woke angry and empty-handed. He abandoned the couch to slam some cabinets around in the kitchen. The milk in the fridge had gone bad, and Matthew had eaten all of the hot dogs the last time he'd come along. Ronan raged into the thin morning light in the screen porch and tore a strange fruit off a potted tree that grew packs of chocolate-covered peanuts. As he paced fitfully, Chainsaw skittered and flapped behind him, stabbing at dark spots that she hoped were dropped peanuts.

Rules for dreamers: DreamMilo had asked him where his dream companion was. Good question. Orphan Girl had haunted his sleep for as long as he could remember, a forlorn little creature with a white skullcap pulled over her white-blond pixie cut. He thought she'd been older once, but maybe he had been younger. She'd helped him hide during nightmares. Now she more often hid behind Ronan, but she still helped him keep his mind on task. It was weird that she hadn't shown up when Milo mentioned her. The whole dream had been weird.

Don't you even know what you are?

Ronan didn't, exactly, but he had thought he was getting better about living with the unfolding mystery of himself. His dream could screw itself.

"*Brek,*" said Chainsaw.

Throwing a peanut at her, Ronan stalked back into the house to search for inspiration. Sometimes putting his hands on something real helped him when he was having a hard time dreaming. To successfully bring back a dream object, he had to know the way it felt and smelled, the way it stretched and bent, the way gravity worked on it or didn't, the things that made it physical instead of ephemeral.

In Matthew's bedroom, a silky pouch of magnetic rocks caught Ronan's eye. As he studied the fabric, Chainsaw waddled blandly between his legs, making a low growling noise. He never understood why she chose to walk and hop so often. If he had wings, all he'd ever do was fly.

"He's not in here," Ronan told her as she stretched her neck long in an attempt to see on top of the bed. Grunting in response, Chainsaw unsucessfully searched for entertainment. Matthew was a loud, joyful kid, but his room was orderly and spare. Ronan used to think that this was because Matthew kept all his clutter inside his curly-haired head. But now he suspected it was because Ronan had not had enough imagination to dream a fully formed human. Three-year-old Ronan had wanted a brother whose love was complete and uncomplicated. Three-year-old Ronan had dreamt Matthew, the opposite of Declan in every way. Was he human? Dream-Adam/Declan didn't seem to think so, but Dream-Adam/Declan was also clearly a liar.

Rules for dreamers.

Dreamers are to be classified as weapons.

Ronan already knew he was a weapon; but he was trying to make up for it. Today's goal was to dream something to keep Gansey safe in the case that he was stung again. Ronan had dreamt antidotes before, of course, EpiPens and cures, but the problem was that he wouldn't know if those worked until it was too late if they didn't.

So now, better plan: a sheer armoured skin. Something that would protect Gansey before he ever got hurt.

Ronan couldn't shake the idea that he was running out of time.

It was gonna work. It was gonna be great.

At lunchtime, Ronan abandoned his bed after two more failures to produce a successful armour. He pulled on muck boots and an already grubby hoodie and went outside.

The Barns was a conglomerate of outbuildings and sheds and big cattle barns; Ronan stopped at one to fill feed buckets and to heave a salt block on top of the pellets, a variation of his childhood routine. Then he set off towards the high pasture, passing the silent lumps of his father's dream-cattle stubbornly sleeping in the fields on either side. On the way, he detoured to one of the big equipment barns. Standing on his toes, he felt around the top of the doorjamb until he found the tiny dream flower he'd left there. When he tossed it, the flower hovered just above his head, throwing out a continuous little yellow glow sufficient to illuminate his immediate path through the windowless barn. He made his dusty way past the broken machinery and unbroken machinery until he found his albino night horror curled on the hood of a rusted old car, all white ragged menace and closed eyes. Its pale and savage claws had scratched the hood down to bare metal; the night horror had spent more than a few hours here already. The creature opened a pinkened eye to regard him.

"Do you need anything, you little bastard?" Ronan asked it.

It closed its eye again.

Ronan left it and continued on his way with the feed buckets rattling productively, letting the dream flower follow him although he didn't need it in the daylight. By the time he passed the largest cattle barn, he was no longer alone. The grass scuffled on either side of him. Groundhogs and rats and creatures that didn't exist pattered out of the field grass to scamper in his footprints, and in front of him, deer emerged from the wood's edge, their dusky hides invisible until they moved.

Some of the animals were real. Most of the deer were ordinary Virginia whitetails, fed and tamed by Ronan for no purpose other than delight. Their domestication had been aided by the presence of a dreamt buckling that lived among them. He was pale and lovely, with long, tremulous eyelashes and foxy red ears. Now, he was the first to accept Ronan's offering of the salt block as he rolled it into the field, and he allowed Ronan to stroke the short, coarse fur of his withers and worry some burrs out of the soft hair behind his ears. One of the wild deer nibbled pellets from Ronan's cupped palms, and the rest stood patiently as he poured it into the grass. Probably it was illegal to feed them. Ronan could never remember what was legal to feed or shoot in Virginia.

The smaller animals crept closer, some pawing at his boots, some alighting on the grass near him, others spooking the deer. He scattered pellets for them, too, and inspected them for wounds and ticks.

He breathed in. He breathed out.

He thought about what he wanted the skin armour to look like. Maybe it didn't have to be invisible. Maybe it could be silver. Maybe it could have lights.

Ronan grinned at the thought, feeling suddenly silly and lazy and foolish. He stood, letting the day's failure roll off his shoulders and fall to the ground. As he stretched, the white buckling lifted his head to observe him keenly. The others noted the buckling's attention and likewise focused their gaze. They were beautiful in a way that Ronan's dreams could be, the way

Cabeswater could be, only now he was awake. Somehow, without Ronan marking the moment, the schism between his waking life and dreaming life had begun to narrow. Although half of this strange herd would fall asleep if Ronan died, so long as he was here, so long as he breathed in and breathed out, he was a king.

He left his bad mood in the field.

Back in the house, he dreamed.

FOUR

The forest was Ronan.

He was lying on his face in the dirt, his arms out-stretched, his fingers digging down into the soil for the ley line's energy. He smelled leaves burning and falling, death and rebirth. The air was his blood. The voices muttering to him from the branches were his own, tracked over themselves. Ronan, looped; Ronan, again; Ronan, again.

"Get up," the Orphan Girl said in Latin.

"No," he replied.

"Are you trapped?" she asked.

"I don't want to leave."

"I do."

He looked at her, somehow, although he was still all tangled up in his root-fingers and the ink branches growing from the tattoo on his bare back. Orphan Girl stood with a feed bucket in her hands. Her eyes were dark and sunken, the eyes of the always hungry or the always wanting. Her white skullcap was pulled down low over her honey-blond pixie cut.

"You're just a piece of dream," he told her. "You're just some kind of subfuckery of my imagination."

She whimpered like a kicked puppy, and he immediately felt cross with her, or himself. Why shouldn't he just say what she was?

"I was looking for you before," he said, because he'd just remembered this. Her presence kept reminding him, again and again, that he was in a dream.

"Kerah," she said, still hurt by his earlier statement. Ronan was annoyed to hear her steal Chainsaw's name for him.

"Find your own," he said, but he'd lost the taste for being firm with her, even if it was just honesty. She sat beside him, pulling her knees up to her chest.

Pressing his cheek against the cool soil, he stretched further into the earth. His fingertips brushed grubs and earthworms, moles and snakes. The grubs uncurled as he passed them. The earthworms joined him in his journey. The moles' fur pressed against him. The snakes coiled around his arms. He was all of them.

He sighed.

Aboveground, Orphan Girl rocked and sang a little lament to herself, looking anxiously up at the sky.

"*Periculosum*," she warned. "*Suscitat.*"

He didn't feel any danger, though. Just earth, and the ley's energy, and the branches of his veins. Home, home.

"It's down here," he said. The dirt swallowed his words and sent up new shoots.

Orphan Girl hunched her back up against his leg and shivered. "*Quid —*" she began, then continued, stumbling, in English, "What is it?"

It was a skin. Shimmering, nearly transparent. Enough of him was below the surface of the forest that he could see the shape of it among the dirt. It was fashioned like a body, like it was germinating beneath the ground, like it was waiting to

35

be dug free. The fabric of it felt like the cloth of the bag in Matthew's room.

"I have it," Ronan said, his fingers brushing the surface. *Help me hold it.* He might have only thought it, not said it out loud.

Orphan Girl began to cry. "Watch out, watch out."

She had barely finished saying it when he felt . . .

Something

Some

one?

It was not the cool, dry scales of the snakes. Nor the warm, rapid heartbeats of the moles. It was not the moving-dirt-softness of earthworms or the smooth, slow flesh of the grubs.

It was dark.

It seeped.

It was not so much a thing as not a thing.

Ronan did not wait. He knew a nightmare when he felt it.

"Girl," he said, "pull me out."

He snatched the dream skin in one of his root-hands, rapidly trying to commit the feeling of it to memory. The weight, the density, the realness.

Orphan Girl was pawing at the soil around him, burrowing like a dog, making frightened little noises. How she hated his dreams.

The darkness that was not darkness crept up through the dirt. It was eating the things it touched. Or rather, they were there, and then they were not.

"Faster," Ronan snapped, retreating with the skin clutched in his root fingers.

He could leave the dream skin behind and wake himself up.

He didn't want to leave it. It could work.

Orphan Girl had a hold of his leg, or his arm, or one of his branches, and she was pulling, pulling, pulling, trying to unearth him.

"Kerah," she wept.

The darkness gnawed up. If it got ahold of Ronan's hand, he might wake up without one. He was going to have to cut his losses —

Orphan Girl fell back, tugging him free of the soil. The blackness burst up through the ground behind him. Without thinking, Ronan threw himself over the girl protectively.

Nothing is impossible, said the forest, or the darkness, or Ronan.

He woke. He was trapped in place, as he always was after he brought something of any size from a dream. He couldn't feel his hands *please,* he thought, *please let me still have hands* — and he couldn't feel his legs — *please,* he thought, *please let me still have legs.* He spent several long minutes staring up at the ceiling. He was in the living room on the old plaid couch, looking at the same three cracks that had made the letter *M* for years. Everything smelled of hickory and boxwood. Chainsaw flapped over him before settling heavily on his left leg.

So he must at least still have one leg.

He couldn't quite formulate what had made the darkness so terrifying, now that he wasn't looking at it.

Slowly, his fingers began to move, so he must still have them, too. The dream skin had come with him and was draped halfway off the couch. It was gauzy and insubstantial looking, stained with dirt and ripped to shreds. He had his limbs, but the suit was a wash. He was also starving.

His phone buzzed, and Chainsaw flapped up to the back of the couch. Ordinarily he would not have checked it, but he was so unnerved by the memory of the nothingness in the dream that he used his newly mobile fingers to pluck it from his pocket to be sure it wasn't Matthew.

It was Gansey. *Parrish wants to know if you killed yourself dreaming just now please advise*

Before Ronan had time to formulate an emotion about this knowledge of Adam's, Chainsaw suddenly ducked her head down low on the back of the couch. The feathers on her neck stood in wary attention. Her gaze was fixed on some point across the room.

Pushing himself up, Ronan followed her attention. At first he saw nothing but the living room's familiar clutter. The coffee table, the TV, the game cabinet, the walking stick basket. Then his eyes caught movement beneath the end table.

He froze.

Slowly, he realized what he was looking at.

He said, "Shit."

FIVE

Blue Sargent had been thrown out of school.

Only for a day. Twenty-four hours was supposed to cure her of willful destruction of property and, *frankly, Blue, a surprisingly bad attitude.* Blue couldn't quite make herself as sorry as she knew she ought to be; nothing about school felt particularly *real* in comparison to the rest of her life. As she had stood in the hallway outside the administration offices, she heard her mother explaining how they'd had a recent death in the family and that Blue's biological father had just returned to town and it was all very traumatic. Probably, Maura added — smelling of mugwort, which meant she'd been doing a ritual with Jimi while Blue was at school — her daughter was acting out even without realizing it.

Oh, Blue realized it all right.

Now she sat beneath the beech tree in 300 Fox Way's backyard, feeling cranky and out of sorts. A very faraway part of her realized that she was in trouble — more serious trouble than she'd been in for a long time. But the more immediate part of her was relieved that for a whole day she didn't have to try to pretend that she cared about her classes. She hurled a bug-eaten beech nut; it bounced off the fence with a crack like a gunshot.

"OK, here's the idea."

The voice came first, then the chill across her skin. A moment later, Noah Czerny joined her, dressed as always in his navy Aglionby sweater. *Joined* was perhaps the wrong verb. *Manifested* was better. The phrase *trick of the light* was even more superior. *Trick of the mind* was the best. Because it was rare that Blue noticed the moment Noah actually appeared. It wasn't that he gently resolved into being. It was that somehow her brain rewrote the minute before to pretend that Noah had been slouching beside her all along.

It was a little creepy, sometimes, to have a dead friend.

Noah continued amiably, "So you get a trailer. Not an Adam trailer. A commercial trailer."

"What? *Me?*"

"You. You. What do you call it when it's everyone, but you say *you*? It's grammary."

"I don't know. Gansey would know. What do you mean *Adam trailer?*"

"Internal you?" he guessed, as if she hadn't said anything. "Whatever. I just mean, like, a general you. So you come up with five, like, super great chicken recipes. Like, rotisserie. Those are the ones that cook for ever, right?" He ticked off his fingers. "Like, uh, Mexican. Honey-curry. Barbecue. Uh. Teriyaki? And. Garlic-Something. The other thing you need is, like, beverages. Crazy addictive beverages. People have to think, I'm craving that honey-curry chicken and that, uh, lemon tea, hell, yeah, to the max, yeah, Chickie-chickie-chicken!"

He was more animated than she'd ever seen him. This cheerfully prattling version of Noah was surely closer to the living version of him, the skateboarding Aglionby student with the bright red Mustang. She was struck by the realization that she probably wouldn't have ever become friends with this Noah. He wasn't terrible. Just *young* in a way that she had never been. It was an uncomfortable, sideways thought.

"— and I would call it — are you ready – CHICKEN OUT. Get it? What do you want tonight? Oh, Mom, please get CHICKEN OUT." Noah smacked Blue's little ponytail so that it hit the top of her head. "You could wear a little paper hat! You could be the *face* of CHICKEN OUT."

All at once, Blue lost patience. She exploded, "OK, Noah, stop beca—"

A cawing laugh from overhead silenced her. A few dry leaves floated down. Blue and Noah tipped their heads back.

Gwenllian, Glendower's daughter, lounged in the sturdy branches above them, her long body leaned into the trunk, her legs braced against a smooth-skinned branch. As usual, she was a terrifying and wonderful sight. Her towering rain cloud of dark hair was full of pens and keys and twists of paper. She was wearing at least three dresses, and all of them had managed to hitch clear up to her hip through either climbing or intention. Noah stared.

"Hi ho, dead thing," Gwenllian sang, taking a cigarette out of one side of her hair and a lighter from the other.

"How long have you been there? Are you smoking?" Blue demanded. "Don't kill my tree."

Gwenllian released a puff of clove-scented smoke. "You sound like Artemus."

"I wouldn't know." Blue tried not to sound resentful, but she was. She hadn't expected Artemus to fill a gaping hole in her heart, but she also hadn't expected him to merely shut himself away in a closet.

Blowing a credible smoke ring through the dried leaves, Gwenllian shoved off the trunk and allowed herself to slide to a lower branch. "Your little shrub dweller of a father is not a very easy thing to know, oh blue lily, lily blue. But then again, that thing down there now is not easy to know, either, is it?"

"What thing — Noah? Noah is not a *thing!*"

"We came across a bird in a bush, a bird in a bush, a bird in a bush," Gwenllian sang. She slipped down, and then down again, enough to dangle her boots at Blue's eye level. "And thirty of its friends! You were feeling pretty alive-oh, little dead thing, between the two of us, weren't you? Lily blue with her mirror-power, and lily gwen with her mirror-power, and you in the middle remembering life?"

It was annoying to realize that Gwenllian was probably right: This effervescent, lively Noah had almost certainly been made possible only by bookended psychic batteries. It was also annoying to see that Gwenllian had completely murdered Noah's good mood. He had ducked his head so that nothing but the whorl of his cowlick was visible.

Blue glared up. "You're horrible."

"Thanks." Gwenllian plunged to the ground with a great, flapping leap and stubbed out her cigarette on the beech's trunk. It left a black mark that Blue felt mirrored on her soul.

She scowled at Gwenllian. Blue was very short and Gwenllian was very tall, but Blue very much wanted to scowl at Gwenllian and Gwenllian seemed intent on being scowled at, so they made it work. "What do you want me to say? That he's dead? What's the point of rubbing that in?"

Gwenllian leaned close enough that their noses brushed. Her words came out in a clove-scented whisper: "Have you ever solved a riddle you weren't asked?"

Calla thought that Gwenllian had begun singing and riddling as a result of being buried alive for six hundred years. But looking at her gleefully bright eyes now, remembering how she'd been buried for trying to stab Owen Glendower's poet to death, Blue also thought there was a very credible chance that Gwenllian had always been this way.

"There is no solving Noah," Blue replied, "except by having him . . . pass on. And he doesn't want that!"

Gwenllian cackled. "*Want* and *need* are different things, my pet." She nudged the back of Noah's head with a lifted boot. "Show her what you've been hiding, dead thing."

"You don't have to do anything she says, Noah." Blue said it so quickly that she knew at once that she both believed Gwenllian and feared the truth of him.

They all knew that Noah's existence was a fragile one, subject to the whims of the ley line and the location of his physical remains. And Blue and Gansey in particular had seen firsthand how Noah seemed to be having a harder and harder time coping with the vagaries of being dead. What Blue already knew of Noah was scary. If there was worse, she wasn't sure she wanted to know.

Noah sighed. "It's what you deserve. Just . . . I'm sorry, Blue."

Nerves started to patter inside her. "There's nothing to be sorry for."

"Yeah," he said in a small voice, "there is. Don't . . . just . . . OK."

Gwenllian stepped back to give him room to stand. He did, slowly, stiffly, turning his back to Blue. He squared his ordinarily slouching shoulders as if preparing himself for battle. She felt the moment that he stopped pulling energy from her. It was as if she'd dropped a backpack to the ground.

Then he turned to face her.

Every summer, a travelling carnival came to Henrietta. They set up in the big stock sale fields behind the Walmart, and for a few nights it was flattened grass and funnel cakes and lights spasming in the dark. Blue always wanted to like it – she'd gone a few times with people from school (she'd always wanted to like them, too) – but in the end she had just felt like she was still waiting for the real event to happen. Thinking she needed thrills, she'd tried the drop tower. It had lifted them all up – *ker-chunk*, *ker-chunk* – and then – nothing. Some sort of malfunction had meant they were not dropped, merely lowered in the same way they'd climbed. Even though they had never plummeted, for a brief moment, Blue's stomach had dropped as if she *had* been set free, a feeling made even stranger for the rest of her body not moving an inch.

It was precisely what she felt now.

"Oh," said Blue.

It was hollow eyes dead and teeth-bared lips and soul threaded through naked bones. It had not been alive for years. It was impossible to not see how decayed the soul was, how removed from humanity, how stretched thin from time away from a pulse.

Noah Czerny had died.

This was all that was left.

That was the truth.

Blue's body was a riot of shivers. She had kissed this. This thin, cold memory of a human.

Because it was only energy, it read her memories as easily as her words. She felt it haunt her thoughts and then pass out the other side.

It hissed, "I said I was sorry."

She took a deep breath. "I said there was nothing to be sorry for."

And she meant it.

Blue didn't care that he — it — Noah — was strange and decaying and frightening. She knew that he — it — Noah — was strange and decayed and frightened, and she knew that she loved him anyway.

She hugged it. Him. Noah. She didn't care if he wasn't quite human any more. She would keep calling whatever this was *Noah* for as long as it wanted to be called Noah. And she was glad that he could read her thoughts in that moment, because she wanted him to know how thoroughly she believed that.

Her body went icily cold as she let Noah draw energy from her, her arms tight around his neck.

"Don't tell the others," he said. When she stepped back, he'd pulled his boyish face over his features again.

"Do you need to go?" Blue asked. She meant *go for ever*, but she couldn't say it out loud.

He whispered, "Not yet."

Blue wiped a tear from her face with the heel of her hand, and he wiped a tear from her other cheek with the heel of his.

His chin dimpled in that way that comes before tears, but she put her fingers against it and it resolved.

They were wheeling towards the end of something, and they both knew it.

"Good," said Gwenllian. "I hate liars and cowards."

Without pause, she began to climb the tree once more. Blue turned back to Noah, but he was gone. Possibly he had gone before Gwenllian had spoken; just as with his arrival, it was hard to tell the exact moment of his leaving. Blue's brain had already rewritten all of the seconds around his disappearance.

Blue's school suspension felt like a faded dream. What was real? This was real.

The kitchen window groaned open, and Jimi shouted out, "Blue! Your boys are out front, looking like they're fixing to bury a body."

Again? Blue thought.

SIX

When Blue climbed into Gansey's black Suburban, she discovered that Ronan was already installed in the backseat, his head freshly shaven, boots up on the seat, dressed for a brawl. His presence in the backseat instead of in his usual passenger-seat throne suggested that trouble was afoot. Adam – in a white T-shirt and a pair of clean work coveralls rolled down to the waist – had his seat instead. Gansey sat behind the wheel, wearing both his Aglionby uniform and an electric expression that startled Blue. It was wide-awake and glittering, a match struck just behind his eyes. She'd seen this vivid Gansey before, but usually only when they were alone.

"Hello, Jane," he said, and his voice was as bright and intense as his eyes. It was hard not to be captured by this Gansey; he was both powerful and worrisome in his tension.

Don't stare – too late. Adam had caught her at it. She averted her eyes and busied herself tugging up her thigh-highs. "Heya."

Gansey asked, "Do you have time to run an errand with us? Do you have work? Homework?"

"No homework. I got suspended," Blue replied.

"Get the fuck out," Ronan said, but with admiration. "Sargent, you asshole."

Blue reluctantly allowed him to bump fists with her as Gansey eyed her meaningfully in the rearview mirror.

Adam swivelled the other way in his seat — to the right, instead of to the left, so that he was peering around the far side of the headrest. It made him look as if he were hiding, but Blue knew it was just because it turned his hearing ear instead of his deaf ear towards them. "For what?"

"Emptying another student's backpack over his car. I don't really want to talk about it."

"I do," Ronan said.

"Well, I don't. I'm not proud of it."

Ronan patted her leg. "I'll be proud for you."

Blue cast a withering look in his direction, but she felt grounded for the first time that day. It was not that the women in 300 Fox Way weren't her family — they were where her roots were buried, and nothing could diminish that. It was just that there was something newly powerful about this assembled family in this car. They were all growing up and into each other like trees striving together for the sun. "So what's happening?"

"If you can believe it," Gansey said, still in his chilly, super-polite tone that meant he was annoyed, "I was originally planning on coming over to talk to Artemus about Glendower. But Ronan has decided to change all that. He has *different* ideas for our afternoon. More *important* uses of our time."

Ronan leaned forward. "Tell me, Dad, are you mad that I fucked up, or are you just mad that I skipped school?"

Gansey said, "I think those both count as fuckups, don't you?"

"Oh, don't," Ronan retorted. "It just sounds vulgar when *you* say it."

As Gansey sent the vehicle off from the kerb at a brisk speed, Adam gave Blue a knowing look. His expression said, *Yes, they've been at this awhile.* Blue was strangely grateful for this nonverbal exchange. After their fractious breakup (had they even been dating?), Blue had reconciled herself to Adam being too hurt or uncomfortable to be good friends with her. But he was trying. And she was trying. And it seemed to be working.

Except that she was in love with his best friend and hadn't told him.

Blue's feeling of calm immediately dissolved, replaced by the exact same sensation that she had experienced right before she had shaken out Holtzclaw's backpack over the hood of his car. All emotions fuzzing to white.

She really needed to find some coping mechanisms.

"GANSEY BOY!"

They all startled at the cry through Gansey's open window. They'd pulled up to the stoplight adjacent to Aglionby's main gate; a group of students stood on the pavement holding placards. Gansey reluctantly offered the group a three-fingered salute, which provoked further cries of *Whoop, whoop, whoop!*

The sight of all the boys in their uniforms immediately provoked an unpleasant emotion in Blue. It was a long-held, multi-headed sensation formed from judgement, experience and envy, and she didn't care for it. It wasn't that she necessarily thought that her negative opinions on raven boys were *wrong.* It was just that knowing Gansey, Adam, Ronan and Noah complicated what she did with those opinions. It had been a lot more straightforward when she'd just assumed that she could despise them all from the thin air of the moral high ground.

Blue craned her neck, trying to see what the signs said, but none of the boys were doing a very good job pointing them towards the road. She wondered if Blue Sargent, Aglionby student, would have been Blue Sargent, placard holder. "What are they protesting?"

"Life," replied Adam drily.

She realized then that she recognized one of the students standing on the pavement. He had an unforgettable tuft of styled black hair and a pair of high-top trainers that could only have looked more expensive if they had been wrapped in dollar bills.

Henry Cheng.

She'd been on a secret date with Gansey the last time she'd seen him. She didn't remember the fine details, only that his electric super car had broken down by the side of the road, that he'd made a joke that she didn't find funny, and that he had reminded her of all the ways Gansey was not like her. It had not been a good end to the date.

Henry clearly remembered her, too, because he gave her a wide smile before pointing two fingers at his eyes and then hers.

Her already mixed feelings were joined by yet more mixed feelings.

"What do you call it when you say 'you' to mean everyone in general?" Blue asked, leaning forward, eyes still on him.

"*Universal you*," Gansey replied. "I think."

"Yes," Adam said.

"What a bunch of fancy posers," Ronan said. It was hard to tell if he meant Gansey and Adam with their grammar prowess or the Aglionby students standing outside with their hand-lettered placards.

"Oh, sure," Gansey said, still cold and annoyed. "God forbid young men display their principles with futile but public protests when they could be skipping school and judging other students from the backseat of a motor vehicle."

"Principles? Henry Cheng's principles are all about getting larger font in the school newsletter," Ronan said. He did a vaguely offensive version of Henry's voice: "Serif? Sans serif? More bold, less italics."

Blue saw Adam both smirk and turn his face away in a hurry so that Gansey wouldn't see, but it was too late.

"Et tu, Brute?" Gansey asked Adam. "Disappointing."

"I didn't say anything," Adam replied.

The light turned green; the Suburban began to pull away from the protestors.

"Gansey! Gansey! Richard-man!" This was Henry's voice; even Blue recognized it. There was no vehicle behind them, so Gansey slowed, leaning his head out the window.

"What can I do for you, Mr Cheng?"

"You've got . . . your tailgate is open, I think." Henry's airy expression had turned complicated. The cheery smile had not quite slipped, but there was something behind it. Blue once again felt the surge of uncertainty; she knew what Henry was like, but she also didn't know all of what he was like.

Gansey scanned the dash for notification lights. "It's not . . . oh." His voice had changed to match Henry's expression. *"Ronan."*

"What?" snapped Ronan. His jealousy of Henry was visible from space.

"Our *tailgate* is open."

A car honked behind them. Gansey waved at them in his rearview mirror, saluted Henry, and hit the gas. Blue looked over her shoulder in time to see Henry turn back to the other students, his expression once more melting into the uncomplicated wide grin he'd worn before.

Interesting.

Meanwhile, Ronan twisted to look in the rear cargo space behind the backseats. He hissed, "Stay *down*."

He was clearly *not* speaking to Blue. She narrowed her eyes and asked warily, "What exactly is this errand again?"

Gansey was glad to answer. "Lynch, in his infinite wisdom, decided to dream instead of going to school, and he brought back more than he asked for."

The Henry encounter had left a ding in Ronan's cheerful aggression, and now he snapped, "You could've just told me to handle this myself. My dreaming's nobody's business but mine."

Adam interjected, "Oh, no, Ronan. I don't take sides — but that's bullshit."

"Thank you," Gansey said.

"Hey, old man —"

"Don't," Gansey said. "Jesse Dittley's dead because of the people interested in your family's dreaming, so don't act like others aren't affected by whether it stays secret or not. It's yours first, but we're all in the blast zone."

This silenced Ronan. He slammed himself back into his seat, looked out the window, and put one of his leather bracelets between his teeth.

Blue had heard enough. She tugged out her seat belt to give herself room to turn around, and then she put her chin on the leather seat to look into the rear cargo area behind her. She did not immediately see anything. Perhaps she *did*, but didn't want to acknowledge it, because once her eyes picked out Ronan's dream, it was impossible to imagine how she hadn't seen it at once.

Blue had been absolutely dead set against shock.

But she was shocked.

She demanded, "Is that — is that a child?"

There was a creature curled small beside a gym bag and Gansey's messenger bag. It had enormous eyes nearly eclipsed by a skullcap pulled down low. It wore a tattered and manky over-sized fisherman's sweater and had either dark gray legs or gray leggings. Those things at the end of the legs were either boots or hooves. Blue's mind was bending.

Ronan's voice was flat. "I used to call her Orphan Girl."

SEVEN

Adam had suggested Cabeswater, so they took her to Cabeswater.

He wasn't sure, yet, what they would do there; it was just the first thing he'd thought of. Actually, it was the second, but his first thought was so shameful that he'd immediately regretted it.

He'd taken one look at her and thought if she'd been another night horror they could have just killed it or left it somewhere.

A second later — no — no, less than a second, half a second, simultaneously — he hated himself for thinking it. It was exactly the sort of thought he'd expect from his father's son. *What, you want to leave? You're going to go? Is that your bag? Believe me, if I was allowed to let you go, I'd have dropped you in a ditch myself. Everything's a production with you.*

He hated himself, and then he hated his father, and then he gave the emotion to Cabeswater in his head and Cabeswater rolled it away.

And now they were at Cabeswater itself, Cabeswater in the flesh, here at Adam's second thought that he wished had been his first, taking the Orphan Girl to Ronan's mother, Aurora. This was the field they had spotted from the air long ago, with a huge raven formed of shells. Gansey could not avoid driving over the scattered shells, but he took care to avoid the raven itself. Adam appreciated this part of Gansey, his endless concern for the things in his care.

The vehicle stopped. Gansey, Blue and Adam got out. Ronan and his strange little girl did not; it seemed there was some negotiation occurring.

They waited.

Outside, the sky was low and gray and torn by the peaks over the brown-red-black of Cabeswater's trees. From where they stood, it was nearly possible to imagine it was just an ordinary forest on an ordinary Virginia mountain. But if one squinted into Cabeswater long enough, in the right way, one could see secrets dart between the trees. The shadows of horned animals that never appeared. The winking lights of another summer's fireflies. The rushing sound of many wings, the sound of a massive flock always out of sight.

Magic.

This close to the forest, Adam felt very . . . Adam. His head was crowded with the ordinary sensation of his coveralls folded at the small of his back, the ordinary thought of the literature exam the next day. It seemed like he should become stranger, more other, when he was near Cabeswater, but in reality, the closer he was to Cabeswater, the more firmly present he remained. His mind didn't have to wander far to communicate with Cabeswater when his body was able to lift a hand to touch it.

Strange he hadn't had a premonition of what this place would become to him all those months ago. But maybe not. So much of magic — of power, in general — required belief as a prerequisite.

Gansey took a phone call. Adam took a piss. Ronan remained in the SUV.

Adam rejoined Blue on the other side of the vehicle. He took pains to stare at neither her breasts nor her lips. Adam and Blue were no longer together — insofar as they had ever been together in the first place — but being broken up and aware that it was good for both of them had not diminished the aesthetic appeal of either set of body parts. Her hair had got wilder since he first met her, less contained by all of her clips, and her mouth had got messier since he met her, more desirous of forbidden kisses, and her stance had got harder, her spine sharpened by grief and peril.

"I think you and I need to talk about," she said. She didn't finish the sentence, but her eyes were on Gansey. He wondered if she knew how transparent her gaze was. Had she ever looked that hungry when she'd looked at him?

"Yes," Adam replied. Too late, he realized she probably meant to discuss the search for Glendower's favour, not to confess her secret relationship with Gansey. Well, they needed to talk about that, too.

"When?"

"I'll call you tonight. Wait — I have work. Tomorrow after school?"

They nodded. It was a plan.

Gansey was still talking to his phone. "No, traffic is nonexistent unless it's a bingo night. A shuttle? How many people are you expecting? I can't imagine — oh. The activity bus could be pressed into service, surely."

"KERAH!"

Both Blue and Gansey started wildly at the feral shriek. Adam, recognizing Chainsaw's name for Ronan, searched the sky.

"Jesus Mary," Ronan snarled. "Stop being impossible."

Because it wasn't Chainsaw who had screamed the raven's name for Ronan. It was the waifish little Orphan Girl. She was folded into an impossibly small shape in the colourless field grass behind the SUV, looking like a pile of clothing. She rocked and refused to stand. When Ronan hissed something else at her, she screamed in his face again. Not a child's scream, but a creature's scream.

Adam had seen many of Ronan's dreams made real by now, and he knew how savage and lovely and terrifying and whimsical they could be. But this girl was the most *Ronan* of any of them that he'd seen. What a frightened monster she was.

"It's the apocalypse. Just text me if you think of anything else." Gansey hung up. "What's wrong with her?" His tone was hesitant, as if he wasn't sure if something *was* wrong with her, or if this was just the way she always was.

"She doesn't want to go in," Ronan said. Without any ceremony, he leaned in, scooped up the girl, and began to march towards the forest's edge. It was clear now, with her spidery legs dangling over one of his arms, that they ended in dainty hooves.

On the other side of Adam, Blue put her fingers to her lips and then dropped them again. In a very low voice, she said, "Oh, Ronan!" But it was in the same way one would whisper, *Oh man!*

Because it was impossible. The dream creature was a girl; she was not; she was an orphan; they were not parents. Adam could not very well judge Ronan for dreaming so vastly; Adam was also trading in magic he didn't understand perfectly. These days, they all had their hands thrust into the sky, hoping for comets. The only difference was that Ronan Lynch's wild and expanding universe existed inside his own head.

"Excelsior," said Gansey.

They followed Ronan in.

Inside the forest, Cabeswater murmured, voices hissing from the old autumn trees, disappearing into the old mossy boulders. This place meant something different to all of them. Adam, the forest's caretaker, was bound by bargain to be its hands and eyes. Blue's power of amplification was somehow connected to it. Ronan, the Greywaren, had been here long before the rest of them, early enough to leave his handwriting scrawled on rocks. Gansey — Gansey just loved it, fearfully, awesomely, worshipfully.

Overhead, the trees whispered in a secret language, and in Latin, and then in a corrupted version of both, with English words thrown in. They hadn't spoken any English when the teens had first found them, but they were learning. Fast. Adam couldn't help but think that there was some secret hidden beneath this language evolution. Were the teens really the first English speakers to encounter the trees? If not, why were the trees only fumbling through English *now?* Why Latin?

Adam could almost see the truth hidden behind this puzzle.

"Salve," Gansey greeted the trees, always polite. Blue reached up to touch a branch; she didn't need words to greet them.

Hello, the trees rustled back. The leaves flickered against Blue's fingertips.

"Adam?" Gansey asked.

"Give me a second."

They waited for Adam to get his bearings. Because time and space were negotiable on the ley line, it was entirely possible that they could emerge from the forest at an entirely different time or place than they had entered. This phenomenon had seemed capricious at first, but slowly, as Adam became more in tune with the ley line, he had begun to realize that it did follow rules, just not the linear ones they took for granted in the ordinary world. It was more like breathing – you could hold a breath; you could breathe faster or slower; you could match your breaths to someone standing close to you. Moving through Cabeswater in a predictable way meant getting oriented to the current breathing patterns. Moving with it, not against it, as you tried to work your way back to the time and place you had left behind.

Closing his eyes, Adam allowed the ley line to seize his heart for a few beats. Now he knew which direction it ran beneath their feet, and he could feel how it intersected with another line many miles to their left and how it intersected with two even further away to his right. Tilting his head back, he sensed the stars pricking overhead, and he *felt* how he was oriented in relation to them. Inside him, Cabeswater unfurled careful vines, testing his mood as it did, never pushing boundaries these days unless under duress, and it used his mind and his eyes to search the ground beneath him, digging to find water and rock for further orientation.

Because Adam practised at many things, Adam was *good* at many things, but this – what was it even called? Scrying, sensing, magic, magic, magic. He was not only good at it, but he longed for it, wanted it, loved it in a way that nearly overwhelmed him with gratitude. He had not known that he could love, not really. Gansey and he had fought about it, once – Gansey had said, with disgust, *Stop saying privilege. Love isn't privilege.* But Gansey had always had love, had always been capable of love. Now that Adam had discovered this feeling in himself, he was more certain than ever that he was right. *Need* was Adam's baseline, his resting pulse. *Love* was a privilege. Adam was privileged; he did not want to give it up. He wanted to remember again and again how it felt.

Now that Adam had fully opened his senses, Cabeswater clumsily attempted to communicate with its human magician. It took his memories and turned them sideways and inside out, repurposing them for a hieroglyphic language of dreams: a fungus on a tree; Blue nearly falling over herself in her haste to get away from him; a scab on his wrist; the particular knit of skin that Adam knew was Ronan's frown just between his eyebrows; a snake disappearing beneath the muddy surface of a lake; Gansey's thumb on his lower lip; Chainsaw's beak parted open and a worm crawling out of it instead of in.

"Adam?" Blue asked.

He withdrew from his thoughts. "Oh, yes. I'm ready."

They proceeded. It was hard to say how long it would take them to get to where Ronan's mother lived – sometimes it took no time at all and sometimes it took ages, a fact Ronan complained about bitterly as he carried the Orphan Girl. He tried to convince her to walk on her own again, but she crumpled at once into boneless resistance on the forest floor. He didn't bother to spend minutes fighting with her; he simply scooped her back up again, his expression cross.

The Orphan Girl seemed to divine that she was pressing

Ronan's buttons too hard, however, because as he walked, jostling her with each step, she released a single purposeful note, kicking her hooved legs in time with it. A second later, an unseen bird sang back another note beautifully pitched three steps above hers. The Orphan Girl piped a tone just above her last one, and a different unseen bird sang another one pitched three steps above. A third note: a third bird. Back and forth they all went until a song spun around the teens, a syncopated reel made from a child's voice and hidden birds that may or may not have really existed.

Ronan glowered at the Orphan Girl, but it was obvious what the scowl really meant. His arms around her were protective.

It did not escape Adam how well they knew each other. The Orphan Girl was no random creature taken from a fitful dream. They had the well-worn emotional ruts of family. She knew just how to navigate his tumultuous moods; he seemed to know just how gruff he could be with her. They were friends, though even Ronan's dreamed friends were not easy to get along with.

The Orphan Girl kept cawing out her part of the reel, and it was clear that the off-kilter song was working on Gansey's mood as well as Ronan's. The argument in the car had obviously slipped from his thoughts, and instead he lifted his arms above his head and swept them in time with the music like a conductor, reaching for falling autumn leaves when they drifted close. Each dead curl that he managed to brush with his fingertips transmuted into a golden fish that swam through the air. Cabeswater listened attentively to his intention; more leaves swirled to him, waiting for his touch. Soon, a flock — school — current of fish surrounded them, flashing and darting and changing colour as their scales caught the light.

"It's always fish with you," Blue said, but she laughed as they tickled round her throat and hands. Gansey glanced at her and away, reaching for another leaf to press into service. Joy gleamed between both of them; how purely and simply Blue and Gansey loved the magic of this place.

Easy for them to be so light.

Cabeswater gently prodded Adam's thoughts, calling up a dozen happy memories in the space of the previous year — well, they would have *had* to be from just the past year, because even Cabeswater would have had a hard time stirring up glad memories in the time before Gansey and Ronan. When Adam still resisted, images of himself flickered through his mind: himself as seen by the others. His private smile, his surprised laugh, his fingers stretched towards the sun. Cabeswater didn't quite understand humans, but it learned. Happiness, it insisted. Happiness.

Adam relented. As they kept walking and the Orphan Girl kept piping her song and the fish kept darting through the air around them, he threw out intention of his own.

The volume of the resulting boom surprised even him; he heard it in one ear and felt it in both feet. The others all startled as another bass-heavy boom sounded at the beginning of the next measure of the tune. By the time the third thud came, it was obviously pounding in time with the music. Each of the trees they passed sounded with a processed thud, until the sound around them was the pulsing electronic beat that invariably played in Ronan's car or headphones.

"Oh God," Gansey said, but he was laughing. "Do we have to endure that here, too? *Ronan!*"

"It wasn't me," Ronan said. He looked to Blue, who shrugged. He caught Adam's eye. When Adam's mouth quirked, Ronan's expression stilled for a moment before turning to the loose smile he ordinarily reserved for Matthew's silliness. Adam felt a surge of both accomplishment and nerves. He skated an edge here. Making Ronan Lynch smile felt as charged as making a bargain with Cabeswater. These weren't forces to play with.

The Orphan Girl abruptly fell silent. Adam thought, at first, that she was somehow picking up on his mood. But no: They had reached the rose glen.

Aurora Lynch lived in a clearing bounded on three sides by lush and fruitful roses growing on bushes, vines and trees. Blossoms carpeted the ground and cascaded over the fourth side — a sheer rock ledge built into the mountain. The air was shot through with sun, like light seen through water, and suspended petals floated as if swimming. Everything was blushed pink or tender white or beaming yellow.

All of Cabeswater was a dream, but the rose glen was a dream even within it.

"Maybe the girl will give Aurora company," Gansey said, watching the last of his fish swim from the clearing.

"I don't think you can just give someone a child and expect them to be thrilled," Blue retorted. "She's not a cat."

Gansey opened his mouth, and Adam could see that a borderline offensive comment was queuing up. He caught Gansey's eye. Gansey closed his mouth. The moment passed.

Gansey wasn't entirely wrong, though. Aurora had been created to love, and love she did, in a fashion specific to the object of her affection. So she hugged her youngest son, Matthew, and she asked Gansey about famous people in history, and she brought Blue strange flowers she found during her walks, and she let Ronan show her what he had dreamt or made in the week before. With Adam, though, she would ask things like, "How do you know that you see the colour yellow like I do?" And she would listen attentively as he reasoned it out. He would sometimes try to get her to reason it out herself, but she didn't care so much for thinking, just hearing other people being happy to think.

So they already knew that she would love the Orphan Girl. Whether or not it was right to give Aurora someone else to love was another question entirely.

"Mom, are you here?" Ronan's voice was different when he spoke to either his mother or Matthew. It was Ronan, unperformed.

No. Ronan, unprotected.

This tone reminded Adam of that unshielded smile from before. *Don't play,* he told himself. *This is not a game.*

But it didn't feel like a game, if he was being honest. Adrenaline whispered in his heart.

Aurora Lynch appeared.

She did not step out of the living area, nor from the path they had used. Instead, she emerged from the wall of roses cascading over the rock. It was impossible for a woman to step through rock and rose, but she did it anyway. Her golden hair hung in a sheet around her head, caught through with rosebuds and braided with pearls. For a brief moment, she was at once the roses and a woman, and then she was fully Aurora. Cabeswater behaved differently for Aurora Lynch than it did for the rest of them; they were human, after all, and she was a dream thing. They vacationed here. Aurora belonged.

"Ronan," Aurora said, genuinely happy, as she was always genuinely happy. "Where's my Matthew?"

"Lacrosse or some shit," Ronan replied. "Something sweaty."

"And how about Declan?" Aurora asked.

There was a pause, just a breath too long.

"Working," Ronan lied.

Everyone in the rose glen looked at Ronan.

"Oh well. He's always been so diligent," Aurora said. She waved at Adam, Blue and Gansey. Adam, Blue, and Gansey waved back. "Have you found that king yet, Gansey?"

"No," replied Gansey.

"Oh well," Aurora said again. She hugged Ronan's neck, pressing her pale cheek to his pale cheek, as if he was holding an armful of groceries instead of a strange little girl. "What have you brought me this time?"

Ronan put the girl down without ceremony. She folded up against his legs, all sweater, and wailed in faintly accented English, "I want to go!"

"And I want to feel my right arm again," Ronan snapped.

"*Amabo te*, Greywaren!" she said. *Please, Greywaren.*

"Oh, stand up." He took her hand and she stood, rail-rod straight beside him, her brown dainty hooves splayed.

Aurora knelt so that she was on eye level with the Orphan Girl. "How beautiful you are!"

The girl didn't look at Aurora. She didn't move at all.

"Here's a lovely flower the colour of your eyes – would you like to hold it?" Aurora offered a rose in her palm. It was indeed the colour of the girl's eyes – a dull, stormy blue. Roses did not occur in that colour, but they did now.

The girl did not so much as turn her head in the direction of the rose. Instead, her eyes were fixed upon some point just past Adam's head, her expression blank or bored. Adam felt a prickle of recognition. There was no petulance or anger in the girl's expression. She was not tantrumming.

Adam had been there, crouched beside the kitchen cabinets, looking at the light fixture across the room, his father spitting in his ear. He recognized this sort of fear when he saw it.

He could not quite bear to look at her.

As Adam gazed up at the autumn-thin branches instead, Ronan and his mother spoke in low voices. Unbelievably, Gansey's phone buzzed; he pulled it out to look at it. Cabeswater pressed at Adam. Blue lined spent rose petals along her arm. The big trees outside the glen kept whispering to them in Latin.

"No, Mom," Ronan said, impatient, this brand-new tone capturing the others' attention. "This wasn't like before. This was an accident."

Aurora looked gently tolerant, which clearly infuriated her middle son.

"It *was*," he insisted, even though she hadn't said anything. "It was a nightmare, and something was different about it."

Blue swiftly interjected, "Different how?"

"Something in this one was f— messed up. There was something black in the dream that felt weird." Ronan scowled at the trees as if they might give him the words to explain it. He added finally, "Decayed."

This word affected them all. Blue and Gansey looked at each other as if it continued a previous conversation. Adam recalled the troubled images Cabeswater had shown him when he first stepped into the forest. Aurora's golden expression tarnished.

She said, "I think I'd better show you all something."

EIGHT

Much to Gansey's annoyance, he had phone reception. Ordinarily, something about Cabeswater interfered with mobile signal, but today his phone vibrated with incoming texts about black-tie Aglionby fund-raisers as he climbed up and then down a mountain.

His mother's texts looked like state documents.

Headmaster Child agrees that the timing will be tight but luckily my team has enough practice by now to bring it together quickly. It will be so wonderful to do this with you and the school.

His father's texts were jovial, man-to-man.

The money's not the point, it's just going to be a "do." Don't call it a fund-raiser, it's just a swingin' good time

His sister Helen's cut through to the important details.

Just tell me how much public debauchery the press is going to have on your classbros so I can start spinning the situation now.

Gansey kept thinking the signal would cut out, but it stayed strong and true. It meant that he was simultaneously getting a text about the Henrietta hotel situation for out-of-town guests while also observing a magical tree seeping some kind of black, toxic-looking liquid.

Greywaren, whispered a voice from distant branches. *Greywaren.*

The liquid beaded from the bark like sweat, collecting into a slow and viscous cascade. They all regarded it, except for the strange girl, who pressed her face into Ronan's side. Gansey did not blame her. The tree was a little . . . difficult to look at straight on. He had not considered how few things in nature were purely black until he saw the tarry sap. The absolute darkness bubbling on the trunk looked poisonous, or artificial.

Gansey's phone buzzed again.

"Gansey, man, is this diseased tree cutting into your digital time?" Ronan asked.

The fact was the digital time was cutting into his diseased tree time. Cabeswater was a haven for him. The presence of the texts here felt as out of place as the darkness oozing from the tree. He switched his phone off and asked, "Is this the only one like this?"

"That I've found in my walks," Aurora replied. Her expression was untroubled, but she kept running a hand over the length of her hair.

"It's hurting the tree," Blue said, craning her head back to look at the wilting canopy.

The dark tree was the opposite of Cabeswater. The longer Gansey spent in Cabeswater, the more awed he was by it. The longer he spent looking at the black sap, the more distressed he was by it. He asked, "Does it do anything?"

Aurora tilted her head. "What do you mean? Other than what it's doing?"

"I don't know," he said. "I don't know what I meant. Is it just an ugly disease, or is it something magical?"

Aurora shrugged. Her problem solving only went as far as finding someone else to solve the problem. As Gansey circled the tree, trying to look useful if nothing else, he saw Adam crouch in front of the hooved orphan girl. She continued staring past him as he unbuckled his cheap watch. He tapped the top of her hand, lightly, just so that she marked that he was offering the watch to her. Gansey expected her to ignore him or to reject the gift like she had Aurora's rose, but the girl accepted it without hesitation. She began to wind it with intense concentration as Adam remained crouched before her for a moment longer, eyebrows knitted.

Gansey joined Ronan directly by the tree. This close, the darkness *hummed* with an absence of sound. Ronan said something in Latin to the tree. There was no audible response.

"It doesn't seem to have a voice," Aurora said. "It just feels very odd. I keep finding myself returning to it, even if I don't mean to."

"It reminds me of Noah," Blue said. "Decaying."

Her voice was so melancholy that Gansey was struck all at once by what he and Blue really lost by keeping their relationship a secret. Blue radiated psychic energy for others, but touch was where she gained hers back. She was always hugging her mother or holding Noah's hand or linking her elbow in Adam's or resting her boots on Ronan's legs as they sat on the sofa. Touching Gansey's neck just between his hair and his collar. This worry in her tone demanded fingers braided together, arms on shoulders, cheeks rested against chests.

But because Gansey was too cowardly to tell Adam about falling in love with her, she had to stand there with her sadness by herself.

Aurora took Blue's hand.

Shame diffused through him, black as the tree sap.

Is this really how you want to spend the rest of your time?

A sudden movement between the trees caught Gansey's attention.

"Oh," Blue said.

Three figures. Familiar, impossible.

It was three women wearing Blue's face — sort of. It was not so much Blue's face as the way one might *remember* Blue's face. Perhaps the difference between those two things might not have been as obvious if Blue herself had not been there with them. She was the reality; they were the dream.

They approached in the way of things in a dream, too. Were they walking? Gansey couldn't remember, even though he was watching it happen. They were getting closer. That was all he knew. Their hands were up by either side of their faces; their palms were red.

"Make way," they said together.

Ronan's eyes darted to Gansey.

"Make way for the Raven King," they said together.

The Orphan Girl began to cry.

Gansey asked in a low voice, "Is Cabeswater trying to tell us something?"

They were closer. Their shadows were black and the ferns beneath them were dying.

"It's a nightmare," Adam said. His right hand held the wrist of his left, thumb pressed into his pulse point. "Mine. I didn't mean to think of them. Cabeswater, take them away."

The shadows stretched to the black on the tree, a black-sap

pedigree proving their lineage. The black bubbled out of the tree a little faster; a branch above them groaned.

"Make way," they said.

"Take them away," the Orphan Girl wailed.

"Cabeswater, *dissolvere*," Ronan said. Aurora had stepped in front of him as if she meant to protect her son. There was nothing vague about her now.

The three women came closer. Again, Gansey missed how they accomplished it. They were far, they were close. Now he smelled rot. Not the too-sweet decay of plants or food, but the musky horror of flesh.

Blue jerked away from them. Gansey thought it was fear, but she was only running to get to him. She seized his hand.

"Yes," Adam said, understanding what she was doing before Gansey did. "Gansey, *say* it."

Say it. They wanted him to tell the women to leave. *Really* tell them. In the cave of bones, Gansey had ordered the bones to wake, and the bones had woken. He had used Blue's energy and his own intention to speak a command that had to be heard. But Gansey didn't understand why it worked, and he didn't understand why it was *him*, and he didn't know how Adam or Ronan or Blue ever came to grips with their magical capabilities, because he certainly couldn't.

"Make way for the Raven King," the women said again. And then they were in front of Gansey. Three false Blues facing Blue and Gansey.

To Gansey's astonishment, Blue flicked out a switchblade in her free hand. He had no doubt that she would use it: She'd stabbed Adam with it once, after all. He had a lot of doubt, though, that it would be effective against these three nightmares before him.

Gansey looked into their black eyes. He pressed certainty into his voice and said, "Cabeswater, make it safe."

The three women rained away.

They splattered on Blue's clothing and on his shoulders, and then the water dissolved into the ground. Blue let out a little sigh that had a tone to it, her shoulders slumping.

Gansey's words had worked once again, and he was none the wiser about why or how he was meant to use this ability. Glendower had controlled the weather with his words and spoken to birds; Gansey clung to the possibility that his king, when found and woken, would explain the intricacies of Gansey *to* Gansey.

"I'm sorry," Adam said. "Stupid of me. I wasn't being careful. And this tree is — I think it amplified it."

"I might be amplifying it, too," Blue said. She was staring at Gansey's rain-spattered shoulders; her expression was so stricken that he glanced at his sweater to be certain that the splash had not eaten holes in the material. "Can we . . . can we get away from it now?"

"I think that's wise," Aurora advised. She did not seem particularly concerned, merely pragmatic, and it occurred to Gansey that to a dream, perhaps a nightmare was simply an unpleasant acquaintance rather than anything uncanny.

"You should stay away from it," Ronan told his mother.

"It finds me," she said.

"Operae pretium est," Orphan Girl said.

"Don't be a weirdo," Ronan told her. "We're not in a dream any more. English."

She didn't translate, though, and Aurora reached out to pat her skullcap-covered head. "She'll be my little helper. Come on, I'll walk you out."

Back at the forest's edge, Aurora walked with them to the SUV. It was outside the boundaries of the forest, but she never fell asleep straightaway. Unlike Kavinsky's dreamt creatures, who fell asleep instantly after his death, Niall Lynch's wife always managed to persist for a bit of time on her own. She'd stayed awake for three days after his death. She had once stayed awake for an hour outside Cabeswater. But in the end, the dream needed the dreamer.

So now Aurora walked them out to the SUV, looking even more like a dream when removed from Cabeswater, a vision wandered into waking life, clothed in flowers and light.

"Give Matthew my love," Aurora said, and hugged Ronan. "It was so nice to see all of you again."

"Stay with her," Ronan ordered Orphan Girl, who swore at him. "Watch your mouth around my mother."

The girl said something else, rapid and lovely, and he snapped, "I can't understand that when I'm awake. You have to use English or Latin. You wanted out; you're out now. Things are different."

His tone drew the keen attention of both Aurora and Adam.

Aurora said, "Don't be sad, Ronan," which made him look

away from all of them, the set of his shoulders unmoving and furious.

She spun in a circle, hands outstretched. "It's going to rain," she said, and then she fell gently to her knees.

Ronan, still and dark and very much real, closed his eyes.

Gansey said, "I'll help you carry her."

NINE

The moment Blue got back from Cabeswater, she promptly got herself into yet more trouble.

After the boys had dropped her off, Blue stormed into 300 Fox Way's kitchen and began a one-sided interrogation of Artemus, who was still hidden behind the closed storage closet door. When he failed to reply to her reasonably asked questions about murder-handed women with Blue's face and about the possible whereabouts of Glendower, she got progressively louder and added door pounding. Her heart was full of the memory of the spattered shoulders of Gansey's Aglionby sweater — precisely what his spirit had been wearing on the church watch — and her head was full of frustration that Artemus knew more about all of this than he was saying.

Gwenllian delightedly watched the proceedings from a perch on the counter.

"Blue!" Her mother's voice broke in from somewhere else in the house. "*Blooooooooo*. Why don't you come chat with us for a moment?"

The gooeyness of her tone was how Blue knew she was in trouble. She lowered her fist from the kitchen closet door and started up the stairs. Her mother's voice was coming from the house's single shared bathroom, and when Blue got there, she found her mother, Calla and Orla all sitting in a full bathtub, all fully clothed and all equally soaking. Jimi was sitting on the closed toilet lid with a burning candle in her hands. They had all been crying but none of them were crying now.

"What?" Blue demanded. Her throat was a little sore, which meant that she'd possibly been shouting even louder than she'd intended.

Her mother peered up at her with more authority than one would think a woman could in her position. "Do you think you would like it if someone pounded on your bedroom door and ordered you to come out?"

"A storage closet is *not* a bedroom," Blue said. "For starters."

"The past decades have been stressful for him," Maura said.

"The past few *centuries* have been stressful for Gwenllian, and she's out on the counter at least!"

From the toilet, Jimi said, "You can't compare one person's coping capacity to another, hon."

Calla snorted.

"Is that why you guys are all in a bathtub?" Blue asked.

"Don't be mean," Maura replied. "We were trying to make contact with Persephone. And no, before you ask, it didn't work. And while we're on the topic of you doing things that are unwise, where exactly did you disappear to? Being suspended is not a vacation."

Blue bristled. "I was not *on vacation*! Ronan dreamt up his inner child, or something, and we had to take her to his mother. While we were there, we saw the three women from that tapestry I told you about, and a tree that looked messed up, and Gansey could have died really easily and I would have been right there beside him!"

The women looked pitying, which maddened Blue further. She said, "I want to warn him."

There was silence.

She hadn't known she was going to say it until it came out of her mouth, but it was out now. She filled the quiet. "I know you said before that it would only ruin someone's life to know, and it wouldn't save them. I get that. But this is different. We're gonna find Glendower, and we're gonna ask for Gansey's life to be saved. So we need Gansey to stay alive until then. And that means he has to stop charging into danger!"

Her thin hope couldn't bear more pity at that point, but luckily, that wasn't what she got. The women all exchanged looks, considering. It was hard to tell if they were making decisions based upon ordinary means or psychic ones.

Then Maura shrugged. "OK."

"OK?"

"Sure, OK," Maura said. She glanced again at Calla for verification; Calla lifted her eyebrows. "Tell him."

"Really?"

Blue must have expected them to push back harder, because when they didn't, she felt like she'd had a chair snatched from under her. It was one thing to inform *them* that she was going to tell Gansey he was going to die. It was another thing to imagine telling him. There was no undoing it once it was done. Blue squeezed her eyes shut — *be sensible, get yourself together* — and opened them.

Mother looked at daughter. Daughter looked at mother. Maura said, "Blue."

Blue allowed herself to deflate.

Jimi blew out the candle she was holding and set it beside the toilet. Then she put her arms around Blue's hips and tugged her on to her lap, like she would have when Blue was small. Well, Blue was still small. When Blue was *young*. The toilet groaned beneath them.

"You're going to collapse the toilet," Blue said, but she let Jimi fold her arms around her and pull her into her ample bosom. She sighed shakily as Jimi rubbed her back and clucked to herself. Blue could not understand how this childish comfort was at once soothing and suffocating. She was both glad for it and wishing that she could be someplace with fewer threads tying her to every challenge or sadness in her life.

"Blue, you know it's not a bad thing that you want to leave Henrietta, right?" her mother asked from the tub. This was so precisely what Blue had been thinking about that she couldn't tell if her mother had brought it up because her mother was a good psychic or merely because she knew her well.

Blue shrugged against Jimi. "Pshaw."

"It's not always running away," Jimi said, her voice deep and rumbling through her chest to Blue's ear. "To leave."

Calla added, "We're not going to think you hate Fox Way."

"I don't hate Fox Way at all."

Maura swatted Orla's hand away; Orla was trying to braid Maura's damp hair. "I know. Because we're great. But the difference between a nice house and a nice prison is really small. We chose Fox Way. We made it, Calla and Persephone and I. But it's only your origin story, not your final destination."

This wisdom of Maura's made Blue quite cross for some reason.

"Say something," Orla said.

Blue didn't quite know how to say it; she didn't know quite what *it* was. "It . . . just feels like such a waste. Falling in love with all of them." All of them really meant all of them: 300 Fox Way, the boys, Jesse Dittley. For a sensible person, Blue thought that maybe she had a problem with love. In a dangerous voice, she added, "Don't say 'it's good life experience.' Do not."

"I've loved a lot of people," Orla said. "I would say it's good life experience. Anyway, I told you ages ago those guys were going to leave you behind."

"Orla," snapped Calla, as Blue's next breath was a little uneven. "It confounds me, sometimes, to imagine what you must tell your poor clients on the phone."

"Whatever," said Orla.

Maura shot Orla a dark look over her shoulder, and then said, "*I* wasn't going to say good life experience. I was going to say that leaving helps, sometimes. And it's not always a for ever goodbye. There's leaving and coming back."

Jimi rocked Blue. The toilet lid creaked.

"I don't think I can go to any of the colleges I want," Blue said. "The counsellor doesn't think so."

"What do you want?" Maura asked. "Not out of college. Out of life."

Blue swallowed the truth once, because she was ready to move from crisis and crying to solutions and stability. Then she said the truth slowly and carefully, so that it would be manageable. "What I always wanted. To see the world. To make it better."

Maura also seemed to be choosing her words carefully. "And are you sure that college is the only way to do that?"

This was the sort of impossible answer Blue's guidance counsellor would give her after looking at her financial and academic situation. Yes, she was sure. How else could she change the world for the better, without finding out first how to do it? How could she get a job that would pay her to be in Haiti or India or Slovakia if she didn't go to college?

Then she remembered that it was not her guidance counsellor asking; it was her psychic mother.

"What do I do?" Blue asked cannily. "What have you guys seen me doing?"

"Travelling," Maura replied. "Changing the world."

"Trees in your eyes," Calla added, more gently than usual. "Stars in your heart."

"How?" Blue asked.

Maura sighed. "Gansey's offered to help you, hasn't he?"

It was a guess that didn't require psychic ability, only a minimal grasp of Gansey's personality. Blue angrily tried to get up; Jimi wouldn't let her. "I'm not going to ride the Gansey charity train."

"Don't be like that," Calla said.

"Like what?"

"Bitter." Maura considered, and then added, "I just want you to look at your future as a world where anything is possible."

Blue shot back, "Like Gansey not dying before April? Like me not killing my true love with a kiss? Any of those possibilities?"

Her mother was quiet for a long minute, during which Blue realized that she was longing naively for her mother to tell her that both of those predictions could be wrong and that Gansey would be all right. But finally, her mother simply replied, "There's going to be life after he dies. You have to think about what you're going to do *after*."

Blue *had* been thinking about what she was going to do after, which was why she'd had a crisis in the first place. "I'm not going to kiss him, anyway, so that can't be how he goes."

"I don't believe in the concept of true love," Orla said. "It's a construct of a monogamous society. We're animals. We make love in the bushes."

"Thanks for your contribution," Calla said. "Let's give Blue's prediction a call and let it know."

"Do you love him?" Maura asked curiously.

"I'd rather not," Blue replied.

"He has lots of negative qualities I can help you hone in on," her mother offered.

"I'm already aware of them. Infinitely. It's stupid, anyway. True love *is* a construct. Was Artemus your true love? Is Mr Gray? Does that make the other one *not* true? Is there just one shot and then it's over?"

This last question was asked with the most flippancy of any of them, but only because it was the one that hurt the most. If Blue was nowhere near ready to take on Gansey's death, she was *certainly* nowhere near ready to take on the idea of him being dead long enough for her to happily waltz into a relationship with someone she had not even met yet. She just wanted to keep being best friends with Gansey for ever, and maybe one day also have carnal knowledge of him. This seemed like a very sensible desire, and Blue, as someone who had sought to be sensible her entire life, was feeling pretty damn put out that this small thing was being denied her.

"Take my mom card," Maura said. "Take my psychic card. I don't know the answers to these questions. I wish I did."

"Poor baby," Jimi murmured into Blue's hair. "Mmm, I'm so glad you never got any taller."

"For crying out loud," Blue said.

Calla heaved herself to standing, grabbing for the shower rod to balance herself. The bathwater churned beneath her. She swore. Orla ducked her head as water drained from Calla's blouse.

Calla said, "Enough crying altogether. Let's go make some pie."

TEN

Five hundred miles away, Laumonier smoked a cigarette in the main room of an old harbour ferry. The room was charmless and utilitarian — dirty glass windows set in raw metal, everything as cold as the black harbour and just as fishy smelling. Birthday decorations remained from a previous celebration, but age and dim lighting rendered them colourless and vaguely ominous as they rattled in a draught.

Laumonier's eyes were on the distant lights of the Boston skyline. But Laumonier's mind was on Henrietta, Virginia.

"First move?" Laumonier asked.

"I don't know if this is an action item," Laumonier replied.

"I would like some answers," Laumonier said.

The Laumonier triplets were mostly identical. There were slight differences — one was a hair shorter, for instance, and one had a noticeably broader jaw. But what individuality they had in appearance they had destroyed by a lifelong practice of only using their surname. An outsider would know he was not speaking to the same Laumonier that he had at a prior visit, but the brothers would have both referred to themselves by the same name, so he would have to treat them as the same person. There were not really Laumonier triplets. There was only Laumonier.

Laumonier sounded dubious. "How do you suppose to get these answers?"

"One of us goes over there," Laumonier said, "and queries him."

Over there meant to the Back Bay home of their old rival Colin Greenmantle and *queries* meant doing something unpleasant to him in return for half a decade of wrongs. Laumonier had been in the magical artefact trade for as long as they'd been in Boston, and they'd had little competition until the preppy upstart Greenmantle had got into it. Sellers had got greedy. Artefacts had got expensive. Hired muscle had become necessary. Laumonier felt that both Colin Greenmantle and his wife, Piper, had watched far too many mob movies.

Now, however, Colin had shown some weakness by retreating from his long-held territory of Henrietta. Alone. There was no sign of Piper.

Laumonier wanted to know what this meant.

"I'm not opposed to that," said Laumonier, breathing a cloud of cigarette smoke into the close room. His insistence on smoking made it impossible for the other two to quit, an excuse all of them appreciated.

"Well, I am," Laumonier replied. "I don't want to make a mess. And that mercenary of his is terrifying."

Laumonier tapped ash off his cigarette and glanced up at the streamers as if imagining setting them alight. "The word is that the Gray Man is no longer working for him. And we're perfectly capable of discretion."

Laumonier shared name and goals, but not methodology. One of them leaned towards caution and one towards fire, leaving the last as peacekeeper and devil's advocate.

"Surely there is another way to find out about —" Laumonier began.

"Don't say that name," the other two interrupted at once.

Laumonier pursed his lips. It was a dramatic gesture, as all of the brothers had quite a lot going on in the mouth area, an effect that skewed handsome, sort of, on one of them and obscene, sort of, on another.

"So we go over there to talk—" Laumonier started again.

"Talk," snorted Laumonier, playing with his cigarette lighter.

"Stop that, please. It is like you are a schoolboy thug." This Laumonier had retained his accent to use in situations just such as this. It added weight to his disdain.

"The lawyer says I shouldn't commit another misdemeanour for at least six months," Laumonier said plaintively. He stubbed out his cigarette.

Laumonier buzzed softly.

Although it would have been unsettling for any of the brothers to randomly buzz, there was an additional creeping discomfort to the sound that immediately chilled the atmosphere.

The other two regarded each other suspiciously – wary not of each other, but of everything that was not each other. They examined the buzzing brother for signs of medical infirmity and then for evidence of an ancient amulet stolen from a French tomb, a mysterious bracelet shadily acquired in Chile, an ominous belt buckle pilfered from Mongolia, or an inscrutable scarf crafted from a Peruvian gravecloth. Anything that might carry supernatural side effects.

They found nothing, but the buzzing did not stop, so they methodically searched the room, running hands under chairs and along ledges, occasionally glancing at the other to be certain that there was only one buzzing Laumonier still. If it was malevolent, Greenmantle was the most likely candidate. They had other enemies, of course, but Greenmantle was the closest to home. In all the ways.

Laumonier found nothing of supernatural interest, only a cache of desiccated ladybirds.

"Hey. It's me."

Laumonier turned back to the buzzing brother, who had both stopped buzzing and dropped his cigarette. It glowed impotently on the pressed metal floor. He frowned off at the harbour in an introspective way somewhat opposed to his usual nature.

"Was that him?" Laumonier asked.

Laumonier frowned. "It was not his voice, was it?"

The previously buzzing brother asked, "Can you hear me? I'm new to this."

It was certainly not his voice. And it was certainly not his facial expression. His eyebrows moved in a way that they had always been capable of, surely, but never been asked to. It made him look at once younger and more intense.

Laumonier collectively felt a twinge of possible understanding.

"Who is this?" demanded Laumonier.

"It's Piper."

It was a name that had an immediate and visceral effect on Laumonier. Rage, betrayal, shock, and then back around to rage and betrayal. Piper Greenmantle. Colin's wife. Her name had not been breathed in conversation before, and yet here she was busting into it anyway.

Laumonier said, "Piper! How is it Piper? Get out of him."

"Oh, is that how this works?" Piper asked with curiosity. "Is it creepy? A possession-phone?"

"It *is* you," said Laumonier wonderingly.

"Hi, Dad," Piper said.

Although it had been years, Laumonier still knew his daughter's mannerisms very well.

Laumonier said, "I cannot believe it. What do you want? How is your p.o.s. husband these days?"

"He's in Boston without me," Piper replied. "Probably."

"I was just asking to see what you would say," Laumonier replied. "I already knew that."

Piper said, "You were right; I was wrong. I don't want to fight any more."

The Laumonier who had stubbed his cigarette now dabbed his eye in a sentimental way.

The Laumonier who never stopped smoking snapped, "Ten years and now you 'don't want to fight any more'?"

"Life's short. I'd like to go into business with you."

"Let me make sure I have my facts straight. You nearly got us sent to jail last year. Your husband killed a supplier for some artefact that doesn't exist. You are possessing us. And you want to do business with us? That does not sound like Colin Greenmantle's pretty little wife."

"No, it sure doesn't. That's why I'm calling. I'm turning over a new leaf."

"What sort of tree is this leaf attached to?" Laumonier asked suspiciously.

"A nice one with supernatural roots," Piper replied. "I've got something amazing down here. Huge. Buy of a lifetime. Of a century. I need you to pull out the stops, get everyone down here to bid for it. It's gonna be big."

Laumonier looked hopeful. "We —"

The only Laumonier still actively smoking interrupted, "After August? I don't think you can expect us to just swing in to business. Call me crazy, my love, but I don't trust you."

"You're just going to have to take my word on it."

"That's the least valuable thing you could offer," Laumonier replied coolly. He handed his cigarette to his other brother so that he could dig under his coat and sweater collar to his rosary beads. "You've devalued that quite a bit in the last ten years."

"You are the worst father," Piper snapped.

"In fairness, you are the worst daughter."

He pressed the rosary against the previously buzzing brother's head. Immediately, he spat blood and fell to his knees, his own expression resolving in his face once more.

"That," Laumonier said, "was what I suspected."

"I can't believe you hung up on her before I could say goodbye," Laumonier replied, wounded.

"I think I was just possessed," Laumonier said. "Did you guys see anything?"

ELEVEN

Back in Henrietta, night proceeded.

Richard Gansey was failing to sleep. When he closed his eyes: Blue's hands, his voice, black bleeding from a tree. It was starting, starting. No. It was ending. He was ending. This was the landscape of his personal apocalypse. What was excitement when he was wakeful melted into dread when he was tired.

He opened his eyes.

He opened Ronan's door just enough to confirm that Ronan was inside, sleeping with his mouth ajar, headphones blaring, Chainsaw a motionless lump in her cage. Then, leaving him, Gansey drove to the school.

He used his old key code to get into Aglionby's indoor athletic complex, and then he stripped and swam in the dark pool in the darker room, all sounds strange and hollow at night. He did endless laps as he used to do when he had first come to the school, back when he had been on the rowing team, back when he had sometimes come earlier than even rowing practice to swim. He had nearly forgotten what it felt like to be in the water: It was as if his body didn't exist; he was just a borderless mind. He pushed himself off a barely visible wall and headed towards the even less visible opposite one, no longer quite able to hold on to his concrete concerns. School, Headmaster Child, even Glendower. He was only this current minute. Why had he given this up? He couldn't remember even that.

In the dark water he was only Gansey, now. He'd never died, he wasn't going to die again. He was only Gansey, now, now, only now.

He could not see him, but Noah stood on the edge of the pool and watched. He had been a swimmer himself, once.

Adam Parrish was working. He had a late shift at the warehouse that night, unloading mason jars and cheap electronics and puzzles. Sometimes when he worked late like this, when he was tired, his mind ran to his life back in the trailer park. Neither fearful nor nostalgic, just forgetful. He'd somehow fail to recall that things had changed, and he would sigh as he pictured driving back to the trailer when his shift ended. Then there would be the jolt of surprise when his conscious mind clicked in with the reality of his apartment over St. Agnes.

Tonight, he once again misremembered his life and had the lurch of recalling he'd improved things, and as relief trickled through him, he remembered instead the Orphan Girl's frightened face. By all accounts, Ronan's dreams were often frightening things, and unlike Ronan, she had no hope of waking up. When he'd brought her back to the real world, she must have thought that she, too, had carved herself a new life. But instead they had merely moved her into another nightmare.

He told himself she wasn't real.

But guilt gnawed at him.

He thought about how tonight he would return to the home he'd made for himself. The Orphan Girl, though, would remain trapped in dreamspace, wearing his old watch and his old fear.

As he picked up the inventory clipboard, thoughts of Cabeswater nagged at him, reminding him that he still needed to consider the origin of that blackened tree. As he signed out, Aglionby pressed at him, reminding him that he still had a three-page paper on economics in the thirties to turn in. As he climbed into the car, the starter whined, reminding him that he needed to take a look at it before it failed entirely.

He didn't have time to devote to Ronan's dream urchin; he had problems of his own.

But he couldn't stop thinking about her.

His thoughts focused as his fingers skittered across the steering wheel in front of him. It took him a moment to realize what was happening, actually, even though he was looking right at it. His hand galloped across the top of the wheel, feeling the edge, testing the pressure of each pad against the surface.

Adam had not told his hand to move.

He made that hand into a fist and pulled it from the wheel. He held his wrist with his other hand.

Cabeswater?

But Cabeswater seemed no more present inside him than it ordinarily did when it wasn't trying to get his attention. Adam studied his palm in the grotty glow of the streetlight, disconcerted by the image of his fingers scuttling like an insect's legs without his mind attached to them. Now that he was looking right at his ordinary hand, the lines dark with cardboard dust and metal flake, it seemed like he may have imagined it. Like Cabeswater may have sent him the image.

Reluctantly, he remembered the wording of the bargain he'd made with the forest: *I will be your hands. I will be your eyes.*

He rested his hand once more on the centre of the steering wheel. It lay there, looking strange with the pale strip of skin where his watch had been. It didn't move.

Cabeswater? he thought again.

Sleepy leaves uncurled in his thoughts, a forest at night, cold and slow. His hand stayed where he had put it. His heart still crawled inside him, though, like the image of his fingers moving of their own accord.

He didn't know if it had been real. *Real* was becoming a less useful term all the time.

Back at Monmouth, Ronan Lynch dreamt.

The dream was a memory. Summer-green Barns, lush and messy with insects and humidity. Water fountained up from a sprinkler nestled in the grass. Matthew ran through it in swim trunks. Young. Pudgy. Curls bleached white from the sun. He was laughing in a rolling, infectious way. A second later, another boy hurtled after him, tackling him without hesitation. Both boys rolled, covered with wet pieces of grass.

This other boy stood. He was taller, sinuous, self-possessed. His hair was long and dark and curled, nearly to his chin.

This was Ronan, before.

Here was a third boy, leaping tidily over the sprinkler. *Jack be nimble, jack be quick.*

Ha, you thought I wouldn't, Gansey said, resting his palms on his bare knees.

Gansey! This was Aurora, already laughing as she said his name. The same wild laughter as Matthew. She directed the sprinkler right at him, soaking him immediately.

Ronan, before, regarded Ronan, after.

He felt the moment he realized he was dreaming — he heard his electronica pounding in his ears — and he knew he could wake himself. But this memory, this perfect memory . . . he became that Ronan, before, or the Ronan, before, became the Ronan, after.

The sun kept getting brighter. Brighter.

Brighter.

It was a white-hot electric eye. The world was seared into light, or shadow, nothing in between. Gansey shielded his eyes. Someone emerged from the house.

Declan. Something in his hand. Black in this harsh light.

A mask.

Round eyes, gaping smile.

Ronan remembered nothing of the mask but horror. Something about it was terrible, but he couldn't remember what right now. Every thought was burning out of him in this nuclear waste of a memory.

The eldest Lynch brother strode out, purposefully, shoes squelching in the soaked lawn.

The dream shuddered.

Declan began to run, right at Matthew.

"Orphan Girl!" Ronan shouted, scrambling to his feet. "Cabeswater! *Tir e e'lintes curralo!*"

The dream shuddered again. An apparition of a forest super-imposed over all of it, a frame snuck into a movie reel.

Ronan pelted across the sick white grass.

Declan reached Matthew first. The youngest Lynch brother tilted his head back to him, trustful, and that was the nightmare.

Grow up, asshole, Declan told Ronan. He slapped the mask on Matthew's face.

That was the nightmare.

Ronan snatched Matthew from Declan; the dream heaved again. He had the familiar form of his younger brother in his arms, but it was too late. The primitive mask was an effortless part of Matthew's face.

A raven flew overhead and vanished mid-sky.

It'll be OK, Ronan told his brother. *You can live like that. You can just never take it off.*

Matthew's eyes were unafraid in the wide eyeholes. That was the nightmare. That was the nightmare That was the

Declan tore the mask off.

A tree behind him oozed black.

Matthew's face was lines and dashes. It was not bloody; it was not horrific; it was simply not a face, and so it was terrible. He was not a person, he was just a drawn thing.

Ronan's chest was shaking in airless, silent sobs. He had not cried like that for so long —

The dream shuddered. And now it was not only Matthew who had fallen apart; everything was undoing. Aurora's hands were pointed at each other, all fingers bent backwards to her chest — lines, unmade. Behind them, Gansey was on his knees, his eyes dead.

Ronan's throat was raw. *I'll do anything! I'll do anything! I'll do anythi*

It was unmaking everything Ronan loved.

Please

In the Aglionby dorms, Matthew Lynch woke. When he stretched, his head hit the wall; he'd rolled right up against it in the night. It was only when his roommate, Stephen Lee, made a noise of grotesque frustration that he realized he was awake because his phone was ringing.

He pawed it to his ear. "Yah?"

There was no reply. He blinked at the screen to see who was calling, then put it back to his ear. Sleepily, he whispered, "Ronan?"

"Where are you? In your room?"

"Dur."

"I'm serious."

"Hur."

"Matthew."

"Yah, yah, I'm in my room. SL hates you. It's like two or sumthin'. Whatdya want?"

Ronan didn't reply right away. Matthew couldn't see him, but he was curled on his bed back at Monmouth, forehead resting on his knees, one hand gripping the back of his own skull, phone pressed to his ear. "Just to know you're all right."

" 'm all right."

"Go to sleep, then."

"Still sleeping now."

The brothers hung up.

Outside of Henrietta, nestled on the ley line, something dark watched all of this, everything in the Henrietta night, and said, *I'm awake I'm awake I'm awake.*

TWELVE

The following morning was over-bright and over-hot.

Gansey and Adam stood by the double doors of the Gladys Francine Mollin Wright Memorial Theatre, hands folded neatly. They had pulled usher service – just Adam had, really, but Gansey had volunteered to take Brand's place as the other usher. Ronan was nowhere in sight. Annoyance simmered inside Gansey.

"Raven Day," said Headmaster Child, "is more than a day of school pride. Because don't we have school pride every day?"

He stood on the stage. Everyone was sweating a little, but not him. He was a lean, rugged cowboy in the cattle drive that was life, skin striated like the face of a bleached canyon wall. Gansey had long maintained that Child was wasted here. To put such a survivor into a light-gray suit and tie was to throw away the opportunity of putting him, instead, on the back of a buckskin horse and on the inside of a ten-gallon hat.

Adam shot Gansey a knowing look. He mouthed *yee haw*. They smirked and had to look away from each other. Gansey's gaze landed right on Henry Cheng and the Vancouver crowd, all seated together near the back. As if feeling his attention, Henry looked over his shoulder. His eyebrow raced upward. Gansey was uncomfortably reminded of how Henry had seen the Orphan

Girl in the back of the SUV. He would, at some point, require an explanation, an evasion, or a lie.

"— for *this* Raven Day," Child insisted.

Gansey was ordinarily charmed by Raven Day. It was composed entirely of things that he liked: students assembled smartly in white T-shirts and khaki trousers like extras from a WWI documentary; hoisting of flags; teams pitted against one another with plenty of hurrahing; pomp, circumstance, in-jokes; ravens painted upon everything. This crop of juniors had made ravens for the entire student body to stage a mock conflict on the common while the school photographers captured shining faces for another year's worth of promotional materials.

Now, everything in Gansey sang urgently for him to spend his time seeking. His quest was a wolf, and it starved.

"Today is the tenth anniversary of Raven Day," Child said. "Ten years ago, the festivities we enjoy today were proposed by a student who had attended Aglionby for years. Sadly, Noah Czerny cannot be here today to celebrate, but before the rest of us do, we are fortunate enough to have one of his younger sisters here to tell us a little more about Noah and the day's origins."

Gansey would have thought he had misheard if Adam hadn't peered at him and mouthed, *Noah?*

Yes, Noah, because here was one of the Czerny sisters climbing on to the stage. Even if Gansey had not recognized her from the funeral, he would have recognized Noah's elfin mouth, the tiny eyes with the cheery bags beneath them, the large ears hidden behind fine hair. It was odd to see Noah's features on a young woman. It was odder to see them on anyone living. She seemed too old to be Noah's younger sister, but it was only because Gansey had forgotten how Noah existed in suspension. He would have been twenty-four now if he had been saved instead of Gansey.

A freshman said something that Gansey didn't catch and got himself promptly escorted from the theatre for his trouble. Noah's sister leaned into the microphone and said something also too faint to catch, and then said something else that was eaten by a squeal as the sound manager tried to adjust the volume. Finally, she said, "Hi, I'm Adele Czerny. I don't really have a long speech. I mean, I sat through these things when I was your age, and they're boring. I'm just going to say a few things about Noah and Raven Day. Did any of you guys know him?"

In unison, Gansey and Adam started to lift their hands and just as quickly dropped them. Yes, they knew him. No, they had not *known* him. Noah, alive, had been before their time here. Noah, dead, was a phenomenon, not an acquaintance.

"Well, you were missing out," she said. "My mom always said he was a firecracker, which just meant he was always getting speeding tickets and jumping on tables at family reunions and stuff. He always had so many ideas. He was so hyper."

Adam and Gansey looked at each other. They had always had the sense that the Noah they knew was not the true Noah. It was just disconcerting to hear how much *Noahness* death had stripped. It was impossible to not wonder what Noah would have done with himself if he had lived.

"Anyway, I'm here because I was actually the first one he told about his idea for Raven Day. He called me one evening, I guess it would've been when he was fourteen, and he told me he'd had this *dream* about ravens fighting and battling. He said they were all different colours and sizes and shapes, and he was inside them, and they were, like, swirling around him." She motioned around herself in a whirlwind; she had Noah's hands, Noah's elbows. "And he told me, 'I think it would be a cool art project.' And I told him, 'I'll bet if everybody at the school made one, I bet you'd have enough.'"

Gansey was aware that his arm hairs were standing up.

"So they're swooping and careening and there's nothing but ravens, nothing but dreams all around you," Adele said, only Gansey wasn't sure if she had actually said it, or if he'd heard her wrong and he was just half-remembering something she'd already said. "Anyway, I know he'd like what it is like nowadays. So, um, thanks for remembering one of his crazy dreams."

She was walking off the stage; Adam was covering one of his eyes with a hand; there was the dutiful double clap that Aglionby students were asked to perform in lieu of unruly applause.

"Let's go, ravens!" Child said.

This was Adam and Gansey's cue to open the doors. Students poured out. Humidity and light poured in. Headmaster Child joined them in the doorway.

He shook Gansey's hand, then Adam's. "Thanks for your service, gentlemen. Mr Gansey, I didn't think your mother could put together this fund-raiser and a guest list by this weekend, but we're pretty much there. She has my vote for running the country."

He and Gansey exchanged the sort of coMr adely smile that comes from having signed legal paperwork together. It would have been a fine moment if it had ended there, but Child lingered, making polite chitchat with Gansey and Adam – his best and his brightest, respectively. For seven excruciating minutes, they mined the weather, Thanksgiving break plans, and shared experiences in Colonial Williamsburg, and then, finally, exhausted, they parted ways as the juniors appeared with their raven warriors.

"Jesus Christ," Gansey said, panting a bit from the effort.

"I thought he would never leave," Adam said. He touched the bottom of his left eyelid, squinting it shut, before looking past Gansey. "If – ah. I'll be right back. I think I have something in my eye."

He left Gansey; Gansey set himself free on Raven Day. He found himself at the foot of the stairs where students were receiving ravens. The flock was composed of paper and aluminium foil and wood and papier-mâché and brass. Some birds floated with helium balloon bellies. Some glided. Some teetered on multiple supports, with separate rods to control flapping wings.

Noah had done this. Noah had *dreamt* this.

"I'm flipping you a bird," said a junior, handing him a dull black raven made of newspaper tacked to a wooden frame.

Gansey stepped off into the crowd. Noah's crowd. In a better world, Noah would have been giving that tenth-anniversary introduction.

At eye level, the landscape was all sticks and arms and white T-shirts, the mechanics and gears. But if one squinted into the too-bright sky, the sticks and the students vanished and the expanse was filled with ravens. They swooped and attacked, plunged and lifted, flapped and spun.

It was very hot.

Gansey felt time slip. Just a little. It was just that this sight was so oddly like something from his other life, his real life; these birds were cousins to Ronan's dream things. It seemed unfair that Noah should have died and Gansey had not. Noah had been *living* when he was murdered. Gansey had been marking time.

"What are the rules of this battle again?" he asked over his shoulder.

"No rules in war except stay alive."

Gansey turned; wings flapped past his face. He was hemmed in by shoulders and backs. He could not tell who had spoken, or even, now, without a face to look at, if someone had.

Time tugged at his soul.

The Aglionby orchestra began to play. The very first measure was a harmonious thicket of sound, but one of the brass instruments got the first note on the next phrase very wrong. At the same moment, an insect buzzed past Gansey's face, close enough that he could feel it. Suddenly, everything went slanting sideways. The sun overhead burned white. Ravens flapped around Gansey as he turned, looking for Adam or Child or anything that wasn't just a white shirt, a hand, a bird flapping. His eyes snagged on his own wrist. His watch said 6:21.

It had been hot when he died.

He was in a forest of wooden sticks, of birds. The brass instruments muttered; the flutes screamed. Wings buzzed and hummed and shivered around him. He could feel the hornets in his ears.

They aren't there

But that big insect whirred by him again, circling.

It had been years since Malory had been forced to stop half-way through a hike to wait as Gansey fell to his knees, hands over his ears, shivering, dying.

He had worked hard to walk away from that.

They aren't there. You are at Raven Day. You are going to eat sandwiches after this. You are going to jump-start the Camaro in the parking lot after school. You are going to drive to 300 Fox Way. You will tell Blue about your day you will

The insects pricked into his nostrils, moved his hair gently, collectively seethed. Sweat ran straight down his spine. The music shimmered. The students had become spirits, brushing past him and around him. His knees would buckle; he would let them.

He could not re-create his death here. Not now, not when it would be fresh on everyone's minds at the fund-raiser — *Gansey Three lost it at Raven Day, did you hear; Mrs Gansey can we have a word about your son?* — he would not make it about him.

But time was slipping; he was slipping. His heart ran with black, black blood.

"GanseyMan."

Gansey couldn't quite focus on the words. Henry Cheng stood before him, all hair and smile, his eyes intense. He took Gansey's raven from him and instead pressed something cool into Gansey's hand. Cool, and getting colder.

"Once, you got me coffee," Henry said. "When I was losing my mind. Consider the favour returned."

Gansey was holding a plastic cup of ice water. It should not have done anything, but something worked: the shocking temperature difference, the ordinary sound of the ice cubes knocking against one another, the eye contact. Students still milled around them, but they were once again students. The music was once again merely a school orchestra playing a new piece on an incredibly hot day.

"There he is," Henry said. "Toga party tonight, Richard, at Litchfield House. You should bring your boys and your child bride."

Then he was gone, ravens flapping where he had been.

THIRTEEN

Adam had thought there was something in his eye. It had begun while he stood in the over-hot theatre. Not so much an irritation as a fatigue, like he'd been staring at a screen for too long. He could have lived with it until the end of the school day if it had stayed like that, but his vision was getting a little blurry now. Not a troubling amount on its own, but combined with being able to *feel* his eye, it seemed like he should take a look at it.

Instead of returning to one of the academic buildings, he slid down the stairs to the theatre's side door. There were bathrooms in the area under the stage, and it was those he headed to, passing many-legged animals made of stacked old chairs, strange silhouettes of stage-set trees, and depthless oceans of black curtain hung over everything. The hallway was dark and close, the walls horrors of chipped green paint, and with one hand cupped over his eye, Adam found it distorted and unnerving. He recalled again the picture of his skittering hand.

He needed to do some work with Cabeswater, he thought, and figure out what was going on with that tree.

The bathroom light was switched off. It was not an obstacle at all — the light switch was just inside the door — but still, Adam didn't quite want to put his hand into the blackness to find it.

He stood there, his heart a little too fast, and he looked behind himself.

The hall was close and dark and unmoving under sickly fluorescent light. The shadows were inseparable from the stage curtains. Big swaths of black connected everything.

Turn on the light, Adam thought.

With his free hand, the one not covering his eye, he reached into the bathroom.

He did it fast, fingers pressing through cold, through dark, touching something —

No, it was only a Cabeswater vine, only in his head. He slammed his hand past it and turned on the light.

The bathroom was empty.

Of course it was empty. Of course it was empty. Of course it was empty.

Two old stalls made of green-painted plywood, nowhere near up to proper accessibility codes, nowhere near up to proper hygiene codes. A urinal. A sink with a yellow ring round the drain. A mirror.

Adam stepped in front of the glass, his hand over his eye, looking at his gaunt face. His nearly colourless eyebrow was pinched with worry. Lowering his hand, he looked again at himself. He saw no pinkness around his left eye. It didn't seem to be watering. It was —

He squinted. Was he slightly walleyed? That was what it was called when your eyes didn't point in the same direction, right?

He blinked.

No, it was fine. It was just a trick of this chilly green light. He leaned in closer to see if there was any redness in the corner.

It *was* walleyed.

Adam blinked, and it was not. He blinked, and it was. It was like one of those bad dreams that was not a nightmare, not really, that was just about trying to put on a pair of socks and finding they suddenly wouldn't fit on your foot.

As he watched, his left eye slowly sank down to look at the floor, unhitched from the gaze of his right eye.

His vision blurred and then focused again as his right eye took dominance. Adam's breath was uneven. He'd already lost hearing in one ear. He couldn't lose sight in one eye, too. Was it from his father? Was this a delayed effect of hitting his head?

The eye rocked slowly, like a marble sliding in a jar of water. He could feel the horror of it in his stomach.

In the mirror, he thought the shadow of one of the stalls changed.

He turned to look: nothing. Nothing.

Cabeswater, are you with me?

He turned back to the mirror. Now his left eye was travelling slowly around, wandering back and forth, up and down.

Adam's chest hitched.

The eye looked at him.

Adam scrambled back from the mirror, hand smacked over his eye. His shoulder blade crashed into the opposite wall, and he stood there, gasping for air, scared, scared, scared, because what kind of help did he need, and who could he ask?

The shadow above the stall *was* changing. It was turning from a square into a triangle because — oh God — one of the stall doors was opening.

The long hallway back to the outside felt like a horror gallery gauntlet. Black spilled out of the stall door.

Adam said, "Cabeswater, I need you."

The darkness spread across the floor.

All Adam could think was that he couldn't let it touch him. The thought of it on his skin was worse than the image of his useless eye. "Cabeswater. Keep me safe. *Cabeswater!*"

There was a sound like a shot — Adam shied away — as the mirror split. A sun from somewhere else burned on the other side of it. Leaves were pressed up against the glass as if it were a window. The forest whispered and hissed in Adam's deaf ear, urging him to help it find a channel.

Gratitude burned through him, as hard to bear as the fear. If something happened to him now, at least he wouldn't be alone.

Water, Cabeswater urged. *Waterwaterwater.*

Scrambling to the sink, Adam twisted on the tap. Water rushed out, scented with rain and rocks. He reached through the flow to smash down the plug. The inky black bled towards him, inches from his shoes.

Don't let it touch you—

He clambered on to the edge of the sink as the darkness reached the bottom of the wall. It would climb, Adam knew. But then, finally, the water filled the plugged basin and flowed over the edge on to the floor. It washed over the blackness, soundless, colourless, sliding towards the drain. It left behind only pale, ordinary concrete.

Even after the blackness was gone, Adam let the sink pour on to the floor for another full minute, soaking his shoes. Then he slipped off the edge of the sink. He scooped the water up in his palms and splashed the earthy-scented water over his face, over his left eye. Again and again, again and again, again and again, until his eye no longer felt tired. Until he could no longer *feel* it at all. It was just his eye again, when he peered into the mirror. Just his face. There was no sign of the other sun or a lazy iris. Drops of Cabeswater's rivers clung damply in Adam's eyelashes. Cabeswater muttered and moaned, vines curling through Adam, dappled light flashing behind his eyes, stones pressing up beneath the palms of his hands.

Cabeswater had taken so long to come to his aid. Only a few weeks before, a heap of roofing tiles had fallen on top of him, and Cabeswater had swept instantaneously to save him. If that had happened today, he would have been dead.

The forest whispered at him in its language that was equal parts pictures and words, and it made him understand why it had been so slow to come to him.

Something had been attacking them both.

FOURTEEN

As Maura had already pointed out, being suspended was not a vacation, so Blue had her after-school shift at Nino's as usual. Although the sun outside was overpowering, the restaurant was strangely dim inside, a trick of the thunderheads darkening the western sky. The shadows beneath the metal-legged tables were gray and diffuse; it was hard to tell if it was dark enough to turn on the lights that hung over each table or not. The decision could wait; there was no one in the restaurant.

With nothing to occupy her mind except for sweeping the Parmesan cheese from the corners of the room, Blue thought about Gansey inviting her to a toga party tonight. To her surprise, her mother had urged her to go. Blue had said that an Aglionby toga party went against everything she stood for. Maura had replied, "Private school boys? Using random pieces of fabric as apparel? That seems like exactly what you stand for these days."

Shoof, shoof. Blue swept the floor aggressively. She could feel herself hurtling towards self-awareness, and she wasn't sure she liked it.

In the kitchen, the shift manager chortled. Dissonant, clunky music warred with the electric guitar playing overhead; he was watching videos on his phone with the cooks. A loud ding sounded as the restaurant door opened. To her surprise, Adam stepped in and warily assessed the empty tables. His uniform was strangely bedraggled: the trousers wrinkled and muddied, his white shirt smudged and damp in places.

"Wasn't I supposed to call you later?" Blue asked. She eyed his uniform. Ordinarily it would have been impeccable. "Are you OK?"

Adam slid into a chair and touched his left eyelid cautiously. "I remembered I had Weights and Discovery after school and didn't want you to miss me. Uh, phys ed and a scientific method extracurricular."

Blue walked her broom over to his table. "You didn't say if you were OK."

He flicked his fingers irritably against one of the damp places on his sleeve. "Cabeswater. Something's up with it. I don't know. I have to do some work with it. I'll need someone to spot me, I guess. What are you doing this evening?"

"Mom says I'm going to a toga party. Are you?"

Disdain dripped from Adam's voice. "I'm not going to a party at Henry Cheng's, no."

Henry Cheng. Things made marginally more sense. In a Venn diagram where one circle held the words *toga party* and one held the words *Henry Cheng*, Gansey might possibly end up where they intersected. Blue's mixed feelings returned in force. "What is the actual deal with you and Henry Cheng? And do you want some pizza? Someone placed a wrong order and we have extras."

"You've seen him. I don't have time for that. And yes, please."

She fetched the pizza and sat opposite Adam as he inhaled it as politely as possible. The truth was that until he'd walked in the door, she'd forgotten that they had arranged a call to talk about Gansey and Glendower. She was feeling pretty short on ideas after discussing it with her family members in the bathtub. She admitted, "I should tell you I don't really have any ideas about Gansey other than finding Glendower, and I don't know what to do next about that."

Adam said, "I didn't get a lot of time to think about it today, either, because of—" He gestured to his rumpled uniform again, though she couldn't tell if he meant Cabeswater or school. "And so I don't have an idea, I only have a question. Do you think Gansey could *order* Glendower to appear?"

Something about this question neatly upended Blue's stomach. It was not that she hadn't thought about Gansey's power of command; it was just that his uncanny authoritative voice was so closely allied with his ordinary bossy voice that it was sometimes difficult to convince herself that she had not imagined it. And then when she did admit that there was something there – for instance, when he had clearly magically dissolved the false Blues during their last visit to Cabeswater – it was still nonetheless somewhat difficult to think of in a magical sense. The knowledge slid sideways, pretending to be normal. Now that she thought of the phenomenon more firmly, though, holding on to the entirety of it as best she could, she realized that it was a lot like Noah's appearing and disappearing, or like the dream logic of Aurora appearing through rock. Her mind was quite happy to let her believe that there was nothing magic about it; to sketchily rewrite it as simply Gansey being Gansey.

"I don't know," Blue said. "If he could, wouldn't he have tried it before now?"

"Honestly —" Adam started, and then stopped. His face changed. "Are you going to the party tonight?"

"I guess so." Too late, she got the sense that the question meant more than the words she'd heard. "Like I said, Mom told me I was going, so . . ."

"With Gansey."

"Yeah, I guess. And Ronan, if he's going."

"Ronan won't go to Henry's."

Carefully, Blue said, "Then, yeah, I guess, with Gansey."

Adam frowned at the edge of the table, looking at his own hand. He was taking his time with something, measuring the words, testing them before he said them. "You know, when I first met Gansey, I couldn't figure out why he was friends with someone like Ronan. Gansey was always in class, always getting stuff done, always a teacher's pet. And here was Ronan, like a heart attack that never stopped. I knew I couldn't complain, 'cause I hadn't come first. Ronan had. But one day, he'd done some stupid shit I don't even remember, and I just couldn't *take* it. And I asked why Gansey was even friends with him if he was such an asshole all the time. And I remember Gansey told me that Ronan always told the truth, and the truth was the most important thing."

It was not at all difficult to imagine Gansey saying such a thing.

Adam looked up to Blue then, and he pinned her with his gaze. Outside, the wind chucked leaves against the glass. "Which is why I wanna know why you two won't tell me the truth about you two."

Now her stomach turned over the other direction. You two. Gansey and her. Her and Gansey. Blue had imagined this conversation dozens of times. Endless permutations of how she brought it up, how he reacted, how it ended. She could do this. She was ready.

No, she wasn't.

"About us?" she said. Lamely.

His expression, if possible, turned more disdainful than it had over Henry Cheng. "Do you know what hurts the most? What this means you think of me. You didn't even give me the chance to be OK with it. You were just so sure I'd be eaten by jealousy. That's how you see me?"

He wasn't *wrong*. But he had been a rather more brittle version of himself back when they'd first made the decision to not tell him. Saying this out loud felt rather unsporting, though, so she just tried, "You – *things* – were different then."

" 'Then'? How long has it been going on?"

"*Going on* isn't exactly what is happening," Blue said. A relationship that was squeezed into stolen glances and secret phone calls was so drastically less than what she wanted that she refused to consider it dating. "And it's not exactly like starting a new job. 'The start date was *x*!' I can't tell you precisely how long it's been going on."

"*You* just said 'going on,' " Adam said.

Blue's mental state surfed the crest of a wave that divided empathy and frustration. "Don't be impossible. I'm sorry. It wasn't supposed to be something, and then it was, and then I didn't know how to say anything. I didn't want to risk messing up our friendship."

"So even though I might have been decent about it, some part of you thought I'd be so shittily in constant competition with Gansey that you figured it was better to just lie?"

"I didn't *lie*."

"Sure, *Ronan*. Lying by omission is still lying," Adam said. He was sort of half-smiling, but in that way people did when they were annoyed rather than when anything was funny.

Outside, a couple paused by the door to read the menu attached to it; both Blue and Adam waited in irritated silence until they moved on, leaving the restaurant empty. Adam opened his hands as if he expected her to tip a satisfactory explanation into them.

The fair part of Blue was well aware that she was in the wrong and so it was her job to defuse his legitimate hurt, but the prideful part of her still would've preferred to point out how difficult he had been back when she and Gansey had first realized they had feelings for each other. With some effort, she went with a middle ground. "It wasn't as calculated as you make it sound like it was."

Adam rejected the middle ground. "But I *saw* you guys trying to hide it. The crazy thing is – like, *I'm right here*. I'm with you guys every day. Do you think I didn't see it? He's my best friend. You think I don't know him?"

"Then why aren't you having this conversation with him? He's half of this, you know."

He spread his hands out at the still-empty restaurant, as if he, too, was amazed by the turn this conversation had taken. "Because I was here to talk to you about how to save him from dying. Then I found out you guys were going to a party together, and I couldn't believe how irresponsible you were being."

Now Blue also spread her hands. It was a rather less elegant gesture than Adam's, more like a fist clench in reverse. *"Irresponsible? Excuse me?"*

"Does he know about your curse?"

Her cheeks felt hot. "Oh, don't."

"You don't think it's a little relevant that the guy who is supposed to die in the next year is *dating* the girl who's supposed to kill her true love with a kiss?"

She was too angry to do anything but shake her head. He merely raised an eyebrow in reply, an action that warmed the temperature of Blue's blood by a single degree.

She snapped, "I can control myself, thanks."

"In any circumstance? You're not gonna fall on him, or get tricked into it, or magic's not gonna go wrong in Cabeswater — can you guarantee? I don't think you can."

Now she'd definitely tipped over the crest of the wave into boiling anger. "You know what, I've been living with this a heck of a lot longer than you have, and I don't really think you can come in here and tell me how to deal with it —"

"I can when it's *my best friend.*"

"He's mine as well!"

"If he really was, you wouldn't be so damn selfish."

"If he really was *yours*, you'd be happy he had someone."

"How could I have been happy about it *when I wasn't supposed to know about it*?"

Blue stood up. "It's amazing, really, how this seems to be about you instead of him."

Adam stood up, too. "Funny, because I was about to say the same thing."

They faced each other, both furious. Blue could feel poisonous words bubbling up in a dark queue like the sap from that tree. She wasn't going to say them. She wasn't. Adam's mouth went very thin, like he was about to retort something, but in the end, he just swiped his keys from the table and walked out of the restaurant.

Outside, thunder growled. There was no sign of the sun; the wind had dragged the clouds across the entire sky. It was going to be a wild night.

FIFTEEN

Many years before this afternoon, a psychic had told Maura Sargent that she was "a judgemental but gifted clairvoyant with a talent for bad decision-making." The two of them had been standing by the side of an I-64 exit ramp about twenty miles outside of Charleston, West Virginia. Both had bags on their backs and their thumbs out. Maura had hitchhiked from points further west. The other psychic had hitchhiked from points south. They did not know each other. Yet.

"I'm gonna take that as a compliment," said Maura.

"Shocking," snarled the other psychic, but in a way that made it kind of another compliment. She was a harder weapon than Maura, more unforgiving, already tempered by blood. Maura liked her at once.

"Where are you headed?" Maura asked. A car approached; they both stuck out their thumbs. The car vanished on to the interstate; they put their thumbs down. They were not yet discouraged; it was a green and rippling summer of the sort that made anything seem possible.

"East, I guess. You?"

"Same. Feet are walking me there."

"My feet are running," the other psychic said, grimacing. "How far east?"

"I guess I'll know when I get there," Maura said thoughtfully. "We could travel together. Set up shop when we get there."

The other psychic raised a knowing eyebrow. "Turning tricks?"

"Continuing education."

They both laughed, which was how they knew they would get along. Another car came; they put out their thumbs; the car went.

The afternoon continued.

"What's this?" said the other psychic.

A mirage had appeared at the end of the exit ramp, only now that they looked a bit harder, it was a real person, behaving like an unreal person. She was walking directly up the middle of the asphalt towards them, gripping an overstuffed butterfly-shaped bag in one hand. She had high, old-fashioned boots laced all the way up beyond where her peculiar dress ended. Her hair was a blond frothy cloud and her skin was chalky. Except for her black eyes, everything about her was as pale as the psychic beside Maura was dark.

Both Maura and the other psychic watched this third person labour up the exit ramp, seemingly unconcerned with the possibility of motorized vehicles.

Just as the pale young woman had nearly reached them, an elderly Cadillac rounded the corner on to the exit ramp. The woman had plenty of time to leap out of the way, but she didn't. Instead, she paused and tugged up the zipper on her butterfly bag as the Cadillac's brakes squealed mightily. The car came to a stop inches away from her legs.

Persephone peered at Maura and Calla.

"I think you'll find," she told them, "that this lady is going to give us a ride."

Twenty years had passed since that meeting in West Virginia, and Maura was still a judgmental but gifted clairvoyant with a talent for bad decisions. But in the years between, she'd grown used to being a member of an inseparable three-headed entity that shared decision making equally. They'd let themselves think that would never end.

It was so much harder to see things clearly without Persephone.

"Picked up anything?" Mr Gray asked.

"Go around again," Maura replied. They headed back through Henrietta as store lights flickered in time with an unseen ley line. The rain had stopped, but evening had come on, and Mr Gray turned on the headlights before rebraiding his fingers with hers. He was acting as driver as Maura tried to solidify an increasingly urgent hunch. It had begun this morning when she woke up, an ominous feeling like one had after waking from a bad dream. Instead of fading as the day went on, however, it only grew more pointed, focusing on Blue, and Fox Way, and a creeping darkness that felt like passing out.

Also her eye hurt.

She'd been doing this for long enough to know that there was nothing wrong with it. There was something wrong with someone else's eye at some point in time, and Maura was just tuned into the station. It irritated her, but it wasn't an action item. The hunch was. The problem with pursuing bad feelings was that it was always difficult to tell if one was running towards a problem to fix it, or running to a problem to create it. It would've been easier if it had still been the three of them. Usually Maura started a project, Calla made it into a tangible thing, and Persephone sent it flying into the ether. Nothing worked the same with just two.

"Go around again, I guess," Maura told Mr Gray. She could feel him thinking as he drove. Poetry and heroes, romance and death. Some poem about a phoenix. He was the worst decision she'd made so far, but she couldn't keep from making it again and again.

"Do you mind if I talk?" he asked. "Will it ruin everything?"

"I'm not having any luck. You might as well. What are you thinking about? Birds rising from ashes?"

He glanced over at her with an appraising nod, and she gave him a cunning smile. It was a parlour trick, the simplest of things she could do – pluck a current thought from an unguarded and sympathetic mind – but it was nice to be appreciated.

"I've been thinking a lot about Adam Parrish and his band of merry men," Mr Gray admitted. "And this dangerous world they tread."

"That's a strange way of putting it. I would have said Richard Gansey and his band of merry men."

He inclined his head as if he could see her point of view as well, even if he didn't share it. "I was just thinking how much danger they've inherited. Colin Greenmantle leaving Henrietta doesn't make it safer; it makes it more perilous."

"Because he kept the others away."

"Just so."

"And now you think others will come here, even though no one is selling anything here? Why would they still be interested?"

Mr Gray indicated a buzzing streetlight as they drove by the courthouse. Three shadows passed over the top of it, cast by nothing Maura could see. "Henrietta is one of those places that looks supernatural even from a distance. It will be a perennial stop for people in the business, poking around for things that might be the cause or effect of it."

"Which is dangerous for the merry men because there is actually something for them to find? Cabeswater?"

Mr Gray inclined his head again. "Mm. And the Lynch property. I don't forget my part in this, either."

Neither did Maura. "You can't undo that."

"No. But —" His pause at this point in the conversation was evidence of the Gray Man regrowing his heart. It was a pity that the seedling of it had to erupt into the same torched ground that had killed it in the first place. Consequences, as Calla often said, were a bitch. "What do you see for me? Do I stay here?" When she didn't answer, he pressed, "Do I die?"

She removed her hand from his. "Do you actually want to know?"

"*Simle þreora sum þinga gehwylce, ær his tid aga, to tweon weorþeð; adl oþþe yldo oþþe ecghete fægum fromweardum feorh oðþringeð.*" He sighed, which told Maura more about his mental state than his untranslated Anglo-Saxon poetry did. "It was easier to tell hero from villain when the stakes were only life and death. Everything in between gets harder."

"Welcome to how the other half lives," she said. With sudden clarity, she drew a loopy symbol in the air. "What's the company with the logo like this?"

"Disney."

"Har."

"Trevon-Bass. It's nearby."

"Is there a dairy farm close to it?"

"Yes," Mr Gray answered. "Yes, there is."

He made a safe but illegal U-turn. In a few minutes, they passed the faded concrete monolith of the Trevon-Bass factory, then turned on to a back road, and finally down a drive bounded by four-board fence. Rightness trickled through Maura, like reaching for a pleasant memory and finding it exactly how you left it.

Maura said, "How did you know it was back here?"

"I've been here before," Mr Gray said in a vaguely ominous tone.

"I hope you didn't kill someone here."

"No. But I did hold a gun to someone's head here, in full disclosure." A barely visible farm sign welcomed them to the vacation property. The drive ended in a gravel lot; the headlights illuminated a barn that had clearly been converted into stylish living space. "This is where the Greenmantles stayed when they were in town. The dairy's way over there."

Maura was already opening the car door. "Do you think we can get inside?"

"I would merely suggest brevity."

The side door was unlocked. Both Maura's clairvoyance and her heart could sense Mr Gray standing close behind her as they stepped inside, tense and watchful. Nearby, some cows lowed and grunted, sounding larger than they must have really been.

The inside of the rental was very dark, all shadows, no corners. Maura closed her eyes, letting them adjust to the idea of total blackness. She was not afraid of the dark, nor of the things in it. Fear was unworthy of her devotion; the rightness was.

She groped for it now.

Opening her eyes, she made her way around a lump that was probably a sofa. Certainty thrummed through her more strongly as she found a staircase and began to climb. At the top was an open-plan kitchen, dimly lit with purple-gray through the massive new windows, green-blue from the microwave clock.

It was unpleasant. She couldn't tell if it was something about the room itself, or merely Mr Gray's memories pressing up against her own. She proceeded.

Here was a pitch-black hallway, no windows, no light at all.

It was more than dark.

As she stepped cautiously into it, the darkness ceased to be darkness and instead became an absence of light. The two conditions are similar in several ways, but none of which were important when you were standing in one instead of the other.

Something whispered *Blue* in Maura's ear.

Every one of her senses was wrung raw; she couldn't tell if she was meant to push forward or not.

Mr Gray touched her back.

Except that it wasn't him. She only had to turn her head slightly to the right to realize that he was still at the edge of the liquid dark. Maura took a moment to visualize a protective shell around herself. Now she could see that the hallway ended at a doorway. Though there were other closed doors on either side, the one at the end was obviously the source.

She glanced back at the light switch beside Mr Gray. He flicked it.

The lights were like losing an argument with the correct answer. They should have been on. They *were* on. When Maura peered at the bulbs, she could tell in an objective way that they were on.

But the hallway was still not lit.

Maura met Mr Gray's narrowed eyes.

They crossed the final few feet, soundless, pushing the absence of light before them, and then Maura hovered her hand above the doorknob. It looked ordinary, which is how the most dangerous things looked. It cast no shadow on the door, because no light reached it.

Maura stretched for the rightness and found terror. Then she stretched beyond that and found the answer.

Turning the knob, she pushed open the door.

The hall lights seeped darkly past her, revealing a large bathroom. A scrying bowl lay beside the bathtub. Three colourless candles had dripped all over the back of the sink. *PIPER PIPER PIPER* was written backwards on the mirror in a substance that looked a lot like pink lipstick.

There was something large on the floor, and it was moving and scraping.

Maura told her hand to find the light switch, and it did.

The thing on the floor was a body – no. It was a human. It was twisting in a way a human shouldn't, though, shoulders unfolding. Fingers claws on the tile. Legs scrabbling, scuttling. An inhuman sound escaped from his mouth, and then Maura understood.

This person was dying.

Maura waited until he had finished, and then she said, "You must be Noah."

SIXTEEN

C alla had also been having a persistently negative hunch that day, but unlike Maura, she had been stuck in an Aglionby Academy office doing paperwork and didn't have the liberty of trying to find out what the source of the bad feeling was. Nonetheless, it grew and grew, filling her mind like a black headache, until she had given in and asked to go home an hour early. She was lying on her face upstairs in the room she shared with Jimi when the front door slammed.

Maura's voice rose clearly from the front hallway. "I've brought home dead people. Cancel every appointment! Hang up your phones! Orla, if you have a boy here, he's gotta go!"

Calla extracted herself from her comforter and scooped up her slippers before heading down the hall. Jimi, benevolent busy-body that she was, smashed her ample hip on the sewing table in her hurry to see what was up.

They both stopped halfway down the stairs.

To her credit, Calla only thought about dropping her slippers when she saw Noah Czerny standing beside Maura and Mr Gray.

Noah Czerny was a very human name to give something that did not look very human to Calla's eyes. She had seen a lot of living humans in her time, and she'd seen a lot of spirits in her time, but she hadn't ever seen something like this. A soul this decayed shouldn't have been — well, it shouldn't have been anything. It should have been a remnant of a ghost, a mindless, repetitive haunting. A hundred-year-old scent in a hallway. A shiver standing next to a certain window.

But somehow, she was looking at a shambles of a soul, and in it, there was still a dead kid.

"Oh, baby," Jimi said, full of instant compassion. "You poor thing. Let me get you some . . ." Jimi, ever the herbalist, generally had an herbal suggestion for every possible mortal ill.

"Some what?" Calla prompted.

Jimi pursed her mouth and rocked a bit on her feet. She was clearly stumped, but could not lose face in front of the others. Also, she did have a tediously good heart, and there was no doubt that Noah's existence distressed her.

"Mimosa," Jimi finished, triumphant, and Calla sighed with grudging appreciation. Jimi wagged a finger at Noah. "Mimosa flowers help make spirits appear, and that'll make you feel stronger!"

As she stomped back up the stairs, Maura asked Mr Gray to show Noah into the reading room, and then she and Calla conferred at the base of the stairs. Rather than telling her how they'd come to have Noah with them, she merely held out her arm and allowed Calla to press her palm against her skin. Calla's psychometry – divination through touch – was often unspecific, but in this case, the event was recent and vivid enough for her to pick it up easily, along with a kiss Maura had shared with Mr Gray beforehand.

"Mr Gray is talented," Calla observed.

Maura looked withering. She said, "Here's the rub. I think I was being shown that mirror with Piper's name on it on purpose, but I don't think it was Noah's purpose. He doesn't remember how he got there or why he was doing it."

Calla kept her voice low. "Could he have been a portent?"

Portents – supernatural warnings of ill tidings to come – were not of particular interest to Calla, mostly because they were usually imaginary. People tended to see portents where there were none: black cats bringing bad luck, a crow promising sadness. But a true portent – an ominous suggestion from a little-understood cosmic presence – was not something to be ignored.

Maura's voice was also hushed. "Could be. I haven't shaken this terrible feeling all day. The only thing is, I didn't think something sentient could be a portent."

"*Is* he sentient?"

"Part of him, anyway. We were talking in the car. I've never seen anything like it. He's decayed enough to appear as a mindless portent, but at the same time, there's a boy in there still. I mean, we had him *in the car.*"

Both women mused upon this.

Calla said, "He's the one who died on the ley line? Maybe Cabeswater made him strong enough to stay conscious for all of this, beyond when he should have passed on. If he's too cowardly to go on, that crazy forest could be giving him enough power to stick it out here."

Maura gave Calla another withering look. "It's called *scared*, Calla Lily Johnson, and he is just a kid. Ish. Remember he was murdered. Remember he's one of Blue's best friends."

"So what's the plan? You want me to get ahold of him and find things out? Or are we trying to send him on?"

Uneasily, Maura said, "Remember the frogs, though."

A few years before, Blue had caught two tree frogs while out performing neighbourly errands. She'd triumphantly set up a makeshift terrarium for them in one of Jimi's largest iced tea pitchers. As soon as she'd gone to school, Maura had immediately divined — through ordinary channels, not psychic ones — that these tree frogs were in for a slow death if tended by a young Blue Sargent. She had set them free in the backyard and thus began one of the largest arguments she and her daughter had yet or since had.

"Fine," Calla hissed. "We won't free any ghosts while she's at a toga party."

"I don't want to go."

Both Maura and Calla jumped.

Of course Noah was standing beside them. His shoulders were slumped and his eyebrows tipped upward. Under it all were threads and black, dust and absence. His words were soft and slurred. "Not yet."

"You don't have much time, boy," Calla told him.

"Not yet," Noah repeated. "Please."

"No one's going to make you do anything you don't want to do," Maura said.

Noah shook his head sadly. "They . . . already have. They . . . will again. But this . . . I want to do it for *me*."

He held his hand out to Calla, palm up, as if he were a beggar. It was a gesture that reminded Calla of another dead person in her life, one who still hung sadness and guilt around her neck, even after two decades. In fact, now that she considered it, the gesture was too perfectly accurate, the wrist too limply similar, the fingers too delicately and intentionally sprawled, an echo of Calla's memories —

"I'm a mirror," Noah said bleakly, responding to her thoughts. He stared at his feet. "Sorry."

He started to drop his hand, but Calla was finally moved to a reluctant and genuine compassion. She took his cool fingers.

Immediately a blow smashed into her face.

She should have expected it, but still, she barely had time to recover when the next came. Fear spewed up, then the pain, and then another blow – Calla nimbly blocked this one. She did not need to relive Noah's entire murder.

She moved around it and found . . . nothing. Ordinarily, her psychometry worked exceptionally well on the past, digging through all recent events to any strong distant events. But Noah was so decayed that his past was mostly gone. All that remained were thready cobwebs of memories. There was more kissing – how did Calla's day end up involving living through so many Sargents with so many tongues in their mouths? There was Ronan, appearing far more kind through Noah's memories. There was Gansey, courageous and solid in ways Noah clearly envied. And Adam – Noah was afraid of him, or for him. This fear tangled through images of him in increasingly dark threads. Then there was the future, spreading out with thinner and thinner images and —

Calla took her hand away from Noah and stared at him. For once, she had nothing clever to say.

"OK, kid," she said finally. "Welcome to the house. You can stay here as long as you can."

SEVENTEEN

Although Gansey liked Henry Cheng, agreeing to go to a party of his felt like a strange shift in power. It was not that he felt threatened by Henry in any way – both Henry and Gansey were kings in their respective territories – but it felt more loaded to meet Henry on his own turf rather than on the neutral ground of Aglionby Academy. The four Vancouver kids all lived off-campus in Litchfield House, and parties there were unheard of. It was an exclusive club. Undeniably Henry's. To dine in fairyland was to be forced to stay there for ever or to pine for it once you left, and all that.

Gansey wasn't sure he was in a position to be making new friends.

Litchfield House was an old Victorian on the opposite edge of downtown from Monmouth. In the damp, cooling night, it rose out of curls of mist, turrets and shingles and porches, every window lit with a tiny electric candle. The driveway was double-parked with four fancy cars, and Henry's silver Fisker was an elegant ghost on the kerb in front, right behind a dutiful-looking old sedan.

Blue was in a terrible mood. Something had clearly happened while she was on shift, but Gansey's attempts to prise it from her had established only that it was neither about the toga party nor him. Now, she was the one driving the Pig, which had a threefold benefit. For starters, Gansey couldn't imagine anyone whose mood wouldn't be marginally lifted by driving a Camaro. Second, Blue said she never got a chance to practise driving in Fox Way's communal vehicle. And third, most importantly, Gansey was outrageously and eternally driven to distraction by the image of her behind the wheel of his car. Ronan and Adam weren't with them, so there was no one to catch them in what felt like an incredibly indecent act.

He had to tell them.

Gansey wasn't sure he was in a position to be falling in love, but he'd done it anyway. He didn't quite grasp the mechanics of it. He understood his friendship with Ronan and Adam – they both represented qualities that he both lacked and admired, and they liked the versions of himself that he also liked. That was true of his friendship with Blue, too, but it was more than that. The better he got to know her, the more it felt like he did when he was swimming. There stopped being dissonant versions of him. There was only Gansey, now, now, now.

Blue paused the Pig at the quiet stop sign opposite Litchfield House's corner, assessing the parking situation.

"Mr uh," she said unpleasantly, eyes on the high-end cars.

"What?"

"I just forgot how Aglionby he was."

"We really don't have to go," Gansey said. "I mean, I just need to stick my head in the door to tell him thanks, but that's it."

They both peered across the road at the house. Gansey thought about how strange it was that he felt uncomfortable doing this, a purposeless visit with a crowd he almost certainly knew in its entirety. He was about to admit this out loud when the front door opened. The act created a square of yellow, like a portal to another dimension, and Julius Caesar stepped out on to the wraparound porch. Julius waved a hand at the Camaro and shouted, "Yo, yo, Dick Gansey!"

Because it was not Julius Caesar; it was Henry in a toga.

Blue's eyebrows disappeared into her bangs. "Are you going to wear one of those?"

This was going to be terrible.

"Absolutely not," Gansey told her. The toga looked more real than he would have liked now that he was looking right at it. "We're not staying long."

"Park around the corner and don't hit any cats!" Henry shouted.

Blue circled the block, successfully avoided a white cat, and did a slow but credible job of parallel parking, even with Gansey watching closely, even with the power steering belt whining a protest.

Although Henry must have known it would not take them long, he had retreated back inside in order to be able to grandly answer the door when they rang the bell. Now he shut the door behind them, sealing them in a slightly over-warm pocket of garlic-and-rose-scented air. Gansey had expected to find students swinging from chandeliers and skating on alcohol, and although he had not necessarily *wanted* that, the discrepancy was off-putting. The interior was fussily tidy; a dark hall hung with carved mirrors and cramped with brittle antique furniture stretched dimly into the guts of the house. It did not look remotely like a place that might host a party. It looked like a place old ladies might go to die and remain undiscovered until the neighbours noticed a strange smell. It was utterly at odds with what Gansey knew of Henry.

It was also very quiet.

Gansey had a sudden, terrible thought that it was possible the party might be simply Henry and the two of them in togas in a fancy sitting room.

"Welcome, welcome," Henry told them, as if he had not just seen Gansey a moment before. "Did you hit the cat?"

He had taken enormous care with his appearance. His toga was tied with more care than any tie Gansey had ever knotted, and Gansey had knotted a lot of ties. He was wearing the most chrome watch Gansey had ever seen, and Gansey had seen a lot of chromed things. His black spiked hair strove frantically upward, and Gansey had seen a lot of things striving frantically upward.

"We zigged," Blue said tersely. "It zagged."

"Wendybird came!" Henry exclaimed, as if he had only just noticed her. "I googled lady togas in case you did. Good work on the cat. Mrs Woo would poison us in our sleep if you'd squashed it. What's your name again?"

"Blue," Gansey said. "Blue Sargent. Blue, do you remember Henry?"

They eyed each other. At their previous brief meeting, Henry had managed to thoroughly offend Blue through casual self-deprecation. Gansey understood on a basic level that Henry made outrageous and offensive fun of himself because the alternative was storming into a room and flipping tables on to the money changers behind them. Blue, however, had clearly thought that he was merely a callow Aglionby princeling. And in her current mood —

"I remember," she said coolly.

"It was not my finest moment," Henry said. "My car and I have since made amends."

"His electric car," Gansey inserted with subtlety, in case Blue had missed the environmental ramifications.

Blue narrowed her eyes at Gansey and then pointed out, "You could bike to Aglionby from here."

Henry wagged a finger. "True, true. But it is important to practise safe bicycling, and they have not yet made a helmet to accommodate my hair." To Gansey, he said, "Did you see Cheng Two out there?"

Gansey didn't really know Cheng2 — Henry Broadway, actually, confusingly nicknamed not because he was the second of two Chengs at Aglionby, but rather because he was the second of Henrys — aside from what everyone knew: that he was a high-speed shaker with energy drinks pumping continual voltage to his extremities. "Not unless he got a CaMr y while I wasn't looking."

This made Henry laugh mirthfully, as if Gansey had touched upon some previous conversation. "That's Mrs Woo's. Our tiny overlord. She's around here somewhere. Check your pockets. She could be there. Sometimes she falls into these cracks between the floorboards — that's the hazard of these great old houses. Where are Lynch and Parrish?"

"Both busy, alas."

"That is incredible. I knew the president did not always have to act in concert with Congress and the Supreme Court; I just never thought I'd live to see the day."

Gansey asked, "Who else is coming?"

"Just the usual suspects," Henry said. "No one wants to see a casual acquaintance in a bedsheet."

"You don't know me," Blue pointed out. It was impossible to tell what her facial expression meant. Nothing good.

"Richard Gansey the Third vouches for you, so close enough."

A door opened at the end of the hallway, and a very small Asian woman of any age stomped out with an armful of folded sheets.

"Hello, auntie," Henry said sweetly. She glared at him before stomping through another doorway. "Mrs Woo was thrown out of Korea for her bad temper, poor thing; ha, she has the charm of a chemical weapon."

Gansey had vaguely figured that some sort of authority figure lived at Litchfield House, but he hadn't thought much harder. Politeness dictated that he should have sourced flowers or food in the case of a small gathering. "Should I have brought something for her?"

"Who?"

"Your aunt."

"No, she's Ryang's," Henry said. "Come, come, let's go further in. Koh is upstairs cataloguing beverages. You do not have to get drunk, but I will be getting drunk. I'm told I don't get loud, but sometimes I can get very philanthropic. Fair warning."

Now Blue looked properly judgemental, which was about two ticks off from her ordinary expression and one tick off from

Ronan's. Gansey was beginning to suspect that these two worlds were not going to mingle.

A mighty crash sounded as Cheng2 and Logan Rutherford appeared through another door, plastic bags in hands. Rutherford had the sense God gave him to keep his mouth shut, but Cheng2 had never learned that skill.

He said, "Holy fuck, we got girls?"

Beside Gansey, Blue grew four times taller; all the sound sucked in from the room in preparation for the explosion.

This was going to be terrible.

EIGHTEEN

It was 6:21.

No, it was 8:31. Ronan had read the car clock wrong.

The sky was black, the trees were black, the road was black. He pulled up to the kerb in front of Adam's. Adam lived in an apartment located above the office of St. Agnes Catholic Church, a fortuitous combination that focused most of the objects of Ronan's worship into one downtown block. Ronan, who had been neglecting his phone as usual, had missed a call from Adam several hours before. The voicemail had been brief: "If you're not going to Cheng's with Gansey tonight, would you come help me with Cabeswater?"

Ronan was not going to Henry Cheng's under any circumstances. All that smiling and activism gave him a rash.

Ronan was certainly going to Adam's.

So now he climbed out of the BMW, clucking to Chainsaw so that she'd stop trying to worry a seam free in the passenger seat, and scanned the lot beside the church for the tri-coloured Hondayota. He spotted it, the headlights still on, engine off. Adam was crouched in front of it, staring unflinchingly into the headlights' brilliance. His fingers were spread on the asphalt and his feet braced like a runner waiting for the starting shot. Three tarot cards splayed before him. He'd taken one of the floor mats out of the car to crouch on to keep from dirtying his uniform trousers. If you combined these two things – the unfathomable and the practical – you were most of the way to understanding Adam Parrish.

"Parrish," Ronan said. Adam didn't respond. His pupils were pinhole cameras to another world. *"Parrish."*

Just one of Adam's hands lifted in the direction of Ronan's leg. His fingers twitched in a way that conveyed *don't bother me* with the absolute minimum of motion.

Ronan crossed his arms to wait, just looking. At Adam's fine cheekbones, his furrowed fair eyebrows, his beautiful hands, everything washed out by the furious light. He had memorized the shape of Adam's hands in particular: the way his thumb jutted awkwardly, boyishly; the roads of the prominent veins; the large knuckles that punctuated his long fingers. In dreams Ronan put them to his mouth.

His feelings for Adam were an oil spill; he'd let them overflow and now there wasn't a damn place in the ocean that wouldn't catch fire if he dropped a match.

Chainsaw flapped to where the tarot cards were laid out, beak parted curiously, and when Ronan silently pointed at her, she sulked underneath the car. Ronan turned his head sideways to read the cards. Something with flames, something with a sword. The Devil. One thousand images were triggered by that single word, *devil*. Red skin, white sunglasses, his brother Matthew's terrified eyes in the trunk of a car. Dread and shame together, thick enough to vomit up. Ronan was uneasily reminded of his recent nightmares.

Adam's fingers tensed, and then he sat back. He blinked, and then blinked again, rapidly, touching the corner of his eye with just the tip of his ring finger. This didn't suffice, so he rubbed his palms over them until they watered. Finally, he tilted his chin up to Ronan.

"Headlights? That's hardcore, Parrish." Ronan held out his hand; Adam took it. Ronan hauled him up, his mind all palm against palm, thumb crossed over thumb, fingers pressed into wrist bone – and then Adam was facing him and he released his hand.

The ocean burned.

"What the hell's wrong with your eyes?" Ronan asked.

Adam's pupils were still tiny. "Takes me a while to come back."

"Creepy bastard. What's with the Devil?"

Adam stared up at the dark stained glass of the church. He was still partway caught in the kingdom of the headlights. "I can't understand what it's telling me. It feels like it's holding me at an arm's length. I need to find a way to scry deeper, but I can't without someone to watch me in case I get too far away from myself."

Someone in this case being Ronan.

"What are you trying to find out?"

Adam described the circumstances surrounding his eye and his hand with the same level tone he would use to answer a question in class. He allowed Ronan to lean in to compare his eyes – close enough that Ronan felt his breath on his cheek – and he allowed Ronan to study the palm of his hand. The latter was not strictly necessary, and they both knew it, but Adam watched Ronan closely as he lightly traced the lines there.

This was like walking the line between dream and sleep. The

night-sharp balance of being asleep enough to dream and awake enough to remember what he wanted.

He knew Adam had figured out how he felt. But he didn't know if he could step off this knife-slender path without destroying what he had.

Adam held Ronan's gaze as Ronan released his hand. "I'm trying to find the source of what's attacking Cabeswater. I can only assume it's the same thing as what was attacking that black tree."

"It's in my head, too," Ronan admitted. His day at the Barns had been marked by dreams that he'd hastily woken himself from.

"Is it? Is that why you look like hell?"

"Thanks, Parrish. I like your face, too." He briefly described how the corruption of the nightmare tree seemed identical to the corruption of his dreams, hiding his relative distress over the content of the dreams and the fact that it was evidence of a larger secret with an excess of swear words. "So, I'm just never sleeping again."

Before Adam could reply to this, movement from above caught their attention. Something light and strange flapped between the dark trees that lined the neighbourhood streets. A monster.

Ronan's monster.

His albino night horror rarely left the protected fields of the Barns, and when it did, it was only to trail after Ronan. Not in a faithful, canine way, but rather in the careless, widening gyre of a cat. But now it flew down the street towards them, straight and purposeful. In the purple-black space, it was as visible as smoke, dragging ragged-edged wings and cloth from its body. The sound of its wings was more prominent than anything else: *thump, thump, thump.* When it opened its pair of beaks, they trembled with a ferocious cry inaudible to human ears.

Both Ronan and Adam tipped their heads back. Ronan shouted, "Hey! Where are you going?" But it glided over them without so much as a pause. Straight on towards the mountains. Ugly fucker was going to get shot by some terrified farmer someday.

He didn't know why he cared. He guessed it had saved his life that one time, probably.

"Creepy bastard," Ronan said again.

Adam frowned after it and then asked, "What time is it?"

"It's 6:21," Ronan replied, and Adam frowned. "No, 8:40. I read my watch wrong."

"Still time if it's not far, then." Adam Parrish was always thinking about his resources: money, time, sleep. On a school night, even one with supernatural threats breathing on his collar, Ronan knew that Adam would be stingy with all of these; this was how he had stayed alive.

"Where are we going?"

"I don't know. I want to try to find out where this devil is — I'm trying to decide if I can scry while you drive. I wish I could drive and scry at the same time, but that's impossible. Really, all I want is to move my body where my mind tells it to go."

Overhead, a streetlight buzzed and then went out. It had not been raining for several hours, but the air still felt as charged as a thunderstorm. Ronan wondered where his night horror was heading. He said, "OK, magician, if I'm driving while you're whacked out, how am I going to know where to go?"

"I guess I'll try to stay present enough to tell you where to go."

"Is that possible?"

Adam shrugged; the definitions of *possible* and *impossible* were negotiable these days. He leaned to offer his arm to Chainsaw. She leapt on, flapping to balance as his sleeve twisted under her weight, and tilted her head as Adam carefully stroked the fine feathers by her beak. He said, "Never know until we try. You up for it?"

Ronan jingled his car keys. As if he was ever not in the mood to drive. He jerked his chin towards the Hondayota. "Are you going to lock your shitbox?"

Adam said, "No point. Hooligans got in anyway."

The hooligan in question smiled thinly.

They drove.

NINETEEN

Adam jerked awake at the sound of a car door closing. He was in his terrible little car — was he supposed to be in his car?

Persephone settled herself in the passenger seat, her froth of pale hair cascading over the console on to the driver's seat. She carefully placed the toolbox that had been on the seat on the floor between her feet.

Adam squinted against the colourless new dawn — was it supposed to be daytime? — his eyes still pinched with exhaustion. It felt like only a few minutes had passed since he'd emerged from his night shift at the factory. The drive home had felt like too enormous an undertaking without a few minutes of sleep; it felt no more doable now.

He couldn't understand if Persephone was really there or not. She must be; her hair was tickling his bare arm.

"Take out the cards," she ordered in her small voice.

"What?"

"Time for a lesson," Persephone said mildly.

His fatigued brain slid out from under him; something about all of this struck him as not entirely *true*. "Persephone — I — I'm too tired to think."

The thin morning light illuminated Persephone's secret smile. "That's what I'm counting on."

As he reached for the cards, fumbling into the door pocket he used to keep them in, it struck him. "You're dead."

She nodded in agreement.

"This is a memory," he said.

She nodded again. Now it made sense. He was wandering in a recollection of one of his early lessons with Persephone. The goals of those sessions were always the same: Escape his conscious mind. Discover his unconscious. Expand that to the collective unconscious. Look for the threads that connected all things. Rinse and repeat. In the beginning, he had never got past the first two. Every session had been spent trying to lure himself out of his own concrete thoughts.

Adam's fingers scraped the bare bottom of the door pocket. The truth of where the cards had been in his memory was bumping up against the knowledge of where he stored them in the present. That window had started to leak after Persephone's death, and he had begun to keep the cards in the glove box instead to prevent damage.

"Why are you here? Is this a dream?" he asked, then corrected himself. "No. I'm scrying. I'm looking for something."

And just like that, he was alone in the car.

He was not only alone, but he was in the passenger seat where she had been, holding a single tarot card in his hand. The art on the card was sketchy and scribbly and looked a little bit like a pile of hornets. Actually, it might have been a face. It was unimportant. What was he looking for? It was difficult to navigate the space between conscious and unconscious. Too much focus, and he would lose the meditation. Too little, and he would lose the purpose.

He let his mind wander slightly closer to his present.

Electronic music bled into his awareness, reminding him that his body was actually in Ronan's car. In this other place, it was easy to tell that the music was the sound of Ronan's soul. Hungry and prayerful, it whispered of dark places, old places, fire and sex.

Adam was grounded by the pulsing backbeat and the memory of Ronan's closeness. The Devil. No, a demon. The knowledge was not there, and then it was.

North, he said.

A ring of glowing white surrounded everything. It was so bright that it seared his vision if he looked directly at it; he had to keep his gaze focused ahead. A very faraway part of him, a part that thudded with electric beat, remembered suddenly that it was the light of the phone charger. That was the part of his brain that was still present enough to whisper directions to Ronan.

Turn right.

Cabeswater muttered into his deaf ear. It whispered of taking apart, of disowning, of violence, of nothingness. A backwards step of self-doubt, a lying promise that you knew would hurt you later, a knowledge that you were going to get hurt and you probably deserved it. Demon, demon, demon.

Go go go

Somewhere, a dark car raced along a night road. A hand gripped the wheel, leather bands looped over the wrist bone. The Greywaren. Ronan. In this dreamplace, all times were the same time, and so Adam had a strange, lucid beat of reliving the moment Ronan had offered his hand to help Adam up from the asphalt. Stripped of context, the physical sensations exploded:

the surprising shock of heat from that skin-to-skin grip; the soft hiss of the bracelets against Adam's wrist; the sudden bite of possibility —

Everything in his mind was ringed by the searing white light.

The deeper Adam moved through the music and the white-ringed dark, the closer he got to some sort of hidden truth about Ronan. It was hidden in things Adam already knew, half-glimpsed behind a forest made of thoughts. For a bare moment, Adam thought he nearly understood something about Ronan, and about Cabeswater – about Ronan-and-Cabeswater – but it slid away. He darted after it, deeper into whatever stuff Cabeswater's thoughts were made of. Here, Cabeswater hurled images at him: a vine strangling a tree, a cancerous growth, a creeping rot.

Adam realized all at once that the demon was *inside*.

He could feel the demon watching him.

Parrish.

He was *seen*.

PARRISH.

Something brushed his hand.

He blinked. Everything was that glowing circle, and then he blinked again, and it resolved into the bright iris of the phone charger plugged into the cigarette lighter.

The car was not moving, though it had only recently stopped. Dust still swirled by its headlights. Ronan was absolutely silent and still, one hand resting on the gearshift, made into a fist. The music had been turned off.

When Adam looked over, Ronan continued looking out the windshield, clenching his jaw.

The dust cleared and Adam finally saw where he had brought them.

He sighed.

Because the helter-skelter drive through the cold night and Adam's subconscious had brought them not to some disaster in Cabeswater, not to some schism in rocks along the ley line, not to whatever threat Adam had seen in the glaring headlights of his car. Instead, Adam — freed from reason and turned loose in his own mind, set upon the task of finding a demon — had directed them back to the trailer park where his parents still lived.

Neither of them spoke. The lights were on in the trailer, but there were no silhouettes in the windows. Ronan hadn't shut off the headlights, so they shone directly on the front of the trailer.

"Why are we here?" he asked.

"Wrong devil," Adam replied quietly.

It had not been that long since the court case against his father. He knew that Ronan remained righteously furious over the outcome: Robert Parrish, a first-time offender in the eyes of the court, had walked away with a fine and probation. What Ronan didn't realize was that the victory hadn't been in the punishment. Adam didn't need his father to go to jail. He had merely needed someone outside the situation to look at it and confirm that yes, a crime had been committed. Adam had not invented it, spurred it, deserved it. It said so on the court paperwork. Robert Parrish, guilty. Adam Parrish, free.

Well, almost. He was still here looking at the trailer, his pulse thudding lowly in his stomach.

"Why," Ronan repeated, "are we here?"

Adam shook his head, his eyes still on the trailer. Ronan had not turned off his headlights yet, and Adam knew that part of him was hoping for Robert Parrish to come to the door to see who it was. Part of Adam was, too, but in the shivery way of waiting for the dentist to just pull your tooth and get it over with.

He felt Ronan's eyes on him.

"Why," Ronan said a third time, "are we at this fucking place?"

But Adam didn't answer because the door opened.

Robert Parrish stood on the steps, the finer details of his expression washed out by the headlights. Adam didn't have to see his face, though, because so much of what his father felt was conveyed by his body. The thrust of his shoulders, the slant of his neck, the curvature of his arms into the dull traps of his hands. So Adam knew that his father recognized the car, and he knew precisely how he felt about that fact. Adam felt a curious thrill of fear, completely discrete from his conscious thoughts. His fingertips had gone numb with a jolt of sick adrenaline that his mind had never ordered his body to produce. Thorns studded his heart.

Adam's father just stood there, looking. And they sat there, looking back. Ronan was coiled and simmering, one hand resting on his door.

"Don't," said Adam.

But Ronan merely hit the window button. The tinted glass hissed down. Ronan hooked his elbow on the edge of the door and continued gazing out the window. Adam knew that Ronan was fully aware of how malevolent he could appear, and he did not soften himself as he stared across the patchy dark grass at Robert Parrish. Ronan Lynch's stare was a snake on the pavement where you wanted to walk. It was a match left on your pillow. It was pressing your lips together and tasting your own blood.

Adam looked at his father, too, but blankly. Adam was there, and he was in Cabeswater, and he was inside the trailer at the same time. He noted with remote curiosity that he was not processing correctly, but even as he marked it, he continued to exist in three split screens.

Robert Parrish didn't move.

Ronan spat into the grass – an indolent, unthreatened gesture. Then he rolled his chin away, contempt spilling over and out of the car, and silently put the window back up.

The interior of the BMW was entirely silent. It was so quiet that when a breeze blew, the sound of dried leaves scuttling up against the tyres was audible.

Adam touched the place on his wrist where his watch normally sat.

He said, "I want to go get Orphan Girl."

Ronan finally looked at him. Adam expected to see gasoline and gravel in his eyes, but he wore an expression Adam wasn't sure he'd seen on his face before: something thoughtful and appraising, a more deliberate, sophisticated version of Ronan. Ronan, growing up. It made Adam feel . . . he didn't know. He didn't have enough information to know how he felt.

The BMW reversed with a show of dirt and menace. Ronan said, "OK."

TWENTY

The toga party was not terrible at all.

It was, in fact, wonderful.

It was this: finding the Vancouver crowd all lounged on sheet-covered furniture in a sitting room, all dressed in sheets themselves, everything black and white, black hair, white teeth, black shadows, white skin, black floor, white cotton. They were people Gansey knew: Henry, Cheng2, Ryang, Lee-Squared, Koh, Rutherford, SickSteve. But here, they were different. At school, they were driven, quiet, invisible, model students, Aglionby Academy's 11-per-cent-of-our-student-body-is-diverse-click-the-link-to-find-out-more-about-our-overseas-exchange-programmes. Here, they *slouched*. They would not slouch at school. Here, they were angry. They could not afford to be angry at school. Here, they were loud. They did not trust themselves to be loud at school.

It was this: Henry giving Gansey and Blue a tour of Litchfield House as the other boys followed in their togas. One of the things about Aglionby that had always appealed to Gansey was the sense of sameness, of continuity, of tradition, of immutability. Time didn't exist there . . . or if it did, it was irrelevant. It had been populated by students for ever and would always be populated by students; they formed a part of something bigger. But at Litchfield House, it was the opposite. It was impossible not to see that each of these boys had come from a place that was not Aglionby and would be headed to a life that was also not Aglionby. The house was messy with books and magazines that were not for school; laptops were tipped open to both games and news sites. Suits hung like bodies in doorways, worn often enough to require easy access. Motorcycle helmets rolled up against used boarding passes and crates of agriculture magazines. Litchfield House boys already had lives. They had pasts and they hurtled on beyond them. Gansey felt strange: He felt he had looked into a funhouse mirror. The details wrong, the colours the same.

It was this: Blue, teetering on the edge of offence, saying, *I don't understand why you keep saying such awful things about Koreans. About yourself.* And Henry saying, *I will do it before anyone else can. It is the only way to not be angry all of the time.* And suddenly Blue was friends with the Vancouver boys. It seemed impossible that they accepted her just like that and that she shed her prickly skin just as fast, but there it was: Gansey saw the moment that it happened. On paper, she was nothing like them. In practice, she was everything like them. The Vancouver crowd wasn't like the rest of the world, and that was how they wanted it. Hungry eyes, hungry smiles, hungry futures.

It was this: Koh demonstrating how to make a toga of a bedsheet and sending Blue and Gansey into a cluttered bedroom to change. It was Gansey politely turning his back as she undressed and then Blue turning hers — maybe turning hers. It was Blue's shoulder and her collarbone and her legs and her throat and her *laugh her laugh her laugh.* He couldn't stop looking at her, and here, it didn't matter, because no one here cared that they were together. Here, he could play his fingers over her fingers as they stood close, she could lean her cheek on his bare shoulder, he could hook his ankle playfully in hers, she could catch herself with an arm around his waist. Here he was unbelievably greedy for that laugh.

It was this: K-pop and opera and hip-hop and eighties power ballads blaring out of a speaker beside Henry's computer. It was Cheng2 getting impossibly high and talking about his plan to improve economics in the southern states. It was Henry getting drunk but not loud and allowing Ryang to trick him into a game of pool played on the floor with lacrosse sticks and golf balls. It was SickSteve putting movies on the projector with the sound turned down to allow for improved voice-overs.

It was this: the future beginning to hang thick in the air, and Henry starting a quiet, drunk conversation about whether or not Blue would like to travel to Venezuela with him. Blue replying softly that she would, she very much would, and Gansey hearing the longing in her voice like he was being undone, like his own feelings were being unbearably mirrored. *I can't come?* Gansey asked. *Yes, you can meet us there in a fancy plane,* Henry said. *Don't be fooled by his nice hair,* Blue interjected, *Gansey would hike.* And warmth filled the empty caverns in Gansey's heart. He felt *known.*

It was this: Gansey starting down the stairs to the kitchen, Blue starting up, meeting in the middle. It was Gansey stepping aside to let her pass, but changing his mind. He caught her arm and then the rest of her. She was warm, alive, vibrant beneath the thin cotton; he was warm, alive, vibrant beneath his. Blue slid her hand over his bare shoulder and then on to his chest, her palm spread out flat on his breastbone, her fingers pressed curiously into his skin.

I thought you would be hairier, she whispered.

Sorry to disappoint. The legs have a bit more going on.

Mine too.

It was this: laughing senselessly into each other's skin, playing, until it was abruptly no longer play, and Gansey stopped himself with his mouth perilously close to hers, and Blue stopped herself with her belly pressed close to his.

It was this: Gansey saying, "I like you an awful lot, Blue Sargent."

It was this: Blue's smile – crooked, wry, ridiculous, flustered. There was a lot of happiness tucked in the corner of that smile, and even though her face was several inches from Gansey, some of it still spilled out and got on him. She put her finger on his cheek where he knew his own smile was dimpling it, and then they took each other's hands, and they climbed back up together.

It was this: this moment and no other moment, and for the first time that Gansey could remember, he knew what it would feel like to be present in his own life.

TWENTY-ONE

Ronan could tell straightaway that something wasn't right.

When they stepped into Cabeswater, Adam said, "Day," at the same time that Ronan said, *"Fiat lux."* The forest was ordinarily quite attuned to the wishes of its human occupants, particularly when those human occupants were either its magician or its Greywaren. But in this case, the darkness around the trees remained stubbornly present.

"I said, *fiat lux,*" Ronan snapped, then, grudgingly, *"Amabo te."*

Slowly, the dark began to rise, like water bleeding through a paper. It never made it quite to full daylight, however, and what they could see was . . . not right. They stood among black trees blossomed with dull gray lichen. The air was gloomy and green. Though there were no leaves left on the trees, the sky felt low, a mossy ceiling. The trees had still said nothing; it was like the dull hush before a storm.

"Huh," said Adam out loud, clearly unsettled. He was not wrong.

"You still up for this?" Ronan asked. Everything was reminding him precisely of his nightmares. The entire evening did: the race to the trailer, Robert Parrish's specter, this sick gloom. Chainsaw would have normally taken flight to explore by now, but instead she ducked on Ronan's shoulder, claws dug tight into his jacket.

And like one of Ronan's dreams, he felt he knew what was going to happen before it did:

Adam hesitated. Then he nodded.

It was always impossible to tell in the dreams if Ronan knew what was going to happen before it did, or if the things only happened because he thought of them first. Did it matter? It did when you were awake.

They took a moment at the edge of the forest to establish their location. For Ronan, it was merely moving around enough for the trees to see that he was among them; they would do their best to do what he wanted, which included not letting anything supernatural murder him. For Adam, it meant linking in to the ley line that pulsed beneath the forest, unwrapping himself and allowing the bigger pattern inside. It was a process that was both eerie and awesome to watch from the outside. Adam; then Adam, vacated; then Adam, more.

Ronan thought about the story of Adam's wandering eye and rogue hand. *I will be your hands. I will be your eyes.*

He sliced the thought out of his head. The memory of Adam bargaining part of himself away was too frequent a visitor in his nightmares already; he didn't need to call it back up again through intention.

"Are you done with your magician business?" Ronan asked.

Adam nodded. "Time?"

Ronan handed him his phone, glad to be rid of it.

Adam studied it. "6:21," he said with a frown. Ronan frowned, too. It was not puzzling because it was unexpected here. Time on the ley line was always uncertain, skipping to and fro, minutes taking hours and vice versa. What was surprising was that 6:21 had now happened enough outside of the ley line to arouse their suspicions. Something was happening, but he did not know what.

"Are you done with your Greywaren business?" Adam asked.

"That's ongoing," Ronan replied. Cupping his hands over his mouth, he shouted into the hush, "Orphan Girl!"

Far off through the still green air, a raven cawed back. *Ha ha ha.*

Chainsaw hissed.

"Good enough for me," Ronan said, and set off through the green trees. He wasn't happy about the gloom, but it wasn't like he was a stranger to working in nightmares. The key was to learn what rules and fears they were playing off as quickly as possible, and lean into them. Panic was how you got hurt in nightmares. Reminding the dream that you were something alien was a good way to get ejected or destroyed.

Ronan was good at being a dream thing, especially in Cabeswater.

They kept going. All the while, the forest continued being *wrong* around them. It was as if they walked on a slant, though the ground beneath them was level enough.

"Tell me again," Adam said carefully, catching up, "how your dreams were wrong. Use less cursing and more specifics."

"Without changing Cabeswater around us?" Even though Cabeswater had been slow to respond to their request for light, it didn't mean that it would be slow to respond to a nightmare prompt. Not when it already looked like this, a gray-green half-world of black trunks.

"Obviously."

"They were wrong like this."

"Like what?"

Ronan said, "Just like this."

He didn't say anything more. He shouted, "Orphan Girl!"

Caw caw caw!

This time it sounded a little more like a girl, a little less like a bird. Ronan picked up the pace a little; now they were climbing. To their right, a bare rock surface slanted steeply down with only a few small trees bursting from cracks in the naked surface. They picked their way cautiously along this precarious edge; a loose step would send them sliding for yards with no fast way to climb back up.

He glanced behind to make sure Adam was following; he was, looking at Ronan with narrowed eyes.

"Do you think your dream is wrong because Cabeswater is wrong?" Adam asked.

"Probably."

"So if we fix Cabeswater, we would fix your dreams."

"Probably."

Adam was still processing, thinking so hard that Ronan imagined he could feel it. Actually, in Cabeswater, with Adam so close to him, it was possible he really did.

"You could dream things into being before we found Cabeswater, right? Can you do it without Cabeswater?"

Ronan stopped and squinted through the gloom. About fifteen yards below, the slanted rock slide they'd been walking along ended in a pool of perfectly clear water. It was tinted green because the air was green, because everything was green, but otherwise the water was clear. Ronan could see all the way to its rocky bottom. It was clearly far deeper than it was wide, a chasm filled with water. It held his attention. "Why?"

"If you cut yourself off from Cabeswater, somehow, until I fixed it, would your dreams be normal?"

Here it was. Adam was finally asking the right questions; the questions that meant he probably already knew the answer. The longer they spent in Cabeswater, the more they worked together with Ronan's dreams, the more Cabeswater's nightmares were reflected in Ronan's and vice versa. The more the evidence piled up.

But now that they were to it, Ronan wasn't sure he wanted to be on the other side. So many days on a pew with his knuckles pressed to his forehead, silently asking *what am I am I the only one what does this mean —*

He said, "I can do it *better* with Cabeswater. With Orphan Girl, too. But —"

He stopped. He looked at the ground.

"Ask me," he said. "Just do it. Just —"

"Ask you what?"

Ronan didn't reply, just looked at the ground. The green air moved all around him, tinting his pale skin, and the trees curved black and real around him, everything in this place looking like his dreams, or everything in his dreams looking like this place.

Adam pressed his lips together, and then he asked, "Did you dream Cabeswater?"

Ronan's blue eyes flicked up to Adam.

TWENTY-TWO

It was 6:21.

"When?" Adam asked. "When did you know that you dreamt Cabeswater? Right away?"

They faced each other at the top of the slanted rock face, that clear pool far down below. Adam's heart was racing with either adrenaline or with sheer proximity to the ley line.

"Always," said Ronan.

It should not have changed the way he saw Ronan. The dreaming had always been impressive, unusual, a god-glitch, a trick of the ley line that allowed a young man to make his thoughts into concrete objects. Magic, but a reasonable magic. But this — to not only dream an entire forest into being, but to create a dreamspace outside of one's own head. Adam stood in Ronan's dreams; that was what this realization meant.

Ronan corrected himself. "Sort of always. Just — the moment we got here, I recognized it. My handwriting on that rock. I guess I knew right away. It just took me longer to believe it."

Every one of Adam's memories of those early forays into the forest were slowly shifting inside him. Pieces falling into place. "That's why it calls you the Greywaren. That's why you're different to it."

Ronan shrugged, but it was a shrug from caring too much instead of too little.

"That's why its Latin grammar is terrible. It's *your* grammar."

Ronan shrugged again. Questions cascaded through Adam, too difficult to say aloud. Was Ronan even human? Half a dreamer, half a dream, maker of ravens and hoofed girls and entire lands. No wonder his Aglionby uniform had choked him, no wonder his father had sworn him to secrecy, no wonder he could not make himself focus on classes. Adam had realized this before, but now he realized it again, more fully, larger, the ridiculousness of Ronan Lynch in a classroom for aspiring politicians.

Adam felt a little hysterical. "That's why it speaks Latin at all, and not Portuguese, or Welsh. Oh, God. Did I —"

He had made a bargain with this forest. When he fell asleep and Cabeswater was in his thoughts, tangled through his dreams, was that *Ronan* —

"No," Ronan said, fast, his tone unschooled. "No, I didn't *invent* it. I asked the trees after I figured it out, why the hell — how the hell this happened. Cabeswater existed, somehow, before me. I just dreamt it. I mean, I made it look this way. I chose these trees and this language and all that shit for it, without knowing. Wherever it was on the ley line before, it got destroyed, and then it didn't have a body, a shape — when I dreamt it, I brought it back into physical form, that's all. What did they call it? *Manifested* it. I just manifested it from whatever other fucking plane it was on. It's not me."

Adam's thoughts spun in the mud; he made no progress.

"Cabeswater isn't me," Ronan repeated. "You're still just you."

It was one thing to say it and another thing to see Ronan Lynch standing among the trees he had dreamt into being, looking of a piece with them because he *was* of a piece with them. Magician – no wonder Ronan was all right with Adam being uncanny. No wonder he *needed* him to be.

"I don't know why the fuck I told you," Ronan said. "I should've lied."

"Just give me a second with it, will you?" Adam asked.

"Whatever."

"You can't be pissed off because I'm thinking this through."

"I said whatever."

"How long did it take *you* to believe it?" Adam demanded.

"I'm still trying," Ronan replied.

"Then you can't —" Adam broke off. He suddenly felt as if he had been dropped from a height. It was the same sensation as when he had known Ronan was dreaming something big. He just had time to wonder if it had truly been the ley line or merely the shock of Ronan's revelation when it happened again. This time, the light around them sagged in time with it.

Ronan's expression had sharpened.

"The ley line . . ." Adam began and then broke off, uncertain of how to finish this thought. "Something is happening to the ley line. It feels like when you're dreaming something big."

Ronan spread his arms out, meaning clear. *It's not me.* "What do you wanna do?"

"I don't know if we should stay here while it's like this," Adam said. "I definitely don't think we should try to make it to the rose glen. Let's call her just a few more times."

Ronan eyed Adam, assessing his status. Correctly seeing that Adam was feeling like he needed to kneel in his apartment with his hands over his head and think about what he had just learned. He said, "How about just once more?"

Together they shouted: *"Orphan Girl!"*

Intention sliced through their shared words, sharper than the gloom.

The forest listened.

The Orphan Girl appeared, her skullcap pulled low over her enormous eyes, sweater even mankier than before. She could not help but be off-putting in this gray-green wood, not arriving like she did, skittering between dark trees. She looked like she belonged in the vintage photographs Adam had seen in the Barns, a lost immigrant child from a destroyed country.

"There you are, you urchin," Ronan said as Chainsaw chattered nervously. "Finally."

The girl offered Adam's watch back to him, reluctantly. The band had acquired some toothmarks since he'd last seen it. The face of it said 6:21. It was very grubby.

"You can keep it," Adam said, "for now." He couldn't really spare the watch, but she didn't have anything, even a name.

She started to say something in the strange, complicated language that Adam knew was the old and basic language of whatever this place was — the language that young Ronan must have mistaken for Latin in his long-ago dreams — and then stopped herself. She said, instead, "Watch out."

"For what?" Ronan asked.

Orphan Girl screamed.

The light dimmed.

Adam felt it in his chest, this plummeting energy. It was as if every artery to his heart had been scissored.

The trees howled; the ground shivered.

Adam dropped to a crouch, pressing his hands into the ground for breath, for help, for Cabeswater to give him back his heartbeat.

Orphan Girl was gone.

No, not gone. She was plummeting yards down the slanted rock face, fingers clawing for purchase, hooves scraping dully, tiny rocks tumbling down with her. She didn't cry for help — she just tried to save herself. They watched her slide straight into that pool of clear water, and because it was so transparent, they could see how far she plummeted into it.

Without pause, Ronan leapt after her.

TWENTY-THREE

It was 6:21.

Ronan hit the water hard enough that he saw sparks behind his vision. The pool was as warm as blood, and the moment he thought about that heat, he realized that he remembered this pool. He had dreamt it before.

It was acid.

The heat was because it was eating him. At the end of this dream there was nothing left of him but bones, white-picked sticks in a uniform, like Noah.

Immediately Ronan threw all of his intention out towards Cabeswater.

Not acid, he thought. *Make it not acid.*

Still his skin warmed.

"Not acid," he said out loud, to the pool, as his eyes stung. Liquid flowed into his mouth, sucked into his nostrils. He could feel it bubbling under his fingernails. Somewhere below him was Orphan Girl, and she'd been in the strange sea for a few seconds longer than he had. How long did he have? He couldn't recall the dream well enough right now to know. He breathed words directly into the acid. *"Make it safe."*

Cabeswater heaved around him, shuddering, shrugging, trying to grant his appeal. Now he could see Orphan Girl sinking slowly just below him. She'd covered her eyes; she didn't know that he'd come after her. Probably didn't expect any help. Orphan girl, orphan boy.

Ronan struggled towards her — he was an OK swimmer, but not without air, not through acid.

The liquid growled against his skin.

He snatched her oversized sweater, and her eyes opened wide and strange and startled. Her mouth formed *Kerah?* and then she seized his arm. For a moment they both sank, but she was not stupid, and she began to paddle with her free hand and kick off the stone walls.

It felt like they had sunk miles beneath the surface.

"Cabeswater," Ronan said, huge bubbles escaping from his mouth. His brain was failing to problem-solve. "Cabeswater, *air*."

Cabeswater would keep him safe, ordinarily. Cabeswater knew how fragile his human body was, ordinarily. But it wasn't listening to him now, or it was, but it couldn't do anything about it.

The pool boiled around them.

He was going to die, and all he could think was how if he did, Matthew's life was over, too.

Suddenly, something hit his feet. Pressed against his hands. Crushed his chest. His breath — he only had time to seize the Orphan Girl before everything went black.

And then he burst out of the water, propelled from below. He was vomited up on to the rocky edge of the pool. Orphan Girl rolled from his arms. Both of them coughed up the liquid; it was pinkish from the blisters on his tongue. Leaves were plastered all over Ronan's arms, all over the Orphan Girl's arms. So many leaves.

Looking woozily over his shoulder, Ronan found that the entire pool was filled with vines and shrubs. Tendrils still grew slowly out of the pool. The submerged parts of the plants were already being eaten away by the acid.

This was what had saved them from drowning. They had been lifted by the branches.

Adam crouched on the other side of the pool, head dropped low like he was about to sprint or pray, his hands pressed to the rock on either side of him, knuckles white. He had placed a few small stones between his hands in a pattern that must have made sense to him. One of the still growing tendrils had tangled around his ankles and his wrists.

The proper truth struck Ronan: The plants had not saved their lives. Adam Parrish had saved their lives.

"Parrish," Ronan said.

Adam looked up, eyes blank. He was quivering.

Orphan Girl scrambled around the pool, keeping well back from the edge, to Adam's side. Hurriedly, she knocked the tiny stones into the pool with her finger and thumb. At once, the vines stopped growing. Adam sat back with a shiver, expression still far away and ill. His right hand twitched in a way that was not quite comfortable to look at. Orphan Girl took his left hand and kissed the palm – he merely closed his eyes – and then she turned her urgent gaze to Ronan.

She said, "Out! We need him out!"

"Out of where?" Ronan asked, picking his way around the pool to them. He looked up at the rock face, at the mountainside around him, trying to plot a path out.

"Cabeswater," Orphan Girl said. "Something is happening. Ah!"

In between the submerged and damaged leaves in the pool, the liquid was turning black. This was a nightmare.

"Get up, Parrish," Ronan said, gripping Adam's arm. "We're getting out of here."

Adam opened his eyes; one lid was drooping. He said, "Don't forget she's coming with us."

TWENTY-FOUR

It was 6:21.

No one had been answering the Fox Way phone for ages. Blue had obediently used Gansey's phone to call home every forty-five minutes as her mother had asked, but no one picked up. This didn't strike her as unusual the first time; if the line was tied up with a long-distance psychic consult, outside calls rang through to voicemail. It *was* unusual when it kept happening, though. Blue tried again in another forty-five minutes, and then another.

"We need to go," Blue said to Gansey.

He did not question it. Neither, to Henry Cheng's credit, did he, even though he was quite philanthropically drunk and would've rather they stayed. Instead, he seemed to instantly divine that this was private and to be left untouched. He accepted their bedsheets and bid them good night and begged Blue once more to travel to Venezuela with him.

In the car, they realized that Gansey's watch kept turning 6:21.

Something was wrong.

At 300 Fox Way, she tried the front door. Although it was late — was it late? It was 6:20, now 6:21, always 6:20, then 6:21 — the door wasn't locked. Beside her, Gansey was both wary and electric.

They closed the front door behind them.

Something was wrong.

In the dark house, Blue could not immediately tell what was amiss, only that she was absolutely certain something was. She was frozen with it, unable to move until she determined what was troubling her. *This*, she thought, *must be what it is like to be psychic.*

Her hands quivered.

What was wrong? It was darker, perhaps, than usual, the ambient light from the kitchen failing to penetrate the night. It was cooler, perhaps, than it ordinarily was, but that might have been her anxiety. It was quieter, with no chattering of television or clink of mugs, but that could have been simply the lateness of the hour. A bulb flickered – no, it was just car lights reflecting off the glass face of the clock on the hallway table. The clock said 6:21.

She couldn't move.

It seemed impossible to be trapped here by dread and nothing more, and yet she stood. She told herself that she had crawled through mysterious caverns, stood under the sparks of a nightmare dragon, and been in the presence of a desperate man with a gun, and so the mere fact of her very own house with no obvious threat shouldn't paralyse her.

But she couldn't move, and Gansey did not stir, either. One finger was pressed absently against his left ear. His eyes had the glassy look that she recalled from his panic attack in the cave not long ago.

She had half a thought that they were the last two people left in the world. She would step into the living room and find nothing but bodies.

Before she could catch herself, a single note of a whimper escaped from her.

Be sensible!

Gansey's hand fumbled into hers. His palm was sweaty, but it didn't matter — hers was, too. They were both terrified.

Now that she thought about it, the house was not silent after all. Beneath the quiet, she heard something crackling and humming like discordant electronics.

Gansey's eyes darted to hers. She squeezed his fingers tightly, gratefully. Then, at the same time, they released each other's hands. They weren't sure if they'd need both hands to defend themselves.

Move, Blue.

They started forward, gently, both hesitating if the floorboards began to creak. Both afraid to make a sound until they were sure of what they found.

Just: afraid.

At the base of the stairs, she rested her hand on the solid knob of the railing and listened. The hum she'd heard before was louder now, more dissonant and alive. It was a buzzing, wordless song, eerily voicing one note before modulating to another further up the unfamiliar scale.

A thud from directly behind them made Gansey start. But Blue was glad for *this* sound, because she knew it. It was the brush-clunk of her cousin's giant clogs on the uneven floor. With relief, she turned to find Orla, comfortingly familiar and silly in her usual bell-bottoms. Her gaze was fixed on some place over Blue's head.

"Orla," Blue said, and her cousin's eyes dropped to meet hers.

Orla screamed.

Blue's hands acted without her mind, cupping over her ears like a child, and her feet followed suit, stumbling back into Gansey. Orla pressed her hands over her heart and screamed again, the sound cracking and pitching higher. It was nothing Blue had ever thought she'd hear out of her cousin. Some part of Blue darted away from it, making it not Orla's face screaming, making it not Blue's body watching, making it a dream instead of reality.

Orla fell silent.

Her eyes, though — she was still looking past Blue at nothingness. At something inside herself. Her shoulders heaved with horror.

And behind everything, that hum continued from somewhere in the house.

"Orla," Gansey whispered. "Orla, can you hear me?"

Orla didn't reply. She was looking at a world that Blue couldn't see.

Blue didn't want to say the truth, but she did anyway. "I think we have to find the sound."

Gansey nodded grimly. Leaving Orla in her unseeing weeping, they crept deeper into the house. At the end of the front hall, the light of the kitchen seemed to promise safety and certainty. But between them and the kitchen was the blackness of the reading room doorway. Although Blue's heart told her that the interior of the room was completely dark, her eyes showed her that there were three candles on the table within. They were lit. But it didn't matter. They didn't affect the blackness.

The strange, multiheaded buzz spilled from inside the reading room.

There was also a dull scuffling, like someone running a broom over the floorboards.

Gansey's knuckles brushed tentatively against hers.

Take a step.

She took a step.

Go in.

They went in.

On the floor of the reading room, Noah twisted and twitched, his body impossible. Somewhere, he was dying. Always dying. Even though Blue had seen him reenact his death before, it never got easier to watch. His face turned to the ceiling, his mouth open in mindless pain.

Gansey's breath hitched audibly.

Above Noah, Calla sat at the large reading table, her eyes focused on nothing at all. Her hands rested on top of scattered tarot cards. A phone sat beside them; she'd been in the middle of a long-distance reading.

The dissonant hum was louder than anything.

It was coming from Calla.

"Are you afraid?" Noah whispered.

Both Gansey and Blue started. They hadn't realized that Noah had stopped twitching, but he had, and he was lying on his back, knees drawn up, looking at them. There was suddenly something a little taunting about his expression, a little un-Noah-like. His skull's teeth smiled through his lips.

Blue and Gansey glanced at each other.

The thing that was Noah suddenly gazed up as if it had heard something approaching. He began to hum, too. It was not musical.

Every mobile in Blue's body burned a warning at her.

Then Noah duplicated and singled.

Blue wasn't sure how else to put it. There was a Noah, then another right beside him, facing the other way, and then the single Noah again. She could not decide if it was an error in Noah, or an error in how she was seeing Noah.

"We should all be afraid," Noah said, his voice thin through the buzzing. "When you play with time —"

He was suddenly close to them, eye to eye, standing, or at least just his face was, and in a blink, he was a few feet away again. He'd pulled some of his Noah-ness — his boy-guise — over himself again. He had his hands on his knees like a runner, and every time he panted out, the hum reluctantly escaped him.

Blue's and Gansey's breath hung in a cloud before them, shimmering, like *they* were the dead ones. Noah was pulling energy from them. A lot of energy.

"Blue, go," Noah said. His voice was strained, but he'd controlled the hideous humming. "Gansey . . . go. It won't be me!" He slid to the right and then back again; it was not the way matter was meant to behave. A lopsided smile snuck across his mouth, utterly at odds with his knitted eyebrows, and vanished. There was a challenge in his face, and then there wasn't.

"We're not leaving," Blue said. But she did begin to throw all of her protection up around herself. She could not keep whatever had Noah from drawing on both Gansey and Calla, but she could cut off her own considerable battery.

"Please," Noah hissed. "Unmaker, unmaker."

"Noah," Gansey said, "you're stronger than this."

Noah's face went black. From skull to ink in the opposite

of a heartbeat. Only the teeth glowed. He gasped or laughed. "YOU'RE ALL GOING TO DIE."

"Get out of him!" Blue snarled.

Gansey shuddered badly with the cold. "Noah, you can do this."

Noah lifted his hands in front of him, the palms and fingers facing each other like a clawsome dance. They were Noah's hands, and then they were scribbly lines.

"Nothing is impossible," Noah said, his voice flat and deep. The darting sketch lines took the place of his hands again, corrupt and useless. Blue could see inside his chest cavity, and there was nothing there but black. "Nothing is impossible. I'm coming for him. I'm coming for him. I'm coming for him."

The only thing that kept Blue planted, the only thing that kept her so close to this creature, was the knowledge that she was witnessing a crime. This wasn't Noah being unintentionally terrifying. This was something *in* Noah, *through* Noah, without permission.

The buzzing voice kept going. "I'm coming for him – *Blue!* – I'm coming for him – *Please! Go!* – I'm coming for him —"

"I won't leave you," Blue said. "I'm not afraid."

Noah let out a wild laugh, a goblin's delight. In a high, sideways voice, he thrilled, "You will be!"

And then he threw himself at her.

Blue caught a glimpse of Gansey snatching for him just as Noah's claws dug into her face.

The reading room went as light as it had been dark. Pain and brilliance, cold and heat —

He was digging out her eye.

She wailed, *"Noah!"*

Everything was squiggling lines.

She threw her hands to her face, but nothing changed. She felt hooked on to claws, his fingers dug in her flesh. Her left eye saw only white; her right eye saw only black. Her fingers felt slick; her cheek felt hot.

Light was exploding from Noah like a flare off the sun.

Suddenly, hands gripped her shoulders, wrenching her away from him. She was surrounded by warmth and mint. Gansey held her so tightly that she could feel him trembling against her. The hum was everywhere. She could feel it in her burning face as Gansey twisted to put himself between her and the buzzing fury that was Noah.

"Oh, Jesus. Blue, I need your energy," Gansey told her, right into her ear, and she heard fear laced through his words. "Now."

Pain exploded with every beat of her heart, but she let him take her slick fingers.

Gansey gripped her hand. She took down all the walls around her energy.

Crisp and certain and loud, he told the thing: *"Be. Noah."*

The room went silent.

TWENTY-FIVE

It was 6:21.

A little less than six hundred miles down the ley line, a million tiny lights winked across the dark, cold ripples of the Charles River. The toothful November air found its way in the balcony door of Colin Greenmantle's Back Bay town house. He had not left the door open, but it was open nonetheless. Just a crack.

In they crawled.

Colin Greenmantle himself was on the ground floor of the townhome, in the golden-brown, windowless room he had reserved for his collection. The cases themselves were beautiful, glass and iron, mesh and gold, suitably outlandish displays for suitably outlandish objects. The floor beneath the cases was made of oak reclaimed from an old farmhouse in Pennsylvania; the Greenmantles always preferred to possess things that used to be someone else's. It was impossible to tell how large the room really was, because the only lights were the spotlights that illuminated each unusual artefact. The bulbs glowed through the blackness in each direction like ships in a night sea.

Greenmantle stood in front of an old mirror. The edge was all carved in acanthus leaves and swans feasting upon other swans, and a brass-rimmed clock was embedded in the topmost frame. The clock face read 6:21 P.M. Supposedly, the mirror itself beaded tears on viewers' reflections if they'd had a recent death in the family. His reflection was dry-eyed, but he felt he looked pitiful, anyway. In one hand he held a bottle of Cabernet Sauvignon whose label promised notes of cherry and graphite. In the other hand he held a pair of earrings he had obtained for his wife, Piper. He was wearing a beautifully cut jacket and a pair of boxers. He was not expecting company.

They came anyway, picking their way across the crown moulding of the second-floor library, crawling over each other's bodies.

Greenmantle took a swig of the wine directly from the bottle — when he'd selected it from the kitchen, he had thought it would look more aesthetically pathetic and desperate than carrying a solitary glass, and it did. He wished there was someone here to see just how aesthetically pathetic and desperate he looked.

"Notes of black powder and abandonment," he told his reflection. He took another swallow; this mouthful he choked on. A little too much black powder and abandonment at once.

His reflection went wide-eyed; his wife stood behind him, fingers wrapped around his throat. A few of her blond hairs strayed from her otherwise smooth hair, and the collection lights behind her burned these strands golden-white fiery. Her eyes were black. One of her eyebrows was raised, but she looked otherwise unperplexed as her fingertips pressed into his skin. His neck purpled.

He blinked.

She wasn't there.

She had never been there. She had left him behind. Well, in fairness, he had left her behind, but she'd started it. She was the one who had chosen to perpetuate a considerable amount of tactless violent crime in the wilds of Virginia, right when he had decided he was ready to take his toys and go.

"I'm alone," Greenmantle told the mirror.

But he wasn't. They buzzed down the stairs, alighting upon the tops of the picture frames, and ricocheted into the kitchen.

Greenmantle turned from the mirror to face his collection. A four-armed suit of armour, a taxidermy unicorn the size of a pygmy goat, a blade that continuously dripped blood on the floor of its glass case. It represented the finest of nearly two decades of collecting. Not really the finest, Greenmantle mused, merely the objects he thought most likely to capture Piper's attention.

He thought he heard something in the hallway to the room. A humming. Or scratching. Not quite scratching – it was too light for that.

"After numerous personal betrayals, Colin Greenmantle had a nervous breakdown in his late thirties," Greenmantle narrated, ignoring the sound, "leading many to believe he would fade into obscurity."

He regarded the earrings in his hand. He had taken steps to acquire them over two years before, but it had taken this long for his suppliers to cut them from a woman's head in Gambia. Rumour had it that the wearer could see through walls. Certain types of walls, anyway. Not brick. Not stone. But drywall. They could handle drywall. Greenmantle didn't have pierced ears, so he hadn't tried them. And with Piper pursuing a new life of crime, it seemed he might never find out.

"But the onlookers had underestimated Colin's personal fortitude," he said. "His ability to bounce back from emotional injury."

He turned to the door just as the visitors exploded through it. He blinked.

They did not disappear.

He blinked, and blinked again, and something was still coming in through the door, something that was neither his imagination nor a cursed mirror image. It took his mind a moment to process the sound and the sight to realize it was not a single visitor: It was many. They poured and tumbled and scrabbled over one another.

It was not until one broke free from the horde and flew at him erratically that he realized that it was insects. As the black wasp landed on his wrist, he told himself not to slap it. It stung him.

"Bitch!" he said, and swung the wine bottle at it.

Another wasp joined the first. Greenmantle shook his arm, dislodging it, but a third flew at him. A fourth, a fifth, a hallwayfull of them. They were all over him. He was wearing a beautiful jacket, and boxers, and wasps.

The earrings fell to the floor as he spun. In the mirror, his reflection dripped tears and he saw not wasps, but Piper, her arms and smile wrapped around him.

"We're through," her mouth said.

The lights went out.

It was 6:22.

TWENTY-SIX

You could say what you liked about Piper Greenmantle, but she wasn't a quitter, even when things didn't turn out exactly as she imagined. She kept going to Pilates long after it was physically satisfying, continued attending book club after she discovered she was a far speedier reader than her fellow members, and persisted in getting fake mink eyelashes sewed into her own every two weeks, even after the salon location closest to her was shut down for health violations.

So when she went looking for a magical sleeping entity supposedly buried near her rental house, she didn't quit until she found it.

Unmaker.

That had been the first thing it had said when she'd found it. It had taken her a moment longer to realize that it was replying to her question ("What the hell?").

In Piper's defence, the sleeper was unsettling. She'd been expecting a human, and instead she'd found a murder-black six-legged creature that she would have called a hornet if she didn't firstly find hornets repellent and secondly think hornets had no business being eleven inches long.

"That is a demon," Neeve had said. Neeve was the third leg on their uncomfortable tripod. She was a mild-voiced, squat woman with pretty hands and bad hair; Piper thought she was a television psychic but could not remember how she'd arrived at this information.

Neeve had not seemed happy to have uncovered a demon, but Piper had been dying at the time and unchoosy with her friends. She'd skipped over all other social niceties and said to the demon, "I woke you. Do I get a favour? Fix my body."

I will favour you.

And it had. The air in the darkened tomb had gone a little shifty, and then Piper had stopped bleeding to death. She had expected that to be the end of it. It turned out, though, that a favour was a one-time affair, but favouring was for ever.

Now look at her. They were out of that cave, the sun was sort of shining, and Piper had just killed her cowardly dirtbag husband. Magic was churning through her and, to be honest, she was feeling pretty badass. Beside her, a waterfall was crashing upward, backwards, the water spraying up into the sky in great gasps. The tree closest to Piper was shedding its bark in peeling, wet clumps.

"Why does the air feel like this?" Piper asked. "It's like it's scratching me. Is it going to twitch like this the entire time?"

"I believe it is calming," Neeve said in her faded voice. "The further we travel from the moment of your husband's death. These are aftershocks. The forest is trying to rid itself of the demon, which seems to use the same power source, focused through the forest. The forest is reacting to being used to kill. I can sense that this place is about creation, and so any step you take that is opposite to that will cause this kind of spiritual quake."

"We all do things we don't want to," Piper said. "And it's not like we're going to be killing loads of people. This was just to prove to my father that I was being serious about making up with him."

The demon asked, *Now what do you wish?*

It was clinging to the marled old bark of a tree, back hunched in the way hornets curl when they are in the cold or damp or breeze off a waterfall. Its antennae quivered in her direction, and it still hummed in time with a swarm that was no longer in evidence. Overhead, the sun shook; Piper had a thought that it wasn't really daytime at all. Another bit of bark sloughed off the tree.

"Are you harmful to the environment?" Piper had always been attentive to her carbon footprint. It seemed pointless to have spent two decades recycling if she was going to destroy an entire ecosystem.

I am a natural product of this environment.

A branch sagged to the ground beside Piper. Its leaves were black and running with a thick yellow liquid. The air continued to shudder.

"Piper." Neeve took Piper's hand in a tender way, looking as serene as someone could when dressed in tattered rags beside a waterfall travelling in reverse. "I know that when you plunged into the sleeper's tomb, pushing me out of the way, ensuring that you and you alone would have the sleeper's favour, you were hoping to cut me out of the loop and continue in a future where you and you alone controlled your own choices and enjoyed the demon's favour, probably leaving me in the cavern to wander at best and die at worst. At the time, I'll admit I was very upset with you, and the feelings I had then are not feelings that I'm proud of now. I see now that you not only have some trust issues, and you didn't know me. But if you want . . ."

Piper missed a large part of this as she noticed Neeve's shapely fingernails. They were enviably perfect little coins of keratin. Piper's own nails were ragged from clawing out of the collapsed cavern.

". . . there are better ways to accomplish your goals. Really it's essential that you learn to rely on my considerable experience in magic."

Piper's attention focused. "All right. I zoned out there, but what? Skip all the feelings parts."

"I don't think it's wise to pair yourself with a demon. They are inherently subtractive rather than additive. They take more than they give."

Piper turned to the demon; it was hard to tell how attentive it was. Hornets didn't have eyelids, so it was possible it was asleep. "How much of this forest will have to die to get my life back?"

Now that I am awake, I will unmake all of it either way. Eventually.

"Well then," Piper said. She had the sense of relief that came from a bad decision being made for her. "That's settled. We might as well make hay while the sun shines. Hey — where are you going? Don't you want to be . . ." Piper listened, and the demon leaned on her thoughts. ". . . famous?"

Neeve blinked. "Respected."

"Same diff," Piper said. "Well, don't go just yet. I did sort of shaft you, before, because I was dying and sort of rude. Just a little? But I want to make it right."

Neeve looked less enthusiastic about this than Piper had hoped, but she at least didn't try to run away again. This was positive; Piper didn't really want to be alone with the demon. Not because she was scared, but because she felt more energized with an audience. She'd taken an online quiz that said she was some special sort of extrovert and that she was likely to be this way for the rest of her life.

"This is going be a new start for both of us," Piper assured Neeve.

The demon tilted its head, its antennae waving again. Hornet eyes were not meant to be so large, Piper thought. They were like big brown-black aviator sunglasses. Possibilities of life and death moved darkly in them.

What now?

Piper said, "Time to call Dad again."

TWENTY-SEVEN

I t was not 6:21.

It was either late at night or early in the morning.

When Adam and Ronan arrived at the Mountain View Urgent Care, they found a small waiting room empty except for Gansey. Music strummed overhead; the fluorescent lights were soulless and innocent. His khakis were bloody, and he sat in a chair with his head in his hands, either sleeping or grieving. A painting of Henrietta hung on the wall opposite him, and water dripped from it, because that was apparently the world they lived in now. Another time, Adam might have tried to understand what such a sign meant; tonight, his mind was already overflowing with data points. His hand had stopped twitching now that Cabeswater had regained some of its strength, but Adam had no illusions that this meant the danger was over.

"Hey, Shitlord," Ronan said to Gansey. "Are you weeping?" He kicked the side of Gansey's shoe. "Sphincter. You asleep?"

Gansey removed his face from his hands and looked up at Adam and Ronan. There was a small smear of blood by his jawline. His expression was sharper than Adam had expected, and only grew sharper when he saw Ronan's filthy clothing. "Where were you?"

"Cabeswater," Ronan said.

"Cabeswa— What is *she* doing here?" Gansey had just caught sight of the Orphan Girl as she stumbled through the door behind Adam. She was clumsy in a pair of muck boots that Ronan had pulled from the trunk of the BMW. They were far too big for her legs and of course entirely the wrong shape for her hooves, but that was kind of the desired effect. "What was the *point* of us using an entire afternoon to take her out there if you were just going to bring her back out again?"

"Whatever, man," Ronan said, an eyebrow raised at Gansey's fury. "It was two hours."

Gansey said, "Maybe two hours doesn't mean anything to you, but some of us go to school, and two hours is what we had for ourselves."

"Whatever, Dad."

"You know what?" Gansey said, standing. There was something unfamiliar in his tone, a bowstring drawn back. "If you call me that one more time —"

"How's Blue?" Adam interrupted. He already assumed that she was not dead, or Gansey would not have had the bandwidth to be arguing with Ronan. He assumed, actually, that it had looked worse than it had really been, or Gansey would have led with a status report.

Gansey's expression was still edged and glistening. "She'll keep the eye."

"*Keep the eye,*" Adam echoed.

"She's getting stitches now."

"*Stitches,*" Ronan echoed.

Gansey said, "Did you think I was just panicking over nothing? I told you: Noah was possessed."

Possessed, like by a devil. Possessed, like Adam's hand. In between that simmering black in Cabeswater and this violent result of Noah's possession, Adam was beginning to get a feel for what his own hand might be capable of if Cabeswater couldn't protect him. Part of him wanted to tell Gansey about it, but part of him had never forgotten Gansey's agonized shout when Adam had made the bargain with Cabeswater in the first place. He didn't really think Gansey would say *I told you so*, but Adam would know that he would have been within his rights to do so, which was worse. Adam had always been the most negative voice in his own head.

Unbelievably, Ronan and Gansey were still fighting. Adam tuned back in as Ronan said, "Oh come *on* – there was no way I cared if Henry Cheng asked me to a party."

"The point was that *I* asked you," Gansey said. "Not that Henry asked. He didn't care; I cared."

"Aw," said Ronan, but not in a kind way.

"Ronan," Adam said.

Gansey flicked at the bloodstain on his slacks. "And instead, you went to Cabeswater. You could have died there, and I wouldn't have even known where you were because you couldn't be bothered to pick up the phone. Do you remember that tapestry that Malory and I were talking about while he was here? The one with Blue's face on it? Oh, of course you do, Adam, because you dredged up those nightmare Blues in Cabeswater. When the Noah thing was over, Blue looked just like it." He lifted his hands, palms out. "Her hands were all red. Her own blood. *You* were the one who told me, Ronan, that something was starting, all those months ago. Now's not the time to be going rogue. Someone's going to get killed. No more playing around. There's no more time for anything but truth. We're supposed to be in this together, whatever *this* is."

There was no effective protest to be made to any of this; it was all unquestionably true. Adam could have said that he had been to Cabeswater countless times to do the ley line's work and that he had thought this was just like any other time, but he knew full well that he had realized something was off about the forest and continued anyway.

The Orphan Girl knocked over the coat hanger behind the office door and skittered away from the crash.

"Quit screwing around," Ronan snapped. Counterintuitively, him losing his temper meant that the argument was over. "Put your hands in your pockets."

She hissed something back to him in a language that was neither English nor Latin. Here in this mundane office, it was especially clear that she had been assembled according to rules from some other world. That old-fashioned sweater, those enormous black eyes, the slender legs with their hooves hidden in boots. It was impossible to believe that Ronan had pulled her from his dreams, but it had been impossible to believe his other outlandish dream objects, too. It seemed obvious now that they had been walking briskly for quite some time towards a world where a demon was plausible.

They all looked up sharply as the door to the back opened. Blue and Maura stepped into the waiting room as a nurse began to shuffle behind the counter. All attention immediately shifted to Blue.

She had two visible stiches in her right eyebrow, pinning together the cleaned-up edges of a gouge that continued down her cheek. Faint scratches on either side of the deepest wound told the story of fingers clawing into her skin. Her right eye was squinted mostly shut, but at least it was still there. Adam could tell that she was hurting.

He knew he cared about her because his stomach was tingling uncomfortably just looking at her wound, the suggestion of violence scratching through him like fingers on a chalkboard. *Noah* had done that. Adam curled his own hand into a fist, remembering what it had felt like for it to move on its own accord.

Gansey was right: Any of them could have died tonight. It was time to stop playing around.

For a strange second, none of them spoke.

Finally, Ronan said, "Jesus God, Sargent. Do you have stitches on your *face*? Bad. Ass. Put it here, you asshole."

With some relief, Blue lifted her fist and bumped it against his.

"Corneal abrasion," Maura said. Her humourless, business-like tone betrayed her concern more than any crying could have. "Antibiotic drops. Should be OK."

She eyed the Orphan Girl. The Orphan Girl eyed her back. Like Ronan, her attentive stare landed somewhere between sullen and aggressive, but the effect was slightly more uncanny when presented by a waif of a girl in muck boots. Maura looked as if she was about to ask something, but instead, she retreated to the counter to pay for the visit.

"Look," Gansey said in a low voice. "I need to say something. This is a strange time to say it, but I — I kept waiting for the right moment to do it and I can't stop thinking about how, if tonight had gone worse, I might have never got that moment. So here it is: I cannot ask you to be truthful if I haven't been myself."

He gathered himself. Adam saw his gaze land on Blue. Judging, perhaps, whether or not she knew what he was about to say, or whether he should say it. He touched his thumb to his lower lip, caught himself at it, lowered his hand.

"Blue and I have been seeing each other," he said. "I don't want to hurt any feelings, but I want to keep seeing her. I don't want to hide it any more. It's eating me, and nights like this, having to stand here and look at Blue with her face like this and pretend like —" He drew himself to a stop, a full stop, a silence so intense that no one tipped any other sound into it. Then he finished, repeating, "I cannot ask you to do things I haven't been doing myself. I'm sorry for being a hypocrite."

Adam had never quite believed that Gansey would acknowledge the relationship in such a pointed way, and now that the confession hung in the air, it was intensely unpleasant. There was no joy to be gained by Gansey looking so miserable, and there was no satisfaction to be gained by Gansey and Blue essentially asking for permission to continue seeing each other. Adam wished that they had just told him the truth all along; then it would have never come to this.

Ronan raised an eyebrow.

Blue drew her fingers into small, tight fists at her sides.

Gansey added nothing else, simply waited for judgement, his uncertain gaze on Adam in particular. He was such a tattered version of the person Adam had first met, and Adam couldn't tell if Gansey was becoming someone different, or if he was returning to someone he'd already been long before. Adam rummaged within himself for anything that he wanted Gansey to say now, but nothing stood out. Respect was what he had wanted all this time, and respect was what he was looking at, even if it was belated.

"Thank you," Adam said. "For finally telling us." He meant *for telling me*. Gansey knew it; he gave an infinitesimal nod. Blue and Adam regarded each other. She sucked in her lip; he lifted a shoulder. They were both sorry.

"Good. I'm glad that's out," Gansey said in an airy voice. Long ago, Adam would have found this breezy response unbearable; he would have assumed it was flippancy. Now he knew that it was the opposite. When pressed too close to something huge and personal, Gansey ducked away into cheery politeness. It was so out of place here in this urgent care, in this tumultuous night, that it was truly unsettling, particularly paired with the continued disarray of his expression.

Blue took Gansey's hand.

Adam was glad she did.

"Gross," Ronan said, which was the most juvenile response possible.

But Gansey said, "Thanks for the input, Ronan," with a proper look on his face again, and Adam saw how cleverly Ronan had released the tension of the moment. They could all breathe again.

Maura returned to them from the counter. Adam got the distinct impression that she had been loitering there intentionally, giving them all room. Now she took out her car keys and said, "Let's get out of here. These places make me nervous."

Adam leaned to bump his knuckles against Gansey's.

No more playing around. There was only time for truth.

TWENTY-EIGHT

D epending on where you began the story, it was about
Declan Lynch.

Although it was hard to believe, he hadn't been born paranoid.

And really, was it paranoia when you weren't necessarily wrong?

Caution. That was what it was called when people really were out to kill you. He'd learned caution, not paranoia.

He'd been born pliant and trusting, but he'd learned. He'd learned to be suspicious of people who asked you where you lived. He'd learned to talk to his father only on disposable mobile phones bought at gas stations. He'd learned not to trust anyone who told you that it wasn't honourable to long for a historical town house in a corrupt city, a master suite with a tiger-skin rug, a case full of beautifully winking bourbons, and a German car that knew more about the world than you did. He'd learned that lies were only dangerous if you sometimes told the truth.

The eldest and most natural son of Niall Lynch stood in his Alexandria, Virginia, town house and leaned his forehead against the glass, staring out at the quiet morning street below. D.C. traffic was only beginning to growl to life, and this neighbourhood had yet to shake itself to waking.

He was holding a phone. It was ringing.

It was clunkier than the work phone that he used for his internship with Mark Randall, political denizen and golf ball killer. He'd intentionally chosen a model with a decidedly different shape for his father's work. Didn't want to scrape his hand through his messenger bag and grab the wrong one. Didn't want to feel the nightstand in the middle of the night and speak easily to the wrong person. Didn't want to give the wrong phone to Ashley to hold for him. Anything he could do to remind himself to be paranoid – cautious – while running the Niall Lynch business was a help.

This phone hadn't rung in weeks. He thought he'd finally got out of it.

It rang.

He debated for a long time if it was more dangerous to pick it up or to ignore it.

He readjusted. He was no longer Declan Lynch, ingratiating political whippersnapper. He was Declan Lynch, Niall Lynch's steel-jawed son.

It rang.

He picked it up.

"Lynch."

"Consider this a courtesy call," said the person on the other end of the phone. Music was playing in the background; some wailing string instrument.

A thin, viscous string of nerves stretched and dribbled down Declan's neck.

He said, "You can't possibly expect me to believe that's all this is."

"I would not expect any such thing," replied the voice on the other line. It was clipped, amused, accented, invariably accompanied by music of some kind. Declan knew her only as Seondeok. She didn't buy many artefacts, but when she did, there was no drama. The understanding was clear: Declan presented a magical object, Seondeok made an offer, Declan handed it over to her, and they parted ways until next time. At no point did Declan feel he might be capriciously stuffed in the trunk of his father's car while listening to his father being roughed up, or handcuffed and forced to watch his parents' barn get tossed in front of him, or beaten senseless and left half dead in his Aglionby dorm room.

Declan appreciated the little things.

But none of them could be trusted.

Caution, not paranoia.

"The situation is very volatile back in Henrietta," Seondeok said. "I have heard it is no longer Greenmantle's store."

Volatile, yes. That was a word. Once upon a time, Niall Lynch had sold his "artefacts" to dealers all over the world. Somehow that had got narrowed down to Colin Greenmantle, Laumonier and Seondeok. Declan assumed it was for security, but maybe he was giving his father too much credit. Maybe he'd just alienated everyone else.

"What else have you heard?" Declan asked, neither confirming nor denying.

"I am glad to hear you do not trust me," Seondeok replied. "Your father talked too much."

"I don't appreciate the tone," Declan said. His father *had* talked too much. But that was for a Lynch to say, not some Korean dealer of illegal magical antiquities.

The music in the background wailed in apology. "Yes, that was rude of me. The word is that someone may be selling something special in Henrietta," Seondeok said.

The nerves drooled down Declan's collar. "Not me."

"I did not think so. Like I said: courtesy call. I thought you might want to know if wolves were coming to your door."

"How many wolves?"

The music tripped; restarted. "There may possibly be packs and packs."

Maybe they had found out about Ronan. Declan's fingers tightened on the phone. "Do you know what they are howling for, *seonsaengnim*?"

"Mm," Seondeok said. It was an evocative noise that conveyed both that she knew he was sucking up and that she accepted it nonetheless. "This secret is still very young. I called in hope that I could give you enough time to act."

"And how do you think that I should act?"

"It is hardly my place to tell you. I am not your parent."

Declan said, "You know I have no parents."

The music whispered and sighed behind her. Finally, she repeated, "I am not your parent. I am just another wolf. Don't forget that."

He pushed off the window. "I'm sorry. Now I was being rude. I appreciate the call. "

His mind was already digging through worst-case scenarios. He needed to get Ronan and Matthew out of Henrietta — that was all that mattered.

Seondeok said, "I miss your father's finds; they are most

beautiful. He was a very troubled man, but he had a most beautiful mind, I think."

She was imagining Niall Lynch going through closets and collections and basements, carefully curating the objects he found. Declan imagined something closer to the truth: his father dreaming at the Barns, in hotel rooms, on couches, in the backseat of the BMW that was now Ronan's.

"Yeah," Declan said. "Yeah, I think so, too."

TWENTY-NINE

Sleep, snatched. Breakfast, skipped. School, attended.

Gansey could not tell how close it had to be to the end of the world – his world – before he could justify taking school off to chase Glendower, and so he kept going. Adam went, because Adam would cling to his Ivy League dreams even if they were being borne skyward in Godzilla's jaws. And, to Gansey's amazement, Ronan went as well, nearly making them both late as he scrounged for a complete uniform in the mess of his room. He suspected that Ronan was only attending to make up for the fight in the urgent care the night before, but Gansey didn't care. He just wanted Ronan to log some time in a classroom.

Henry caught up to Gansey in the hallway of Borden House as he left class (French, to replace his defunct Latin studies – Gansey preferred Latin, but he was not terrible at French, so *n'y a pas de quoi fouetter un chat*). Henry skipped until he was in step with Gansey. "Hey, Junior. Is everything joy in your world after last night?"

"Two steps down from joy. We had a very good time last night, at Litchfield. It was rude of us to run out when we did."

"We only watched music videos on our phones after you left. The mood sagged. I tucked in the children and read them stories but they kept asking after you."

This made Gansey laugh. "We were having adventures."

"I thought so. That's what I told them."

Carefully, Gansey added, "An old friend wasn't feeling well." It was not a lie. Just not an entire truth. It was the edge of a truth.

Henry raised an eyebrow to demonstrate that he clearly spotted this edge, but he didn't tug at it. "They'll be all right?"

Noah's face went to inky black. Noah's sister stood on the auditorium stage. Bones yellowed beneath an Aglionby sweater.

Gansey said, "We remain optimistic."

He did not think there was anything off about the tone of his voice when he said it, but Henry's gaze darted over to him, quickly. That eyebrow quirked again. "Optimistic. Yes, you are an optimistic person, Gansey Boy. Would you like to see something interesting before lunch?"

A glance at his watch told Gansey that Adam, at least, would be looking for him at the dining hall soon.

Henry swiftly interpreted this look. "It's right here. In Borden. It's cool. It's Ganseylike."

This struck Gansey as patently absurd. No one knew what Ganseylike was, even Gansey. Teachers and family friends were always collecting articles and stories that they thought might capture his attention, things they thought were Ganseylike. The well-meaning items always addressed the most obvious parts of him. Welsh kings or old Camaros or other young people who had travelled the world for bizarre reasons no one else understood. No one dug down past that, and he supposed he didn't much encourage it. There was a lot of night in those days behind him, and he preferred to turn his face into the sun. Ganseylike. What was Ganseylike?

"Does that smile mean yes? Yes, good, follow me," Henry said. He immediately pitched left through a narrow door labelled STAFF USE ONLY. Borden House had originally been a house, not an academic building, and the door opened into a narrow staircase. One fussy sconce lit the way; the light was swallowed by hideously busy wallpaper. They started down the stairs. "This is a very old building, Dick Three. Seventeen fifty-one. Imagine the things it has seen. Or heard, since houses don't have eyes."

"Currency Act," Gansey said.

"What?"

"Was passed in 1751," Gansey said. "Banning the issue of currency by New England. And George the Third became Prince of Wales in 1751, if I remember right."

"Also" — Henry reached for a light switch. It barely illuminated a low-ceilinged basement with a dirt floor. A glorified crawl space, with nothing but a few cardboard boxes shoved against one of the foundation walls — "the first performing monkey act in the United States." He had to duck his head to keep from tangling his hair in the exposed wooden beams supporting the floor above them. The air smelled like a concentrated version of Borden House's aboveground floors — which was to say, like mould and navy blue carpet — but with the additional damp, living scent peculiar to caves and very old basements.

"Really?" Gansey asked.

"Maybe," Henry said. "I tried to find primary sources, but you know the Internet, man. Here we are."

They had come to the far corner of the basement, and the single lightbulb by the base of the stairs did not quite illuminate what Henry was pointing at. It took Gansey a moment to realize what the blacker square in the already dark dirt floor was.

"Is it a tunnel?" he asked.

"Nah."

"A hidey hole?" Gansey asked. He crouched. It seemed like it. The hole was no more than three feet square with edges worn by the centuries. Gansey touched a groove in one edge. "It had a door at one point, I guess. They called them priest's holes in the UK. Must've been for slaves, or for . . . alcohol during prohibition, maybe?"

"Something like that. Interesting, yes?"

"Mmm," Gansey said. It was historical. That was Ganseylike, he supposed. He was vaguely disappointed, which must have meant that he had hoped for something more, even if he didn't know what that something more would have been.

"No, the Ganseylike part is inside," Henry said. To his surprise, Henry slid into the pit, landing at the bottom with a dull thud. "Check it out."

"I assume you have a plan for getting back out if I do."

"There's handholds." When Gansey did not move, Henry explained, "Also, this is a test."

"Of what?"

"Merit. No. Ma— No. There's an *m* word for bravery, but I can't recall it. My frontal lobe is still drunk from last night."

"Mettle."

"Yes, yes, that's it. This is a test of mettle. That's the Ganseylike part."

Gansey knew that Henry was right by the *zing* of feeling in his heart. It was very similar to the sensation he'd felt at the toga party. That feeling of being known. Not in a superficial way, but in something deeper and truer. He asked, "What is my prize if I pass?"

"What is ever any prize of a test of mettle? The prize is your honour, Mr Gansey."

Doubly known. Triply known.

Gansey wasn't precisely sure how to cope with being so accurately pegged by a person who was, after all, only a recent acquaintance.

So there was nothing left but to lower himself into the hole.

It was almost completely dark, and the walls intruded. He was close enough to Henry to both smell the bite of Henry's hair product and hear his slightly accelerated breathing.

"History, that complicated bitch," Henry said. "Are you claustrophobic?"

"No, I have other vices." If this had been Cabeswater, it would have been rapidly working with Gansey's fear to produce stinging insects. Gansey was grateful that intention was not such a powerful thing outside of Cabeswater. This hole in the ground could remain simply a hole in the ground. In this world, he only had to worry about schooling his exterior, not his interior. "Can you imagine having to hide in one of these? Did I pass the test?"

Henry scratched at the wall or something similar; it made a dead, hissing sound as dirt crumbled to the floor. "Have you ever been kidnapped, Richard Gansey?"

"No. Am I being kidnapped now?"

"Not on a school night. I was kidnapped once," Henry said. His tone was so light and ordinary that Gansey wasn't certain if he was making a joke or not. "For ransom. My parents were not in the same country, and so communication was not good. They put me in a hole like this. It was perhaps a bit smaller."

He was not joking.

"Jesus," said Gansey. He could not see Henry's face in the darkness to know how he felt about the story he was telling; his voice was still light.

"Jesus was not there, unfortunately," Henry said. "Or perhaps fortunately. The hole was barely big enough for me."

Gansey could hear Henry rubbing his fingers against each other, or making and unmaking fists; every sound was amplified in this dusty chamber. And now he could smell that peculiar scent that came with fear: the body producing chemicals that reeked of anxiety. He could not tell, however, if it was his or Henry's. Because Gansey's mind knew that this hole would not produce a sudden swarm of bees to kill him. But Gansey's heart remembered hanging in the cave in Cabeswater and hearing the swarms develop beneath him.

"This is Ganseylike too, yes?" Henry asked.

"Which part?"

"Secrets."

"True enough," Gansey admitted, because admitting you had secrets was not the same as telling them. "What happened?"

"What happened, he asks. My mother knew that to pay the ransom right away was only to encourage others to kidnap her children while she was not watching, and so she haggled with my captors. They did not like this, as you can imagine, and they had me tell her on the phone what they intended to do to me every day she did not pay."

"They had *you* tell her?"

"Yes, yes. You see, that is part of the haggling. If the parent knows that the child is afraid, it will make them pay faster, and more, that is the wisdom."

"I had no idea."

"Who does? Now you do." The walls felt closer. Henry went on, with a little laugh — a *laugh*. "She said, 'I do not pay for damaged goods.' And they said that was all she would get, so on and so forth. But my mother is very good at bargains. And so after five days, I was returned to her, with all of my fingers and both of my eyes still. For a good price, they say. I was a little hoarse, but that was my own fault."

Gansey didn't know how he felt about this. He had been given this secret, but he didn't know why. He didn't know what Henry wanted from him. He had many assembled reactions prepared to deploy — sympathy, advice, concern, support, indignation, sorrow — but he didn't know which combination was called for. He was used to knowing. He didn't think Henry *needed* anything from him. This was a landscape with no map.

Finally, he said, "And now we're standing in a hole just like that, and you sound quite calm."

"Yes. That's the point. I have spent . . . I have spent many years in the pursuit of being able to do this," Henry said. He took a short, thin breath, and Gansey was certain that his face was telling a far different story than his still airy voice. "Instead of hiding, facing the thing I was afraid of."

"How many years? How old were you?"

"Ten." Henry's sweater rustled; Gansey sensed him repositioning. His voice went a little different. "How old were you, Whoop Whoop Gansey Boy, when you were stung by those bees?"

Gansey knew the factual answer, but he wasn't sure if that was the answer Henry wanted. He still didn't know why this conversation was happening. "I was ten as well."

"And how have those years treated you?"

He hesitated. "Some better than others. You saw, I suppose."

"Do you trust me?" Henry asked.

It was a loaded question here in the dark and the more dark. Here in the test of mettle. Did he? Gansey's trust had always been based in instinct. His subconscious rapidly assembling all markers into a picture that he understood without knowing why he understood it. Why was he in this hole? He already knew the answer to this question.

"Yes."

"Give me your hand," Henry said. With one of his hands, he found Gansey's palm in the darkness. And with the other, he placed an insect in it.

THIRTY

Gansey did not breathe.

At first, he didn't think it really was an insect. In the dark, in this closeness, he was imagining it. But then he felt it shift its weight on his palm. Familiar. Slender legs supporting a more vast body.

"Richardman," Henry said.

Gansey did not breathe.

He could not snatch his hand away: That was a losing game he'd played before. Then, terribly, it buzzed, once, without lifting off. It was a noise that Gansey had long since stopped interpreting as a sound. It was a weapon. It was a crisis where he who flinched first died first.

"Dick."

Gansey did not breathe.

The odds of being stung by an insect were astonishingly low, actually. *Think about it*, Gansey had often told a worried friend of the family as they stood outside, insects bright in the dusk. *When's the last time you were stung?* He could not process why Henry had done this. He didn't know what he was supposed to be thinking. Was he supposed to be remembering all that had happened to him? All of the good and the bad? Because if so, the recorder was stuck, playing only this moment.

"Gansey," Henry said. *"Breathe."*

Little lights moved at the corner of Gansey's vision. He was breathing, just not enough. He couldn't risk moving.

Henry touched the back of Gansey's hand, and then he cupped his other hand over the top of Gansey's. The insect was trapped against Gansey and Henry, inside a globe of fingers.

"Here is what I have learned," Henry said. "If you cannot be unafraid —"

There was a place where terror stopped and became nothingness. But today, in this hole, with an insect on his skin, with a promise that he was to die soon, the nothingness never came.

Henry finished, "— be afraid *and* happy. Think of your child bride, Gansey, and the times we had last night. Think about what you are afraid of. That weight that tells you it is a bee? Does it have to be something that kills you? No. It is just a little thing. It could be anything. It could be something beautiful instead."

Gansey could not hold his breath any longer; he had to pass out or take a proper breath. He released a ragged stream of worthless air and sucked in another. The dark became just the dark again; the dancing lights were gone. His heart was still making a racket in his chest, but it was slowing.

"There he is," Henry said, same as he had at Raven Day. "It is a terrible thing to see someone else scared, isn't it?"

"What is in my hand?"

"A secret. I am going to trust you with this secret," Henry said. Now he sounded a little uncertain himself. "Because I want you to trust me. But to do that, if we are to be friends, you have to know the truth."

Henry took a deep breath, and then he took his hand off the top of Gansey's palm to reveal a bee of extraordinary size.

Gansey barely had time to react when Henry touched his fingers again.

"Easy, Mr Gansey. Look again."

Now that Gansey had settled, he could see that it wasn't an ordinary bee at all; it was a beautiful robotic insect. *Beautiful* was perhaps not the best word, but Gansey couldn't immediately think of another. The wings, antennae, and legs were clearly fashioned of metal, with fine articulated joints and thin wire wings, but it was as delicately and elegantly coloured as a flower petal everywhere else. It was not alive, but it looked vital. He could see it in this darkness because it had a tiny heart that emitted an amber glow.

Gansey knew that Henry's family was in the business of robotic bees, but he had not thought of *this* when he considered robotic bees. He felt fairly certain that he had seen images of robotic bees, and while they had been impressive bits of nano-robotics, they were nothing like actual bees, having more in common with tiny helicopters than with living insects. Henry's bee, though, was fearfully and impossibly constructed. It reminded him so strongly of Ronan's dream objects that it was hard to shake the idea once it had occurred to him.

Henry dug his phone out of his pocket. Tapping rapidly, he brought up a rainbow-slicked screen that was somehow just as strange to look at. "RoboBee interfaces with ChengPhone via this app. It's fingerprint specific, so you see I press my finger here and tell it what I want it to find — RoboBee, find great hair! — oh and look, there it goes."

Gansey startled violently as the bee took flight with the same sound as before, lifting into the air and alighting upon his hair. The weight of it there was even worse than having it in his palm. Stiffly, he said, "Could you remove that? It makes me very uncomfortable."

Henry pressed his finger to the screen again, and the bee lifted back into the air, buzzing on to his shoulder.

Gansey said, "You didn't say anything that time."

"No, I don't have to say anything. It reads my thoughts through my fingerprint," Henry said. He didn't look up from the screen as he said this, but Gansey could see in the light that he was gauging Gansey's reaction. "So I just tell it what to do and — *whoosh!* — off it goes, thank you, thank you, little bee."

Henry held his hand out and the bee whirred into it like a mobile blossom; the light extinguished. He tucked it back into his pocket. It was impossible, of course, and Henry was waiting for Gansey to say it was impossible. This was why it was secret, because it couldn't exist.

The net looped down around Gansey; he felt it.

"Your parents make robotic bees," he started carefully.

"My father. My father's company, yes." There was a line drawn there, though Gansey didn't understand it.

"And it makes bees like this." Gansey did not try to make it sound like he believed it.

"Gansey Boy, I think we have to decide if we trust each other or not," Henry said. "I think this is the moment in our young friendship."

Gansey considered his words, "But trusting someone and confiding in them are not the same thing."

Henry laughed approvingly. "No. But I have already both trusted in you and confided in you. I have kept the secret of what you had in the back of your SUV and the secret of Adam Parrish not getting killed by those roof tiles. That is trust. And I have confided in you: I showed you RoboBee."

All of this was true. But Gansey knew enough people with secrets to not be dazzled into easily using them as currency. And so much of what Gansey lived with now put other people's lives on the line, not just his own. That was a lot of trust for a toga party and a hole in the ground. He said, "There's a psychological principle that car salesmen use. They buy you a drink from a Coke machine with their own money, and then you feel obligated to buy a car from them."

There was humour in Henry's voice. "Are you saying your secrets are to my secrets as an automobile is to a carbonated beverage?"

Now there was humour in Gansey's. "Your father's company didn't build that bee, did it?"

"No."

He might as well get it over with. "What do you want me to say? The word *magic*?"

"You've seen magic like my RoboBee before," Henry said. "That's not the same sort of magic as watching Parrish deflect a ton of slate. Where have you seen this kind of magic?"

Gansey couldn't. "That's not my secret."

Henry said, "I'll spare you the agony; I know it. Declan Lynch. He sold my mother two of them."

This was so unexpected that Gansey was glad they were in total dark again; he was sure the shock had made it to his face.

He struggled to piece this information together. Declan — so this bee was Niall's work. If Henry's mother was a client, did that mean Declan was selling to people at the school? Surely Declan wasn't that stupid. "How did your mother know to buy them? Did you tell her about them?"

"You have it backwards. She doesn't know because I'm here. I'm here because she knows. Don't you see? I am her excuse. She visits me. Buys something from Declan Lynch. Back she goes. No one the wiser. Ah! I have wanted to say this out loud for two years. They fester, secrets."

"Your mother sent you to Aglionby just so she could have a cover for when she does business with Declan?" Gansey asked.

"Magical artefacts, bro. Big business. Scary business. Good way to get yourself kneecapped. Or killed like our man Kavinsky."

Gansey was going to choke on revelations. "She did business with him?"

"No way. He only dealt drugs, but she said they were magic, too. And come on. You were at that Fourth of July party this year. Explain the dragons."

"I can't," Gansey said. "We both know."

"Yes, we do," Henry said, satisfied. "Once, he nearly killed Cheng Two for the fun of it. He was the worst."

Gansey leaned back against the dusty wall.

"Are you collapsing? Are you fine? I thought we were conversing."

They *were* conversing, just not in any way that Gansey had anticipated. He had spoken to plenty of uncanny people in his pursuit of Glendower. In many ways, his travels were defined not by cities or countries travelled between, but people and phenomena. The difference was that Gansey had gone looking for them. They had never come looking for him. He had never really met anyone else like himself, and even though Henry was far from Gansey's twin, he was the closest that Gansey had yet found.

He hadn't realized the loneliness of this belief until it was tested. He asked, "Are there any other magical people at Aglionby I should know about?"

"Other than the ones who run with you? No one that I know. I've been trying to get your number for a year."

"It's in the student directory."

"No, you fool. Idiomatically. Get. Your. Number. See if you were a creeper like K or not. Get. Your. Number. Who here is English as a second language? Hint, not you."

Gansey laughed, then he laughed some more. He felt he'd gone through every emotion known to man in the last few days.

"I'm not a creeper," he said. "I'm just a guy looking for a king. You said your mother bought two of those things. Where's the other?"

Henry shuffled the jewelled insect back out of his pocket. It amber heart warmed light through the pit again. "Back in the lab, of course, as father dear tries to copy it with nonmagical parts. My mother told me to keep this one to remind me of what I am."

"And what is that?"

The bee illuminated both itself and Henry: its translucent wings, Henry's wickedly cut eyebrows.

"Something more."

Gansey looked at him sharply. Somewhere along the way,

during this hunt for Glendower, he'd forgotten to notice how much magic there was in the world. How much magic that wasn't just buried in a tomb. He was feeling it now.

"Here is the thing I need to tell you before we are friends," Henry said. "My mother sells magic. She told me to watch you to find your secrets. I do not mean to use you now, but that is what I was supposed to do. I did not begin this game looking for a friend."

"What do you want me to say?"

"Nothing yet," Henry said. "I want you to think about it. And then I hope you will choose to trust me. Because I'm over-full on secrets and underfed on friends."

He held the bee between them so that Gansey was looking at him through the glow of its marvellous body. Henry's eyes were lively and ferocious.

He tossed the bee into the air. "Let's get out of this hole."

THIRTY-ONE

The world didn't have words to measure hate. There were tons, yards, years. Volts, knots, watts. Ronan could explain how fast his car was going. He could describe exactly how warm the day was. He could specifically convey his heart rate. But there was no way for him to tell anyone else exactly how much he hated Aglionby Academy.

Any unit of measurement would have to include both the volume and the weight of the hate. And it would also have to include a component of time. The days logged in class, wasted, useless, learning skills for a life he didn't want. No single word existed, probably, to contain the concept. *All*, perhaps. He had all the hate for Aglionby Academy.

Thief? Aglionby was the thief. Ronan's life was the dream, pillaged.

He had told himself that he would let himself quit: that was his eighteenth birthday present to himself.

And yet here he was.

Quit. Just quit. Either he believed he could do it or he didn't.

He could hear Gansey's voice: *Just stick it out until graduation; that's only a couple more months. Surely you can make it that long.*

So now he tried.

The school day was a pillow over his head. He would suffocate before the final bell. The only oxygen to be found was the pale band of skin on Adam's wrist where his watch had been and the glimpse of the sky between classes.

Four more hours to go.

Declan wouldn't stop texting him. *When you have a minute, give me a text.* Ronan did not just give people texts. *Hey I know you're at school but maybe in between let me know.* This was a lie, Declan's super-power. He assumed Ronan was not at school. *Hey I'm in town I need to talk to you.*

This got Ronan's attention. Now that Declan had graduated, he was generally safely stored two hours away in D.C., a distance that had, in Ronan's estimation, improved their relationship in all the ways it could possibly be improved. He returned only for Sunday Mass, an extravagant four-hour round-trip that Matthew took for granted and Ronan only partially understood. Surely Declan had better things to be doing in D.eclan C.ity than spending half his day in a town he hated with a family he had never wanted to be a part of.

Ronan did not care for any of this. It made him feel as if he had won nothing over the summer. Back at Aglionby, his dreams fearful things, trying to avoid Declan.

Three more hours to go.

"Lynch," said Jiang, passing him in the dining hall. "I thought you'd died."

Ronan shot him a cool look. He didn't want to see Jiang's face unless it was behind the wheel of a car.

Two more hours to go.

Declan called during a guest presentation. The phone, on silent, hummed to itself. The sky outside was blue torn by clouds; Ronan longed to be out in it. His species died in captivity.

One more hour.

"I thought I was hallucinating," Adam said, next to the lockers, an announcement droning on over the hall speakers. "Ronan Lynch in the halls of Aglionby."

Ronan slammed his locker. He had not put anything in it and had no reason to open or close it, but he liked the satisfying bang of the metal down the hall, the way it drowned out the announcements. He did it again for good measure. "Is this a real conversation, Parrish?"

Adam didn't bother to reply. He merely exchanged three textbooks for his gym hoodie.

Ronan wrenched his tie loose. "You working after school?"

"With a dreamer."

He held Ronan's gaze over his locker door.

School had improved.

Adam gently closed his locker. "I'm done at four thirty. If you're up for brainstorming some repair of your dream forest. Unless you have homework."

"Asshole," Ronan said.

Adam smiled cheerily. Ronan would start wars and burn cities for that true smile, elastic and amiable.

Ronan's good mood lasted only as long as the hallway and the set of stairs at the end of it, because outside, Declan's sleek Volvo was parked on the kerb. Declan himself stood next to it, talking to Gansey. Gansey had dirt on the elbows of his uniform shirt — how he'd managed to get them so dirty during the course of the school day was mystifying to Ronan. Declan was dressed in a suit, but it never seemed like a special occasion when he did.

He wore a suit the way other people wore pyjama bottoms.

They did not make words to measure Ronan's hatred for his older brother, or vice versa. There was no unit of measurement for an emotion that was equal parts hatred and betrayal, judgement and habit.

Ronan pressed his hands into fists.

One of the back windows rolled down, revealing Matthew's golden curls and pathologically sunny smile. He windmilled a single wave at Ronan.

It had been months since the three of them had been in the same place outside of a church.

"Ronan," said Declan. The word was loaded with additional meaning: *I see you've only just come out of school and already your uniform looks like hell; nothing is shocking here.* He gestured to the Volvo. "Join me in my office."

Ronan did not want to join him in his office. Ronan wanted to stop feeling like he had drunk battery acid.

"What do you need with Ronan?" Gansey asked. His "Ronan" was loaded with additional meaning, too: *Was this pre-arranged and tell me what is happening and do you need me to intervene?*

"Just a little family chat," Declan said.

Ronan looked at Gansey entreatingly.

"Is it a family chat that could happen on the way to Fox Way?" Gansey asked, all polite power. "Because he and I were just headed over there."

Ordinarily, Declan would have stepped off at the slightest pressure from Gansey, but he said, "Oh, I can drop him off there after we're done. Just a few minutes."

"Ronan!" Matthew reached his hand out the window

towards Ronan. His ebullient "Ronan" was another version of *please*.

Trapped.

"*Miseria fortes viros*, Ronan," Adam said.

When he said "Ronan," it meant: *Ronan*.

"Asshole," Ronan said again, but he felt a little better. He got in.

Once they were both in the car, Declan didn't drive far, just to the other side of the parking lot, out of the way of departing cars and buses. He leaned back in his seat, eyes on Aglionby, looking nothing like their mother, only a little like their father. His eyes were pouched with fatigue.

Matthew had resumed playing a game on his phone, his mouth curved into an inattentive smile.

Declan started: "We need to talk about your future."

"No," Ronan said. "No, no, we don't."

He was already most of the way out of the car, leaves snapping dead under his shoes.

"Ronan, wait!"

Ronan did not wait.

"*Ronan!* Before he died, when he and I were out together, Dad told me a story about you."

It was wickedly unfair.

It was wickedly unfair because there was nothing else that would have stopped Ronan from walking away.

It was wickedly unfair because Declan knew it, and he'd known Ronan would try to walk away, and he'd had it at the ready, a rare meal from a diminishing pantry.

Ronan's feet were burned on to the asphalt. The electricity in the atmosphere crackled beneath his skin. He didn't know if he was more furious with his brother, for knowing precisely how to loop the wire around his neck, or with himself, for his inability to duck out of the noose.

"About me," Ronan echoed finally, his voice as dead as he could manage.

His brother didn't reply. He just waited.

Ronan got back inside the car. He slammed the door. He opened it and slammed it again. He opened it a third time and slammed it another time before hurling the knob of his skull against the headrest and staring through the windshield at the turbulent clouds.

"All done?" Declan asked. He glanced back at Matthew, but the youngest Lynch was still playing pleasantly on his phone.

"I was done months ago," Ronan replied. "If this is a lie . . ."

"I was too angry to tell you before." In an entirely different tone, Declan added, "Are you going to be quiet?"

This, too, was an unfair shot, because it was what their father used to say when he was about to tell them a story. Ronan was already going to listen; this made him lay his head against the window and close his eyes.

Declan was unlike his father in many ways, but, like Niall Lynch, he could tell a story. A story, after all, is a lot like a lie, and Declan was an excellent liar. He began:

"There was an old Irish hero once, long ago, back when Ireland was not so much about men and towns and was instead mostly island and magic. The hero had a name, but I'm not telling it to you until the end. He was a god-hero, terrifying and wise and impetuous. He came to have a spear — the story is about the spear — that was thirsty for blood and nothing else. Whoever had this spear would rule the battlefield, because there was nothing that could stand against its killing magic. It was so voraciously bloodthirsty that it had to be covered to hide its eyes and stop the killing. Only blind would it rest."

Declan paused then, sighing, as if the weight of the story was a tangible thing, and he needed to take a moment to regain his strength. It was true that the memory of the ritual was heavy enough. Ronan was all tangled up in half-formed images of his father sitting on the end of Matthew's bed, the brothers tumbled together at its head, his mother perched on that tatty desk chair no one else would sit at. She loved these stories, too, especially the ones about her.

A sound like fingernails tapping pattered on the roof of the car, and a second later, a flock of dried leaves skittered across the windshield. It reminded Ronan of the night horror's claws; he wondered if it had returned to the Barns yet.

Declan went on. "Once the spear was uncovered, it wouldn't matter if the hero's truest love or family was in the room with him; the spear would kill them anyway. Killing was what it was good at, and so killing was what it did."

In the backseat, Matthew gasped dramatically to lighten the mood. Like Chainsaw, he could not bear to see Ronan distressed.

"It was a fine weapon, shaped for fighting and for nothing else," Declan said. "The hero, defender of the island, tried to use the spear for good. But it cut through enemies and friends, villains and lovers, and the hero saw that the single-minded spear was meant to be kept apart."

Ronan picked angrily at his leather wristbands. He was reminded precisely of the dream he'd had only days before. "I thought you said this story was about me."

"The spear, Dad told me, was him." Declan looked at Ronan. "He told me to make sure Ronan was the name of the hero, and not the name of just another spear."

He let the words linger.

On the outside, the three Lynch brothers appeared remarkably dissimilar: Declan, a butter-smooth politician; Ronan, a bull in a china-shop world; Matthew, a sunlit child.

On the inside, the Lynch brothers were remarkably similar: They all loved cars, themselves, and each other.

"I know you're a dreamer like him," Declan said in a low voice. "I know you're good at it. I know it's pointless to ask you to stop. But Dad didn't want you to be alone like he was. Like he made himself."

Ronan twisted the leather bands tighter and tighter.

"Oh, I get it," Matthew said finally. He laughed gently at himself. "Duh."

"Why are you telling me this now?" Ronan asked finally.

"I got word that something big is about to go down here in Henrietta," Declan said.

"Who?"

"Who what?"

"Where did this word come from?"

Declan looked at him heavily.

"How did they know to call you?"

Declan replied, "Did you really think Dad kept track of this stuff on his own?"

Ronan had, but he didn't say anything.

"Why do you even think I was in D.C.?"

Ronan had thought Declan was there to get into politics, but that was so clearly not the correct answer that he kept his mouth shut.

"Matthew, put your earbuds in," Declan said.

"I don't have them with me."

"Pretend you have your earbuds in," Ronan said. He turned on the radio for a little background cover.

"I want you to give me a straight answer," Declan said. "Are you even thinking about going to college?"

"No." It was satisfying and terrible to say it out loud, a trigger pulled, the explosion over within a second. Ronan looked around for bodies.

Declan swayed; the bullet had clearly at least grazed him near a vital organ. With effort, he got the arterial spray under control. "Yeah. I figured. So the endgame is making this a career for you, isn't it?"

This was not, in fact, what Ronan wanted. Although he wanted to be free to dream, and free to live at the Barns, he did not want to dream in order to be able to live at the Barns. He wanted to be left alone to repair all of the buildings, to raise his father's cattle from their supernatural sleep, to populate the fields with new animals to be eaten and sold, and to turn the very rearmost field into a giant mudslick suitable for driving cars around in circles. This, to Ronan, represented a romantic ideal that he would do much to achieve. He wasn't sure how to tell his brother this in a persuasive, unembarrassing way, though, so he said, in an unfriendly way, "I was actually thinkin' of being a farmer."

"Ronan, for fuck's sake," Declan said. "Can we have a serious conversation for once?"

Ronan flipped him the bird with swift proficiency.

"Whatever," Declan said. "So it might not feel like Henrietta's hot now, but that's only because I've been working my ass off to keep them out of town. I've been handling Dad's sales for a while, so I told everyone I was handling them from D.C."

"If Dad wasn't dreaming you new stuff, what were you selling?"

"You've seen the Barns. It's just a question of parceling out the old stuff slowly enough that it seems like I'm getting it from other sources instead of just going into the backyard. That's why Dad travelled all the time, to keep up the ruse that it came from all over."

"If Dad wasn't dreaming you new stuff, *why* were you selling?"

Declan ran his hand around the steering wheel. "Dad dug us all a grave. He promised people stuff he hadn't even dreamt yet. He made deals with people who didn't always care about paying and who knew where we lived. He pretended he'd found this artefact – the Greywaren – that let people take shit out of dreams. Yeah. Sound familiar? When people came to him to buy it, he foisted something else on them instead. It became legendary. Then, of course he had to play them off each other and tease that psychopath Greenmantle and end up dead. So here we are."

Earlier this year, this sort of statement would've been enough to instigate a fight, but now the bitter misery in Declan's voice outweighed the anger. Ronan could step back to weigh these statements against what he knew of his father. He could weigh it against what he knew of Declan.

He didn't like it. He believed it, but he didn't like it. It had been easier to merely fight with Declan.

"Why didn't you tell me?" he asked.

Declan closed his eyes. "I tried."

"The hell you did."

"I tried to tell you he wasn't who you thought."

But that wasn't exactly true. Niall Lynch was exactly what Ronan had thought, but he was also this thing Declan had known. The two versions were not mutually exclusive. "I meant, why didn't you tell me you were up against all these people?"

Declan opened his eyes. They were brilliantly blue, same as all the Lynch brothers'. "I was trying to protect you, you little pissant."

"Well, it would've been a fuckton easier if I'd known more," Ronan snapped back. "Instead Adam and I had to run Greenmantle out on our own, while you played cloak and daggers."

His brother eyed him appraisingly. "That was you? How – oh."

Ronan enjoyed a full minute of his brother's appreciation.

"Parrish always was a creepily clever little fuck," Declan observed, sounding a little like their father despite himself. "Look, here's the thing. This buyer called me this morning and told me someone's offering to sell something big here, like I said. People are gonna come from all over to look at it, whatever it is. It's not going to take much effort to find you and Matthew and the Barns and that forest here."

"Who is this person selling something?"

"I don't know. I don't care. It hardly even matters. Don't you see? Even after that deal is over, they're gonna show up because Henrietta's a giant supernatural beacon. And because who knows what of Dad's business I haven't cleaned up yet. And if they find out you can dream — God help you, because it'll be over. I'm just —" Declan stopped speaking and closed his eyes; when he did, Ronan could see the brother he'd grown up with instead of the brother he'd grown away from. "I'm tired, Ronan."

The car was very quiet.

"Please —" Declan began. "Just come with me, OK? You can quit Aglionby and Matthew can transfer to a school in D.C., and I'll pour gasoline on everything Dad built and we can just leave the Barns behind. Let's just go."

It was not at all what Ronan had expected him to say, and he found he had no response. Quit Aglionby; leave Henrietta; quit Adam; leave Gansey.

Once, when Ronan was quite young, young enough that he had attended Sunday school, he had woken holding an actual flaming sword. His pyjamas, which adhered to rigorous safety codes that had to that point seemed academic in interest, had melted and saved him, but his blankets and the better part of his curtains had been entirely destroyed in a small inferno. Declan had been the one who had dragged Ronan from his room and woken their parents; he had never said anything about it, and Ronan had never thanked him.

When it came to it, it wasn't like there was an option. The Lynches would always save one another's lives, if they had to.

"Take Matthew," Ronan said.

"What?"

"Take Matthew to D.C. and keep him safe," Ronan repeated.

"Yeah? And what about you?"

They looked at each other, warped mirror images of each other.

"This is my home," Ronan said.

THIRTY-TWO

The stormy weather perfectly mirrored Blue Sargent's soul. Her first day back at school after suspension had been interminable. A small part of it was that the time away from school had been extraordinary: the absolute opposite of the mundane experience at Mountain View High. But the much bigger part of it was the memory of the most unmagical element of her suspension: Henry Cheng's toga party. The enchantment of that experience was made more impressive by the fact that it had actually contained no magic. And her instant kinship with the students there only underlined how she had absolutely failed to experience anything like it in her years at Mountain View. What was it that had made her feel so instantly comfortable with the Vancouver crowd? And why did that kinship have to be with people who belonged to a different world? Actually, she knew the answer to that. The Vancouver crowd had their eyes on the stars, not trained on the ground. They didn't know everything, but they wanted to. In a different world, she could have been friends with people like Henry for her entire teen years. But in this world, she stayed in Henrietta and watched people like that move away. She was not going to Venezuela.

Blue was filled with frustration that her life was so clearly demarcated.

Things that were *not enough*, but that she could have.

Things that were *something more*, that she couldn't.

So she stood like a prickly old lady, hunched over in a long mutilated hoodie that she'd made into a dress, waiting for the buses to pull out and free up her bike. She wished she had a phone or a Bible so she could pretend to be super busy with it like the handful of shy teens standing in the bus line ahead of her. Four classmates stood perilously close, holding a conversation about whether or not the bank robbery sequence in that movie everyone had seen was indeed awesome, and Blue was afraid they would ask her opinion on it. She knew, in a broad way, that there was nothing wrong with their topic, but she also knew in a more specific way that there was no way she could talk about the movie without sounding like a condescending brat. She felt one thousand years old. She also felt like maybe she *was* a condescending brat. She wanted her bike. She wanted her friends, who were also one-thousand-year-old condescending brats. She wanted to live in a world where she was surrounded by one-thousand-year-old condescending brats.

She wanted to go to Venezuela.

"Hey, hey, lady! Want to come for the ride of your life?"

Blue didn't immediately realize that the words were being directed at her. Truth only dawned after she realized that all of the faces around her were pointed at her. She pivoted slowly to discover that there was a very silver and expensive car parked in the fire lane.

Blue had managed to go months hanging out with Aglionby boys without *looking* like she hung out with Aglionby boys, but here was the most raven-boy-looking raven boy of them all parked in the fire lane next to her. The driver wore a watch that even Gansey would have considered gauche. The driver had hair tall enough to touch the ceiling of the car. The driver was wearing big black-framed sunglasses despite a notable lack of sun. The driver was Henry Cheng.

"Whoooooooooooo," said Burton, one of the bank robbery boys, swivelling slowly. "Not Your Bitch has a date? Is that who roughed you up?"

Cody, the second of the bank robbers, stepped towards the kerb to gape at the Fisker. He asked Henry, "Is that a Ferrari?"

"No, it's a Bugatti, man," Henry said through the open passenger window. "Ha-ha, I'm kidding you, man. It's totally a Ferrari. Sargent! Don't keep me waiting!"

Half the bus line was looking at her. Until that moment, Blue had never really stacked up all of her public statements against gratuitous commercialism, offensive boyfriends, and Aglionby students in one place. Now that everyone was looking at Henry and then at her, though, she was eyeing the stack and finding it enormous. She was also seeing how every student was slowly labelling the stack *BLUE SARGENT IS A HYPOCRITE.*

There was no easy way to establish that Henry was not her boyfriend, and moreover, it seemed somewhat pointless in light of the fact that her secret boyfriend was only slightly less overwhelmingly Aglionby than the specimen currently in front of her.

Blue was filled with the uncomfortable certainty that she probably needed to label the stack *BLUE SARGENT IS A HYPOCRITE* in her own handwriting.

She stomped over to the passenger window.

"Don't blow him here, Sargent!" someone shouted. "Make him get you steak first!"

Henry smiled sunnily. "Ho! The natives are restless. Hello, my people! Don't worry, I'll establish a higher minimum wage for you all!" Looking back at Blue, or at least turning his sunglasses towards her, he said, "Hi, hi, Sargent."

"What are you doing here!" Blue demanded. She was feeling — she wasn't sure. She was feeling *a lot*.

"I'm here to talk about the men in your life. To talk about the men in my life. I like the dress, by the way. Very boho chic or whatever. I was on my way home, and I wanted to find out if you had a good time at the toga party and also make sure that our plans for Zimbabwe were still on. I see you tried to claw your own eye out; it's edgy."

"I thought . . . I guess . . . it was Venezuela."

"Oh, right, we'll do that on the way."

"God," she said.

Henry inclined his head in humble acknowledgement.

"Graduation breathes on us, redneck lady," he said. "Now is the time to make sure we have the strings to all the balloons we want to keep before they all float away."

Blue looked at him cannily. It would have been easy to reply that she was not floating anywhere, that this balloon was going to slowly lose its helium and sink to the floor in the same place it had been born, but she thought of her mother's predictions for her and didn't. Instead she thought of how she wanted to travel to Venezuela and so did Henry Cheng, and that meant something in this minute, even if it didn't mean something next week.

A thought occurred to her. "I don't have to remind you I'm with Gansey, right?"

"Naturally not. I'm Henrysexual, anyway. Can I take you home?"

Stay away from Aglionby boys, because they are bastards.

Blue said, "I can't get in this car. Do you see what's happening behind me? I don't even want to look."

Henry said, "How about you give me the finger and shout at me now and withdraw with your principles?" He smiled winningly and held up three fingers. He counted to two with devil horns.

"This is incredibly unnecessary," Blue told him, but she could feel herself smiling.

"Life's a show," he replied. He counted one with his middle finger, and then his face melted into exaggerated shock.

Blue shouted, "Drop dead, you bastard!"

"FINE!" Henry screamed back, with slightly more hysteria than the role required. He attempted to squeal out of the lot, stopped to take off the parking brake, and then limped out more sedately.

She had not even had time to turn to see the results of their play in three parts before she heard a very familiar rumble. *Oh no —*

But sure enough, before she could live down her last visitor, a bright orange Camaro pulled up to the kerb in front of her. The engine was bucking a little bit; it was not quite as happy to be alive as the vehicle that had previously occupied the fire lane, but it was doing its best. It was also just as obviously an Aglionby car holding an Aglionby boy as the one that had just left.

Before, Blue had had half of the bus line's attention. Now she had all of it.

Gansey leaned across the passenger seat. Unlike Henry, he at least had the good grace to acknowledge the school's attention with a grimace. "Jane, I'm sorry this couldn't wait. But Ronan just called me."

"He *called* you?"

"Yes. He wants us. Can you come?"

The letters *BLUE SARGENT IS A HYPOCRITE* were most certainly scrawled in her own handwriting. She felt she had some self-examination to do later.

There was relative silence.

The self-examination was happening now.

"Stupid raven boys," she said, and got in the car.

THIRTY-THREE

No one could quite believe that Ronan had used his phone.

Ronan Lynch had many habits that irritated his friends and loved ones — swearing, drinking, street-racing — but the one that maddened his acquaintances the most was his inability to answer phone calls or send texts. When Adam had first met Ronan, he had found Ronan's aversion to the fancy phone so complete that he assumed there must have been a story behind it. Some reason why, even in the press of an emergency, Ronan's first response was to hand his phone to someone else. Now that Adam knew him better, he realized it had more to do with a phone not allowing for any posturing. Ninety per cent of how Ronan conveyed his feelings was through his body language, and a phone simply didn't care.

And yet he'd used it. While waiting for Declan to be done with Ronan, Adam had gone to Boyd's to get a few oil changes out of the way. He'd been there a few hours when Ronan had called. Then Ronan had texted Gansey and called Fox Way. He said the same thing to each of them: *Come to the Barns*, he'd said. *We need to talk.*

And because Ronan had never really asked them to do anything by phone, they all dropped everything to go.

By the time Adam got to the Barns, the others had already arrived — or at least the Camaro was there, and Adam assumed Gansey would have brought Blue, especially now that their secret was out. Ronan's BMW was parked sideways with the wheels jacked in a way that suggested it had slid into its current position. And to Adam's astonishment, Declan's Volvo was also parked there, backed into a spot, already ready to leave.

Adam got out.

The Barns had a strange effect on Adam. He had not known how to diagnose this feeling the first few times he had visited, because he had not truly believed in the two things that the Barns was made of: magic and love. Now that he had at least a passing acquaintance with both of those things, it affected him in a different way. He used to wonder what he would have looked like if he had grown up in a place like this. Now he thought about how, if he wanted it, he could one day live in a place like this. He did not quite understand what had changed.

Inside, he found the others in various states of celebration. It took Adam a moment to realize that this was Ronan's birthday: The grill smoked out back and there were store-bought cupcakes on the kitchen table and a few inflated balloons rolling around the corners of the room. Blue was sitting on the tiles tying strings on to balloons, her bad eye squinted shut, while Gansey and Declan stood by the counter, heads lowered, talking in low, serious voices that made them seem older than they were. Ronan and Matthew jostled into the kitchen from the backyard. They were noisy and brotherly, horsing around, impossibly physical. Was this what it was to have brothers?

Ronan looked up and caught Adam's eye.

"Take your shoes off before you go wandering around, shit-head," Ronan said.

Adam checked himself and leaned to untie his shoe.

"Not you – I meant Matthew." Ronan held Adam's gaze a moment longer and then watched Matthew chuck off his shoes. As he closely attended to Matthew skidding into the dining room on sock feet, Adam understood: This celebration was for Matthew's benefit.

Blue clambered to her feet to join Adam. In a low voice, she explained, "Matthew is going to stay with Declan. He's moving from Aglionby."

The picture grew clearer: This was a going-away celebration.

Slowly, over the next hour, the story came out in fits and starts, delivered in fragments by each of the people there. The upshot was this: The Barns was changing hands by way of a bloodless revolution, the crown passing from father to middle son as the eldest son abdicated. And if Declan was to be believed, rival states slavered just on the other side of the border.

This was both a goodbye party and a war council.

Adam could not quite believe it; he didn't know if he'd ever seen Ronan and Declan in the same space together without a fight. But it was true that these were the brothers as he hadn't seen them before. Declan, relieved and exhausted; Ronan, intense and powerful with purpose and joy; Matthew, unchanging and ebullient like the happy dream that he was.

Something about all of this made Adam feel off-balance. He didn't quite understand it. He would catch a whiff of boxwood from the open window in the kitchen, and it would make him think of scrying in Ronan's car. He would catch sight of Orphan Girl hiding with Chainsaw beneath the dining room table with a box of tinker toys and once again remember the shock of discovering that Ronan dreamt Cabeswater. He had wandered into Ronan Lynch's dream; Ronan had remade everything in this kingdom in the shape of his imagination.

"Why isn't it in *here*?" Ronan's voice came from the kitchen, exasperated.

Matthew rumbled in reply.

A moment later, Ronan hooked his fingers on the doorway of the dining room, looking out. "Parrish. Parrish. Would you see if you could find a damn roll of aluminium foil somewhere? Maybe in Matthew's room."

Adam didn't quite remember where Matthew's room was, but he was glad for the excuse to wander. As conversation continued in the kitchen, he made his way through the hallways and up hidden stairways into other half-hallways and to other half-staircases. Downstairs, Ronan said something and Matthew let out a howl of laughter so unholy that it must have been terrible. To Adam's surprise, he heard Ronan laugh, too, a real thing, unself-conscious, kind.

He found himself in what must have been Niall and Aurora's room. The light through the window splashed over the white bedspread, tender and drowsy. *Come away o human child* said a framed quote beside the bed. There was a framed photo above the dresser: Aurora, mouth open in a wide, surprised, guileless laugh, looking like Matthew. Niall grabbing her, smiling, sharp and handsome, his chin-length dark hair tucked behind his ears. His face was Ronan's.

Adam stood looking at the photo for a long time, unsure of why it held him. It could have been surprise, he reasoned, because he had just assumed Aurora was a blank palette, mild and quiet as she was in Cabeswater. It should have occurred to him that she was capable of happiness and dynamism, for Ronan to have believed for so long that she was real, not a dream.

What was real?

But it was possible that what kept him was Niall Lynch, that older version of Ronan. The likeness was not perfect, of course, but it was close enough to see Ronan's mannerisms in it. This ferocious, wild father; this wild, happy mother. Something inside Adam hurt.

He didn't understand anything.

He found Ronan's room. He knew it was Ronan's room by its clutter and its whimsy; it was a brighter cousin to his room at Monmouth. Strange little objects were tucked into all of the corners and stuffed under the bed: a younger Ronan's dreams, or maybe a father's gifts. There were ordinary things as well – a skateboard, a tattered roller-board suitcase, a complicated-looking instrument that must have been bagpipes lying dustily in an open case. Adam lifted a shiny model car from the shelf and it began to play an eerie, lovely tune.

Adam had to sit.

He sat on the edge of the downy white bedspread, a square of pure white light splashed across his knees. He felt drunk. Everything in this house felt so certain of its identity, so sure of its place. So certain it was wanted. He still held the model car balanced on his knees, although it had fallen silent. It was not any particular sort of car – it was every-muscle-car-ever dreamt into a form that was no-muscle-car-ever — but it reminded Adam of the first thing he had ever bought himself. It was a hateful memory, the sort of memory he would sometimes skirt the edges of by accident as he was falling asleep, his thoughts rolling close to it and then recoiling, burned. He couldn't remember how old he had been; his grandmother had sent him a card with ten dollars in it, back when his grandmother still sent cards. He had bought a model car with it, about this size, a Pontiac. He didn't remember anything about where he had bought the model, or why that model, or even what the occasion for the card had been. All he remembered was lying on the floor of his bedroom, driving tyre tracks into the carpet, and hearing his father say from the other room —

Adam's thoughts rolled close to the memory and jerked back.

But he touched the hood of the dream model and remembered the moment anyway. The fearsome anticipation of recalling the memory was worse than the memory itself, because it would go on for as long as Adam resisted it. Sometimes it was better to just give in at once.

I regret the minute I squirted him into you, Adam's father had said. He didn't shout it. He wasn't angry. It was just a fact.

Adam remembered the moment he realized *him* was Adam. He didn't remember exactly what his mother had said afterwards, only the sentiment of her reply — something like *I didn't imagine it this way, either* or *This isn't what I wanted.* The only thing he remembered with precision was that car, and the word *squirted.*

Adam sighed. It was impossible how some memories never decayed. In the old days — maybe even a few months before — Adam would have recalled that memory again, and again, it playing on a miserable, obsessive loop in his head. Once he had given in, he wouldn't have known how to stop. But now, at least, he could merely feel its sting once and then put it away for some other day. He was ever so slowly moving himself out of that trailer.

A floorboard cracked; knuckles tapped once on the open door. Adam looked up to see Niall Lynch standing in the doorway. No, it was Ronan, face lit bright on one side, in stark shadow on the other, looking powerful and at ease with his thumbs tucked in the pockets of his jeans, leather bracelets looped over his wrist, feet bare.

He wordlessly crossed the floor and sat beside Adam on the mattress. When he held out his hand, Adam put the model into it.

"This old thing," Ronan said. He turned the front tyre, and again the music played out of it. They sat like that for a few minutes, as Ronan examined the car and turned each wheel to play a different tune. Adam watched how intently Ronan studied the seams, his eyelashes low over his light eyes. Ronan let out a breath, put the model down on the bed beside him, and kissed Adam.

Once, when Adam had still lived in the trailer park, he had been pushing the lawn mower around the scraggly side yard when he realized that it was raining a mile away. He could smell it, the earthy scent of rain on dirt, but also the electric, restless smell of ozone. And he could see it: a hazy gray sheet of water blocking his view of the mountains. He could track the line of rain travelling across the vast dry field towards him. It was heavy and dark, and he knew he would get drenched if he stayed outside. It was coming from so far away that he had plenty of time to put the mower away and get under cover. Instead, though, he just stood there and watched it approach. Even at the last minute, as he heard the rain pounding the grass flat, he just stood there. He closed his eyes and let the storm soak him.

That was this kiss.

They kissed again. Adam felt it in more than his lips.

Ronan sat back, his eyes closed, swallowing. Adam watched his chest rise and fall, his eyebrows furrow. He felt as bright and dreamy and imaginary as the light through the window.

He did not understand anything.

It was a long moment before Ronan opened his eyes, and when he did, his expression was complicated. He stood up. He was still looking at Adam, and Adam was looking back, but neither said anything. Probably Ronan wanted something from him, but Adam didn't know what to say. He was a magician, Persephone had said, and his magic was making connections between disparate things. Only now he was too full of white, fuzzy light to make any sort of logical connections. He knew that of all the options in the world, Ronan Lynch was the most difficult version of any of them. He knew that Ronan was not a thing to be experimented with. He knew his mouth still felt warm. He knew he had started his entire time at Aglionby certain that all he wanted to do was get as far away from this state and everything in it as possible.

He was pretty sure he had just been Ronan's first kiss.

"I'm gonna go downstairs," Ronan said.

THIRTY-FOUR

There was a story Niall had once told Ronan that he couldn't quite remember but always liked. It was something about a boy – who sounded an awful lot like Ronan, as the boys often did in Niall's stories – and about an old man – who sounded an awful lot like Niall, as the men often did in Niall's stories. The old man might have been a wizard, actually, and the boy might have been his apprentice, though Ronan may have conflated it with a movie he'd seen once. In the story, there'd been a magical salmon who would confer happiness on the person who ate it. Or perhaps it was wisdom, not happiness. In any case, the old man had been too lazy or busy or on a business trip to spend the time trying to catch the salmon, and so he had set the boy on catching it for him. When the boy caught it, he was to cook it and bring it to the old man. The boy did as he was told, since he was just as clever as the old wizard, but as he'd cooked up the salmon, he'd burned himself. Before he thought about it, he put his burned finger in his mouth and thus got the salmon's magic for himself.

Ronan felt that he had caught happiness without meaning to. He could do anything.

"Ronan, bro, what are you doing up there?" Declan called. "Dinner's done!"

Ronan was on the roof of one of the small equipment

sheds. It was as high as he could get on short notice without wings. He didn't lower his arms. Fireflies and baubles and his dream flower were glowing and swirling all around him, and they kept sweeping by his vision as he gazed up at the pink-streaked sky.

After a moment, the roof groaned, and Declan groaned, and then his older brother pulled himself up beside Ronan. He stood looking not at the sky but at the things floating around his younger brother.

He sighed. "You sure have done a lot with the place." He reached out to catch one of the fireflies. "Jesus Mary, Ronan, there's not even any bug here."

Ronan lowered his arms and looked at the light Declan had snagged. He shrugged.

Declan released the light back into the air. It floated right in front of him, illuminating the sharp Lynch features, the knot of worry between his eyebrows, the press of disappointment to his mouth.

"It wants to go with you," Ronan said.

"I can't take a glowing ball with me."

"Here," Ronan said. "Wait."

He shifted his weight to remove something from his pocket and proffered it to Declan in the palm of his hand. It looked like a crude heavy-duty metal washer, about an inch and a half across, a steampunk paperweight from a strange machine.

"You're right, that's much less likely to stick out," Declan said wryly.

Ronan delivered a sharp tap to the object, and a small cloud of fiery orbs sprayed up with a sparkling hiss.

"Jesus, Ronan!" Declan jerked his chin away.

"Please. Did you think I'd blow your face off?"

He demonstrated it again, that quick tap, that burst of brilliant orbs. He tipped it into Declan's hand, and before Declan could say anything, jabbed it to activate it once more.

Orbs gasped up into the air. For a moment, he saw how his brother was caught inside them, watching them soar furiously around his face, each gold sun firing gold and white, and when he saw the spacious longing in Declan's face, he realized how much Declan had missed by growing up neither dreamer nor dreamt. This had never been his home. The Lynches had never tried to make it Declan's home.

"Declan?" Ronan asked.

Declan's face cleared. "This is the most useful thing you've ever dreamt. You should name it."

"I have. ORBMASTER. All caps."

"Technically you're the orbmaster, though, right? And that's just an orb."

"Anyone who holds it becomes an ORBMASTER. You're an ORBMASTER right now. There, keep it, put it in your pocket. D.C. ORBMASTER."

Declan reached out and scuffed Ronan's shaved head. "You're such a little asshole."

The last time they'd stood on this roof together, their parents had both been alive, and the cattle in these fields had been slowly grazing, and the world had been a smaller place. That time was gone, but for once, it was all right.

The brothers both looked back over the place that had made them, and then they climbed down from the roof together.

THIRTY—FIVE

Depending on where you began the story, it was about Neeve Mullen.

Neeve had the sort of career that most psychics longed to have. Part of this was because she had a very easily monetized variety of clairvoyance: She was good with specific numbers, specific letters, pulling telephone numbers out of people's wallets, birthdays out of people's heads, accurately pinpointing the times of future events. And part of this was because she was single-mindedly ambitious. Nothing was ever enough. Her career was a glass that never seemed to get full. She started with a phone line, and then published some books, landed herself a television gig that came on very early in the morning. She had respect within the community.

But.

Outside of the community, she was always going to be just a psychic. These days, this century, even the very best psychic had the nose-wrinkled stigma of a witch and none of the awe.

Neeve could put her hands on the future and the past and other worlds, and *nobody cared*. And so she'd done the spells and dreamt the dreams and asked her spirit guides for a path. *Tell me how to become powerful in a way people can't ignore.*

Henrietta, whispered one of her guides. Her television screen stuck on weather maps of Virginia. She dreamt of the ley line.

Her half sister called. "Come to Henrietta and help me!" Mirrors showed her a future with all eyes on her. The universe was pointing the way.

And here she was in a blackened forest with Piper Greenmantle and a demon.

Neeve should have guessed that her fixation with power would bring her to an opportunity to bargain with a demon, but she hadn't. She wasn't 100 per cent on ethics, but she was no idiot: She knew there was no happy ending to such a bargain. So this was a dead end. Probably literally.

Morale was low.

Piper, on the other hand, remained enthusiastic. She had replaced her tattered rags with a perfect sky-blue dress with pumps to match; she was a shock of colour in an increasingly colourless landscape. She told Neeve, "No one wants to buy a luxury item from a hobo."

"What are you selling?" Neeve asked.

"The demon," Piper replied.

Neeve wasn't sure if it was a failure of imagination or psychic perception on her part, but she hadn't anticipated *this* either. A rush of bad feeling accompanied Piper's answer. Neeve attempted to articulate it. "It seems to me that the demon is tied in with this geographical location and exists for a specific purpose, i.e., in this case unmaking all energy artefacts associated with this place, and so it seems unlikely to me that you would be able to move it without considerable har—"

"Is time weird here?" Piper interrupted. "I can't tell if we've been here for a couple of minutes or not."

Neeve was fairly certain they had been here far longer, but that the forest was manipulating their sense of time in order to stall Piper. She didn't want to say this out loud, though, because she was afraid that Piper would then use that information in some dreadful way. She wondered if she could kill Piper — *what.* No, she didn't. That was the demon, whispering into her thoughts as it always was.

She wondered what it was whispering to Piper.

Neeve looked at the demon. It looked back. It was beginning to look more at home here among the forest, which was probably a bad sign for the trees. In a low voice, she said, "I do not see how you expect to sell this demon. This is an exercise in arrogance. You cannot control it."

The lowered voice was pointless, as the demon was right there, but Neeve couldn't help herself.

"It is favouring me," Piper said. "That's what it said."

"Yes, but in the end, the demon has its own agenda. You are a tool."

The demon's thoughts whispered through the trees; the trees quivered. A bird cried out, but it was a sound in reverse. A few feet away from Neeve, a mouth had opened in the ground and it was slowly opening and closing in a hungry, neglected way. It was not possible, but the demon didn't care about *possible.* The forest now lived by nightmare rules.

Piper seemed unfussed. "And you are a downer. Demon, make me a house. House cave. Whatever you can do fast around here. As long as I can have a bath, I'm on board. Let it be thus, or whatever."

It was thus, or whatever, according to the word of Piper.

The demon's magic was unlike anything Neeve had ever used before. It was negative, a magical debit card; a psychic proof of energy was neither created nor destroyed. If they wanted to make a building, the demon would have to unmake part of the forest. And it was not an easy process to watch. If it had been a simple deletion, Neeve might not have had such a hard time with it. But it was a corruption. Vines grew and grew and grew, flowering and budding with ceaseless growth until they strangled themselves and rotted. Delicate thorn trees grew razors and spines that twisted and curled until they cut the branch growing them. Birds began to vomit their guts, which became snakes, which ate the birds and then devoured themselves in thrashing agony.

The worst were the big trees. They were holy – Neeve *knew* they were holy – and they resisted change for longer than anything else living in the forest. First they bled black sap. Then, slowly, their leaves shrivelled. The branches fell against each other, collapsing in black muck. Bark sloughed in peeling slabs like ruined skin. The trees began to moan. It was not a sound a human could produce. It was not a *voice*. It was a tonal version of the sound a branch makes groaning in the wind. It was a song of a tree falling in a storm.

It was against everything Neeve stood for.

She made herself watch it, though. She owed it to this old holy forest to watch it die. She wondered if she had been brought to this forest to save it.

Everything was a nightmare.

Piper's new home filled a massive deep cleft in the rocks, suspended and secured by means magical. The structure was a strange marriage of both Piper's desires and the stuccoed-wasp-nest sensibility of the demon. In the very centre of the main room was a deep, tear-shaped bathing pool.

As in any good compromise, both parties were vaguely displeased, but said nothing about it. Piper sneered prettily but merely said, "Great. Time to check in with my father."

"Instead of possession, you could scry in the bathtub to communicate with your father," Neeve suggested quickly. What she didn't say was that she felt scrying would use far less energy than possession. It might not save a tree, but it might preserve it for a little longer.

The demon twitched its antennae towards Neeve. It knew what she was doing. A second later, Piper looked over appraisingly; the demon had clearly tattled directly into her head. Neeve waited for a retort, but Piper merely ran her edges around the edge of the bathing pool in a thoughtful way. She said, "They'll be more moved to love if they see my face, anyway. Demon, connect my father on that thing. Let it be thus, or whatever."

It was thus, or whatever.

Laumonier was in a public men's room. He stood in front of the mirror, and also in front of the door to the men's room to make sure no one came in.

Piper squinted into the pool. "Are you at Legal Sea Foods? I can't believe it. I hate everything."

"Yes, we wanted oysters," Laumonier said, his voice emanating from the demon instead of the pool. His eyes were narrowed, trying to get a better view of wherever his daughter was. "Are you in a wasp's nest?"

"It's a shrine," Piper said.

"To what?"

"Me. Oh, I'm glad you asked it like that. You set up my punch line perfectly. Look, I'll make this quick, since I'm dying for a bath. What have you done on your end?"

"We have set up a look-see for your item," Laumonier said, stepping out of one of the stalls. "We have timed it to happen the day after a Congressional fund-raiser at a boys' school there, in order to allow out-of-town guests to blend in. What is it we're selling?"

Piper described the demon. The demon took flight and circled the pool, and from Laumonier's expression, Neeve could tell that the demon was *also* describing the demon to them. They were clearly impressed by the twisting of their thoughts.

"Good find," Laumonier said. "Let's be in touch."

They vanished from the scrying pool.

"Bath time," Piper said triumphantly. She did not tell Neeve to give her privacy, but Neeve did anyway. She needed to get out. She needed to be alone. She needed to find calm, so that she could see things truthfully.

She wasn't sure she would ever be calm again.

Outside, at the top of the waspy stairs, Neeve clutched at her hair. In retrospect, she knew that she had used the universe's power only for personal gain. That was how she had got here. She could not be angry at this lesson. She was going to have to try to save it. That was what it came down to. She could not live with herself otherwise, knowing she'd stood by while a holy place was destroyed.

She began to run.

Neeve did not ordinarily run, but once she had started, she couldn't believe that she had not done it immediately. She should have started running the moment she saw the demon, and not stopped until it was too far away to hear it in her head. Fear and revulsion suddenly caught up to her, and as she heaved through the forest, sobs gasped from her. *Demon, demon, demon.* She was so afraid. The dry leaves beneath her feet turned into tarot cards with her face on them. She slipped on their surfaces, but as they flipped from under her shoes, they were leaves once more.

Water, she thought to the forest. *I need a mirror if I'm to help you.*

Leaves stirred listlessly over her. A drop of rain spattered on her cheek, mingling with her tears.

Not rain. Water for a mirror, Neeve thought. She looked over her shoulder as she ran. Stumbled. She felt watched, but of course she would feel watched. This entire place was watching. Skidding down a slope, her hands catching only on dry leaves that shifted her further, she found herself looking at a hollowed-out stump.

Water, water. As she watched, water gurgled to fill it. Neeve placed her hand in it and prayed to a few select goddesses, and then she held her hands over it to scry. Her mind filled with images of Fox Way. The attic she had stayed in, the rituals she had done there. The mirrors that she had set to propel her through possibilities that had eventually taken her here.

She badly wanted to look over her shoulder.

She couldn't break focus.

Neeve felt the moment it took hold. She didn't recognize the face, but it didn't matter. If it was a woman in 300 Fox Way, the information would get to people who wanted to do something about it. Neeve whispered, "Can you hear me? There's a demon. It's unmaking the forest and everything attached to it. I'm going to try to —"

"You know," Piper said, "if you had a problem with me, I wish you would have come to me first."

Neeve's connection was broken. The water in the stump rippled, just water, and then the hard black shell of the demon rose up through the surface. With a little shake of its antennae, it crawled on to her arm. Heavy. Malevolent. Whispering terrible possibilities that were increasingly terrible probabilities. Piper came into focus on the other side of the stump, walking through the leaves to them. Her hair was still damp from the bath.

Neeve did not bother to beg.

"God, Neeve. You New Age types are the worst." Piper flipped her hand towards the demon. "Unmake her."

THIRTY-SIX

There was something *living* about the night.

Declan and Matthew had gone. Gansey, Blue, Ronan and Adam remained at the Barns, sitting in a circle in the hickory-scented living room. The only lights were the things Ronan had dreamt. They hovered overhead and danced in the fireplace. It felt like magic hung between all of them, even in the places the light didn't touch. Gansey was aware that they all were happier than they had been in a long time, which seemed strange in light of the frightening events of the night before and the ominous news they had just received from Declan.

"This is a night for truth," Gansey said, and any other time, they would have laughed at him for it, perhaps. But not tonight. Tonight, they all could tell they were part of a slow, wheeling machine, and the enormity of it staggered them. "Let's piece this thing together."

Slowly they described what had happened to them the day before, pausing to allow Gansey to write it in his journal. As he jotted down the facts – the ley line seizing at 6:21, Noah's attack, the black-oozing tree, Adam's eye moving of its own accord – he began to feel the shape of the roles they played. He could nearly see the end if he looked hard enough.

They discussed whether they felt they had a responsibility to protect Cabeswater and the ley line – they all did. Whether they thought Artemus knew more than he was saying – they all did. Whether they thought he would ever talk freely about it – they were all unconvinced.

Partway through this, Ronan got up to pace. Adam went to the kitchen and returned with a coffee for himself. Blue made herself a nest of sofa cushions beside Gansey and put her head in his lap.

This was not allowed.

But it was. The truth was sliding into the light.

They also talked about the town. Whether or not it was wiser to hide from or to fight with outsiders coming to Henrietta to dig for supernatural relics. As they threw around ideas for dreamt defences and dangerous allies, weaponized monsters and acid moats, Gansey gently touched the hair above Blue's ear, careful not to brush the skin near her eyebrow because of her wound, careful not to meet Ronan's or Adam's eyes because of self-consciousness.

It was allowed. He was allowed to want this.

They talked about Henry. Gansey was mindful that he was telling Henry's closely guarded secrets, but he had also decided by the end of the school day that to tell Gansey something was to tell Adam and Ronan and Blue. They were a package deal; Gansey could not be expected to be won without winning them as well. Adam and Ronan made puerile jokes at Henry's expense (*"He's half Chinese" "Which half?"*) and sniggered clannishly; Blue called them on it (*"Jealous, much?"*); Gansey told them to put aside their preconceptions and think about him.

No one had yet said the word *demon*.

It hung there, unspoken, defined by the shape of the conversation around it. The thing Adam and Ronan had driven in pursuit of, the thing that had inhabited Noah, the thing that was possibly attacking Cabeswater. It was quite possible that they might have gone the entire evening not addressing it if Maura had not called from 300 Fox Way. Gwenllian had seen something in the attic mirrors, she said. It had taken this long to work out what she had really seen, but it seemed like it had been Neeve with a warning.

Demon.

Unmaker.

Unmaking the forest and everything attached to it.

This revelation made Ronan stop in his pacing and Adam go completely silent. Neither Blue nor Gansey interrupted this curious silence, and then, at the end of it, Adam said, "Ronan, I think you need to tell *them*, too."

Ronan's expression, if anything, was betrayed. This was wearying; Gansey could see precisely the argument that it was heaving towards. Adam would shoot something cool and truthful over the bow, Ronan would fire back a profanity cannon, Adam would drip gasoline in the path of the projectile, and then everything would be on fire for hours.

But Adam merely said, in an earnest tone, "It's not gonna change anything, Ronan. We're sitting here with dream lights around us, and I can see a hooved girl you dreamt up eating Styrofoam in the hall. We ride around in a car you pulled out of your dreams. It's surprising, but it's not going to change the way they see you."

And Ronan retorted, "*You* didn't handle the revelation well."

In his hurt tone, Gansey thought that he suddenly understood something about Ronan.

"I had other things going on," Adam replied. "That made it a little hard to take on."

Gansey *definitely* felt like he understood something about Ronan.

Blue and Gansey exchanged looks. Blue had an eyebrow raised into her bangs; her other eye was still squinted shut. It made her appear even more curious than she would have normally looked.

Ronan plucked at his leather wristbands. "Whatever. I dreamt Cabeswater."

It was once more absolutely quiet in the room.

On a certain level, Gansey realized why Ronan had been hesitant to tell them: The ability to pull a magical forest out of your head added an otherworldly cast to your persona. But on every other level, Gansey was slightly confused. He felt as if he was being told a secret that he'd already been told before. He couldn't tell if this was because Cabeswater itself had possibly already whispered this truth to them on one of their walks there, or if it was merely that the weight of evidence was already so conclusive that his subconscious had accepted ownership of the secret before the parcel had been officially delivered.

"To think you could have been dreaming the cure for cancer," Blue said.

"Look, Sargent," Ronan retorted. "I was gonna dream you some eye cream last night since clearly modern medicine's doing jack shit for you, but I nearly had my ass handed to me by a death snake from the fourth circle of dream hell, so you're welcome."

Blue looked appropriately touched. "Ah, thanks, man."

"No problem, bro."

Gansey tapped his pen on his journal. "While we're being forthright, have you dreamt any other geographical locations that you should tell us about? Mountains? Water features?"

"No," Ronan said. "But I did dream Matthew."

"For God's sake," Gansey said. He lived in a continuous state of impossibility, occasionally agitating to a higher state of even more impossibility. All of this was hard to believe, but things had been hard to believe for months. He had already drawn the conclusion that Ronan was unlike anyone else; this was only another piece of supporting evidence. "Does that mean you know what the visions in that tree mean?"

He meant the hollowed-out tree that delivered visions to whomever was standing in it; they had discovered it the first time they explored Cabeswater. Gansey had seen two visions in it: one where he seemed quite on the verge of kissing Blue Sargent, and one where he seemed quite on the verge of finding Owen Glendower. He had a keen interest in both of these things. Both had felt very real.

"Nightmares," Ronan replied dismissively.

Both Blue and Adam blinked. Blue echoed, "Nightmares? Is that all? Not visions of the future?"

Ronan said, "When I dreamt that tree, that's what it did. Worst-case scenarios. Whatever mindfuckery it thought would be most likely to mess you up the next day."

Gansey was not certain that he would have classified either of his visions as *worst-case scenarios*, but it was true that they had both provided a certain measure of mindfuckery. Blue's bemused expression suggested she agreed. Adam, on the other hand, let out a breath so enormous that it seemed he'd been holding it for months. This was not surprising. Adam's real life had already been a nightmare when he'd stepped into that tree. Mindfuckery above and beyond the truth must have been truly terrible.

"Is it possible," Gansey started, and then stopped, thinking. "Is it possible that you could dream some protection for Cabeswater?"

Ronan shrugged. "Black stuff in Cabeswater means black stuff in my dreams. I told you, I couldn't even get some eyeball ChapStick out for Sargent last night, and that's a nothing-thing. A child could manifest that. I got nothing."

"I can try to help you," Adam said. "I could scry while you dream. I might be able to clear the energy enough for you to get something useful."

"That feels so insubstantial," Gansey said. He really meant *the monster feels so enormous.*

Blue sat up and groaned, holding her eye. "I'm fine with *insubstantial*. I don't think we should do anything *substantial* until we talk to Mom. I want to hear more about what Gwenllian saw. Ugh. I think you have to take me home, Gansey. My eye is driving me crazy and making me feel like I'm more tired than I am. Sorry, guys."

But there were no more ideas to be had without more information, so the rest of them used this as excuse to get up and stretch, too. Blue headed towards the kitchen and Ronan jogged on ahead of her, jostling her intentionally with his hip. "You *asshole*," she said, and he laughed merrily.

Gansey was deeply moved by the sound of that laugh, here of all places, here in the Barns, here in a room that was only fifty feet from where Ronan had found his father dead and his life in pieces. It was such a throwaway sound now, that laugh. An easy one that said it could be spent so easily because there were more where that one came from. The wound was healing against all odds; the victim would make it after all.

He and Adam remained in the living room, standing, thinking. A window looked out at the dark parking area where the BMW and Adam's shitbox and the glorious Camaro sat. The Pig looked like a rocket ship in the porch light; Gansey's heart still felt full with promise and magic, both dark and light.

"You know about Blue's curse, right?" Adam asked in a low voice.

If you kiss your true love, he'll die.

Yes, he knew. He also knew why Adam was asking, and he could feel the temptation to bluster and joke his way out of it, because it was strangely embarrassing to be talking about him and Blue. Blue and him. He had been transformed into a middle schooler again. But this was a night for truth, and Adam's voice was serious, so he said, "I do."

"Do you think it applies to you?" Adam asked.

Carefully, Gansey replied, "I think so."

Adam glanced to see that Ronan and Blue were still safely in the kitchen; they were. "What about you?"

"What about me?"

"The curse says you're *her* true love. What about you? Do *you* love *her*?" Adam pronounced *love* very carefully, as if it were an unfamiliar element on the periodic table. Gansey *was* prepared to deflect this answer, but a glance at Adam told him both that his friend was quite invested in the answer and that the question was probably really about something else entirely.

"Yes," Gansey answered plainly.

Now Adam turned to him, intense. "What does that *mean*? How did you know it was different than just being her friend?"

Now it was *really* obvious that Adam was thinking about something else entirely, and so Gansey wasn't sure how to answer. It reminded him in a flash of being in the hole with Henry earlier that day, when Henry hadn't needed anything from him but for Gansey to listen. This was not that. Adam needed something. So he tried to find a way to articulate it. "I suppose . . . she makes me quiet. Like Henrietta." He had told Adam this once before; about how the moment he had found the town, something inside him had gone still — something he hadn't even realized was always agitating inside him. Adam hadn't understood, but then again, Henrietta had always meant something different to him.

"And that's it? It's that simple?"

"I don't *know*, Adam! You're asking me to define an abstract concept that no one has managed to explain since time began. You sort of sprang it on me," Gansey said. "Why do we breathe air? Because we love air? Because we don't want to suffocate. Why do we eat? Because we don't want to starve. How do I know I love her? Because I can sleep after I talk to her. Why?"

"Nothing," said Adam, a lie so outrageous that they both

looked out into the yard again in silence. He tapped the fingers of one hand on the palm of his other.

Ordinarily, Gansey would have given him room to roam; it was always dubiously productive to bully either Adam or Ronan into talking before they were ready. But in this case, it was late, and Gansey didn't have months to wait for Adam to come round to the topic of discussion. He said, "I thought this was a night for truth."

"Ronan kissed me," Adam said immediately. The words had clearly been queued up. He gazed studiously into the front yard. When Gansey didn't immediately say anything, Adam added, "I also kissed him."

"Jesus," Gansey said. "Christ."

"Are you surprised?"

He was chiefly surprised Adam had *told* him. It had taken *Gansey* several furtive months of dating Blue before he'd been able to bring himself to tell the others, and then, only under extreme circumstances. "No. Yes. I don't know. I've been given about one thousand surprises today and so I can't tell any more. Were *you* surprised?"

"No. Yes. I don't know."

Now that Gansey had had more than a second to think about it, he considered all the ways such a thing might have played out. He imagined Adam, ever the scientist. Ronan, ferocious and loyal and fragile. "Don't break him, Adam."

Adam continued peering out the window. The only tell to the furious working of his mind was the slow twisting together of his fingers. "I'm not an idiot, Gansey."

"I'm serious." Now Gansey's imagination had run ahead to imagine a future where Ronan might have to exist without him, without Declan, without Matthew, and with a freshly broken heart. "He's not as tough as he seems."

"I'm *not an idiot*, Gansey."

Gansey didn't think Adam was an idiot. But he had had his own feelings hurt over and over by Adam, even when Adam had meant no harm. Some of the worst fractures had appeared *because* Adam hadn't realized that he was causing them.

"I think you're the opposite of an idiot," Gansey said. "I don't mean to imply otherwise. I just meant . . ."

Everything Ronan had ever said about Adam restructured itself in Gansey's mind. What a strange constellation they all were.

"I'm not going to mess with his head. Why do you think I'm talking to you? I don't even know how I . . ." Adam trailed off. It was a night for truth, but they both had run out of things they were sure about.

They looked out the window again. Gansey took a mint leaf out of his pocket and put it in his mouth. The feeling of magic that he had felt at the beginning of the night was even more pronounced. Everything was possible, good and bad.

"I think," Gansey said slowly, "that it's about being honest with yourself. That's all you can do."

Adam released his hands from each other. "I think that's what I needed to hear."

"I do my best."

"I know."

In the quiet, they heard Blue and Ronan talking to the

Orphan Girl in the kitchen. There was something quite comforting about the fond and familiar murmur of their voices, and
Gansey felt that uncanny tugging of time again. That he had
lived this moment before, or would live it in the future. Of wanting and having, both the same. He was startled to realize that he
longed to be done with the quest for Glendower. He wanted the
rest of his life. Until this night, he hadn't really thought that he
believed that there *was* anything more to his life.

He said, "I think it's time to find Glendower."

Adam said, "I think you're right."

THIRTY-SEVEN

Depending on where you began the story, it was about Henry Cheng.

Henry had never been good with words. Case in point: The first month he'd been at Aglionby, he had tried to explain this to Jonah Milo, the English teacher, and had been told that he was being hard on himself. *You've got a great vocabulary,* Milo had said. Henry was aware he had a great vocabulary. It was not the same thing as having the words you needed to express yourself. *You're very well-spoken for a kid your age,* Milo had added. *Hell, ha, even for a guy my age.* But sounding like you were saying what you felt was not the same as actually pulling it off. *A lot of ESL folks feel that way,* Milo had finished. *My mom said she was never herself in English.*

But it wasn't that Henry was less of himself in English. He was less of himself *out loud.* His native language was *thought.*

So he had no real way to explain how he felt about trying to befriend Richard Gansey and the members of Gansey's royal family. He had no words to articulate his reasons for offering up his most closely guarded secret in the basement of Borden House. There was no description for how difficult it was to wait to see if his peace branch was accepted.

Which meant he just had to kill time.

He kept himself busy.

He delighted Murs in history with his focused study on the spread of personal electronics through the first world; he aggravated Adler in administration with his focused study on the disparity between Aglionby's publicity budget versus their scholarship budget. He screamed himself hoarse at the sidelines of Koh's soccer match (they lost). He spray-painted the words *PEACE, BITCHES* on the Dumpster behind a gelato parlour.

There was so much day left. Was he expecting Gansey to call? He didn't have words for what he was expecting. A weather event. No. Climate change. A permanent difference in the way that crops were grown in the northwest.

The sun went down. The Vancouver crowd returned to Litchfield to roost and receive marching orders from Henry. He felt 20 per cent guilty for longing to become friends with Gansey and Sargent and Lynch and Parrish. The Vancouver crowd was great. They just weren't enough, but words failed him to say why. Because they were always looking up to him? Because they didn't know his secrets? Because he no longer wanted followers, he wanted friends? No. It was something more.

"Take out the trash," Mrs Woo told Henry.

"I'm very busy, aunt," Henry replied, although he was clearly watching video game walk-throughs in his underwear.

"Busy carrying these," she said, and dropped two bags next to him.

So now he found himself stepping out the back door of Litchfield House into the gravel lot in just a Madonna T-shirt and his favourite black trainers. The sky overhead was purple-gray. Somewhere close by, a mourning dove swooned dreamily. The feelings inside Henry that had no words rushed up anyway.

His mother was the only one who knew what Henry meant when he said that he wasn't good with words. She was always trying to explain things to his father, especially when she had decided to become Seondeok instead of his wife. *It is that*, she for ever said, *but also something more.* The phrase had come to live in Henry's head. *Something more* explained perfectly why he could never say what he meant — *something more*, by its definition, would always be different than what you already had in your hand.

He let the feelings out with a breath through his teeth and then minced across the gravel to the trash bins.

When he turned around, there was a man standing in the door he had just come from.

Henry stopped walking. He did not know the name of the man — wiry, white, self-possessed — but he felt he knew the sort of man he was. Earlier he'd told Richard Gansey about his mother's career, and now, hours later, he faced someone who was undoubtedly here about his mother's career.

The man said, "Do you think we could have a chat?"

"No," Henry replied. "I do not think we can." He reached for his phone in his back pocket before remembering, partway through, that he was not wearing trousers. He glanced up at the windows of the house. He was looking not for help — no one inside knew enough about Henry's mother to even suspect the kind of peril he was in, even if they were looking right at it — but for any cracked windows that might allow RoboBee to come to him.

The man made a great show of displaying his palms so Henry could see he didn't have any weapons. As if that made a difference. "I assure you we have the same goals."

"My goal was to finish watching the walkthrough for *EndWarden II*. I can't believe I've finally found someone who shares my vision."

The man regarded him. He seemed to be considering options. "Word has come to me that something is moving here in Henrietta. I do not like people moving things around in Henrietta. I assumed you, too, preferred to not have people milling about in your life."

"And yet," Henry said lightly, "here we are."

"Are you going to do this the easy way? Save me the trouble."

Henry shook his head.

The man sighed. Before Henry had time to react, he closed the distance between the two of them, embraced Henry in a less than friendly way, and perfunctorily performed a manoeuvre that made Henry emit a soft squeak and stagger back holding his shoulder. Some people might have screamed, but Henry was as committed as the man to keeping secrets.

"Do not waste my time," the man said, "when I began this in a very civil way."

RoboBee, Henry thought. *Come find me.*

There had to be a window cracked somewhere in the house; Mrs Woo always turned the heat on too high.

"If you are trying to get a secret out of me," Henry replied, touching his shoulder gingerly, "you're wasting your own time."

"For God's sake," the man said. He leaned to pull his pistol out of his ankle holster. "Any other time I'd find this really honourable. But now just get in my car before I shoot you."

The gun won, as it usually does. Henry cast a last glance at the house before making his way to the car across the road. He recognized the white car, though he didn't understand what that meant. He began to get into the back.

"The passenger seat is fine," the man said. "I told you, this is a chat."

Henry did as he was told, glancing back at the house a third time as the man settled behind the wheel and pulled away from the kerb. The man turned down the radio (they sang *Yes, I'm a lover not a fighter*) and said, "I just want to know who to expect and if they're going to be trouble. I have no interest in ever interacting with you again."

In the passenger seat, Henry looked out the window before buckling the seat belt. He pulled up his knees and put his arms around his bare legs. He was starting to shiver a little. The man turned up the heater.

"Where are you taking me?" Henry asked.

"We're circling the block like reasonable people do when they are trying to have a conversation."

Henry thought about a hole in the ground.

"I have never had a reasonable conversation with someone with a pistol." He looked out the window again, craning his neck to look behind him. It was dark apart from the streetlights. He would be too far away from the RoboBee to communicate with it soon, but he sent out a last plea: *Tell someone who can make this stop.*

It wasn't a request that made sense in words, but it made sense in Henry's thoughts, and that was all that mattered to the bee.

"Look," said the man. "I regret your shoulder. That was habit."

A metallic *clink* sounded at the top of the windshield. As the man craned his neck to see what had hit the car, Henry sat up attentively. Leaning forward, he saw three slender black lines at the edge of the window.

A phone rang.

The man made a noise before flipping the phone over in the centre console. Whoever it was earned his attention, because he picked it up and wedged it on his shoulder in order to allow himself to still use the stick shift. To the phone, he said, "That's a very strange question to ask."

Henry took the opportunity to roll down his window an inch. RoboBee immediately whirred off the windshield and through the crack.

"Hey —" the man said.

The bee flew into Henry's palm. He cupped it gladly to his chest. The weight of it felt like security.

The man frowned at him, and then said to the phone, "I haven't kidnapped anyone in years, but I do have a student in my car right now." A pause. "Both of those statements are accurate. I was trying to get some clarification on some rumours. Would you like to talk to him?"

Henry's eyebrows shot up.

The man handed Henry his phone.

"Hello?" Henry said.

"Well," Gansey said on the other side of the phone, "I hear you've met Mr Gray."

THIRTY-EIGHT

enry was wearing trousers by the time Blue and Gansey met up with him and the Gray Man in the Fresh Eagle. The grocery store was almost completely empty and had the glittering timelessness that such places began to take on after a certain hour of night. Overhead, a song played about getting out of someone's dreams and into their car. There was only one cashier, and she didn't look up as they walked through the automatic doors. They found Henry standing in the cereal aisle looking at his phone, while Mr Gray stood at the end of the aisle convincingly reading the back of a tin of steel cut oats. Neither drew attention. Mr Gray blended in because his profession had taught him to blend in. Henry did *not* blend in — he reeked of money from his snazzy jacket and Madonna shirt down to his black trainers — but he nonetheless failed to stand out in any remarkable way: Henrietta was no stranger to his sort of youthful Aglionby money.

Henry had been holding a box of cereal of the sort that was bad for you but good for marshmallows, but he put it back on the shelf when he spotted them. He seemed far more jittery than he had been at the toga party. Probably, Blue mused, a side effect of being held at gunpoint earlier.

"The question I'm asking myself," Gansey said, "is why I'm in the Fresh-Fresh-Eagle at eleven P.M."

"The question I was asking *myself*," Henry replied, "was why I was in a thug's car at I-don't-even-know P.M. Sargent, tell me you are not part of this sordid ring of thieves."

Blue, hands in the pockets of her hoodie, shrugged apologetically and gestured with her chin to the Gray Man. "He's sort of dating my mom."

"What a tangled web we weave," Gansey said in an electric, jagged sort of way. He was keyed up after the night at the Barns, and Henry's presence only encouraged it. "This wasn't the next step I wanted to take in our friendship, though. Mr Gray?"

He had to repeat Mr Gray's name, because it turned out that the Gray Man had not been pretending to look at the oatmeal tin; he had actually been reading the back of it.

He joined them. He and Blue exchanged a side hug and then he turned her by her shoulders to examine the stitches above her eyebrow. "Those are neatly done."

"Are they?"

"You probably won't have a scar."

"Damn," Blue said.

Gansey asked him, "Was the Fresh Eagle your idea or Henry's?"

Mr Gray replied, "I thought it might be comforting. It's well-lit, on camera, but not audio-recorded. Safe and secure."

Blue had not thought about the Fresh Eagle that way before.

Mr Gray added cordially, "I am sorry about the fright."

Henry had been watching this entire exchange closely. "You were doing your job. I was doing my job."

What a truth this was. While Blue had grown up learning the principles of internal energy and getting told bedtime stories,

Henry Cheng had grown up contemplating how far he would go to protect his mother's secrets under duress. The idea that they had been any part of this made her feel so uncomfortable that she said, "Let's stop doing jobs now and start doing solutions. Can we talk about who's coming here and why? Wasn't that the whole point of this exchange? Someone's coming somewhere to get something, and everybody's freaked out?"

Henry said, "You're a lady of action. I see why R. Gansey added you to his cabinet. Walk with me, President."

They walked with him. They walked through the cereal aisle, the baking aisle and the canned goods aisle. As they did, Henry described what he had been told about the upcoming sale with all the enthusiasm of a good student delivering a presentation on a natural disaster. The meeting of artefact-selling denizens was to happen the day after the Aglionby fund-raiser, the better to disguise the influx of strange cars and people into Henrietta. An unknown number of parties would descend for a viewing of the object for sale – a magical entity – so that these potential buyers could confirm for themselves the otherworldliness of the product. Then an auction would follow – payment and the exchange of the item, as always, to take place in a separate location out of the view of prying eyes; no one wanted to have their proverbial wallet lifted by a fellow buyer. Further pieces might be available for sale; inquire within.

"A magical entity?" Blue and Gansey echoed at the same time that the Gray Man said, "Further pieces?"

"Magical entity. That was all the description was. It is meant to be a big secret. Worth the trip! They say." Henry traced a smiley face on the exterior of a box of microwave macaroni and cheese. The logo was a tiny bear with a lot of teeth; it was hard to tell if it was smiling or grimacing. "I have been told to keep myself busy and to not accept candy from any strange men."

"Magical entity. Could it be Ronan?" Gansey asked anxiously.

"We just saw Ronan; they wouldn't try to sell him without having him in hand, right? Could it be a demon?" Blue said.

Gansey frowned. "Surely no one would try to sell a demon."

"Laumonier might," Mr Gray said. He did not sound fond. "I don't like the sound of 'further pieces.' Not when it is Laumonier."

"What's it sound like?" Gansey asked.

"Pillaging," Henry answered for him. "What do you mean Ronan's a magical entity? Is *he* a demon? Because this all makes sense if so."

Neither Blue nor Gansey hurried to answer this question; the truth of Ronan was such an enormous and dangerous secret that neither of them was willing to play with it, even with someone they both liked as well as Henry.

"Not exactly," Gansey said. "Mr Gray, what are you thinking about the idea of all of these people descending? Declan seemed worried."

"These people are not the most innocent of folks," the Gray Man said. "They come from all walks of life, and the only thing that they have in common is a certain opportunism and flexibility of morality. Unpredictable enough on their own, but put them together in a place with something they really want, and it's hard to say what could happen. There's a reason they were told not to bring their money with them. And if Greenmantle rears his head again to squabble with Laumonier? There's bad blood between all of them and the Lynches."

"Colin Greenmantle is dead," Henry said in a very precise way. "He will not be rearing anywhere soon, and if he does, we'll have bigger problems to consider."

"He's dead?" the Gray Man said sharply. "Who sa— wait."

The Gray Man's eyes were abruptly cast upward. It took Blue a moment to realize that he was looking at a convex mirror meant to prevent shoplifting. Whatever he saw in the mirror instantly transformed him into something abrupt and powerful.

"Blue," he said in a low voice, "do you have your knife?"

Her pulse slowly revved up to speed; she felt it in her stitches. "Yes."

"Go around with the boys to the next aisle over. Not that way. The other. Quietly. I don't remember if the entrance to the back room is on that wall, but if it is, go out that way. Don't go out any door that might set off an alarm."

Whatever he had seen in the mirror was gone now, but they didn't hesitate. Blue led the way quickly down the end of the canned goods aisle, glanced to either side, and rounded the other side. Laundry detergent. Boxes and boxes in an aggressive assembly of colours. On the other side of them was a large case of butter and eggs. No storeroom exit. The front of the store seemed far away.

On the other side of the aisle, they heard the Gray Man's voice, low and level and dangerous. It was a chillier tone than he had just used with them. Another voice replied, and Henry went very still beside them. His fingers touched the edge of one of the shelves — *$3.99 price slash!* — and he turned his head, listening.

"That's —" he whispered. "That's Laumonier."

Laumonier. It was a name that carried more emotion than fact. Blue had heard it whispered in conversations about Greenmantle. *Laumonier.* Danger.

They heard Laumonier say in his accented voice, "It is so surprising to see you here in Henrietta. Where is your master, hound?"

"I think we both know the answer to that," Mr Gray said, voice so even that it was impossible to know that he had himself just discovered the news about Colin Greenmantle. "And in any case, I have been working alone since this summer. I thought that was common knowledge. It is more interesting to me to see *you* here in Henrietta."

"Well, the town belongs to no one now," Laumonier said, "so it is, as they say, a free country."

"Not so free," the Gray Man said. "I understand that you have something to sell here. I'd like you in and then out again: Henrietta is now my home, and I'm not a fan of houseguests."

There was some mirth over this. "Is this the part where I say 'or what'? Because it seems like it would be."

Their voices dropped for a time — it seemed like it might be getting unpleasant — and Gansey began to text furiously. He turned the phone to Blue and Henry.

He is stalling for us to get out. Henry can robobee find a door?

Henry took Gansey's phone and added to the text:

I will have to keep robobee out of sight tho bc they have always wanted it that is part of why they took me

Blue snatched the phone from him and texted, more slowly, because she had rather less practice than they did:

Who is Mr Gray trying to keep hidden from them? All of us or just you Henry

Henry touched his chest lightly.

Blue typed:

Leave when you can. I'll catch up

She handed Gansey's phone back to him, swiftly removed several price tags from the shelves until she had a bouquet of them, and stepped around the end of the aisle. She was startled to discover that it was not one man with Mr Gray, but two. It took her too long to realize that the tilting feeling she got while looking at the strangers was because they looked eerily similar to each other. Brothers. Twins, maybe. Both had a look that she had grown to despise during her time working at Nino's. Customers who wouldn't take no for an answer, who weren't easily negotiated with, who always ended up getting part of their meal taken off the ticket. In addition, they had a slow, bullish way about them that somehow smacked of a lifetime of blunt trauma.

They were a little terrifying.

Mr Gray blinked at Blue in a vague way, no recognition in his face.

The other two men eyed Blue's hoodie first – not very professional looking – and then her handful of price tags. She ran her thumb over the ends of them in a bored, casual way and said,

"Sir? Guys? I'm sorry for the inconvenience, but I'm going to need you to move your vehicles."

"Excuse me, why?" asked the first. Now that she could hear him better, his accent was more pronounced. French? Maybe.

"We are shopping," said the other, with vague amusement.

Blue leaned on her Henrietta accent; she'd learned early on that it rendered her innocuous and invisible to outsiders. "I know. I'm sorry. We have a street sweeper coming in to do the lot, and he wants the whole thing cleared out. He'll be right pissed if there's still cars here when he starts."

Mr Gray made a great show of rummaging for his keys in such a way that he twitched up his pant leg to reveal a gun. Laumonier muttered and exchanged looks with each other.

"Sorry again," Blue said. "You can just ease over to the laundromat lot if you're not done here."

"Street sweeper," said Laumonier, as if only just hearing the phrase.

"Corporate makes us do it to keep the franchise," Blue replied. "I don't make the rules."

"Let's keep things civil," Mr Gray said, with a thin smile at the other two. He did not look at Blue. She continued looking bored and beleaguered, running her thumbs over the price tags every time she felt her heart thump. "I'll catch you two later."

The three of them moved towards the front door with the uneasy, widening formation of opposing magnets, and by the time they had gone, Blue had skidded hastily down the aisle, through the back-room doors, past the grubby bathrooms, into a warehouse room stacked with boxes and bins, and outside to where

Gansey and Henry had just reached the trash bins full of cardboard behind the store.

Her shadow reached them first, cast by the lights fixed to the back of the supermarket, and they both flinched at the movement before realizing who it belonged to.

"You magical thing," Gansey said, and hugged her head, freeing much of her hair from its clips. They were both shivering in the cold. Everything felt false and stark under this black sky, with Laumonier's two faces still in her memory. She heard car doors shutting, maybe from the front parking lot, every sound both far and close in the night.

"That was brilliant." Henry held his hand above his head, palm to the sky. An insect swirled from it, momentarily lit dark by the streetlights, and then lost to the blackness. He watched it go and then fished out his phone.

Blue demanded, "What did they want? Why did Mr Gray think they would be interested in you?"

Henry watched a text feed scroll across the face of his phone. "RoboBee – did Gansey Boy tell you what it was? Good – RoboBee was one of the first things Laumonier and Greenmantle fought about. Lynch was talking about selling it to one of them but sold it to my mother instead because she wanted it for me; she never forgot that; that is why they hate her and she hates them."

"But Laumonier isn't here for you, right?" Gansey asked. He, too, was reading Henry's phone screen. It seemed to be reporting back where Laumonier was.

"No, no," said Henry. "I would bet they recognized your man Gray's car from the old days and came to see if there was anything to be had from Kavinsky while they were down here. I do not pretend to know the ways of the French. I do not know if they would still recognize me from that hole in the ground; I'm older now. But still. Your assassin man seemed to think they might. He did me a favour. I will not forget that."

He turned the phone around so that Blue could watch the live reporting of Laumonier's actions. The text came in fits and starts, and was strangely conversational, describing Laumonier's slow progress out of the parking lot in the same way that Henry had described the upcoming artefact sale. Henry's thoughts, on screen. It was a weird and specific magic.

As they watched it together, Gansey opened up his overcoat and tucked Blue inside it with him. This, too, was a weird and specific magic, the ease of it, the warmth of him around her, his heartbeat thumping against her back. He cupped a hand over her injured eye as if to protect it from something, but it was only an excuse for his fingertips to touch her.

Henry was unaffected by this public display of closeness. He pressed fingers against the screen of his phone; it blinked a few times and reported something to him in Hangul.

"Do you want . . ." Blue started, and hesitated. "Should you stay with one of us tonight?"

Surprise lit Henry's smile, but he shook his head. "No, I can't. I must go back to Litchfield, a captain to his ship. I wouldn't forgive myself if they came looking for me and found Cheng Two and the others instead. I will set RoboBee watch until we can —" He circled one finger in a gesture that indicated something like a rendezvous.

"Tomorrow?" Gansey asked. "I'm supposed to meet my sister for lunch. Both of you please come."

Neither Henry nor Blue had to say anything out loud; Gansey surely had to know that merely by asking, he'd assured both would come.

"I take it we're friends now," Henry said.

"We must be," Gansey replied. "Jane says it should be so."

"It should be so," Blue agreed.

Now something else lit Henry's smile. It was genuine and pleased but also *something more*, and there were not quite words for it. He pocketed his phone. "Good, good. The coast is clear; I leave you. Until tomorrow."

THIRTY-NINE

That night, Ronan didn't dream.

After Gansey and Blue had left the Barns, he leaned against one of the front porch pillars and looked out at his fireflies winking in the chilly darkness. He was so raw and electric that it was hard to believe that he was awake. Normally it took sleep to strip him to this naked energy. But this was not a dream. This was his life, his home, his night.

After a few moments, he heard the door ease open behind him and Adam joined him. Silently they looked over the dancing lights in the fields. It was not difficult to see that Adam was working intensely with his own thoughts. Words kept rising up inside Ronan and bursting before they ever escaped. He felt he'd already asked the question; he couldn't also give the answer.

Three deer appeared at the tree line, just at the edge of the porch light's reach. One of them was the beautiful pale buck, his antlers like branches or roots. He watched them, and they watched him, and then Ronan could not stand it. "Adam?"

When Adam kissed him, it was every mile per hour Ronan had ever gone over the speed limit. It was every window-down, goose-bumps-on-skin, teeth-chattering-cold night drive. It was Adam's ribs under Ronan's hands and Adam's mouth on his mouth, again and again and again. It was stubble on lips and Ronan having to stop, to get his breath, to restart his heart. They were both hungry animals, but Adam had been starving for longer.

Inside, they pretended they would dream, but they did not. They sprawled on the living room sofa and Adam studied the tattoo that covered Ronan's back: all the sharp edges that hooked wondrously and fearfully into each other.

"*Unguibus et rostro*," Adam said.

Ronan put Adam's fingers to his mouth.

He was never sleeping again.

FORTY

That night, the demon didn't sleep.

While Piper Greenmantle slept fitfully, dreaming of the upcoming sale and her rise to fame in the magical artefact community, the demon unmade.

It unmade the physical trappings of Cabeswater – the trees, the creatures, the ferns, the rivers, the stones – but it also unmade the dreamy ideas of the forest. The memories caught in groves, the songs invented only in night-time, the creeping euphoria that ebbed and flowed around one of the waterfalls. Everything that had been dreamt into this place it undreamt.

The dreamer it would unmake last.

He would fight.

They always fought.

As the demon unwound and undid, it kept encountering threads of its own story teased through the underbrush. Its origin story. This fertile place, rich with the energy of the ley line, was not just good for growing trees and kings. It was also good for growing demons, if there was enough bad blood spilled on it.

There was more than enough bad blood pooled in this forest to make a demon.

Little stopped its work. It was the forest's natural enemy, and the one thing that would stop the demon in its tracks had not yet occurred to anyone. Only the oldest of the trees put up a fight, because they were the only things that remembered how. Slowly and methodically, the demon unpicked them from the inside. Black beaded from their decaying branches; they crashed down as their roots rotted to nothing.

One tree resisted for longer than the others. She was the oldest, and had seen a demon before, and knew that sometimes it wasn't about saving yourself, it was about holding out for long enough until someone else could save you. So she held out, and stretched for the stars even as her roots were being dug away, and she held out, and she sang to other trees even as her trunk was rotting out, and she held out, and she dreamt of the sky even as she was unmade.

The other trees wailed; if she had been unmade, who could stand?

The demon did not sleep.

FORTY-ONE

Depending on where you began the story, it was about Gwenllian.

She awoke with a scream that morning at dawn.

"Get up!" she howled to herself as she leapt from her bed. Her hair hit the slanted attic ceiling, and then her skull did; she pressed her hand to her head. It was still dull gray outside, early morning, but she hit switches and scrolled knobs and pulled cords until every light was on in the space. Shadows keeled this way and that.

"Get up!" she said again. "Mother, mother!"

Her dreams still clung to her, trees melting black and demons hissing unmaking; she waved her hands around her to clear the cobwebs from her hair and ears. She tugged a dress over her head, and then pulled on another skirt, and her boots, and her sweater; she needed her armour. Then she weaved through the cards she had left spread on the floor and the plants she had burned for meditation and headed directly to the two mirrors that her predecessor had left there in the attic. Neeve, Neeve, lovely Neeve. Gwenllian would have known her name even if the others had not told her, because the mirrors whispered and sang and hissed it all the time. How they loved her and hated her. They judged her and admired her. Lifted her up and tore her down. Neeve, Neeve, hateful Neeve, had wanted the whole world's respect and had done everything to get it. It was Neeve, Neeve, lovely Neeve, who hadn't respected herself in the end.

The full-length mirrors were set up to face each other, eternally reflecting a reflection. Neeve had performed some complicated ritual to ensure that they were full of all the possibilities she could imagine for herself and then some, and in the end, one of them had eaten her. Proper witchery, the women of Sycharth would have said. They would have all been shipped off to the woods.

Gwenllian stood between the mirrors. The magic of them tugged and howled. The glass was not meant to show so many times at once; most people were not built to process so many possibilities at once. Gwenllian was just another mirror, though, and so the magic glanced off her harmlessly as she pressed her palms to either glass. She reached into all the possibilities and looked around, darting from one false truth to another.

"Mother, mother," Gwenllian said out loud. Her disordered thoughts transmuted if she didn't say them out loud at once.

And there her mother was: in this real present, this current possibility, this reality where Neeve herself was dead. A forest, being unmade, and Gwenllian's mother, unmade with them.

Unmade

Unmade

Un

With a scream, Gwenllian smashed the mirrors to the ground. A cry came from downstairs; the house was waking. Screaming again, Gwenllian cast about her room for a tool, a weapon. There was little in this attic that could make a dent — ah. She snatched up a lamp, the cord slapping from the wall, and clattered down the stairs. *Thump thump thump thump* each foot on the stair, double time.

"Artemussssssssss!" she cooed, her voice snapping halfway through. She slid into the dim kitchen. It was lit only by the little bulb over the oven and the diffuse gray through the window above the sink. It was only fog, no sun. "Artemusssss!"

He was awake; probably he had had the same dream as she. They had the same starry stuff in their veins, after all. His voice came through the door. "Go away."

"Open the door, Artemusssss!" Gwenllian said. She was out of breath. She was shaking. The forest, unmade, her mother, unmade. This coward magician hiding in this closet having killed everyone through his inactivity. She tried the door; he had secured it with something from the inside.

"Not today!" Artemus said. "No, thank you! Too many events this decade. Perhaps later! Cannot do the shock! Thank you for your time."

He had been an adviser to *kings*.

Gwenllian smashed the lamp against the door. The bulb shattered with a silvery sound; the end of the lamp split the thin laminate of the door. She sang, "Little rabbit down the hole, down the hole, / Little foxen down the hole, down the hole, / Little houndlet down the hole, down the hole! Come out, little rabbit, I have questions. About *demons*."

"I am a slow-growing creature!" Artemus wailed. "I cannot adapt so quickly!"

"If someone is robbing us, come back after business hours!" Calla's voice came from upstairs.

"Do you know what has happened to my mother, foul

branch?" Gwenllian ripped the lamp free from the door so that she could smash it against the surface once more. The crack widened. "I will tell you what I saw in my mirror mirrors!"

"Go away, Gwenllian," Artemus said. "I can do nothing for any of you! Leave me alone!"

"You can tell me where my father is, little shrub! What hole did you throw him in?"

Shwack

The door cleaved in two; Artemus shrank back into the darkness. He was folded over among Tupperware and reusable grocery bags and sacks of flour. He shielded his long face from her as she wielded the lamp.

"Gwenllian!" Blue said. "What are you *doing*? Doors cost *money.*"

Here was Artemus's little daughter – he did not deserve her in any way – come to rescue him. She had caught hold of Gwenllian's arm to stop her from cleaving his coward's skull with the lamp.

"Don't you want to riddle him, blue lily?" Gwenllian screamed. "I'm not the only one who wants answers. Did you hear my mother's scream, Artemussss?"

Blue said, "Gwenllian, come on, it's early, we're sleeping. Or we *were.*"

Gwenllian dropped the lamp, pulled her arm free and instead snatched Artemus by a hand and his hair. She dragged him from the closet as he whimpered like a dog.

"Mom!" Blue shouted, her hand cupped over one eye. Artemus sprawled between them, peering up at them.

"Tell me how strong this demon is, Artemus," Gwenllian hissed. "Tell me who it is coming for next. Tell me where my father is. Tell me, tell me."

Suddenly, he was up and on his feet. He ran for it, as Gwenllian pawed and grasped for him, slipping and sliding on the shattered glass bulb. She went down on one hip, hard, and clawed her way back up. He was through the sliding glass door to the backyard before she found her footing, and by the time she burst into the foggy backyard, he had already made it up to the first branch of the beech tree.

"It won't have you, you coward!" Gwenllian shouted, although she feared it would. She hurtled after him, beginning to climb herself. She was no stranger to trees and their branches, and she was quicker than him. She snarled, "You schemer, you dreamer, you —"

Her dress caught on a branch, rescuing him for half a moment. Artemus threw his hands up, found a branch, and clambered up a level. As she began to climb again, leaves clattered urgently and smaller twigs snapped.

"Help," he said, only he did not say it like that. He said, "*Auxiril!*" The word came out rapid and terrified and desperate and hopeless.

"My mother," Gwenllian said. Thoughts to words without pause. "My mother, my mother, my mother."

The dead leaves of the beech shuddered above them, raining down around both of them.

Gwenllian leapt for him.

"*Auxiril!*" he begged again.

"This won't save you!"

"*Auxiril,*" he whispered, and he hung on to the tree.

The remaining fall leaves rattled down. Branches thrashed. The ground buckled as roots tugged urgently through dirt. Gwenllian snatched for a handhold, got it, lost it. The branch beneath her shrugged and bucked in a violent wind. The dirt whispered down below as roots heaved – they were too far from the corpse road for this, and Artemus was going to do it anyway, typical, typical, typical – and then Gwenllian fell free as the branch twitched below her.

She crashed down heavily on her shoulder, all breath escaping her, and looked up to see Blue and her dead friend staring at her. Others stood in the doorway to the house, but Gwenllian was too dazzled by the fall to identify them.

"What!" Blue exclaimed. "What just happened? Is he —?"

"In the tree?" finished Noah.

"My mother was in a tree and she's dead," Gwenllian snapped. "Your father is in a tree and he's a coward. You're the unlucky one. I'll just kill you when you come out, you poisoned branch!" This was in the direction of the tree. Artemus could hear her, she knew, his soul curled inside that tree as he was, damned treelight, damned magician. It infuriated Gwenllian to know that he could hide there as long as the beech survived. There was no reason for the demon to be interested in a tree so far outside Cabeswater, and so even after everyone else and everything else had died, he would once again emerge unscathed.

Oh, the *fury.*

Blue looked at the beech tree with her mouth gently agape. "He's . . . he's *in* it?"

"Of course!" Gwenllian said. She pushed herself up from the ground and took big handfuls of her skirt in her hands so she wouldn't trip on it again. "That's who he is! That's your blood. Didn't you feel roots in your veins? *Curses!* Curses."

She stomped back to the house, shoving past Maura and Calla.

"Gwenllian," Maura said, "*what* is going on?"

Gwenllian paused in the hallway. "Demon's coming! Everyone dies. Except for her useless father. He'll live for ever."

FORTY-TWO

On Saturday, Adam woke up to perfect silence. He had forgotten what such a thing was like. Fog moved lightly outside the windows of Declan's bedroom, muting any birds. The farmhouse was too far from a road for the sounds of any cars to reach him. There was no church administration office clunking behind him, no one walking a dog on the pavement, no children shrilling on to a school bus. There was only a quiet so deep that it felt like it was pressing on his ears.

Then Cabeswater gasped back into existence inside him, and he sat up. If it had come back, it meant it had gone.

Are you there?

He felt his own thoughts, and more of his own thoughts, and then, quietly, barely there, Cabeswater. Something wasn't right.

But Adam lingered for a moment after he cast off the covers and stood. Here he was, waking in the Lynch home, wearing last night's clothing that still smelled of smoke from the grill, having overslept the weight class he had this morning by a magnitude of hours. His mouth remembered Ronan Lynch's.

What was he doing? Ronan was not something to be played with. He didn't think he was playing.

You're leaving this state, he told himself.

But he hadn't felt the fire on his heels for a long time. There was no longer the understood second half of the statement: *and never coming back.*

He headed downstairs, peering into each room that he passed, but he seemed to be alone. For a brief, trippy moment, he imagined that he was dreaming, walking through this desaturated farmhouse in his sleep. Then his stomach growled and he found the kitchen. He ate two leftover hamburger buns with nothing on them since he couldn't find butter, and then drank the remainder of the milk directly from the carton. He borrowed a jacket from the coat rack and went out.

Outside, the fields drifted mist and dew. Autumn leaves stuck to the tops of his boots as he walked down the path between the pastures. He listened for sounds of activity in any of the barns, but on an essential level, he was fine with the silence. This quiet, this absolute quiet, nothing but the low gray sky and Adam's thoughts.

He was so still inside.

The silence was interrupted as a creature darted up to him. She skittered so quickly and so oddly on her hooves that it wasn't until her hand had slid into his that he realized it was the Orphan Girl. She held a black-wet stick, and when he looked down at her, he saw that she had bits of bark stuck to her teeth.

"Should you eat that?" he asked her. "Where's Ronan?"

She pressed her cheek to the back of his hand with affection. *"Savende e'lintes i firen —"*

"English or Latin," he said.

"This way!" But instead of leading him in any particular direction, she released his hand and galloped around him in circles, flapping her arms like a bird. He kept walking, and she kept circling, and overhead, a flying bird checked itself mid-flight. Chainsaw had spotted the movement of the Orphan Girl, and now she cawed, wheeled, and headed back towards the upper fields. This was where Adam found Ronan, a black smudge in fog-washed field. He had been watching something else, but Chainsaw had alerted him, and so now he turned, hands in the pockets of his dark jacket, and watched Adam approach.

"Parrish," Ronan said. He eyed Adam. He was clearly taking nothing for granted.

Adam said, "Lynch."

Orphan Girl trotted up between them and poked Ronan with the end of her stick.

"You little puke," Ronan told her.

"Should she be eating that?"

"I don't know. I don't even know if she has internal organs."

Adam laughed at that, at the ridiculousness of all of it.

"Did you eat?" Ronan asked.

"Other than sticks? Yeah. I missed weights."

"Jesus weeps. You want to carry some hay bales? That'll put hair on your chest. Hey. You poke me with that one more time —" This was to the Orphan Girl.

As they scuffled in the grass, Adam closed his eyes and leaned his head back. He could nearly scry just like this. The quiet and the cold breeze on his throat would take him away and the dampness of his toes in his shoes and the scent of living creatures would keep him here. Within and without. He couldn't tell if he was letting himself idolize this place or Ronan, and he wasn't sure there was a difference.

When he opened his eyes, he saw that Ronan was looking at him, as he had been looking at him for months. Adam looked back, as he had been looking back for months.

"I need to dream," Ronan said.

Adam took Orphan Girl's hand. He corrected, "*We* need to dream."

FORTY-THREE

Twenty-five minutes away, Gansey was wide awake, and he was in trouble.

He didn't know yet what he was in trouble for, and knowing the Gansey family, he might never know. He could feel it, though, sure as he could feel the net of the Glendower story lowering over him. Annoyance in the Gansey household was like a fine vanilla extract. It was used sparingly, rarely on its own, and was generally only identifiable in retrospect. With practice, one could learn to identify the taste of it, but to what end? *There's some anger in this scone, don't you think? Oh, yes, I think a little —*

Helen was pissed at Gansey. That was the upshot.

The Gansey family had convened at the schoolhouse, one of the Gansey investment properties. It was a comfortably shabby old stone schoolhouse located in the verdant and remote hills between Washington, D.C., and Henrietta, where it earned its keep as a short-term rental. The rest of the family had stayed the night there — they'd tried to convince Gansey to come spend the night with them, a request he might have fulfilled if not for Ronan, if not for Henry. Maybe that was why Helen was annoyed with him.

In any case, surely he had made up for it by bringing interesting friends for them to play with. The Ganseys loved to delight other people. Guests meant more people to display elaborate cooking skills for.

But he was still in trouble. Not with his parents. They were delighted to see him — *How tan you are, Dick* — and they were, as predicted, even more delighted to see Henry and Blue. Henry immediately passed some sort of friend-peer test that Adam and Ronan had always seemed to struggle with, and Blue was — well, whatever it was about Blue's sharply curious expression that had attracted the youngest Gansey in the first place clearly also caught the older Ganseys. They immediately began to question Blue about her family's profession as they diced eggplant.

Blue described an average day at 300 Fox Way with rather less wonder and bewilderment than she'd just used in the car to tell Gansey about the unaverage experience of her father disappearing into a tree. She listed the psychic hotline, the cleansing of houses, the meditation circles, and the laying out of cards. Her perfunctory method of describing it only charmed Gansey's parents more; if she had tried to sell it to them, it would have never worked. But she was just telling them how it was and not asking a thing from them and they loved it.

With Blue there, Gansey was excruciatingly aware of how they all must look through her eyes — the old Mercedes in the drive, the hemmed trousers, even skin, straight teeth, Burberry sunglasses, Hermes scarves. He could even see the schoolhouse through her lens now. In the past, he wouldn't have thought that it looked particularly moneyed — it was sparsely decorated, and he would've assumed that came off as austere. But now that he had spent time with Blue, he could see that the sparseness was exactly what *made* it look rich. The Ganseys did not need to have a lot of things in the house because every object they *did* have was exactly the right thing for its purpose. There was not a cheap bookshelf also pressed into service as a repository for extra dishes. There was not a desk that had to carry paperwork as well as sewing materials as well as toys. There were not pots and pans piled on cabinets or toilet plungers sitting in cheap plastic buckets. Instead, even in this crumbling schoolhouse, everything was aesthetic. That was what money did. It put plungers in copper pots, and extra dishes behind glass doors, and toys into carved hope chests, and hung skillets from iron pot racks.

He felt quite squirmy about it.

Gansey kept trying to catch Blue's and Henry's gazes to see if they were all right, but the trick with trying to be subtle in a room full of Ganseys was that subtlety was a language they all spoke. There was no discreetly asking if rescue was needed; all messages would be intercepted. And so light conversation proceeded until lunch could be removed to the porch out back. Henry and Blue were seated in chairs too far away for him to air-drop aid to them.

Helen made a point to sit next to him. He was tasting vanilla by the bucket load.

"Headmaster Child said you were a bit late with your college applications," Mr Gansey said as he leaned forward to spoon quinoa on to plates.

Gansey busied himself getting a gnat from his iced tea.

Mrs Gansey waved her hand at an invisible gnat out of solidarity. "It seems like it should be too cold for insects. There must be standing water around here."

Gansey carefully wiped the dead insect on the edge of the table.

"I'm still in touch with Dromand these days," Mr Gansey said. "He's still got his fingers stuck in all the pies in the Harvard history department, if that's what you're still thinking about."

"Jesus, no," Mrs Gansey said. "Yale, surely."

"What, like Ehrlich?" Mr Gansey laughed gently at some private joke. "Let this be a lesson to us *all*."

"Ehrlich's an outlier," Mrs Gansey replied. They clinked their glasses together in a mysterious toast.

"What have you put in already?" Helen asked. There was danger in her voice. Unidentifiable to non-Ganseys, but enough that their father frowned at her.

Gansey blinked up. "None, yet."

"I can't remember the timing for these things," Mrs Gansey said. "Soon, though, right?"

"Time got away from me." It was the simplest possible version of *theoretically I am to die before it matters so I used my evenings for other things.*

"I've read a study on gap years," Henry said. He smiled at his plate as Mrs Gansey placed it before him, and in that smile was an understanding that he was fluent in this language of subtlety. "It is supposed to be good for people like us."

"What are people like us?" Gansey's mother asked, in a way that suggested she enjoyed the idea of commonality between them.

"Oh, you know, overeducated young people who drive themselves to nervous breakdowns in the worthy pursuit of excellence," Henry said. Gansey's parents laughed. Blue picked at her napkin. Gansey had been rescued; Blue had been stranded.

Mr Gansey saw it, though, and he caught the ball before it even hit the ground. "I would love to read something from you, Blue, on growing up in a house of psychics. You could go academic or you could go memoir, and either way, it would just be fascinating. You have such a distinct voice, even when speaking."

"Oh yes, I noticed that, too, the Henrietta cadence," Mrs Gansey said warmly; they were excellent team players. Good save, point to the Ganseys, win for Team Good Feeling.

Helen said, "I nearly forgot about the bruschetta; it's going to burn. *Dick*, would you help me carry it in?"

Team Good Feeling was abruptly disbanded. Gansey was about to find out why he was in trouble.

"Right, sure," he said. "Can I get anyone anything while I'm inside?"

"Actually, if you'd bring back my schedule by the Ellie-furniture, that would be great, thanks," his mother said. "I need to call Martina to make sure she's going to be there in enough time."

The Gansey siblings headed inside, where Helen first removed the toast from the oven and then turned to him. She demanded, "Do you remember when I said, 'tell me what kind of dirt I will find on your brodude friends so that I can spin it before Mom gets out here'?"

"I trust that's a rhetorical question," Gansey said. He garnished bruschetta.

Helen said, "You did not get back to me with any information on that front."

"I sent you clippings of the Turk Week pranks."

"And yet you failed to mention that you had *bribed the headmaster.*"

Gansey stopped garnishing bruschetta.

"You really did," Helen said, reading him effortlessly. Gansey siblings were tuned to the same radio frequency. "Which one did you do it for? Which friend? The trailer park one."

"Don't be insulting," Gansey replied crisply. "Who told you?"

"Paperwork told me. You're not eighteen yet, you know. How did you even manage to convince Brulio to write that document for you? I thought he was supposed to be Dad's attorney."

"This has nothing to do with Dad. I didn't spend his money."

"You're seventeen. What other money do you have?"

Gansey looked at her. "I take it you only read the first page of the document then."

"That's all that would open on my phone," Helen said. "Why? What does the second page say? *Jesus Christ.* You gave Child that warehouse of yours, didn't you?"

It sounded so clean when she put it that way. He supposed it was. One Aglionby diploma in exchange for Monmouth Manufacturing.

You probably won't be around to miss it, he told himself.

"First of all, what has he *possibly* done to deserve such a thing?" Helen demanded. "Are you sleeping with him?"

Indignation cooled his voice. "Because friendship isn't worthy enough?"

"Dick, I see you stretching to stand on the high ground, but trust me, you're failing. You don't just need a morality ladder to get there, you need a booster chair to put the ladder on. Do you understand what an incredibly bad position this puts Mom in if this stupidity of yours comes to light?"

"It's not Mom. It's me."

Helen put her head on its side. Ordinarily he didn't notice the age difference between them, but just then, she was very obviously a polished adult and he was a — whatever he was. "Do you think the press would care? You're seventeen. It was the family lawyer, for God's sake. Example of family corruption, et cetera, et cetera. I cannot believe you wouldn't at least wait until after the election to do it."

But Gansey didn't know how long he had. He didn't know if he had until after the election. This made his chest feel tight and his breaths go instantly small, so he pushed the thought away from himself as quickly as he could.

"I didn't think about the ramifications," he said. "For the campaign."

"Obviously! I don't even know what you were thinking. I was trying all the way out here to put it together and I just couldn't."

Gansey pushed around a lump of tomato on the cutting board. His heart was still feathered inside him. In a much smaller voice, he said, "I didn't want him to throw it all away because his father died. He doesn't want it now, but I wanted him to have it later, when he realized he did."

Helen said nothing, and he knew that his sister was studying him, reading him again. He just kept pushing that lump of tomato around, thinking about how he really wasn't even sure that Ronan needed the degree after all, and how he regretted making the deal with Child even as he hadn't been unable to sleep until he did it. He had been wrong about a lot of things, and it was too late, now, with time running out, to fix them. It had been a lonesome and guilty secret to keep.

To his surprise, Helen hugged him.

"Little brother," she whispered, "what's wrong with you?"

The Ganseys were not huggers, and Helen would not ordinarily risk wrinkling her blouse, and her fine gold bracelets pressed lines into his arm, and something about all of these things combined made Gansey feel dangerously close to tears.

"What if I don't find him," Gansey said finally. "Glendower."

Helen let out a sigh and released him. "You and that king. When will it end?"

"When I find him."

"What then? What if you *do* find him?"

"That's all there is."

It wasn't a good answer, and she didn't like it, but she merely narrowed her eyes. She patted some wrinkles out of her blouse.

"I'm sorry I ruined Mom's campaign," he said.

"You didn't ruin it. I'll just have to, I don't know. I'll find some skeletons in Child's closet to make sure he's compliant." Helen didn't look entirely displeased by the task. She liked organizing facts. "Jesus. To think I thought I'd have to be dealing with hazing and marijuana possession. Who's that girl out there, by the way? You kissed her?"

"No," Gansey replied truthfully.

"You should," she said.

"Do you like her?"

"She's weird. You're weird."

The Gansey siblings smiled at each other.

"Let's get this bruschetta out of here," Helen said. "So we can get out of this weekend alive."

FORTY-FOUR

I t was a mistake.

Adam knew it the moment he fell into the dark mouth of the scrying bowl, but it wasn't like he could leave Ronan there in his dream alone.

His physical body sat cross-legged back at the Barns, a ceramic dog dish serving as his scrying bowl. Ronan's body curled on the sofa. Orphan Girl sat close to Adam, peering into the bowl along with him.

That was real.

But this was also real: this diseased symphony that was Cabeswater. The forest vomited black around him. Trees melted into black, but in reverse — long black strings of goo dripping up towards the sky. The air shuddered and darted. Adam's mind didn't understand how to process what it was seeing. It was the horror of the black-bleeding tree they'd seen before, only it had spread to the entire forest, atmosphere included. If there had been nothing of the true Cabeswater left, it would have been less horrifying — more easily dismissed as a nightmare — but he could still see the forest he had come to know struggling to maintain itself.

Cabeswater?

There was no answer.

He didn't know what happened to him if Cabeswater died.

"Ronan!" Adam shouted. "Are you here?"

Maybe Ronan was only sleeping, not dreaming. Maybe he was dreaming somewhere else. Maybe he had arrived here before Adam and had already been killed in his dreams. *"Ronan!"*

"Kerah," moaned the Orphan Girl.

When he looked for her, though, she was nowhere to be seen. Had she come with him, scrying after him into the bowl? Could Ronan dream another one of her into his dreams? Adam knew the answer to this: yes. He'd watched a dreamt Ronan die in front of the real Ronan. There could be infinite Orphan Girls here in this forest. *Damn it.* He didn't know how to call for her. He tried: "Orphan Girl!"

As soon as he shouted it, he was sorry. Things were what you named them in this place. In any case, there was no reply.

He began to move through the forest. He was careful to cling to his body back at the Barns. His hands on the cold scrying bowl. His hip bones against the wooden floor. The smell of the fireplace behind him. *Remember where you are, Adam.*

He didn't want to call again for Ronan; he didn't want this nightmare to forge a duplicate. Everything he saw was terrible. Here a snake dissolving while still alive, here a stag in slow-motion pedal on the ground, vines growing up through its still-living flesh. Here was a creature that was not Adam but was nonetheless somehow clothed like him. Adam flinched, but the strange boy was not attending to him. He was instead slowly eating his own hands.

Adam shuddered. *"Cabeswater, where is he?"*

His voice cracked, and Cabeswater heaved, trying to appease its magician. A rock had manifested before him. Or rather, it had always been there, in the way of dreams, in the way Noah appeared or disappeared. Adam had seen this boulder before; its striated surface was covered with purple-black letters in Ronan's handwriting.

Adam moved past it as something screamed behind him.

Here was Ronan. Finally. Finally.

Ronan was circling something in the burned-out grass between ruined trees; when Adam drew closer he saw that it was a carcass. It was hard to tell what it had first looked like. It seemed to have chalky white skin, but deep slashes bit through the flesh; the edges of them curled in on themselves pinkly. A snarl of intestines roped out from under a greasy gray flap and hooked on a red-tipped claw. Mushrooms burst through parts of all of it, and there was something terribly wrong about them; they were difficult to look at.

"No," Ronan said. "Oh no. You bastard."

"What is it?" Adam asked.

Ronan's hand hovered over two parted beaks, side by side, both rimmed with black and something purple-red that Adam didn't want to consider too deeply. "My night horror. God. Shit."

"Why would it be here?"

"I don't know. It cares about what I care about," Ronan said. He peered up at Adam. "Is this a nightmare, or is this real?"

Adam held his gaze. This was where they were now: Nightmares *were* real. There was no difference between dreams and reality when they stood here in Cabeswater together.

"What's doing this?" Ronan asked. "I can't hear the trees. Nothing's talking to me."

Adam held his gaze. He didn't want to say *demon* out loud.

Ronan said, "I want to wake up. Can we? I don't want to bring any of it back. And I can't keep my thoughts — I can't —"

"Yes," Adam interrupted. He couldn't, either. "We need to talk to the others. Let's —"

"Kerah!"

The Orphan Girl's thin cry caught Ronan immediately; he craned his neck to see her among the dark branches and pools.

"Leave her," Adam said. "She's with us in real life."

But Ronan hesitated.

"*Kerah!*" she wailed again, and this time Adam heard the pain in her voice. It was small and childlike and piteous, and everything in him had been coded to respond to it. "*Kerah, succurro!*"

It was impossible to tell if this was the Orphan Girl they had back at the Barns, or if this was a copy, or if it was a monstrous devil bird with her voice. Ronan didn't care. He ran anyway. Adam crashed after him. Everything he passed was hideous: a forest of willows sagged into each other, a bird singing a note backwards, a fist of black insects crawling over the stub of a rabbit carcass.

The voice did not belong to a monstrous devil bird. It was the Orphan Girl, or something that looked just like her, and she knelt in a scruff of dry grass. She had not been crying, but she burst into tears when she saw Ronan. As he reached her, out of breath, she held out her arms to him imploringly. Adam did not think she was a copy; she wore his watch with its bite marks on the band, and in any case, this feeble Cabeswater lacked the strength to produce such an incorrupt version of her.

"*Succurro, succurro,*" she sobbed. *Help, help* – The arms she stretched to Ronan were coated and spattered in blood up to the elbow.

Ronan skidded to his knees, his arms around her, and it hurt Adam, somehow, to watch how ferociously he hugged his little strange dream creature, and how she buried her face into his shoulder. He stood with her in his arms, holding her tightly, and he heard her saying, *No, you did good, it's going to be OK, we're waking up.*

Then Adam saw *it*. He saw it before Ronan did, because Ronan had not yet looked beyond the Orphan Girl. *No, no.* The Orphan Girl had not stopped here because it was all the further she could run. She had knelt there because that was all the further she could drag the body. *Body* was a tender word for it. Long strands of hair stuck to the largest of pieces; all of it was strung out long like a string of viscous pearls. This was how Orphan Girl's arms had got painted with blood; this futile rescue effort.

"Ronan," Adam warned as dread welled up in him.

At the tone in Adam's voice, Ronan turned.

There was a brief moment where he was looking just at Adam, and Adam wished that he could keep him in it for ever. *Just wake up*, he thought, but he knew Ronan wouldn't.

Ronan's gaze dropped.

"Mom?"

FORTY-FIVE

Depending on where you began the story, it was about the Gray Man.

The Gray Man liked kings.

He liked official kings, the sorts who had the title and crown and all that, but he also liked unofficial kings, who ruled and led and stewarded without any noble bloodline or proper throne. He liked kings who lived in the past and kings who lived in the future. Kings who had become legends only after their death and kings who had become legends during their lives and kings who had become legends without living at all. His favourites were the kings who used their power in the pursuit of learning and peace rather than status and property, who used violence only to create a country that did not have to live by violence. Alfred, the king the Gray Man most idolized, epitomized this, having conquered the squabbling kinglings of Anglo-Saxon England to create a unified country. How acutely the Gray Man admired such a man, even as he found himself a hit man instead of a king.

It seemed peculiar that he couldn't quite remember his decision to become a hit man.

He remembered the academic portions of his life as a historian back in Boston: the lectures, the papers, the parties, the archives. Kings and warriors, honour and wergild. He remembered the Greenmantles, of course. But everything else was difficult to piece together. Hard to discern what was true recollection and what was merely dream. Back then he'd strung one gray day into another, and it seemed likely that he had lost weeks or months or years to this foggy dissociation. Somewhere in there someone had breathed the word *mercenary*, and somewhere in there someone had given up his identity and become the Gray Man.

"What are we expecting to find here?" Maura asked him now.

They were in the car together, headed out towards Singer's Falls. The presence of only two parts of Laumonier at the grocery store had been gnawing at the Gray Man ever since he had left them, and he'd spent much of the night in a dedicated search for the third and most unpleasant brother. Now, although they'd lost sight of his rental car, they continued on towards the Barns.

"We are *hoping* to find nothing," the Gray Man said. "We are expecting, however, to find Laumonier rifling through Niall Lynch's closets."

The part of the Gray Man who used to be a hit man was not thrilled by the idea of Maura insisting on coming with him; the part of him that was very in love with her was deeply satisfied.

"Still no answer from Ronan," Maura said, peering at the Gray Man's phone. Blue had told them that morning that Ronan Lynch and Adam Parrish were working at the Barns.

"Possibly he wouldn't pick up my number," the Gray Man demurred. Also, possibly he was dead. Laumonier could be very difficult when cornered.

"Possibly," Maura echoed with a frown.

They found the Barns looking idyllic as usual, with only

two cars in the gravel area – the Lynch BMW and the Parrish tri-colour jalopy. There was no sign of Laumonier's rental, but that didn't mean he hadn't parked nearby and walked in.

"Don't tell me to stay in the car," Maura said.

"I wouldn't dream of it," he replied, opening the door slowly to avoid jamming it into a plum tree still growing barely hidden fruit. "A parked car is a vulnerable place."

He retrieved his gun and Maura put his phone in her back pocket and they tried the front door – unlocked. It took them very little time to discover Adam and Ronan in the living room.

They were not dead.

But they were not quite alive, either. Ronan Lynch was unresponsive on the faded leather couch, and Adam Parrish was keeled back beside the fireplace. A young girl sat bolt upright in front of a dog bowl, unblinking. She had hooves. None of the room's occupants responded to Maura's voice.

The Gray Man found himself strangely affected by the sight of them in such a state, which seemed contradictory given that he had killed Ronan's father. But it was precisely *because* he had killed Niall that he now felt responsibility and guilt howling in the corridors of his heart. He was his own man now, and in his position as someone else's tool, he had left Ronan and the Barns without a protector.

"Is this magic or poison?" the Gray Man asked Maura. "Laumonier loves his poisons."

Maura leaned over the scrying bowl before flinching back from it. "I think it's magic. Not that I'm any good at whatever kind of magic they've been playing with."

"Should we shake them?" he asked.

"Adam. Adam, come back." She touched his face. "I don't want to wake Ronan, in case he's keeping Adam's soul close by. I guess . . . I will go in and get Adam. Hold my hand. Don't let me go for more than, I don't know, ninety seconds."

"Is it dangerous?"

"It's how Persephone died. The body can't live with the soul too far away. I don't intend on wandering. If he's not close, I'll come back."

The Gray Man trusted Maura to know her own limits, as he assumed she trusted him. He placed his gun on the floor beside his foot — out of easy reach of the girl, if that's what she was — and took Maura's hand.

She leaned into the scrying bowl, and as her eyes went blank, he began to count. *One, two, three —*

Adam gasped and twitched. One hand flailed out, grabbing for a handhold that wasn't there, nails scratching against the plaster in a thin attack. His gaze swam on to the Gray Man with obvious effort.

"Wake him," he said in a slurred voice. "Don't let him stay there by himself!" The hooved girl leapt up from her position without any sluggishness. (Maybe, the Gray Man thought in retrospect, she had actually not been scrying at all, and had instead remained perfectly still only as camouflage when Maura and the Gray Man came into the house, a chilling but perfectly plausible thought.) She threw her arms around Ronan where he sprawled, then began to agitate at him, hands pressed flat against his cheeks, pounding his chest, speaking all the while in something that sounded like Latin but was not.

Then a peculiar thing happened. In principle, the Gray Man

knew what was happening, but it was a very different thing to see it actually occur before one's eyes.

Ronan Lynch brought something back from his dreams.

In this case: blood.

In one moment, he was asleep, and in the next he was awake, and his hands were mired in gore. The Gray Man's brain moved uneasily between those moments, and he felt that it had neatly removed the most difficult image, the one in the middle.

Adam had clambered unsteadily to his feet. "*Bring Maura back! You have no idea —*"

Yes, ninety seconds, it had been ninety seconds. The Gray Man used Maura's hand to tug her away from the scrying bowl, and because she had only wandered in shallowly, she returned to him at once.

"Oh no," she said. "It's awful. It's so awful. The demon — oh no."

She looked at once to Ronan on the couch. He had not moved even a fraction, although his eyebrows had become more intentional over his closed eyes. There was not a lot of blood on the outside of him, in comparison to how much a human generally carried on the inside, but there was nonetheless something fatal-looking about the display. It was the combination of blood and mud, the bits of bone and viscera stuck to the heels of his hands.

"*Fuck,*" said Adam vehemently. He had begun to shake, though his face had not changed.

"Is Ronan hurt?" Maura asked.

"He doesn't move right after," Adam said. "If he brings

something back. Give him a second. *Fuck!* His mother's dead."

"Look out!" the girl shouted. And it was that, and only that, that kept the Gray Man from dying when Laumonier appeared around the corner with a gun.

Laumonier did not hesitate for even a second when he saw the Gray Man: To see him in this context was to shoot him.

The sound was bigger than the room.

The girl let out a shriek that had nothing to do with the sound a human girl would make and everything to do with the sound that a crow would make.

The Gray Man had hit the deck immediately, taking Maura down with him. He found, in that bare second on the worn floorboards, that he was facing a choice.

He could try to disarm this part of Laumonier, securing the area and reminding him that now that Greenmantle was dead, Laumonier should not have had any quarrel with the Gray Man. It was not as impossible as it sounded: The Gray Man had a gun within easy reach of his hand as well, and Adam Parrish had already proven himself extremely cool and resourceful. Such a negotiation would leave the Barns open to Laumonier's interest, of course, and once Laumonier caught sight of the girl with the hooves, that interest would be undying. This part of the world — and along with it 300 Fox Way and Maura and Blue — would for ever be open to threat unless they fled as Declan and Matthew Lynch had. If he chose this path, he would have to be constantly vigilant to protect them from the interested parties. Constantly on the defensive.

Or the Gray Man could shoot Laumonier.

It would be a declaration of war. The other two parts of Laumonier would not let it pass without remark. But perhaps a war was what this twisted business needed. It had been devolving into a dangerous anarchy of alleyways and basements and kidnappings and hit men since some time before him, and had only become more unruly. Perhaps what it needed was someone to impose some rules from the top down, to get these messy kings in line. But it would not be easy, and it would take years, and there was no version of it that meant that the Gray Man got to stay with Maura and her family. He'd have to take the danger elsewhere, and he'd have to once again throw himself into that world.

He wanted to stay so badly, in this place where he had begun to put violence down. In the place where he'd learned how to feel again. In this place that he loved.

Only a second had passed.

Maura sighed.

The Gray Man shot Laumonier.

He was a king.

FORTy-SIX

I
t was not at all impossible for Blue to believe that a demon had killed Ronan's mother and was killing Cabeswater, too. When they came back from the lunch at the schoolhouse — having received dozens of calls from both Ronan's phone and 300 Fox Way — it felt like the end of the world. Knots of clouds snarled over the town and inside the house, where the Gray Man was packing the few small things that he had left behind there.

"You kill the demon," he told them all. "I will do my best to handle the rest. Will I be back some day?"

Maura just put her hand on his cheek.

He kissed her, hugged Blue, and was gone.

Jimi and Orla, shockingly, were gone as well. They did not deserve to be in the line of fire, Maura said, and had gone to stay with old friends in West Virginia until it was certain what would happen to Henrietta and the psychics in it.

Every appointment had been cancelled, so there were no clients, and the hotline was set up to send every caller straight to voicemail.

Only Maura, Calla and Gwenllian remained.

It felt like the end of everything.

Blue asked Adam, "Where's Ronan?"

Adam led Blue and Gansey out of Fox Way into the chilly day, moving carefully to avoid unseating Chainsaw, who perched on his shoulder with her head hung low. Ronan's car was parked on the kerb a few houses away.

Ronan sat motionless behind the wheel of the BMW, eyes fixed on some point down the road behind them. A trick of the light played over the passenger seat – no, it was no trick. Noah sat there, barely present, also motionless. He was already slouching, but when he caught a look at Blue's stitches, he slouched down even further.

Blue and Gansey walked to the driver's side and waited. Ronan did not roll down the window or look at him, so Gansey tried the door, found it unlocked, opened it.

"Ronan," he said. The gentle way he said it nearly made Blue cry.

Ronan did not turn his head. His feet rested on the pedals; his hands rested on the bottom of the steering wheel. His face was quite composed.

How miserable it was to imagine that he was the last Lynch left here.

Beside Blue, Adam shuddered violently. Blue looped her arm around him. It was terrible to imagine that while Gansey and she had been having lunch, Ronan and Adam had been wandering through a hellscape together. Gansey's gallant magicians, both felled by horror.

Adam shook again.

"Ronan," Gansey said again.

In a very low voice, Ronan replied, "I'm waiting for you to tell me what to do, Gansey. Tell me where to go."

"We can't undo this," Gansey said. "I can't undo it."

This did not make a dent in Ronan's expression. It was terrible to see him without any fire or acid in his eyes.

"Come inside," Blue said.

Ronan didn't acknowledge this. "I know I can't undo it. I'm not stupid. I want to *kill* it."

A car groaned by them, giving the three of them a wide berth where they stood by Ronan's open door. The neighbourhood felt close and present and watching. Inside the car, Noah leaned forward to make eye contact with them. His face was miserable; he touched his own eyebrow where Blue's was scratched.

It wasn't your fault, Blue thought at him. *I'm not upset with you. Please stop hiding from me.*

"I'm not going to let it get to Matthew," Ronan said. He took a breath through his mouth, released it through his nostrils. Slow and intentional. Everything was slow and intentional, flattened into a state of tenuous control. "I could feel it in the dream. I could feel what it wanted. It's unmaking everything I've dreamt. I'm not going to let that happen. I'm not going to lose anyone else. You know how to kill it."

Gansey said, "I don't know how to find Glendower."

"You do, Gansey," Ronan replied, voice uneven for the first time. "I know you do. And when you're ready to get him, I'll be sitting right here, waiting to go where you tell me."

Oh, Ronan.

Ronan's eyes were still trained on the road ahead of them. A tear ran down his nose and clung to his chin, but he didn't so much as blink. When Gansey said nothing else, Ronan reached for the door handle without looking, with the thoughtless stretch of familiarity. He tugged the door free of Gansey's hand. It closed with less of a bang than Blue had thought Ronan was capable of.

They stood there outside their friend's car, none of them speaking or moving. The breeze shuffled dried leaves down the street in the direction of Ronan's line of sight. Somewhere out there was a monster eating his heart. Blue couldn't think too hard upon the trees of Cabeswater under attack, or she became too restless to even stand.

She said, "Is that the language puzzle box in the backseat? I'm going to need it. I'm going to go talk to Artemus."

"Isn't he in a tree?" Adam asked.

"Yeah," Blue said. "But we've been talking to trees for a while."

Only a few minutes later, she picked her way out across the exposed roots of the beech tree to its trunk. Gansey and Adam had joined her, but had been given strict orders to remain on the patio outside the back door and to come no closer. This was going to be about her, her father, and her tree.

Hopefully.

She could not count how many times she had sat beneath this beech tree. Where others had a favourite sweater or favourite song, a favourite chair or a favourite food, Blue had always had the beech tree in the backyard. It wasn't just this tree, of course — she loved all trees — but this tree had been a constant her entire life. She knew the dips in its bark and how much it grew each year and even the particular smell of its leaves when they first began to bud in the spring. She knew it as well as she knew anyone else in 300 Fox Way.

Now she sat cross-legged among its torn-up roots with the puzzle box resting on her calves and a notebook resting on top of it. The jostled ground was damp and cold against her thighs; probably if she was being *really* practical, she would have brought something to sit on.

Or perhaps it was better to feel the same ground the tree felt.

"Artemus," she said, "can you hear me? It's Blue. Your daughter." Right after she said this, she thought maybe it had been a mistake. Maybe he would rather not be reminded of that fact. She corrected, "Maura's daughter. I'm sorry in advance for my pronunciation, but they don't really offer books for this."

She had first begun to have the idea to use this puzzle box of Ronan's earlier that day while talking to Henry. He had explained to her how the bee translated his thoughts more purely than words did, how the bee was more essentially *Henry* than anything that actually came out of his mouth. It got her thinking about how the trees of Cabeswater had always struggled to communicate with the humans, first in Latin, then in English, and how they had another language that they seemed to speak with each other — the dream language that was featured on this translation box of Ronan's. Artemus didn't seem remotely able to express himself. Maybe this would help. At least it might look like Blue was trying to make an effort.

Now she spun the wheel around to translate the things she wanted to say into the dream language, and jotted down the words that appeared. She read the written sentences out loud, slowly and without surety. She was aware of Adam and Gansey's presence, but it was comforting, not awkward. She'd done stupider-looking rituals in front of them. Out loud, the sentences sounded a little like Latin. In Blue's head, they meant:

"Mom always told me that you were interested in the world, in nature, and the way people interact with it, just like me. I thought maybe we could talk about that, in your language."

She wanted to ask about the demon straightaway, but she'd seen how badly that had gone for Gwenllian. So now she simply waited. The backyard was the same as it had been before. Her hands were clammy. She wasn't entirely sure what she expected to happen.

Slowly, she moved the dials on the puzzle box to translate another phrase from English. Touching the smooth, skinlike bark of the beech tree, she asked it out loud: "Please, could you at least tell me if you're listening?"

There was not so much as a rustle from the remaining dry leaves.

When Blue was much younger, she had spent hours setting up elaborate versions of the psychic rituals she'd seen her family undertaking. She'd read countless books on tarot; watched web videos on palmistry; studied tea leaves; conducted séances in the bathroom in the middle of the night. While her cousins effortlessly spoke to the dead and her mother saw the future, Blue struggled for even a hint of the supernatural. She spent hours straining her ears for an otherworldly voice. Trying to predict which tarot card she was about to overturn. Waiting to feel something dead touch her hand.

This was exactly that.

The only thing that was slightly different was that Blue had started this process somewhat optimistic. It had been a very long time since she'd fooled herself into thinking that she herself had any connection with the otherworld. If she wasn't being bitter about it, it was because she hadn't thought that this was about the otherworld.

"I love this tree," Blue said finally, in English. "You don't have any claim to it. If anyone could live inside it, it should be *me*. I've loved it way longer than you could have."

With a sigh, she stood up, brushing muck off the back of her legs. She gave Gansey and Adam a rueful look.

"Wait."

Blue froze. Gansey and Adam both looked sharply behind her.

"Say what you just said." Artemus's voice emanated from the tree. Not like the voice of God, but rather like a voice coming from just behind the trunk.

"What?" Blue asked.

"Say what you just said."

"I've loved this tree?"

Artemus stepped from the tree. It was the same as when Aurora had stepped out of the rock back in Cabeswater. There was tree, and then man-and-tree, and then just man. Artemus held out his hands for the puzzle box, and she put it in them. He sank to the ground with the box in his lap, folding his long limbs around it, turning the dials slowly and looking at each side. Watching his long face and tired mouth and slumped shoulders, Blue was amazed by how differently Artemus and Gwenllian wore their age. Gwenllian had been made young and angry by six hundred years of marking time. Artemus looked defeated. She wondered if that was from the six hundred years in total, or only the past seventeen.

She simply said it: "You look tired."

He peered up at her, small eyes bright in his long face, wrinkles deep-set around them. "I am tired."

Blue sat down opposite him. She didn't say anything at all as he continued testing the box. It was strange to be able to identify the origin of her hands in his hands, though his fingers were longer and knobbier.

"I am one of the *tir e e'lintes*," Artemus said finally. "This is my language."

He turned the dials on the unknown language side to spell *tir e e'lintes*. The translation shifted on the English side, which he showed to her.

"'Tree-lights,'" she read. "Because you can hide in trees?"

"They are our . . ." He faltered. Then he turned the dials and showed her the box again. *Skin-house.*

"You live in trees?"

"In? With." He considered. "I was a tree when Maura and the other two women pulled me out of it years ago."

"I don't understand," Blue said, but kindly. She was not uncomfortable because of the truth of him. She was uncomfortable because the truth of him suggested a truth in her. "You were a tree, or you were in a tree?"

He looked at her, doleful, tired, strange, and then he spread his hand for her. With the fingers of his other hand, he traced the lines in his palm. "These remind me of my roots." He took her hand and placed it flat on the skin of the beech. His long, knobby fingers entirely eclipsed her small hand. "My roots are yours, too. Do you miss your home?"

She closed her eyes. She could feel the familiar cool bark beneath her skin, and felt once again the comfort of being under its branches, on top of its roots, pressed to its trunk.

"You loved this tree," Artemus said. "You already told me."

She opened her eyes. She nodded.

"Sometimes we *tir e e'lintes* wear this," he continued, dropping her hand so he could gesture to himself. Then he touched the tree again. "Sometimes we wear this."

"I wish," Blue said, then stopped. She didn't have to finish the sentence anyway.

He nodded once. He said, "Here is how it began."

He told the story just as a tree grows, beginning with a seed. Then he dug in fine roots to support it as the main trunk began to stretch upward.

"When Wales was young," Artemus told Blue, "there were trees. It is no longer all trees, or it wasn't when I left. At first, it was all right. There were more trees than there were *tir e e'lintes*. Some trees cannot hold a *tir e e'lintes*. You know these trees; even the dullest man knows these trees. They are —" He glanced around. His eyes found the weedy, fast-growing locusts on the other side of the fence and the decorative plum tree in a neighbour's yard. "They do not have a soul of their own, and they aren't built to hold anyone else's."

Blue ran her fingers over an exposed beech root next to her leg. Yes, she knew.

Artemus spread more roots for his story: "There were enough trees that could hold us in Wales. But as the years went by, Wales turned from a place of forests to a place of fires and ploughs and boats and houses; it became a place for all the things that trees could be except for alive."

The roots were dug in; he began on the trunk. "The *amae vias* were failing. The *tir e e'lintes* can only exist in trees near them, but we feed the *amae vias* too. We are *oce iteres*. Like the sky, and the water. Mirrors."

Despite the heat, Blue put her arms around herself, as chilled as she would have been by Noah's presence.

Artemus looked wistfully at the beech tree, or at something past it, something older. "A forest of *tir e e'lintes* is something, indeed, mirrors pointed to mirrors pointed to mirrors, the *amae vias* churning up below us, dreams held between us."

Blue asked, "What about one of them? What is one of them?"

He regarded his hands ruefully. "Tired." He regarded hers. "Other."

"And the demon?"

But this was skipping ahead. He shook his head, backed up.

"Owain was not like common men," he said. "He could speak to the birds. He could speak to us. He wanted his country to be a wild place of magic, a place of dreams and songs, crossed by powerful *amae vias*. So we fought for him. We all lost everything. He lost everything."

"All of his family died," Blue said. "I heard."

Artemus nodded. "It is dangerous to spill blood on an *ama via*. Even a little can plant dark things."

Blue's eyes widened. "A demon."

His eyebrows tipped much further along towards the sad side of things. His face was a portrait called *Worry*. "Wales was unmade. We were unmade. The *tir e e'lintes* who were left were to hide Owain Glyndŵr until a time when he could rise again. We were to hide him for a time. To slow him as we are slow in trees. But there were not enough places of power left on the Welsh *amae vias* after the demon's work. And so we fled here; we died here. It is a hard journey."

"How did you meet my mother?"

"She came to the spirit road intending to communicate with trees, and that is what she did."

Blue started, then stopped, then started again. "Am I human?"

"Maura is human." He did not say *and so am I*. He was not a wizard, a human who could be in trees. He was something else.

"Tell me," Artemus whispered, "when you dream, do you dream of the stars?"

It was too much: the demon, Ronan's grief, the fact of the trees. To her surprise, a tear welled in her eye and escaped; another was queued up behind it.

Artemus watched it fall from her chin, and then he said, "All of the *tir e e'lintes* are full of potential, always moving, always restless, always looking for possibilities to reach out and be somewhere else, be something else. This tree, that tree, that forest, that forest. But more than anything, we love the stars." He cast his eyes up, as if he could see them during the day. "If only we could reach them, maybe we could be them. Any one of them could be our skin-house."

Blue sighed.

Artemus looked at his own hands again; they always seemed to make him anxious. "This form is not the easiest for us. I long – I just want to go back to a forest on the spirit road. But the demon unmakes it."

"How do we get rid of it?"

Very reluctantly, Artemus said, "Someone must willingly die on the corpse road."

Darkness descended so rapidly on Blue's thoughts that she reached to balance herself on the beech tree. She saw Gansey's spirit walking the ley line in her mind. She remembered abruptly that Adam and Gansey were within earshot; she had completely forgotten that it was not just Artemus and her.

"Is there another way?" she asked.

Artemus's voice was quieter still. "Willing death to pay for unwilling death. That's the way."

There was silence, and then more silence, and finally, Gansey asked, his voice raised from next to the house, "What about waking Glendower and using that favour?"

But Artemus did not reply. She had missed the moment of him going: He was in the tree and the puzzle box sat askew in the roots. Blue was left holding this terrible truth and nothing else, not even a scrap of heroism.

"Please come back!" she said.

But there was only the stirring of dried leaves overhead.

"Well," Adam said, his voice as tired as Artemus's. "That's that."

FORTY-SEVEN

Night fell; that, at least, could still be relied upon.

Adam opened the driver's-side door to the BMW. Ronan had not moved a bit since they had seen him last; he was still looking down the road, feet on the pedals, hands resting on the steering wheel. Ready to go. Waiting for Gansey. It was not grief; it was a safer, more vacant place beyond it. Adam told Ronan, "You can't sleep here."

"No," Ronan agreed.

Adam stood in the dark street, shivering in the cold, stepping from foot to foot, looking for any evidence that Ronan might budge. It was late. Adam had called Boyd an hour ago to tell him that he would not be getting to the Chevelle with the exhaust leak he'd promised he would look at. Even if he could have forced himself awake – Adam could nearly always accomplish this – he wouldn't have been able to stand working in the garage knowing that Cabeswater was under attack, Laumonier was conspiring, and Ronan was mourning.

"Are you going to come inside and at least eat something?"

"No," Ronan said.

He was impossible and terrible.

Adam shut the door and lightly pounded his fist three times on the roof. Then he went to the other side of the car, opened the door, made sure Noah wasn't in there, and climbed in.

As Ronan watched him, he fumbled around with the seat controls until he found the one that made it recline all the way, and then he clawed for Ronan's Aglionby jacket. Both it and the Orphan Girl were hopelessly balled up among the other things in the backseat – the Orphan Girl snuffled and pushed the jacket towards his hand. He wadded it beneath his neck as a pillow, draping the sleeve over his eyes to block out the streetlight.

"Wake me up if you have to," he said, and closed his eyes.

Inside 300 Fox Way, Blue watched Gansey let himself be convinced to stay there instead of returning to Monmouth for the night. Even though there were now plenty of empty beds in the house, he took the couch, accepting just a quilt and a pillow with a light pink pillowcase. His eyes weren't closed by the time she went upstairs and put herself to bed in her own room. Everything felt too quiet inside the house, with everyone gone, and too loud outside the house, with everything menacing.

She did not sleep. She thought of her father becoming one with a tree, and she thought about Gansey sitting in the Camaro with his head ducked, and she thought about the whispered voice of the dark sleeper she'd encountered in the cave. Things felt like they were spooling to the end.

Sleep, she told herself.

Gansey slept in a room a dozen feet below her. It should not have mattered – it did not matter. But she could not stop thinking of the nearness of him, the impossibility of him. The promise of his death.

She was dreaming. It was dark. Her eyes didn't get used to it; her heart did. There was no light to speak of. It was so completely dark that eyes were unimportant. Now that she thought about it, she wasn't sure she had eyes. This was a strange idea. What did she have?

Cool damp at her feet. No. Her roots. Stars pressing down above her, so close that they could surely be reachable if only she grew a few more inches. A warm, vital skin of bark.

This was the shape of her soul. This was what she had been missing. This was how she felt in her human skin, tree-shaped feelings in a human body. What a slow, stretching joy.

Jane?

Gansey was there. He must have been there all along, because now that she thought about it, she couldn't stop sensing him there. She was something more; he was still human. He was a king stolen away into this tree by the *tir e e'lint* that was Blue. She was all around him. The joy from her previous revelation overlapped slowly on to this joy. He was still alive, she had him with her, she was as close to him as she could possibly be.

Where are we?

We're a tree. I'm a tree. You're — haha I can't say that. It would be filthy.

Are you laughing?

Yes, because I'm happy.

Slowly, her joy tapered, though, as she felt his rapid pulse against her. He was afraid.

What are you afraid of?

I don't want to die.

This felt true, but it was hard to put together thoughts with any speed. This tree was just as ill-fitted to her essential Blueness as her human body. She remained half one, half the other.

Can you see if Ronan has come in from the car?

I can try. I don't really have eyes.

She stretched out with all of the senses available to her. They were ever so much better than her human ones, but they were interested in very different things. It was exceptionally difficult to focus on the affairs of the humans around the base of the trunk. She had not properly appreciated how much effort it had taken the trees to attend to their needs before now.

I don't know. She held him tightly, loving him and keeping him. *We could just stay here.*

I love you, Blue, but I know what I have to do. I don't want to. But I know what I have to do.

FORTY-EIGHT

All of the sounds and smells of Fox Way were magnified after dark, when all of its human occupants were quiet. All of the fragrant teas and candles and spices became more distinct, each declaring their origin, when in daytime they mingled into something Gansey had only previously identified as *Fox Way*. Now it struck him as something both powerful and homey, secret and knowing. This house was a place of magic, same as Cabeswater, but one had to listen harder for it. Gansey lay on the couch with a quilt over him, his eyes closed against the dark, and listened to the rattle of air or breath through a vent somewhere, to the scratch of leaves or nails against a window somewhere, to the thump of popping wood or footsteps from the other room.

He opened his eyes, and there was Noah.

This was Noah without any daylight to cloud what he really had become. He was very close, because he had forgotten that the living could not focus on things closer than three inches. He was very cold, because he now required massive amounts of energy to remain visible. He was very afraid, and because Gansey was afraid, their thoughts tangled.

Gansey kicked off the quilt. He tied on his shoes and put on his jacket. Quietly, taking great care to tread lightly on these old floors, he followed Noah out of the living room. He didn't turn on any lights, because his mind was still tossed together with Noah's, and he was using Noah's eyes, which no longer cared if it was dark or not. The dead boy didn't take him outside, as he'd expected, however, but up the stairs to the second floor. For the first half of the stairs, Gansey thought that he was being led on Noah's usual haunt around the house, and for the second, he thought that he was being taken to Blue. But Noah passed her door and instead waited at the base of the attic stairs.

The attic was a charged location, having been occupied first by Neeve and then by Gwenllian, two people difficult in different ways. Gansey would not have regarded either of them as possible paths forward, but Noah had led him there, and so Gansey hesitated there with his hand over the knob. He did not want to knock; he would wake the rest of the house.

Noah pushed on the door.

It fell open lightly – it had not been latched – and Noah proceeded up the stairs. Wan light came from the top of them, accompanied by a biting chill scented with oak. It felt like a window was open.

Gansey followed Noah.

A window *was* open.

Gwenllian had turned the room to witchy clutter, and it was currently full of every strange thing but herself. Her bed was empty. Cold night air came through a round porthole window.

By the time Gansey had climbed through it, Noah had vanished.

"Hello, little king," Gwenllian greeted. She was far out on one of the house's small, mismatched roof angles, boots braced against the shingles, a dark and strange silhouette in the ambient and flickering light of the haunted streetlights below. There was nonetheless something noble about her, a brave and arrogant tilt to her chin. She patted the roof beside her.

"Is it safe?"

She cocked her head. "Is this how you die?"

He joined her, picking his way carefully, dirt and tree litter crumbling beneath his shoes, and then sat beside her. From this vantage point, there were trees and more trees. The oaks that were merely featureless trunks at ground level were complicated worlds of ascending branches at roof level, the patterns of them made more complex by the shadows thrown by the orange glow below.

"Hi ho hi ho," Gwenllian sang in a low, disdainful voice. "Are you coming to *me* for wisdom?"

Gansey shook his head. "Courage."

She appraised him.

"You tried to stop your father's war," Gansey said. "By stabbing his poet at the dinner table. You had to be almost certain it wouldn't end well for you. How did you do it?"

Her act of bravery had happened hundreds of years before. Glendower had not been fighting on Welsh soil for centuries now, and the man Gwenllian had tried to kill had been dead for generations. She'd been trying to save a family that now no longer existed; she'd lost everything to sit upon this roof of 300 Fox Way in a different world entirely.

"Haven't you learned yet? A king acts so that others will act. Nothing comes from nothing comes from nothing. But *something* makes *something*." She drew in the air with her long fingers, but Gansey did not think that she was drawing anything intended for a gaze other than her own. "I am Gwenllian Glen Dŵr, and I am the daughter of a king and the daughter of a tree-light, and I did *something* so that others would do *something*. That is kingly."

"But how?" Gansey asked. "How did you manage it?"

She pretended to stab him in the ribs. Then, when he looked at her ruefully, she laughed wildly and freely. After she had been merry for a full minute, she said, "I stopped asking *how*. I just did it. The head is too wise. The heart is all fire."

She did not say anything more, and he did not ask anything more. They sat there beside each other on the roof, she dancing her fingers through the air, he watching the lights of Henrietta dance similarly in time to some hidden and sputtering ley line.

Finally, he said, "Would you take my hand?"

Her fingers stopped moving, and she looked at him cannily, holding his gaze for a long minute, as if daring him to look away or change his mind. He did not.

Gwenllian leaned close, smelling of clove cigarettes and coffee, and much to his great surprise, kissed his cheek.

"Godspeed, King," she said, and took his hand.

In the end, it was such a simple, small thing. He had felt flashes of it before in his life, the absolute certainty. But the truth was that he'd kept walking away from it. It was a far more terrifying idea to imagine how much control he really had over how his life turned out. Easier to believe that he was a gallant ship tossed by fate than to captain it himself.

He would steer it now, and if there were rocks near shore, so be it.

"Tell me where Owen Glendower is," he said to the darkness. Crisp and sure, with the same power he had used to command Noah, to command the skeletons in the cave. "Show me where the Raven King is."

FORTY-NINE

The night began to wail.

The sound came from everywhere – a wild scream. A primal scream. A battle cry.

It got louder and louder, and Gansey clambered to his feet, his hands half-held over his ears. Gwenllian shouted something in delight and fervour, but the sound drowned out her voice. It drowned out the rattle of the remaining dry oak leaves in the trees, and it drowned out the sound of Gansey's shoes scuffing on the roof as he minced towards the edge for a better vantage point. The sound drowned out the lights, and the street was plunged into blackness. The scream drowned out everything, and when the sound stopped and the lights returned, a dull white-horned beast stood askance in the middle of the street down below, hooves splayed on the asphalt.

Somewhere there was the ordinary world, a world of stoplights and shopping malls, of fluorescent lights at gas stations and light blue carpet in a suburban home. But here, now: There was only the moment before the scream and the moment after.

Gansey's ears rang.

The creature lifted its head to look at him with brilliant eyes. It was the sort of animal that everyone thought they knew the name of until they saw it, and then the name ran away and left behind only the feeling of seeing it. It was older than anything, more lovely than anything, more terrible than anything.

Something winning and frightened sang in Gansey's chest; it was the precise same feeling that had taken him the first time he'd seen Cabeswater. He realized that he had seen something like this creature before: the herd of white beasts that had stampeded through Cabeswater. Now that he was looking at this one, though, he realized that those were copies of this, descendants of this, dreamt memories of this.

The beast twitched an ear. Then it plunged into the night.

Gwenllian asked Gansey, "Well, aren't you going to follow it?"

Yes.

She pointed at the oak branches, and he did not question her. He edged quickly to where a great branch overhung the roof, climbed out on to it, getting a handhold here and there on upright spurs. He slipped down from branch to branch and then jumped the eight or nine feet to the ground, feeling the jolt of the landing from the balls of his feet to his teeth.

The beast was gone.

There was not even time for Gansey to register disappointment, though, because of the birds.

They were everywhere: The air dazzled and shimmered with feathers and down. The birds swirled and dived and plummeted around the neighbourhood street, the streetlights catching wings, beaks, claws. Most of them were ravens, but there were others, too. Little chickadees, streamlined mourning doves, compact jays. These smaller birds seemed more chaotic than the ravens, though, as if they had gotten caught up in the spirit of the night without understanding the purpose. Some of them let out little squawks or cries, but mostly the sound was *wings*. The humming, rushing whoosh of frantic flight.

Gansey stepped into the yard and the dense flock immediately rushed up around him. They swirled around him, wings brushing against him, feathers touching his cheek. He couldn't see anything but the birds, every shape and colour. His heart was a winged thing itself. He couldn't catch his breath.

He was so afraid.

If you can't be unafraid, Henry said, *be afraid and happy.*

The flock dipped away. They meant to be followed, and they meant to be followed *now*. They swirled up in a great column over the Camaro.

Make way! they shouted. *Make way for the Raven King!* It was loud enough now that lights were beginning to come on in the houses.

Gansey climbed into the car and turned the key – *start, Pig, start.* It growled to life. Gansey was all things at once: elated, terrified, overcome, satiated.

With a squeal of tires, he pursued his king.

FIFTY

Ronan was operating on emergency battery power. Running on cruise control. He was a drop of water beaded on a windshield. The slightest jolt would be enough to send him skidding downward.

Because he was practising such a delicate balancing act between waking and sleep, it wasn't until the driver's-side door of the BMW wrenched open that he realized something had happened. The noise was terrific, particularly because Chainsaw flew into the car as soon as the door had opened. The Orphan Girl shrieked in the backseat and Adam jolted awake.

"I don't *know*," Blue said.

Ronan wasn't sure what this meant until he realized that she wasn't addressing him, but the people behind her. Maura, Calla and Gwenllian stood in the road in various states of night-time disarray.

"I told you, I told you," Gwenllian cawed. Her hair was a tangle of feathers and oak leaves.

"Were you sleeping?" Blue asked Ronan. He had not been sleeping. He hadn't been awake, though, either, not really. He stared at her. He had forgotten her wound until he was staring at it again; it was such a violent signature, written on her skin. So against everything Noah would ordinarily do. Everything backwards. *Demon, demon.* "Ronan. Did you see where Gansey went?"

Now he was awake.

"He's on the hunt!" Gwenllian shrilled gleefully.

"Shut *up*," Blue said, with unexpected rudeness. "Gansey's gone after Glendower. The Pig's gone. Gwenllian says he went after birds. Did you see where he went? He's not picking up his phone!"

She swept her hand dramatically behind her to demonstrate this truth. The empty kerb in front of 300 Fox Way, the street littered with feathers of all colours, the neighbours' doors opening and closing with curiosity.

"He can't go alone," Adam said. "He'll do something stupid."

"I'm infinitely aware," Blue replied. "I've called him. I've called Henry, to see if we could use RoboBee. No one's picking up. I don't even know if calls are going through."

"Can you locate him?" Adam asked Maura and Calla.

"He's tied into the ley line," Maura said. "Somehow. Somewhere. So I can't see him. That's all I know."

Ronan's mind was wobbling as reality began to jostle at him. The horror of every nightmare being made into truth jittered his fingers on the steering wheel.

"Maybe I can scry," Adam said. "I don't know that I'll know where it is, though. If he's somewhere I haven't been, I won't recognize it and we'll have to piece together clues."

Blue spun in an angry circle. "That will take for ever."

The feathers scattered across the street struck Ronan. Every fine edge of them seemed sharp and real and important against the fuzzed events of the days before. Gansey had gone after Glendower. Gansey had gone without them. Gansey had gone without *him*.

"I'll dream something," he said. No one heard him the first time, so he said it again.

"What?" Blue asked, at the same time that Maura said, "What kind of something?" and Adam said, "But the *demon*."

Ronan's mind was still a fresh horror of seeing his mother's body. The recent memory effortlessly cross-pollinated with the older one of finding his father's body, creating a toxic and expanding flower. He did not want to go back into his head right now. But he would. "Something to find Gansey. Like Henry Cheng's RoboBee. It only has to have one purpose. Something small. I can do it fast."

"You could be killed fast, you mean," Adam said.

Ronan did not reply to this. Already he was trying to think of what form he could swiftly invest with such a skill. What could he most reliably create, even with the hurricane of the demon distracting him? What could he be certain the demon wouldn't corrupt even as he manifested it?

"Cabeswater can't help you," Adam pressed. "It can only hinder you. You'd have to try to create something not terrible among all that, which seems impossible to start, and then you'd have to bring back that, *and only that*, from the dream, which sounds even *more* impossible."

Ronan addressed the steering wheel. "I'm aware of how dreaming works, Parrish."

He did not say *I can't stand the idea of finding Gansey's body, too.* He did not say *If I can't save my old family, I can save my new one.* He did not say *I will not let the demon have everything.*

He did not say that the only true nightmare was not being able to do something and that this, at least, was *something*.

He just said, "I'm going to try," and hoped that Adam knew all of the rest already.

Adam did. So did the others.

Maura said, "We'll do our best to support your energy and hold back some of the worst."

Adam put the seatback in its fully upright and locked position. He said, "I'll scry."

"Blue," Ronan said, "I think you'd better hold his hand."

FIFTY-ONE

The Camaro broke down.

It was *always* breaking down and living again, but tonight – tonight, Gansey needed it.

It broke down anyway. He'd only got to the outskirts of town when it coughed, and the lights inside dimmed. Before Gansey even had time to react, the car had died. His power brakes and steering vanished and he had to wrestle it to the shoulder. He tried the key, looked in the mirror, tried to see if the birds were waiting. They were not.

Make way for the Raven King! they shouted, sailing on. *Make way!*
Damn this car!

Not so long ago, the car had died in just the same way in a pitch-black night, leaving him stranded by the side of the road, nearly getting him killed. Adrenaline hit him in the same way as it had that night, immediate and complete, like time had never progressed.

He pumped the gas, let it sit, pumped the gas, let it sit.

The birds were drawing away. He could not follow.

"Come on," he pleaded. *"Come on."*

The Camaro did not *come on*. The ravens cried furiously; they did not seem to want to leave him, but also seemed to be pulled by a force beyond them. With a soft swear, he scrambled out of the car and slammed the door. He didn't know what he would do. He would give chase on foot, until he had lost them. He would —

"Gansey."

Henry Cheng. He stood before Gansey, his Fisker parked askance in the street behind him, door hanging open. "What's happening?"

The impossibility of Henry's presence hit Gansey harder than anything else that night, even though it was actually the least impossible thing. They were not far from Litchfield's side of town, and Henry had clearly arrived to this place by means automotive rather than magical. But still, the timing was too clearly on Gansey's side, and Henry, unlike the ravens, could not have appeared just because Gansey bade him to.

"How are you here?" Gansey demanded.

Henry pointed up into the sky. Not at the birds, but at the tiny, winking body of RoboBee. "RoboBee was told to tell me if you needed me. So I say again unto thee: What's happening?"

The ravens were still crying for Gansey to follow. They were getting even further; soon he wouldn't be able to see them. His pulse rummaged in his chest. With great effort, he made himself focus on Henry's question. "The Camaro won't start. Those birds. They're taking me to Glendower. I have to *go*, I have to follow them or they'll be —"

"Stop. Stop. Get in my car. You know what? You drive. This thing scares the piss out of me."

Henry tossed him the keys.

He got in.

There was a sick rightness to it, as if somehow, Gansey had always known this was how the chase would go. As they left the

Camaro behind, time was slipping and he was inside of it. Above them, the ravens burst and tumbled through the black. They were sometimes stark against buildings, sometimes invisible against trees. They flashed and flickered before the last of the town's streetlights like fan blades. Gansey and Henry drove through the last vestiges of civilization into the countryside. Henrietta was so large in Gansey's mind that he was somewhat surprised to see, when he was not paying attention to it, how quickly the lights of the small town vanished in his rearview mirror.

Out of Henrietta, the ravens streamed and bobbed north. They flew faster than Gansey thought birds ought to be able to fly, ducking into trees and valleys. Pursuing them was not a simple matter; the ravens flew dead-on straight, while the Fisker had to stick to roads. His heart screamed at him, *Don't lose them. Don't lose him. Not now.*

He could not shake the idea that this was his only chance.

His head was not thinking. His heart was thinking.

"Go, go, go," Henry said. "I'll watch for cops. *Go, go, go.*"

He typed something into the phone and then ducked his head to look out of the car to watch RoboBee spin away to do his work.

Gansey went went went.

Northeast, through tangled roads Gansey had probably been on before but didn't remember. Hadn't he crawled over this entire state? The ravens led them over the mountains on twisting roads that turned to dirt and then back to asphalt. At one point, the Fisker clung to the side of a mountain and looked down a steep drop with nary a guardrail in sight. Then the road turned back to asphalt and trees hid the sky.

The ravens were instantly invisible behind the night-black branches, flying off in some direction without them.

Gansey slammed on the brakes and rolled down the window. Henry, without any questions, did the same. Both boys tilted their heads and listened. Winter trees creaked in the breeze; distant trucks rolled on the highway below; ravens called urgently to one another.

"There," Henry said immediately. "Right."

The Fisker charged ahead. They were headed along the ley line, Gansey thought. How far would the ravens fly? Washington, D.C.? Boston? All the way across the Atlantic? He had to believe they wouldn't go where he could not follow. It ended tonight, because Gansey had said it ended tonight, and he had meant it.

The birds continued on, unerring. An interstate sign loomed in the dark.

"Does that say 66?" Gansey said. "Is that the ramp for 66?"

"I don't know, man. Numbers confuse me."

It was I-66. The birds swept forward; Gansey got on to the interstate. It was faster, but a little risky. There were no options to turn off if the ravens altered their path.

The birds didn't waver. Gansey poured on speed, and more speed.

The birds were headed along the ley line, taking Gansey back towards Washington, D.C., and his childhood home. He had a sudden, terrible thought that that was precisely where they were leading him. Back to the Gansey home in Georgetown, where he learned that his ending was his beginning, and he finally accepted that he had to grow up to be just another Gansey with all that entailed.

"What did you say this was? I-66?" Henry asked, typing in his phone again as another sign flew by them proclaiming the fact of I-66.

"However do you drive?"

"I don't. You do. Mile marker?"

"Eleven."

Henry studied his phone, his face blue by its light. "Hey. Hey. Slow up. Cop in a mile."

Gansey let the Fisker glide down to something closer to the speed limit. Sure enough, the dark paint of an unmarked police car glistened in the median a little less than a mile from when Henry had noted it. Henry saluted him as they drove by.

"Thank you for your service, RoboBee."

Gansey let out a breathless laugh. "OK, now you – wait. Can RoboBee find us an exit?"

The ravens had been getting slightly further away from the interstate with each mile, and now it was becoming quite clear that they were diverging in a permanent way.

Henry tapped into his phone. "Two miles. Exit 23."

Two miles in an ever-widening triangle would put a lot of space between the ravens and the car. "Can RoboBee keep up with the birds?"

"I'll find out."

So they barreled on ahead as the flock grew harder to see in the darkness and eventually disappeared. Gansey's pulse raced. He had to trust Henry; Henry had to trust RoboBee. At the exit, Gansey sent the Fisker racing off the interstate. There was no sign of the ravens: only ordinary Virginia night all around them. He felt strange as he recognized where they were, near Delaplane, quite far from Henrietta now. This was a world of old money, horse farms, and politicians and tyre-company billionaires. It was not a place of archaic wild magic. By day it would reveal itself as a place of genteel loveliness, a place so long beloved and cultivated that it was impossible to imagine it running amok.

"Where now?" Gansey asked. They were driving into nowhere, into ordinariness, into a life Gansey had already lived.

Henry didn't immediately reply, his head bowed over his phone. Gansey wanted to stomp the gas, but there was no point if they were going the wrong way.

"Henry."

"Sorry sorry. Got it! Floor it, turn right when you can."

Gansey did as directed with such efficiency that Henry placed a hand on the ceiling to brace himself.

"Yay," said Henry. "Also, woo."

And then, suddenly, there were the ravens again, the flock tumbling and remaking itself above the tree line, perfect black against the deep purple sky. Henry pounded the ceiling in silent triumph. The Fisker wheeled on to a broad, four-lane highway, empty in both directions. Gansey had only begun to accelerate again when the ravens swirled up in a tornado of birds, tossed aloft by an invisible updraught, changing course abruptly. The Fisker's headlights found a real-estate sign at the end of a driveway.

"There. There!" Henry said. "Stop!"

He was right. The birds had peeled up the driveway. Gansey had already blown by it. He scanned ahead; there was no turn-around immediately in view. He would not lose the birds. He would *not* lose them. Rolling down his window, he craned his head out the window to be sure the night road behind him was still black, then backed up, the transmission whining in excitement.

"Aight," said Henry.

The Fisker climbed the steep driveway. Gansey didn't even pause as he considered that someone might be home. It was late, he was strange and memorable in this fancy car, and this was a private corner of an old-fashioned world. It didn't matter. He would think of something to say to the home owners if it came to that. He would not leave the ravens. Not this time.

The headlights illuminated ill-kept grandeur: the oversized teeth of landscaping stones lining the driveway, grass growing between them; a four-board fence with a board hanging loose; asphalt cracked and spewing dead weeds.

The sensation of time slipping was even greater now. He had been here before. He had done this, or lived this life before.

"This place, man," Henry said, craning his neck, trying to look. "It's a museum."

The driveway climbed until it rose above the tree line and reached the crest. There was a grand circle at the end of the drive, and behind that, a dark and looming house. No, not house. Gansey, who had grown up in a mansion, knew a mansion when he saw one. This one was far larger than his parents' current home, adorned with columns and roof decks and porticoes and conservatories, a sprawling entity of brick and cream. Unlike his parents' home, however, this mansion's boxwoods were overgrown by weedy tall locust trees, and the ivy had crawled off the brick walls on to the stairs leading to the front door. The rosebushes had shot up uneven and ugly.

"Not a lot of kerb appeal," Henry noted. "Bit of a fixer-upper. Would be some great zombie parties on the roof though, yo."

As the Fisker pulled slowly around the circle, the ravens watched them from the roof and the roof deck railings. Déjà vu plucked at Gansey's mind, like looking at Noah and seeing both the living and dead version of him.

Gansey touched his lower lip pensively. "I've been here."

Henry peered up at the ravens, who peered back, unmoving. Waiting. "When?"

"This is where I died."

FIFTY-TWO

Ronan had known before he fell asleep that Cabeswater was going to be unbearable, but he had not realized how unbearable.

It was not the sights that were the worst; it was the emotions. The demon was still working on the trees and the ground and the sky, but it was also corrupting the *feel* of the forest, the things that make a dream a dream even if there is no scenery in it. Now it was every guilty breath sucked in after a sort-of lie. It was the drop of the stomach after finding a body. It was the gnawing suspicion that you were leavable, that you were too much trouble, that you were better off dead. It was the shame of wanting something you shouldn't; it was the ugly thrill of nearly being dead. It was all of those things, all at once.

Ronan's nightmares used to be one or two of these things. Only rarely were they all. That was back when they wanted him dead.

The difference was that he'd been alone in those. Now Maura and Calla were supporting him in the waking world — Calla sitting on his hood and Maura sitting in the backseat. He could feel their energy like hands around his head, blocking out some of the dreadful sound. And he had Adam's mind here in the dream with him. In the real world, he was scrying in the passenger seat again, and in this one, he stood in this ruined forest, hunched over, face unsure.

No. Ronan had to admit to himself that even though they made it easier, their presence wasn't the real difference between his old nightmares and this one. The real difference was that, back then, the nightmares had wanted him dead, and so had Ronan.

He looked around for some safe place in the dream, someplace that his creation might possibly develop in safety. There was no such place. The only uncorrupted things in the dream were Adam and himself.

So he would hold it himself. Ronan pressed his palms together, imagining a tiny ball of light forming there. The demon did not care for this. In his ear, he heard a gasp. Unmistakably his father. Unmistakably in pain. Dying alone.

Your fault.

Ronan pushed it away. He kept thinking about the tiny brilliant thing that he was forming to find Gansey. He imagined its weight, its size, the pattern of its miniature wings.

"Did you really think I'm going to stay in this place for you?" Adam said in his other ear, all chilly dismissal.

The real Adam was standing with his head turned to the side as an unreasonable facsimile of his father screamed in his face, the cadence of his voice perfectly and eerily matched to the real Robert Parrish. There was a firm set to Adam's mouth that was less fear and more stubbornness. He had been slowly untangling himself from his real father for weeks; this duplicate was easier to resist.

Leavable.

I'm not asking him to stay, Ronan thought. *Only to come back.* He wanted badly to check if the object in his hands was what he intended it to be, but he could feel how the demon longed to corrupt the object, to turn it inside out, to make it opposite and ugly. Better to keep it hidden from sight for now, trusting only that he was creating something positive. He had to hold on to the idea of what it was supposed to do when it was brought back to waking life, and not the demon's idea of what it wanted the object to do when brought back to waking life.

Something was scratching at Ronan's neck. Lightly, harmlessly, repeatedly, relentlessly, until it had worked its way through the topmost layer of his skin and found blood.

Ronan ignored it and felt the object in his hand stir to life against his fingers.

The dream splattered a body in front of him. Black and torn, ripped and corrupt. Gansey. Eyes still alive, mouth moving. Ruined and helpless. A claw from one of Ronan's night horrors was still hooked in the corner of his mouth, punched through his cheek.

Powerless.

No. Ronan didn't think so. He felt the dream fluttering against the palms of his hands.

Adam met Ronan's gaze, even as the duplicate version of his father kept screaming at him. The strain of whatever energy balance he was doing was visible on his face. "Are you ready?"

Ronan hoped so. The truth was that they really wouldn't know who'd won this round until he opened his eyes in the BMW. He said, "Wake me up."

FIFTY-THREE

Gansey had been here before — seven years and some change. Impossibly, it had been for another Congressional fund-raiser. Gansey remembered that he had been excited to go. Washington, D.C., in the summer was airless and close, its inhabitants reluctant hostages, bags over their heads. Although the Ganseys had just taken an overseas trip to visit mint farms in Punjab (a political trip that Gansey still didn't fully understand the purpose of), the travel had only served to make the youngest Gansey more restless. The only backyard their Georgetown house had was filled wall to wall with flowers older than Gansey, and he was forbidden to go into it during high summer, because the backyard drowsed with bees. And although his parents took him to antiques shows and museums, horse races and art shindigs, Gansey's feet grew itchier. He had seen all of these things. He felt greedy for new curiosities and wonders, for things he had never seen before and things he couldn't understand. He wanted to go.

So although he was not excited by the idea of politics, he had been excited by the idea of leaving.

"It will be fun," his father had said. "There will be other children there."

"Martin's kids," his mother had added, and the two of them exchanged a private snigger over a long-ago slight.

It had taken Gansey a moment to realize that they were offering this as an incentive rather than merely reporting the fact as a weather update. Gansey had never found children fun, including the child he had been. He had always looked to a future where he could change his own address at will.

Now, years later, Gansey stood on the ivy-tangled staircase and looked at the plaque by the door. THE GREEN HOUSE, it read. EST. 1824. Up close, it was hard to say precisely why the property looked grotesque rather than merely shaggy. The attendance of ravens on every horizontal surface of the house didn't hurt. He tried the front door: locked. He clicked on the torch function on his phone and leaned against the sidelight windows, trying to see inside. He didn't know what he was looking for. He would know it when he saw it, maybe. Perhaps a back door was unlocked, or a window could be slid open. Though there was no particular reason why the interior of the neglected house should hold any secrets relevant to Gansey, the part of him that was good at finding things battered silently against the glass, wanting in.

"Look at this," Henry called from a few yards away. His voice was theatrically shocked. "I have discovered that, at some point, this side door was broken into by a teenage Korean vandal."

Gansey had to pick across a bed of dead lilies to join him at a less elaborate side entrance. Henry had finished the work of a cracked windowpane in order to reach inside and open the lock. "Kids these days. 'Cheng' isn't Korean, is it?"

"My father isn't," Henry said. "I am. I got that, and the vandal part, from my mother. Let us enter, Dick, as I've already broken."

Gansey hesitated, though, outside the door. "You had RoboBee looking out for me."

"It was friendly. That was a friend thing."

He seemed anxious for Gansey to believe that his motives were pure, so Gansey said quickly, "I know that. Just – I don't meet many people who make friends like I do. So – fast."

Henry flipped crazy devil horns at him. "*Jeong*, bro."

"What's that mean?"

"Who knows," Henry said. "It means being Henry. It means being Richardman. *Jeong. You* never say the word, but you live it anyway. I will be honest, I did not expect to find it in a guy such as yourself. It's like we've met each other before. No, not really. We are friends at once, we would instantly do what friends would do for each other. Not just pals. Friends. Blood brothers. You just feel it. *We* instead of *you* and *me*. That's *jeong*."

Gansey was aware on a certain level that the description was melodramatic, heightened, illogical. But on a deeper level, it felt true, and familiar, and like it explained much of Gansey's life. It was how he felt about Ronan and Adam and Noah and Blue. With each of them, it had felt instantly right: relieving. Finally, he'd thought, he'd found them. *We* instead of *you* and *me*.

"OK," he said.

Henry smiled brilliantly, and then opened the door he had just broken. "Now, what are we looking for?"

"I'm not sure," Gansey admitted. He was captured by the familiar scent of the house: whatever it was that made all these old rambling Colonials smell like they did. Mould and boxwood and old floor polish, perhaps. He was struck by not a precise memory, but rather a more carefree era. "Something unusual, I suppose. I think it'll be obvious."

"Should we split up, or is this a horror movie?"

"Scream if something eats you," Gansey said, relieved that Henry had offered to split up. He wanted to be alone with his thoughts. He switched off his torch just as Henry switched his on. Henry looked as if he was about to ask why, and then Gansey would be forced to say *Makes my instincts louder*, but Henry merely shrugged as they parted ways.

In the silence, Gansey wandered through the dim halls of the Green House, ghosts dogging his heels. Here had been a buffet; here had been a piano; here had been a pack of political interns that had seemed so worldly. He stood in the very centre of what had been the ballroom. A motion light triggered outside as Gansey walked further into the room, startling him. There was a wide fireplace with an ugly, dated hearth and an ominous black mouth. Dead flies littered the windowsills. Gansey felt as if he were the last man left alive.

The room had seemed enormous before. If he squinted his eyes, he could still see the party. It was always happening at some point in time. If this were Cabeswater, perhaps he could replay that party, skipping back in time to watch it again. The thought was at once wistful and unpleasant: He had been younger and easier then, unfettered by anything like responsibility or wisdom. But he had done so much between now and then. The idea of living through it again, learning all the hard lessons again, struggling to once again ensure that he met Ronan and Adam, Noah and Blue — it was exhausting, nerve-racking.

Leaving the ballroom, he trailed through hallways, ducking under arms no longer there, excusing himself as he pressed through conversations long since ended. There was champagne; there was music; there was the pervasive smell of cologne. *How are you, Dick?* He was fine, excellent, capital, the only possible answers to that question. The sun always shone on him.

He stepped on to a screen porch and looked out at the black November. The ragged grass was gray in the motion light; the naked trees were black; the sky was dully purple from the distant threat of Washington, D.C. Everything was dead.

Did he still know any of the children he'd played with at that party? Hide-and-seek: He'd hidden so well that he'd become dead, and even when he'd been resurrected, he was still obscured from them. He had stumbled on to a different road by accident.

He pushed open the screen door and stepped on to the damp dead grass of the backyard. The party had been here, too, the older children playing a frustrated game of croquet, the wickets hooked on the toes of servers.

The gray motion light Gansey had triggered before shone across the backyard. He crossed the lawn to the edge of the trees. The porch light filtered all the way out here, and penetrated further than he would have expected. It was not as unruly as he remembered it, though he couldn't decide if it was because he was older and had prowled through more woods now, or if it was merely because it was a leaner season of the year. It did not look like a place one could hide now.

When Gansey had gone to Wales to search for Glendower, he had stood on the edge of many fields like this, places where battles had been fought. He'd tried to imagine what it had been like to be there in that moment, sword in hand, horse beneath him, men sweating and bleeding. What had it been to be Owen Glendower, to know that they fought because you called them to?

While Malory had loitered on the path or hovered by the car, Gansey had strode to the middle of the fields, as far away as he could get from anything modern. He had closed his eyes, tuned out the sound of faraway airplanes, tried to hear the sounds of six hundred years previous. The youngest version of him had borne tiny hope that he might be haunted; that the field might be haunted; that he might open his eyes and see something more than what he had before.

But he had not the slightest psychic inclinations, and the minute that began with Gansey alone in a battlefield ended with Gansey alone in a battlefield.

Now he stood there on the edge of the Virginia forest for perhaps a minute, until the very act of standing felt odd, as if his legs shook, though they didn't. Then he stepped in.

The bare branches overhead creaked in the breeze, but the leaves beneath his feet were damp and soundless.

Seven years ago he had stepped on the hornets here. Seven years ago he had died. Seven years ago he had been born again.

He had been so afraid.

Why had they brought him back?

Twigs caught the sleeves of his sweater. He was not yet to the place it had happened. He told himself that the nest would no longer be there; the fallen tree he had collapsed beside would have rotted; it was too dark in this ghost light; he wouldn't recognize it.

He recognized it.

The tree had not rotted. It was unchanged, as sturdy as before, but black with damp and with night.

This was where he had felt the first sting. Gansey stretched out his arm, examining the back of his own hand in shocked wonder. He took another step, faltering. This was where he'd felt them on the back of his neck, crawling along his hairline. He didn't smack the sensation; it never helped to brush them away. His fingers, though, twitched upward, resisting.

He took another uncertain step. He was a foot away from that old, unchanged black tree. That long-ago Gansey had stumbled to his knees. They had crawled over his face here, over his closed eyelids, along quivering lips.

He had not run. There was no running from them, and in any case, the weapon had done its work already. He remembered thinking that it would only ruin the party by reappearing covered with hornets.

He caught himself on his hands, only for a moment, and then rolled on to his elbow. Poison razed his veins. He was on his side. He was curled. Wet leaves pressed against his cheek as every part of him seemed to suffocate. He was shaking and done and afraid, so afraid.

Why? he wondered. *Why me? What was the purpose of it?*

He opened his eyes.

He was standing, hands fisted, looking at the place it had happened. He must have been saved to find Glendower. He must have been saved to kill this demon.

"Dick! Gansey! Dick! Gansey!" Henry's voice carried across the yard. "You'll want to see this."

FIFTY-FOUR

There was a cave opening beneath the house. Not a grand, aboveground opening like the cave they'd entered in Cabeswater. And not the sheltered hole-in-the-ground entrance they'd used to enter the cavern Gwenllian had been buried in. This was a wet, wide-open maw of an opening, all collapsed ramps of dirt spread over concrete bones and bits of furniture, the ground splitting and part of a basement falling into the resulting pit. The freshness of it made Gansey warily suspect that it had opened as a result of his command to Chainsaw back at Fox Way.

He had asked to see the Raven King. He was being shown the way to the Raven King, no matter what earth had to be moved to make that happen.

"It really is a helluva fixer-upper," Henry said, because someone had to say it. "I feel like they should possibly renovate this basement if they want to get a good sale price. Hardwood floors, update the doorknobs, *maybe put the wall back.*"

Gansey joined him at the edge of the chasm and peered in. Both of them shone the lights on their phones into the pit. Unlike the fresh wound of the opening, the cavern below looked worn and dry and dusty, like it had always existed beneath the house. It was merely this entrance that had been invented in response to his request.

Gansey looked out the window at the Fisker parked out front, mentally aligning himself with the highway, with Henrietta, with the ley line. Of course, he already knew this house was on the ley line. Hadn't it been said at the very beginning that he had only survived his death on the ley line because someone else was dying elsewhere on it?

He wondered if there had ever been an easier way to get to this cavern. Was there another natural opening elsewhere along the line, or had it been waiting all along for him to order it to reveal itself?

"Well," Gansey said eventually. "I'm going in."

Henry laughed, and then realized that he was serious. "Shouldn't you have a helmet and a manservant for expeditions like that?"

"Probably. But I don't think I have time to go back to Henrietta for my equipment. I'll just have to go slowly."

He didn't ask Henry to come along, because he didn't want Henry to have to feel bad when he said that he wasn't coming along. He didn't want Henry to feel that Gansey had ever expected him to do such a thing along with him, to climb into a hole in the ground when the only thing Henry really feared was holes in the ground.

Gansey removed his watch and put it in his pocket so it would not catch on anything if he had to climb. Then he cuffed his trousers and considered the entrance once more. It was not a terrible drop down, but he wanted to be sure he could get back out of it if he returned and no one else was there to help him out. With a frown, he fetched one of the chairs that had not been destroyed in the collapse. He lowered it into the blackness; once he righted it, it would give him the few extra feet he'd need to scramble back out.

Henry watched all of this and then said, "Wait. You're going to junk up your nice coat, white man. Take this." He shouldered out of his Aglionby sweater and proffered it.

"So you're literally giving me the shirt off your back," Gansey said, swapping him for his coat. He was grateful. He looked up to Henry. "See you on the other side. *Excelsior.*"

FIFTY-FIVE

As Gansey walked through the tunnel, he felt a sort of insane joy and sadness rising in him, higher and higher. There was nothing around him but a featureless stone pathway, but still, he could not shake the rightness of it. He had imagined this moment so many times, and now that he was in it, he could not remember the difference between imagining it and experiencing it. There was no dissonance between expectation and reality, as there always had been before. He had meant to find Glendower, and now he was finding Glendower.

Joy and sadness, too big for his body to contain.

He could feel the time-slipping sensation again. Down here, it was palpable, like water rushing over his thoughts. He had a thought that it was not just time that was slipping around him, but distance. It was possible this tunnel was folding back in on itself and taking him to an entirely different location along the ley line. He kept an eye on his mobile phone battery as he walked; it drained quickly with the torch function on. Every time he glanced at the screen, the time had changed in some impossible way: sometimes moving forward twice as fast, sometimes jerking backwards, sometimes sitting on the same minute for four hundred of Gansey's steps. Sometimes the screen flickered and went out entirely, taking the torch with it, leaving him in a second of blackness, two seconds, four.

He wasn't sure what he would do once he was left in darkness. He had already discovered on previous caving missions that it was very easy to fall into a hole, even with a torch. Even though the cave now appeared to be more hallway than cavern, there was no telling where it would end up.

He had nothing to trust but the ravens and the feeling of rightness. All of his footsteps had led him to this moment, surely.

He had to believe the light wouldn't go out before he got there. This was the night, this was the hour; all of this time he was supposed to be alone for this.

So he walked and walked, as his battery flickered up and down. Mostly down.

When it was only a warning-red sliver, he hesitated. He could turn back now, and he might have light for a little bit. The rest of the walk would be in darkness, but at least he knew there had been no pitfalls in it during his trip down. Or he could keep going until the very last bit of light was gone, hoping to find something. Hoping he wouldn't need it once he got to wherever he was going.

"Jesus," Gansey breathed out loud. He was a book, and he was holding his final pages, and he wanted to get to the end to find out how it went, and he didn't want it to be over.

He kept walking.

Sometime later, the light went out. His phone was dead. He was in utter blackness.

Now that he was standing still, he realized it was also chilly. A cool bit of water dripped on the crown of his head, and another slid down the collar of his shirt. He could feel the shoulders of

Henry's borrowed sweater getting wet. The darkness was like an actual thing, crowding him.

He could not decide what to do. Did he press forward in the dark, inch by inch? Now that he was in absolute blackness, he remembered well the sensation of the ground being robbed from him in the cave of the ravens. There was no safety rope to catch him here. No Adam to keep him from sliding in further. No Ronan to tell the humming swarms to be ravens instead of wasps. No Blue to whisper to him until he was once again brave enough to rescue himself.

The darkness wasn't just in the tunnel; it was inside him.

"Do you not want me to find you?" he whispered. "Are you here?"

The tunnel was silent except for the faint pat of water dropping from the ceiling to the stone floor.

Fear mounted in him. Fear, when it was Gansey, had a very specific form. And unlike the hole beneath Borden House, fear had power in a place like this.

He realized that the tunnel was no longer quiet. Instead, a sound had begun to form in the distance: an intensely familiar note.

Swarm.

This was not a single insect travelling down the hall. Not RoboBee. This was the oscillating wail of hundreds of bodies bouncing off the walls as they approached.

And even though it was dark in the tunnel, Gansey could *feel* the blackness that had bled out of that Cabeswater tree.

Gansey could see the entire story spread out in his head: how he had been saved from a death by stinging a little over seven years before, as Noah died. And now, as Noah's spirit decayed, Gansey would die by stinging again. Perhaps there had never been a purpose to all this except to return to the status quo.

The hum came closer. Now the gaps in the buzzing were punctuated by nearly inaudible taps, insects ricocheting through the dark towards him.

He remembered what Henry had said when he put the bee in Gansey's hand. He'd told him not to think of it as something that could kill him, but rather as something that might be beautiful.

He could do that. He thought he could do that.

Something beautiful, he told himself. *Something noble.*

The buzzing hummed-struck-hummed against the walls close to him. It was hideously loud.

They were here.

"Something that won't hurt me," he said out loud.

His vision went red and then black.

Red, then black.

Then just black.

"Leaves," Ronan Lynch's voice said, full of intention.

"Dust," Adam Parrish said.

"Wind," Blue Sargent said.

"Shit," Henry Cheng added.

Light striped across Gansey and away, red and then black again. A torch.

In the first sweep of the light, Gansey thought the walls were trembling with hornets, but in the second, he saw that they were only leaves and dust and a breeze that sent them all scuttling down the tunnel. And in this new light, Gansey saw his friends shivering in the tunnel where the leaves had been.

"You dumb shit," said Ronan. His shirt was very grubby, and the side of his face had dried blood on it, although it was impossible to tell if it was his own.

Gansey couldn't immediately find his voice, and when he did, he said, "I thought you were staying behind."

"Yeah, me too," Henry said. "Then I thought, I can't let Gansey Three wander around in the mysterious pit alone. We have such few old treasures left; it would be so careless to let them get destroyed. Plus, someone had to bring the rest of your court."

"Why would you go alone?" Blue asked. She flung her arms around him, and he felt her trembling.

"I was trying to be heroic," Gansey said, holding her tight. She was real. They were all real. They'd all come here for him, in the middle of the night. The completeness of his shock told him that no part of him had really thought they would do such a thing for him. "I didn't want you guys to hurt any more."

Adam said, "You dumb shit."

They laughed restlessly, uneasily, because they needed to. Gansey pressed his cheek against the top of Blue's head. "How did you find me?"

"Ronan nearly died making something to track you," Adam said. He pointed, and Ronan opened his hand to show a firefly nestled in his palm. The moment his fingers stopped being a cage for it, it flew to Gansey and stuck upon his sweater.

Gansey plucked it carefully from the fabric and cradled it in his own hand. He glanced up at Ronan. He didn't say *I'm sorry*, but he was, and Ronan knew. Instead, he said, "Now what?"

"Tell me to ask RoboBee to find your king," Henry replied immediately.

But Gansey had only ever been in the business of ordering magic and never in the business of ordering people. It was not the Gansey way to *command* anyone to do anything. They asked, and hoped. Did unto others and silently hoped that they would do unto them.

They'd come here for him. They'd come here for him.

They'd come here for him.

"Please," Gansey said. "Please help me."

Henry tossed the bee into the air. "I thought you'd never ask."

FIFTY-SIX

Gansey wasn't sure how long they'd been walking when he finally found it.

In the end, this was how it looked: a raven-carved stone door and a dreamt bee crawling over the ivy. The tunnel behind them had led out of a house from Gansey's unmagical youth, not a forest from Gansey's extraordinary present. It was nothing as he had daydreamed it might look.

It felt exactly right.

He stood before the carving, feeling time slipping around him, him motionless in the rushing pool of it.

"Do you feel it?" he asked the others. *Or is it only me?*

Blue said, "Come closer with the torch."

Henry had been hanging back, a newcomer to this search, waiting politely. Instead of crowding them, he handed her the torch. Blue held it close to the stone, illuminating the fine details. Unlike the previous tomb they'd found, which was carved with a likeness of a knight, this one was carved with ravens upon ravens. Ronan had kicked in the previous tomb they had discovered, but he touched this one carefully. Adam just looked at it in a distant way, his hands clasped together as if they were cold. Gansey reached for his phone to take the usual photo to document the search, remembered his phone was dead, and then wondered if there was any point to it if this was indeed Glendower's tomb.

No. This moment was for him, not the general public.

He put his hand on the door, flat, fingers splayed, experimental. The easy rocking of it indicated that it would open easily.

"There's no chance this guy is evil, is there?" Henry asked. "I'm really too young to die. Really, really too young."

Gansey had been given enough time in seven years to contemplate every possible option for the king behind this door. He had read the accounts of Glendower's life enough to know that Glendower could be either a hero or a villain depending on where you regarded him from. He had pulled Glendower's daughter from her tomb and found that it had driven her mad. He had read legends that promised favours and legends that promised death. Some stories had Glendower alone; some stories had him surrounded by dozens of sleeping knights who woke with him.

Some stories – their story – had a demon in them.

"You can wait outside if you're worried, Cheng," Ronan said, but his bravado was thin as a spiderweb, and Henry brushed it away as easily as one.

Gansey said, "I can't guarantee anything about what's on the other side of this. We're all in agreement that the favour is to kill the demon, right?"

They were.

Gansey pressed his hands to the death-cold stone. It shifted easily beneath the weight of him, some clever mechanism allowing the heavy stone to turn. Or perhaps no mechanism at all, Gansey thought. Perhaps some dreamstuff, some fanciful creation that didn't have to follow the rules of physics.

The torch illuminated the interior of the tomb.

Gansey stepped inside.

The walls of Gwenllian's tomb had been richly painted, birds upon birds chasing more birds, in reds and blues unfaded by light. Armour and swords hung on the walls, waiting for the sleeper to be woken. The coffin had been elevated and covered with an intricately carved lid featuring an effigy of Glendower. The entire tomb had been befitting royalty.

This tomb, on the other hand, was simply a room.

The ceiling was low and hewn into the rock: Gansey had to duck his head a little; Ronan had to duck his head a lot. The walls were bare rock. The torch beam found a broad, dark bowl sitting on the floor; there was a darker circle in the bottom of it. Gansey knew enough by now to recognize a scrying bowl. Blue swept the torch further. A square slab sat in the middle of the room; a knight in armour lay on top of it, uncovered and unburied. There was a sword by his left hand, a cup by his right.

It was Glendower.

Gansey had seen this moment.

Time slid more generously around him. He could feel it eddying around his ankles, weighting his legs. There was no noise. There was nothing to make noise, except for the five watchful teens in the room.

He did not feel particularly real.

"Gansey," whispered Adam. The room swallowed the sound.

Blue's torch pointed past the armoured figure to the floor beyond. It was a second body. They all exchanged a dark look before beginning to creep slowly towards it. Gansey was hyperaware of the dry scrape of his footsteps, and as one, they all paused and looked back at the tomb door. In a normal world, it would be a simple thing to talk themselves out of the fear of the door slamming shut. But they hadn't lived in a normal world for a long time.

Blue continued to illuminate the body with the torch. It was boots and bones and some sort of disintegrating garment of indeterminate colour. It was sprawled partially against the wall, skull propped up as if gazing at its own feet.

What am I doing? Gansey thought.

"Did they die trying to do what we're doing?" Adam asked.

"Only if waking kings was a historical pastime," Henry replied, "because this guy was packing some medieval heat."

Gansey and Ronan knelt beside the bones. The body was wearing a sword. Well, *wearing* was a poor verb. The rib cage was wearing the sword, which had been stabbed through it, the tip of it jammed evocatively into a shoulder blade.

"Correct to Glendower's period," Gansey said, mostly to make himself feel more himself.

There was a heavy silence. Everyone was regarding Gansey. He felt as if he were about to give a speech to a crowd.

"OK," he said, "I'm doing it."

"Do it fast," Blue suggested. "I'm incredibly creeped out."

This was the moment, then. Gansey drew close to Glendower's body in its suit of armour.

His hands hovered just over the helmet. His heart was racing so hard that he couldn't catch a breath.

Gansey closed his eyes.

I am ready.

He gently freed the leather chin strap from the cool metal, and then he carefully pulled the helmet free.

Adam inhaled.

Gansey didn't. He didn't breathe at all. He just stood, frozen, his hands gripped around his king's helmet. He told himself to breathe in, and he did. He told himself to breathe out, and he did. He didn't move, though, and he didn't speak.

Glendower was dead.

FIFTY-SEVEN

B
ones.

Dust.

"Is that — is that what he's supposed to look like?" Henry asked.

Gansey did not reply.

It was not what Glendower was supposed to look like, and yet it did not feel untrue. Everything that day had felt lived before, dreamt, redone. How many times had Gansey feared that he would find Glendower, only to discover him dead? The only thing was that Gansey had always feared that he would find Glendower just a little too late. Minutes, days, months after death. But this man had been dead for centuries. The helmet and skull were only metal and bone. The gambeson beneath the plate mail was threads and dust.

"Are we . . ." Adam started and then stopped, uncertain. He put his hand on the wall of the tomb.

Gansey covered his mouth with his hand; he felt his breath would blast the remainder of Glendower away. The others still stood in shocked assembly. None of them had words. It had been longer for him, but they had been just as hopeful.

"Are we supposed to wake his bones?" Blue asked. "Like the skeletons in the cave of bones?"

Adam said, "That's what I was going to say, but . . ."

He trailed off again, and Gansey knew why. The cave of bones had been filled with skeletons, but it had still felt inherently *vital*. Magic and possibility had crackled in the air. The idea of waking those bones had felt incredible, but not impossible.

"I don't have my dream amplifier," Ronan said.

"Wake. His. Bones," echoed Henry. "I really don't mean to sound like the naysayer here, as you are all clearly experts at this, but."

But.

Ronan said, "Then let's do it. Let's do it fast. I hate this place. It feels like it's eating my life."

This vehemence served to focus Gansey's clouded thoughts.

"Yes," he said, although he didn't feel remotely certain. "Let's do it. Perhaps the cave of bones was a practice run for this and that's why Cabeswater led us there." The bones hadn't stayed alive long in that cave, but it didn't matter, he supposed. They only needed Glendower to be awake long enough to grant a favour.

Gansey's heart stumbled inside him at the idea of trying to extract both a favour and a purpose for his existence before Glendower turned to dust.

Better than nothing.

So the teens attempted to assemble as they had in the cave of bones, with Henry standing back, curious or wary. Adam splayed his fingers on the tomb walls, feeling for some semblance of energy to project. He moved around and around the tomb, clearly unhappy with what he was finding. Eventually, he stopped where he had begun and put his hand on the wall.

"Here is as good as any place," he said, but he didn't sound hopeful. Blue took his hand. Ronan crossed his arms. Gansey carefully put his hand on Glendower's chest.

It felt pretend. Ridiculous. Gansey tried to summon up intention, but he felt empty. His knees were knocking, not out of fear or anger, but some more vast emotion that he refused to acknowledge as grief.

Grief meant he'd already given up.

"Wake up," he said. Then, again, trying a little harder, "Wake up."

But they were just words.

"Wake," Gansey said again. "Up."

A voice and nothing more. *Vox et praeterea nihil.*

The first moment of realization was giving way to a second, and third, and each new minute revealed some facet that Gansey had not yet let himself consider. There would be no waking of Glendower, so there was no favour. Noah's life would not be begged for, the demon would not be bargained away. There may have never been magic involved with Glendower; his corpse may have been brought to the New World only to be buried out of reach of the English; it was possible that Gansey needed to notify the historian community of this find, if it was even findable by normal means. If Glendower had always been dead, it could not have been him who spared Gansey.

If Glendower had not saved Gansey's life, he did not know who to thank, or who to be, or how to live.

No one said anything.

Gansey touched the skull, the raised cheekbone, the face of his promised and ruined king. Everything was dry and gray.

It was over.

This man was not going to ever be anything to Gansey.

"Gansey?" Blue asked.

Every minute was giving way to another and then another, and slowly it sank into his heart, all the way to the centre:

It was over.

FIFTY-EIGHT

Gansey had forgotten how many times he had been told he was destined for greatness.

Was this all there was?

They had emerged into sun. The tricky ley line had stolen hours from them without them feeling it, and now they sat in the tattered Green House, just a few hundred yards away from where Gansey had died. Gansey sat in the ballroom, leaning against the wall, all of him contained in a square of sunlight coming through the dusty, many-paned windows. He rubbed a hand over his forehead, although he wasn't tired — he was so awake that he was certain the ley line had somehow affected that as well.

It was over.

Glendower was dead.

Destined for greatness, the psychics had said. One in Stuttgart. One in Chicago. One in Guadalajara. Two in London. Where was it, then? Perhaps he'd used it all up. Perhaps the greatness had only ever been the ability to find historical trinkets. Perhaps the greatness was only in what he could be to others.

"Let's get out of here," Gansey said.

They started back to Henrietta, the two cars travelling close together.

It only took a few minutes for Gansey's phone to regain charge after being being plugged into the cigarette lighter, and it only took a few seconds after that for texts to begin pouring in — all the texts that had come in while they were underground. A buzz sounded for each; the phone did not stop buzzing.

They had missed the fund-raiser.

The ley line had not taken hours from them. It had taken a *day* from them.

Gansey had Blue read the texts to him until he couldn't bear it any more. They began with polite query, wondering if he was running a few minutes late. Wandered into concern, contemplating why he wasn't answering his phone. Descended into irritation, uncertain why he would think it was appropriate to be late to a school function. And then skipped right over anger and headed into hurt.

I know you have your own life, his mother said to his voicemail. *I was just hoping to be part of it for a few hours.*

Gansey felt the sword go right through his ribs and out the other side.

Before, he had been replaying the failure to wake Glendower over and over again. Now he couldn't stop replaying the image of his family waiting at Aglionby for him. His mother thinking he was just running late. His father thinking he was hurt. Helen Helen knowing he'd been doing something for himself, instead. Her only text had come at the end of the night: *I suppose the king will always win, won't he?*

He would have to call them. But what would he say?

Guilt was building in his chest and his throat and behind his eyes.

"You know what?" Henry said eventually. "Pull over. There."

Gansey silently pulled the Fisker in to the rest stop that he had indicated; the BMW pulled in behind them. They parked in the single row of spots in front of the fancy brick building that held toilets; they were the only cars there. The sun had given way to clouds; it looked like rain.

"Now get out," Henry said.

Gansey looked at him. "I beg your pardon?"

"Stop driving," he said. "I know you need to. You've needed to since we left. Get. Out."

Gansey was about to protest this, but he discovered that his words felt rather unsteady in his mouth. It was like his shaking knees in the tomb; the wobble had snuck up on him.

So he said nothing and he got out. Very quietly. He thought about walking into the toilets, but at the last moment veered to the picnic area beside the rest stop. Out of view of the cars. Very calmly. He made it to one of the picnic benches, but didn't sit on it. Instead, he slowly sat down just in front of it and curled his hands over his head. He folded himself down small enough that his forehead brushed the grass.

He could not remember the last time he had cried.

It was not just Glendower he was mourning. It was all the versions of Gansey he had been in the last seven years. It was the Gansey who had pursued him with youthful optimism and purpose. And it was the Gansey who had pursued him with increasing worry. And it was this Gansey, who was going to have to die. Because it made a fatal sort of sense. They required a death to save Ronan and Adam. Blue's kiss was supposed to be deadly to her true love. Gansey's death had been foretold for this year. It was him. It was always going to be him.

Glendower was dead. He'd always been dead.

And Gansey kind of wanted to live.

Eventually, Gansey heard footsteps approaching in the leaves. This was terrible, too. He did not want to stand and show them his teary face and receive their pity; the idea of this well-meaning kindness was nearly as unbearable a thought as his approaching death. For the very first time, Gansey understood Adam Parrish perfectly.

He unfolded himself and stood with as much dignity as he could muster. But it was just Blue, and somehow there was no humiliation to her seeing that he'd been levelled. She just looked at him while he brushed the pine needles off his trousers, and then, after he had sat on the top of the picnic table, she sat beside him until the others left the cars to see what they were doing.

They stood in a half circle around his picnic table throne.

"About the sacrifice," Gansey said.

No one said anything. He couldn't even tell if he had said it out loud.

"Did I say anything?" Gansey asked.

"Yeah," Blue replied. "But we didn't want to talk about it."

"I apologize if this is a rudimentary question," Henry interjected, "as I arrived to class late. But I don't suppose your treefather gave you any other demon-killing advice?"

"No, just the sacrifice," Blue said. Gingerly, she added, "I think . . . he might have known about Glendower. Not all along, maybe. He might have figured it out while he was wandering around down there after getting with my mom, or maybe from the beginning. But I think he was one of Glendower's magicians. Maybe also that . . . other guy."

She meant the other body in the tomb. It wasn't difficult to follow the story she imagined, of Artemus trying to put Glendower to sleep and doing something wrong.

"So we're left with the sacrifice," Gansey pressed. "Unless you have any better ideas, Adam?"

Adam had been frowning off into the sparse pine trees that bordered the picnic area. He said, "I am trying to think of what else would satisfy the ley line magic, but *willing life for unwilling life* doesn't suggest substitutions."

Gansey felt a prickle of dread in his stomach. "Well then."

"No," said Ronan. He didn't say it in a protesting way, or an angry way, or an upset way. He simply said *no*. Factual.

"Ronan—"

"*No*." *Factual.* "I didn't just come get you out of this hole for you to die on purpose."

Gansey matched his tone. "Blue saw my spirit on the ley line, so I already know that I die this year. Occam's razor suggests the simplest explanation is the right one: We decide that it is me."

"Blue did *what*?" Ronan demanded. "When were you going to tell me?"

"Never," Blue said. She didn't say it in a protesting way, or an angry way, or an upset way. Just *never*. Factual.

"Don't look at me like that," Gansey said. "I don't *want* to die. I'm terrified, actually. But I don't see any other option. And the fact is that I want to make something of myself before I die, and I thought it was going to be something about Glendower. It's obviously not. So I might as well do something meaningful. And – kingly." The last bit was a little melodramatic, but it was a melodramatic situation.

"I think you're getting *king* confused with *martyr*," Henry said.

"I'm open to other options," Gansey said. "In fact, I'd prefer them."

Blue said abruptly, "We're your magicians, right?"

Yes, his magicians, his court, him their pointless king, nothing to offer but his pulse. How *right* it had felt at each moment that he met them all. How certain that they plunged towards something bigger than even this moment.

"Yes," he said.

"I just – I feel like there has to be something we can all do, like in the cave of bones," she said. "It was wrong in the tomb because there was no life there to start with. Or something. There was no energy. But if we had more of the pieces right?"

Gansey said, "I don't understand the magic well enough."

Ronan said, "Parrish does."

"No," Adam protested. "I don't think I do."

"Better than any of the rest of us," Ronan said. "Give us an idea."

Adam shrugged. His hands were gripped together so tightly that his knuckles were white. "Maybe," he started, then stopped. "Maybe you could die and then come back. If we used Cabeswater to kill you in some way that didn't damage your body, then it would provoke the time-holding like 6:21. A minute playing out over and over again, so you wouldn't have time to get, I don't know, too far away from your body. Too dead. And then . . ." Gansey could hear that Adam was making this up as he went along, spinning a plausible fairy tale for Ronan. "It would have to take place in Cabeswater. I could scry into the dreamspace while Blue amplified it, and during one of the time spasms we could tell your soul to return to your body before you were ever really dead. So you'd fulfil the requirements of the sacrifice to die. Nothing says you have to stay dead."

There was a long pause.

"Yes," Gansey said. Factual. "That feels right. Is that kingly enough for you, Ronan? Not martyrdom, Henry?"

They didn't look thrilled, but they looked willing, which was all that mattered. They only had to want to believe it, not really believe it.

"Let's go to Cabeswater," Gansey said.

They had only just started back towards the cars when Adam attacked Ronan.

FIFTY-NINE

It took Ronan too long to realize that Adam was killing him. Adam's hands were around Ronan's neck, thumbs pressed knuckle white into his arteries, his eyes rolled back up in his head. Ronan's vision produced flashes of light; his body had only been without air for a minute and it already missed it. He could feel his pulse in his eyeballs.

"*Adam?*" demanded Blue.

Part of Ronan still thought there was a mistake.

Ronan's breath hitched as the two of them stumbled back through the pine trees around the picnic area. The others were circling them, but Ronan couldn't focus on what they were doing.

"Fight back," Adam growled at Ronan, thin, desperate, an animal dragged by the neck. At the same time that his voice protested, though, his body jammed Ronan's back against a trunk of a pine tree. "Hit me. Knock me down!"

The demon. The demon had taken his hands.

Every beat of Ronan's heart was an articulated part in a collapsing train. He grabbed Adam's wrists. They felt frail, snappable, cold. The choice was death or hurting Adam, which wasn't much of a choice at all.

Adam suddenly lost his grip, stumbling to his knees before clambering quickly back up. Henry leapt back as Adam snatched for his face in a way that was terrifying in its wrongness. No human would fight in such a way, but the thing that had his hands and his eyes was not human.

"Stop me!" Adam begged.

Gansey grabbed for Adam's fingers, but Adam pulled them free easily. Instead, he snarled fingers into Ronan's ear, ripping at it, and his other hand hooked into Ronan's jaw, tearing the other way. His eyes stared hard to his left, waiting for intruders to stop him.

"Stop me —"

Pain was a torn piece of paper. Ronan thought about how much it hurt, and then he allowed himself one deeper measure of pain, and he ripped himself free of Adam's grip. In that moment of opportunity, Blue darted forward and got a handful of Adam's hair. Instantly Adam whirled on her, and with razor-fast precision, he tore her stitches open.

Blue exhaled in shock as the blood began to drip blackly over her eyelid again. Gansey dragged her back before Adam could scratch again.

"Just hit me," Adam said miserably. "Don't let me do this."

It seemed it should have been simple: There were four of them, one of Adam. But none of them wanted to hurt Adam Parrish, no matter how violent he had become. And the demon operating Adam's limbs had a superpower: It did not care about the limitations of the human they belonged to. It did not care about pain. It did not care about longevity. So Adam's knuckles careened past Ronan and smashed into the trunk of a pine tree without the slightest hesitation, even as Adam gasped. Everyone's breath puffed white all around them, looking like dust clouds.

"It's going to break his fucking hands," Ronan said.

Blue snatched one of Adam's wrists. There was a terrible pop as Adam swung around in the opposite direction and snatched her switchblade out of the loose pocket of her sweater. The blade snicked out.

He had their full attention.

His rolling eyes, controlled by the demon, focused on Ronan.

But Adam — the real Adam — was also paying attention. He heaved his body away from the group, crashing himself against the picnic bench, then crashing again, trying to jar the arm that held the knife. As he successfully pinned it under his own weight, though, his other hand clawed up. Quick as a cat, it scratch-scratch-scratched at his own face. Blood beaded instantly. It was digging harder. Punishing.

"No," Gansey said. He could not bear it. He ran at Adam. As he slid to him, snatching that angry hand, Henry skidded right on his heels. So when Adam lifted the switchblade over Gansey, Henry was there to catch Adam's wrist in his hands, pressing his entire weight against the strength of Adam's right arm. Adam's eyes darted furiously, weighing his next move. The demon's next move.

All Adam cared about was his autonomy.

As Adam jerked his wrist in Henry's grasp — "Stop, you idiot, you're going to break it!" — and knocked his fist back against Gansey's teeth — "You're OK, Adam, we know it's not you!" — Ronan wrapped his arms around Adam, pinning Adam's upper arms against him.

He was contained.

"Forsan et haec olim meminisse juvabit," Ronan said into Adam's hearing ear, and Adam's body sagged against Ronan, chest heaving. His hands still jerked and strained to violence. He gasped, "You asshole," but Ronan could hear how near tears he was.

"Let's tie his hands while we figure this out," Blue said. "Could you – oh, you're so clever, thank you."

This was because the Orphan Girl had already anticipated how this might end and fetched a long red ribbon of unknown origin. Blue accepted it and then squeezed between Henry and Gansey. "Give me some room – put his wrists together."

"No, President," Henry said out of breath, "cross them like this. Haven't you seen any cop dramas?"

Blue braided Adam's fingers together, which took some doing as they still had a mind of their own, and then tied his still bucking wrists together. She wrapped the length of them with the ribbon and tied it. Adam's shoulders still twitched, but he couldn't unlink his fingers once they were braided together and tied.

Finally it was quiet.

With a great sigh, she stepped back. Gansey touched her bloody forehead with care and then looked at Henry's knuckles, which had somehow got abraded in the scuffle.

Adam's hands had stopped jerking as the demon realized that they were well secured. His head rested miserably on Ronan's shoulder, everything shaking, standing only because Ronan did not allow him to sink. The fresh horror of it kept rising in him. The permanence of it, the corruption of Adam Parrish, the deadness of Glendower.

The Orphan Girl crept in close. She carefully undid the dirty watch on her wrist, and then she fastened it on one of Adam's, loosely, above where he was tied. Then she kissed his arm.

"Thank you," he said, dully. Then, to Gansey, in a low voice, "*I* might as well be the sacrifice. I'm ruined."

"*No,*" Blue, Gansey and Ronan said at once.

"Let's not get carried away just because you just tried to kill someone," Henry clarified. He sucked on his bloody knuckles.

Adam finally lifted his head. "Then you better cover my eyes."

Gansey looked puzzled. "What?"

"Because," Adam said bitterly, "otherwise they'll betray you."

SIXTY

Depending on where you began the story, it was about Seondeok.

She had not meant to be an international art dealer and small-time crime boss. It had begun as a mere desire for *something more*, and then a slow realization that *something more* was never going to be reachable on her current path. She was married to a clever man she'd met in Hong Kong, and she had several bright children who mostly took after him except for the one, and she had seen how her life would play out.

Then she had gone mad.

It hadn't been a long madness. A year, perhaps, of fits and visions and being found prowling through the streets. And when she had come out the other side, she had discovered that she had a psychic's eyes and a shaman's touch and that she was going to make a career of it. She'd renamed herself Seondeok and the legend had been born.

She handled wonder every day.

The robotic bee was the moment she realized she was on a fated path. Henry, her middle son, shone brightly, but he never seemed able to direct that light outside of himself. And so when Niall Lynch offered to find her a bauble, a token, a magical toy, that would help him, she was listening. The beautiful bee struck her the moment she saw it. Of course he had also shown it to

Laumonier and to Greenmantle and to Valquez and to Mackey and to Xi, but that was to be expected because he was a scoundrel and could not help himself. But when he had met Henry, he had let Seondeok have it for nearly nothing, and she would not forget that.

Of course, it had been a gift and a penalty, since later, Laumonier had kidnapped Henry for it.

She would have revenge for that.

She didn't regret it. She couldn't make herself regret it, even when it threatened her children. This was a fated path, and she felt right on it, even when it was hard.

When she found herself next to the Gray Man, Greenmantle's old hired muscle, in an off-campus Aglionby Academy lot, and discovered that the blood on his shoes was Laumonier's, she was instantly interested in what he had to say.

"A brave new way of doing business," the Gray Man said in a low voice, as the parking lot was quickly beginning to fill up with a small but potent number of forbidding-looking people. It was not that they looked dangerous, necessarily. Just odd in a way that suggested they didn't look at the world at all like you did. They were a very different group than the people who had come to the school the night before. Technically both gatherings had a lot to do with politics. "An ethical way. There are no armed guards outside of furniture stores to prevent people from bludgeoning employees and carrying out sofas. That is the business I want."

"That will not be an easy goal," Seondeok said, her voice also low. She kept her eyes on the cars pulling up, and also on her phone. She knew that Henry had been told to stay away, and she trusted him to keep his head down, but she also didn't trust

Laumonier in the slightest. There was no point tempting them by showing that Henry — and by extension, his bee — were within close proximity. "The people have got used to carrying sofas, and one does not like to stop stealing sofas when others haven't yet agreed to."

"Persuasion might be required at the beginning," the Gray Man admitted.

"You are talking years."

"I am committed," he replied. "So long as I can get a decent number of people who are interested in that vision. People I like."

Here was Laumonier, finally, one of them on the phone. His face suggested he was trying to contact the third one, but the third one was not in a condition to answer. The Gray Man would discuss this with them after the sale had happened. In a persuasive way aided with some truly fantastic weapons that he had found on the Lynch farm.

Seondeok said, "I am not people you like."

"You are people I respect, which is nearly the same."

Her smile said she knew he was sucking up to her and she accepted it nonetheless. "Perhaps, Mr Gray. This is according to my interest."

This was when Piper Greenmantle arrived.

Well, it was not her, at first. It was dread first, then Piper. The feeling struck them like a wave of nausea, rocking from feet to head, sending hands to throats and knees to pavement. It was early afternoon, but the sky suddenly seemed darker. This was the first sign that this sale was going to be something remarkable.

So, first dread, then Piper. She arrived flying, which was the second sign that things were going to be somewhat unusual.

When she landed, it became obvious that she had arrived on a rug of tiny black wasps, which dissolved when they touched the asphalt.

She looked good.

This was striking for a several reasons, first because rumour had it that she had died before her smarmy husband had been killed by wasps in his apartment, and she was clearly not dead. And secondly because she was holding a black wasp that was nearly a foot long, and most people didn't look as serene and put together as she did when holding a stinging insect of any size.

She strode over to Laumonier, clearly intending to cheek-kiss, but they both bowed back from the insect. This was the third sign that things were going to be somewhat unusual, because Laumonier ordinarily made a point to never look alarmed.

"This is not good," the Gray Man said under his breath.

Because it was obvious now that the dread was coming from either Piper or the wasp. The sensation kept hitting Seondeok in ill waves, reminding her painfully of her year of being mad. It took a moment for her to realize that it was *verbally* reminding her of her year of being mad — she could hear the words being said directly into her head. In Korean.

"Thank you all for coming," Piper said grandly. She cocked her head, eyes narrowed, and Seondeok knew that she was being whispered to also. "Now that I am single, I intend to move independently into the business of luxury magical items, curating only the most extraordinary and otherworldly of crazy shit. I hope you all start to trust me to be a quality source. And our kickoff piece – the thing you've come all this way for – is this." She lifted her arm, and the wasp stepped a little further towards her hand. The crowd shuddered as one; there was something quite wrong about it. The dread, plus the size, the real weight of it moving the fabric of her sleeve. "This is a demon."

Yes. Seondeok believed this.

"It's favoured me, as you can probably tell by my fabulous hair and skin, but I'm ready to pass it along to the next user so I can find the next great thing! It's all about the journey, right? Right!"

"Is it —" started one of the men in the group. Rodney, Seondeok believed his name was. He didn't seem to know how to finish his question.

"How does it work?" Seondeok asked.

"Mostly I just ask it to do stuff," Piper said, "and it goes for it. I'm not really religious, but I feel like somebody with some religious background could really make it do some cool tricks. It made me a house, and these pumps. What could it do for you? Stuff. Shall we start the bidding, Dad?"

Laumonier was still not quite recovered. The thing about being in the demon's presence was that it got worse instead of better. The opposite of getting used to it – that was the sensation. It was a wound that increased from ache to stab. The whispers were hard to bear, because they were not really whispers. They were thoughts, mingling helplessly with one's own, difficult to prioritize. Seondeok had survived a year of madness, though, and she could bear this. It was not impossible to tell which thoughts were the demon's: They were the ugliest, the most backwards, the ones that would unmake the thinker.

A few of the folks in the back were leaving, retreating wordlessly towards their cars before things got ugly. Uglier. Ugliest.

"Hey!" Piper said. "Don't just *walk* away from me. Demon!"

The wasp twitched its antennae and the people twitched in rhythm. They twirled, eyes wide.

"You see," Piper said through gritted teeth, "it's really quite handy."

"I think," Laumonier said cautiously, looking at the frozen buyers, and then at the faces of their peers, and then at his daughter, "this might not be the best method of displaying this particular good."

What he meant was, the demon was creeping everyone out and it was hard to shake the idea that they might all die at any time, which was bad for business both present and future.

"Don't use that passive-aggressive stuff on me," Piper said. "I read an article on how you have basically been undercutting my personhood for my entire life and that is *totally* an example."

"This is totally an example of you overstepping your knowledge," Laumonier said. "Your ambition is constantly outstripping your education! You don't even know how to transfer a demon."

"I'll *wish* it, don't you get it?" Piper asked. "It has to favour me! It has to do what I say."

But Seondeok wasn't sure that was the same thing.

"Do you think?" Laumonier asked. "Do you control it, or does it control you?"

"Oh, *please*," Piper said. "Demon, unfreeze those people! Demon, make it sunny! Demon, change my clothing to all white! Demon, do as I say, do as I say!"

The people unfroze; the sky turned white-hot bright for just a second; her clothing bleached; the demon buzzed up into the air. The whispering in Seondeok's head had become something fierce.

Laumonier shot his daughter.

It made a little *oonph* sound because of the silencer. Laumonier looked shocked. Both said nothing, just stared at her body, then up at the demon who had whispered it to them.

Now everyone fled. If Laumonier would shoot his daughter, anything could happen.

The demon had landed upon the wound in Piper's neck, its legs sinking into the blood, its head lowered to the hole.

It was changing. She was changing. Everything was unmaking and violence and perversion.

"Call me," Seondeok told the Gray Man, "and get out of here."

Piper's scream played backwards. Seondeok had not realized she was still alive.

The blood around her neck was black.

Ambition greed hatred violence contempt ambition greed hatred violence contempt

She was dead.

The demon began to rise.

Unmaker, unmaker, I wake, I wake, I wake

SIXTY-ONE

Adam could not decide if this was the worst thing that had happened to him, or if it felt that way because he had been so recently and senselessly happy that the comparison was making it so.

He was in the backseat of the BMW, his hands still bound, his eyes still covered, one ear deaf. He didn't even feel real. He felt tired but not sleepy, worn by the effort of being unable to participate in his senses. And still the demon occasionally worked against the ribbon – how his skin sang with pain – and rolled his eyes against his will. Blue sat beside him, and the Orphan Girl on the other side of her, by his request. He didn't know if he could escape from the ribbon, but he knew that the demon would only hurt Blue in an effort to get to Ronan or the Orphan Girl. So at least they would have a warning if it happened again.

God, God. He'd nearly killed Ronan. He *would* have killed him. He had only just been making out with Ronan, and his hands would have nonetheless murdered him while Adam watched.

How would he go to school? How would he do *anything* —

His breath betrayed him, because Blue leaned against his shoulder.

"Don't —" he warned.

She lifted her head, but then he felt her fingers in his hair instead, stroking it gently, and then touching the skin on his cheek where he had gouged himself. She didn't say anything.

He closed his eyes behind the blindfold, listening to the slow patter of the rain on the windshield, the shoosh of the wipers. He had no idea how close they were to Cabeswater.

Why couldn't he think of another way around the sacrifice? Gansey was only hurrying to do this because of him, because of how his bargain had turned this into an emergency. In the end, Adam was killing him anyway, just like in his vision. A backwards, sideways version of the blame, but Adam at its helm just the same. But it was undeniable that Adam was the one who'd made it an emergency.

Bad feeling hissed inside Adam, but he couldn't tell if it was guilt or a warning from Cabeswater.

"What's that?" Gansey's voice came from the passenger seat. "On the road?"

Blue drew away from Adam; he heard her pull herself between the driver's and passenger's seats. She sounded dubious. "Is it . . . blood?"

"From what?" Ronan asked.

"Maybe not from anything," Gansey said. "Is it real?"

Ronan said, "The rain's hitting it."

"Should we . . . should we drive through it?" Gansey asked. "Blue, what's Henry's face look like? Can you see it?"

Adam felt Blue's body brush him as she swivelled to look in the Fisker behind them. His hands strained and twitched, endlessly hungry. The demon felt . . . close.

Blue said, "Give me your phone. I'm going to call Mom."

"What's happening?" Adam asked.

"The road is flooded," Blue said. "It looks like blood, though. And there's something floating in it. What is that, Gansey? Is it . . . petals? Blue petals?"

There was a heavy silence in the car.

"Do you ever feel like things are coming full circle?" Ronan said in a low voice. "Do you . . ."

He didn't finish his sentence. The car was quiet again, unmoving – apparently he hadn't decided whether or not to drive through the flood yet. Rain spattered. The windshield wipers clunk-sighed again.

"I guess we – Jesus," Gansey broke off. "*Jesus*. Ronan?"

Terror coated his words.

"*Ronan?*" repeated Gansey. There was a metallic slap. Groan of a seat. Scuffling. The car shifted beneath them with the ferocity of Gansey shifting his weight. Ronan still hadn't replied. A roar pitched low behind his words. The engine: Ronan was hitting the gas while the car was out of gear.

The sick warning in Adam had risen to an alarm.

The roar suddenly stopped; the car had been turned off.

"Oh no," Blue said. "Oh no, the girl, too!" She moved away from Adam, fast; he heard her open the door on the other side of the car. Cool, moist air sucked into the BMW. Another door opened, another. All of them but Adam's. Henry's voice came from outside, deep and serious and completely devoid of humour.

"What's happening?" Adam demanded.

"Can we —" Blue's voice was halfway to a sob, coming from outside the driver's-side door. "Can we pick it off him?"

"Don't," Ronan gasped. "Don't touch it – don't —"

The driver's seat knocked back so hard that it smashed into Adam's knees. Adam heard a sound that was unmistakably Ronan sucking in his breath.

"Oh, Jesus," Gansey said again. "Tell me what I can do."

Again the seat bucked. Adam's hands clawed back against the seat behind him, quite against his will. Whatever was happening, they wanted to help it happen faster. From the front seat, Ronan's phone began to ring and ring and ring. It was the low dull ring that Ronan had programmed for when Declan's number called.

The worst was that Adam knew what that meant: something was happening to Matthew. No, the worst was that Adam *couldn't do anything about any of it.*

"Ronan, Ronan, don't close your eyes," Blue said, and now she was crying. "I'm calling — I'm calling Mom."

"Whoa, stand back!" Gansey shouted.

The entire car rocked.

Henry demanded, "What was *that*?"

"He's brought it back from his dreams," Gansey said. "When he passed out. It won't hurt us."

"What's happening?" Adam demanded.

Gansey's voice was low and miserable. It reached the edge and cracked. "He's being unmade."

SIXTY-TWO

It was impossible to believe that Adam had thought that the previous moment was the worst.

This was the worst: being blindfolded and tied in the back of a car and knowing that the soft, gasping sound was Ronan Lynch choking for breath every time he waded back to consciousness.

So much of Ronan was bravado, and there was none left.

And Adam was nothing but a weapon to kill him faster.

It felt like years ago that he had made his bargain with Cabeswater. *I will be your hands. I will be your eyes.* How horrified Gansey had been, and maybe he had been right. Because here was Adam stripped of all of his options. Rendered so easily and simply powerless.

His thoughts were a battlefield now, and Adam ran away into the blackness of the blindfold. It was a dangerous game, scrying when Cabeswater was so endangered, when everyone else would be too busy to notice if he also began to die in the backseat, but it was the only way he could survive being so close to Ronan's pained gasps.

He wheeled far and fast, throwing his unconscious far away from his conscious thoughts, as far away as he could get from the truth of the car as quickly as he could manage it. There was very, very little Cabeswater left. Mostly darkness. Maybe he wouldn't find his way back to his corrupted body. Maybe he would be lost, like

Persephone

Persephone

As soon as he thought her name, he realized that she was with him. He couldn't tell how he knew, since he couldn't see her. In fact, he couldn't see anything. In fact, he found that he was once more intensely aware of the fabric of the blindfold against his eyes and the dull ache of his fingers braided and jammed against each other. Once more intensely aware of his physical reality; once more grounded inside his useless body.

"You pushed me back here," he accused.

Ish, she replied. *Mostly you let yourself get pushed.*

He didn't know what to say to her. He was too painfully glad to feel her presence again. It was not that Persephone, vague Persephone, was a creature given to providing comfort. But her brand of sense and wisdom and rules had comforted him greatly when he was chaos, and even though she had not yet really said anything to him, the mere recollection of that comfort gave him a burst of outsized happiness.

"I'm ruined."

Mmm.

"It's my fault."

Mmm.

"Gansey was right."

Mmm.

"Stop saying *mmm!*"

Then perhaps you should stop saying things you got tired of saying to me weeks ago.

"My hands, though. My eyes." When he named them, he felt them. The clawing hands. The rolling eyes. They were thrilled by the destruction of Ronan. This was their purpose. How they longed to help in that dreadful task.

Who did you make that deal with?

"Cabeswater."

Who is using your hands?

"The demon."

That is not the same thing.

Adam didn't reply. Once again Persephone was giving him advice that sounded good but was impossible to use in the real world. It was wisdom, not an actionable item.

You made your deal with Cabeswater, not with a demon. Even though they look the same and feel the same, they are not the same.

"They feel the same."

They are not the same. The demon has no claim to you. You didn't choose the demon. You chose Cabeswater.

"I don't know what to do," Adam said.

Yes, you do. You have to keep choosing it.

But Cabeswater was dying. Soon there might be no Cabeswater left to choose. Soon it might just be Adam's mind, Adam's body, and the demon. He didn't say it out loud. It didn't matter. In this place, his thoughts and his words were the same thing.

That does not make you a demon. You will be one of those gods without magic powers. What are they called?

"I don't think there is a word."

King. Probably. I am going to go now.

"Persephone, please — I —" *miss you.*

He was alone; she had gone. He was left, as always, with

equal parts comfort and uncertainty. The feeling that he knew how to move forward; the doubt that he was capable of executing it. But this time, she'd come an awfully long way to give him his lesson. He didn't know if she could see him any more now, but he didn't want to let her down.

And the truth was that if he thought about the things that he loved about Cabeswater, it wasn't difficult at all to tell the difference between the demon and it. They grew from the same soil, but they were nothing like each other.

These eyes and hands are mine, Adam thought.

And they were. He didn't have to prove it. It was a fact as soon as he believed it.

He turned his head and rubbed the blindfold off his eyes.

He saw the end of the world.

SIXTY-THREE

The demon slowly worked at the fibres of the dreamer.

They were difficult things to unmake, dreamers. So much of a dreamer didn't exist inside a physical body. So many complicated parts of them snarled in the stars and tangled in tree roots. So much of them fled down rivers and exploded through the air between raindrops.

This dreamer fought.

The demon was about unmaking and nothingness, and dreamers were about making and fullness. This dreamer was all of that to an extreme, a new king in his invented kingdom.

He fought.

The demon kept pulling him unconscious, and in those short bursts of blackness, the dreamer snatched at light, and when he swam back to consciousness, he thrust the dream into reality. He shaped them into flapping creatures and earthbound stars and flaming crowns and golden notes that sang by themselves and mint leaves scattered across the blood-streaked pavement and scraps of paper with jagged handwriting on them: *Unguibus et rostro.*

But he was dying.

SIXTY-FOUR

Wanting to live, but accepting death to save others: that was courage. That was to be Gansey's greatness.

"It has to happen now," he said. "I have to do the sacrifice now."

Now that the moment had come, there was a certain glory to it. He didn't want to die, but at least he was doing it for these people, his found family. At least he was doing it for people who he knew were going to really *live.* At least he was not dying pointlessly, stung by wasps. At least this time it would matter.

This was where he was going to die: on a sloped field speckled with oak leaves. Black cattle grazed far up the hill, tails swishing as the rain fell in fitful spells. The grass was strikingly green for October, and the shock of colour against the fall-bright leaves made it look like a calendar photo. There was no one else around for miles. The only thing out of place was the flower-strewn river of blood across the winding road, and the young man dying in his car.

"But we're nowhere near Cabeswater!" Blue said.

Ronan's phone was ringing again: *Declan, Declan, Declan.* Everything was falling apart everywhere.

Ronan flickered briefly back into consciousness, his eyes awash with black, a rain of flickering pebbles scattering from his hand and skidding to a mucky stop on the bloody pavement. Terribly, the Orphan Girl was just watching blankly from the backseat, black slowly running from her closest ear. When she saw Gansey looking at her, she simply mouthed *Kerah* without any sound coming out.

"Are we on the ley line?" All that mattered was that they were on the line, so the sacrifice would count to kill the demon.

"Yes, but we're nowhere near *Cabeswater*. You'll just *die*."

One of the great things about Blue Sargent was that she never really gave up hope. He would have told her this, but he knew it would only upset her more. He said, "I can't watch Ronan die, Blue. And Adam – and Matthew – and all this? We don't have anything else. You already *saw* my spirit. You already know what we chose!"

Blue closed her eyes, and two tears ran out of them. She did not cry noisily, or in a way that asked him to say anything different. She was a hopeful creature, but she was also a sensible creature.

"Untie me," Adam said from the backseat. "If you're going to do it now, for God's sake, untie me." His blindfold was off and he was looking at Gansey, his eyes his own instead of the demon's. His chest was moving fast. If there was any other way, Gansey knew Adam would have told him.

"Is it safe?" Gansey asked.

"Safe as life," Adam replied. *"Untie me."*

Henry had been waiting for something to do – he clearly did not know how to process this without having a task – so he leapt to untie Adam. Shaking his reddened wrists free of the ribbon, Adam first touched the top of the Orphan Girl's head and whispered, "It's going to be all right." And then he climbed out of the car and stood before Gansey. What could they possibly say?

Gansey bumped fists with Adam and they nodded at each other. It was stupid, inadequate.

Ronan clawed briefly back to consciousness; flowers spilled out of the car in shades of blue Gansey had never seen. Ronan was frozen in place, as he always was after a dream, and black slowly oozed out of one of his nostrils.

Gansey had never understood really what it meant for Ronan to have to live with his nightmares.

He understood it now.

There was no time.

"Thanks for everything, Henry," Gansey said. "You're a prince among men."

Henry's face was blank.

Blue said, "I hate this."

It was right, though. Gansey felt the feeling of time slipping — one last time. The sense of having done this before. He gently laid the backs of his hands on her cheeks. He whispered, "It'll be OK. I'm ready. Blue, kiss me."

The rain spattered about them, kicking up splashes of red-black, making the petals around them twitch. Dream things from Ronan's newly healed imagination piled around their feet. In the rain, everything smelled of these mountains in fall: oak leaves and hay fields, ozone and dirt turned over. It was beautiful here, and Gansey loved it. It had taken a long time, but he'd ended up where he wanted after all.

Blue kissed him.

He had dreamt of it often enough, and here it was, willed into life. In another world, it would just be this: a girl softly pressing her lips to a boy's. But in this one, Gansey felt the effects of it at once. Blue, a mirror, an amplifier, a strange half-tree soul with ley line magic running through her. And Gansey, restored once by the ley line's power, given a ley line heart, another kind of mirror. And when they were pointed at each other, the weaker one gave.

Gansey's ley line heart had been gifted, not grown.

He pulled back from her.

Out loud, with intention, with the voice that left no room for doubt, he said, "Let it be to kill the demon."

Right after he spoke, Blue threw her arms tightly around his neck. Right after he spoke, she pressed her face into the side of his. Right after he spoke, she held him like a shouted word. *Love, love, love.*

He fell quietly from her arms.

He was a king.

SIXTY–FIVE

Depending on where you began the story, it was about Noah Czerny.

The problem with being dead was that your stories stopped being lines and started being circles. They started to begin and end in the same moment: the moment of dying. It was difficult to focus on other ways of telling stories, and to remember that the living were interested in the specific order of events. *Chronology.* That was the word. Noah was more interested in the spiritual weight of a minute. Getting killed. There was a story. He never stopped noticing that moment. Every time he saw it, he slowed and watched it, remembering precisely every physical sensation that he had experienced during the murder.

Murder.

Sometimes he got caught on a loop of constantly understanding that he had been murdered, and rage made him smash things in Ronan's room or kick the mint pot off Gansey's desk or punch in a pane of glass on the stairs up to the apartment.

Sometimes he got caught in *this* moment instead. Gansey's death. Watching Gansey die, again and again and again. Wondering if he would have been that brave in the forest if Whelk had asked him to die instead of forcing him to. He didn't think he would have. He wasn't sure they'd been that sort of friends.

Sometimes when he went back to see the still-living Gansey, he forgot whether or not this Gansey already knew that he was going to die. It was easy to know everything when time was circular, but it was hard to remember how to use it.

"Gansey," he said. "That's all there is."

This was not the right moment. Noah had been sucked into Gansey's spirit life instead, which was a different line entirely. He moved away from it. It was not a spatial consideration but a timing one. It was a bit like playing skip rope with three – Noah could no longer remember who he had done such a thing with, only that he must have done it at some point to remember it – you had to wait for the right moment to move forward or you got repelled by rope.

He didn't always remember why he was doing this, but he remembered what he was doing: looking for the first time Gansey had died.

He couldn't remember the first time that he'd made this choice. It was hard, now, to remember what was remembering and what was actually repeating. He wasn't even certain now which he was doing.

Noah just knew he had to keep doing it until the moment. He only had to stay solid long enough to make sure it stuck.

Here he was: Gansey, so young, twitching and dying in the leaves of a wood at the same time that Noah, miles away, had been twitching and dying in the leaves of a different wood.

All times were the same. As soon as Noah died, his spirit, full of the ley line, favoured by Cabeswater, had felt spread over every moment he had experienced and was going to experience. It was easy to look wise when time was a circle.

Noah crouched over Gansey's body. He said, for the last time, "You will live because of Glendower. Someone else on the ley line is dying when they should not, and so you will live when you should not."

Gansey died.

"Goodbye," Noah said. "Don't throw it away."

He quietly slid from time.

SIXTY-SIX

Blue Sargent had forgotten how many times she'd been told that she would kill her true love.

Her family traded in predictions. They read cards and they held séances and they upturned teacups on to saucers. Blue had never been part of this, except in one important way: She was the person with the longest-standing prediction in the household.

If you kiss your true love, he'll die.

For most of her life, she'd considered how it would happen. She'd been warned by all sorts of clairvoyants. Even without a hint of psychic ability, she had lived enmeshed in a world that was equal parts present and future, always knowing in a certain sense where she was headed.

But not any more.

Now she was looking at Gansey's dead body in its rain-spattered V-neck sweater and thinking, *I have no idea what happens now.*

The blood was draining off the highway, and crows had landed a few yards off to peck at it. All active signs of demonic activity had vanished at once.

"Get him," Ronan started, and then had to gather himself to finish, in a snarl, "Get him off the road. He's not an *animal*."

They dragged Gansey's body into the green grass by the side of the little road instead. He still looked entirely alive; he had only been dead for a minute or two, and there just wasn't a lot of difference between being dead and sleeping until things started to go bad.

Ronan crouched beside him, black still smeared on his face under his nose and around his ears. His dreamt firefly rested on Gansey's heart. "Wake up, you bastard," he said. "You fucker. I can't believe that you would . . ."

And he began to cry.

Beside Blue and Henry, Adam was dry-cheeked and dead-eyed, but the Orphan Girl hugged his arm as if comforting a weeper as he stared off into nothingness. His watch twitched the same minute over and over.

Blue had stopped crying. She'd used up all her tears beforehand.

The sounds of Henrietta made their way to them; an ambulance or a fire truck was wailing somewhere. Engines were revving. A loudspeaker was going. In a tree close by, little birds were singing. The cows were starting to move down the field towards them, curious about how long they'd been parked there.

"I don't really know what to do," Henry confessed. "This isn't how I thought it would end. I thought we were all going to Venezuela."

He was wry and pragmatic, and Blue saw that this was the only way he could cope with the fact of Richard Gansey's dead body lying in the grass.

"I can't think about that," Blue said truthfully. She couldn't really think about anything. Everything had come to an end at once. Every bit of her future was now unwritten for the first time in her life. Were they supposed to call 911? Practical concerns of dead true loves stretched out in front of her and she found she couldn't focus on any of them clearly. "I can't really . . . think at all. It's like I have a lampshade over my head. I keep waiting for — I don't know."

Adam suddenly sat down. He said nothing at all, but he covered his face with his hands.

Henry sucked in a very uneven breath. "We should get the cars out of the road," he said. "Now that things are not bleeding, traffic will . . ." He stopped himself. "This isn't right."

Blue shook her head.

"I just don't understand," Henry said. "I was so sure that this was going to . . . change everything. I didn't think it would end like this."

"I always knew it was going to end like this," she said, "but it still doesn't feel right. Would this ever feel right?"

Henry shifted from foot to foot, looking for other cars, making no move towards their cars despite his earlier care about traffic. He looked at his watch — like Adam's, it was still restlessly trying out the same few minutes, though not as violently as before — and repeated, "I just don't understand. What is the point of magic, if not for this?"

"For what?"

Henry stretched a hand over Gansey's body. "For him to be dead. You said you were Gansey's magicians. *Do something.*"

"*I'm* not a magician."

"You just *killed* him with your *mouth*." Henry pointed at Ronan. "That one just dreamed that pile of shit beside the car! That one saved his own life at the school when things fell from a roof!"

Adam's attention focused sharply at this. Grief sharpened his tone to a knife's edge. "That's different."

"Different how! It breaks the rules, too!"

"Because it is one thing to break the rules of physics with magic," Adam snapped. "It's a different thing to bring someone back from the dead."

But Henry was relentless. "Why? He's already come back once."

It was impossible to argue with that. Blue said, "That required a sacrifice, though. Noah's death."

Henry said, "So find another sacrifice."

Adam growled, "Are *you* offering?"

Blue understood his anger, though. Any degree of hope was impossible to bear in this situation.

There was silence. Henry looked down the road again. Finally, he said, *"Be magicians."*

"Shut *up*," Ronan suddenly snapped. "Shut *up*! I can't take it. Just *leave it*."

Henry actually stepped back a step, so fierce was Ronan's grief. They all fell silent. Blue couldn't stop looking at the time twitching away on Henry's watch. It was becoming ever less frantic the further they got from the kiss, and Blue couldn't help but dread when time returned entirely to normal. It felt like Gansey would really, truly be dead when it did.

The minute hand quivered. It quivered again.

Blue was already tired of a timeline without Gansey in it.

Adam looked up from where he was folded in the grass. His voice was small. "What about Cabeswater?"

"What about it?" Ronan asked. "It's not powerful enough to do anything any more."

"I know," Adam replied. "But if you asked — it might die for him."

SIXTY-SEVEN

Depending on where you began the story, it was about Cabeswater.

Cabeswater was not a forest. Cabeswater was a thing that happened to look like a forest right now. This was a peculiar magic that meant that it was always very old and very young at once. It had always been and yet it was always learning itself. It was always alive and waiting to be alive again.

It had never died on purpose before.

But it had never been asked.

Please, the Greywaren said. *Amabo te.*

It was not possible. Not like he thought. A life for a life was a good sacrifice, a brilliant base for a fantastic and peculiar magic, but Cabeswater was not quite mortal, and the boy the humans wanted to save was. It was not as simple as Cabeswater dying and him rising. If it was going to be anything at all, it would have to be about Cabeswater making some essential part of itself human-shaped, and even Cabeswater wasn't certain if that was possible.

The magician-boy's mind moved through Cabeswater's tattered thoughts, trying to understand what *was* possible, projecting images of his own to help Cabeswater understand the goal of resurrection. He did not realize that it was a much harder concept for him to grasp than Cabeswater; Cabeswater was always dying and rising again; when all times were the same, resurrection was merely a matter of moving consciousness from one minute to another. Living for ever was not difficult for Cabeswater to imagine; reanimating a human body with a finite timeline was.

Cabeswater did its best to show him the reality of this, though nuance was difficult with the ley line as worn down as it was. What little communication they could muster was only possible because the psychic's daughter was there with him, as she had always been there in some form, amplifying both Cabeswater and the magician.

What Cabeswater was trying to make them understand was that Cabeswater was about creation. Making. Building. It could not unmake itself for this sacrifice, because it was against its nature. It could not quite *die* to bring a human back just as before. It would have been easier to make a copy of the human who had just died, but they did not want a copy. They wanted the one they had just lost. It was impossible to bring him back unchanged; this body of his was irreversibly dead.

But it might be able to refashion him into something new.

It just had to remember what humans were like.

Images flashed from Cabeswater to the magician, and he whispered them to the psychic's daughter. She began to direct her mirror-magic at the trees that remained in Cabeswater, and she whispered *please* as she did, and the *tir e 'e'lintes* recognized her as one of theirs.

Then Cabeswater began to work.

Humans were such tricky and complicated things.

As it began to spin life and being out of its dreamstuff, the remaining trees began to hum and sing together. Once upon a time, their songs had sounded different, but in this time, they sang the songs the Greywaren had given to them. It was a wailing, ascending tune, full of both misery and joy at once. And as Cabeswater distilled its magic, these trees began to fall, one by one.

The psychic's daughter's sadness burst through the forest, and Cabeswater accepted that, too, and put it into the life it was building.

Another tree fell, and another, and Cabeswater kept returning again and again to the humans who had made the request. It had to remember what they felt like. It had to remember to make itself small enough.

As the forest diminished, the Greywaren's despair and wonder surged through Cabeswater. The trees sang soothingly back to him, a song of possibility and power and dreams, and then Cabeswater collected his wonder and put it into the life it was building.

And finally, the magician's wistful regret twisted through what remained of the trees. Without this, what was he? Simply human, human, human. Cabeswater pressed leaves against his cheek one last time, and then they took that humanity for the life it was building.

It was nearly human-shaped. It would fit well enough. Nothing was ever perfect.

Make way for the Raven King.

The last tree fell, and the forest was gone, and everything was absolutely silent.

Blue touched Gansey's face. She whispered, "Wake up."

EPILOGUE

June evenings in Singer's Falls were beautiful things. Lush and dark, the world painted in complicated greens. Trees: everywhere trees. Adam drove the winding road back to Henrietta in a slick little BMW that smelled of Ronan. The radio was playing Ronan's terrible techno, but Adam didn't turn it off. The world felt enormous.

He was going back to the trailer park.

It was time.

It was a thirty-minute drive from the Barns to the trailer park, so he had plenty of time to change his mind, to go back to St. Agnes or Monmouth Manufacturing instead.

But he drove past Henrietta to the trailer park, and then he drove down the long, bumpy drive to the trailers, his tyres kicking up a disintegrating thunderhead of dust behind him. Dogs leapt out to chase the car, vanishing by the time he arrived in front of his old home.

He didn't have to ask if he was really doing this.

He was here, wasn't he?

Adam climbed the rickety stairs. These stairs, once painted, now peeled and cracked, drilled with the perfectly round tracks of carpenter bees, weren't very different from the stairs up to his apartment above St. Agnes. Just fewer of them here.

At the top of the stairs, he studied the door, trying to decide if he should knock or not. It had not been that many months since he had lived here, coming and going without announcement, but it felt like it had been years. He felt taller than he had been when he had been here last, too, although he surely couldn't have grown that much since the summer before.

This was not his real home any more, so he knocked.

He waited, hands in the pockets of his pressed khaki slacks, looking at the clean toes of his shoes and then up again at the dusty door.

The door opened, and his father stood there, eye to eye with him. Adam felt a little more kindly to the past version of himself, the one who had been afraid of turning out like this man. Because although Robert Parrish and Adam Parrish didn't look alike at first glance, there was something introverted and turned-inward about Robert Parrish's gaze that reminded Adam of himself. Something about the knit of the eyebrows was similar, too; the shape of the furrow between them was precisely the shape of the continued difference between what life was supposed to be and what life was actually like.

Adam was not Robert, but he could have been, and he forgave that past Adam for being afraid of the possibility.

Robert Parrish stared at his son. Just behind him, in the dim room, Adam saw his mother, who was looking past Adam to the BMW.

"Invite me in," Adam said.

His father lingered, one nostril flaring, but he retreated back into the house. He turned a hand in a sort of mocking invitation, a gesture of pretend fealty to a false king.

Adam stepped in. He had forgotten how compressed their lives were here. He had forgotten how the kitchen was the same as the living room was the same as the master bedroom, and on the other side of the main room, Adam's tiny bedroom. He could not blame them for resentfully carving out that space; there was no other place to be in this house that was not looking at each other. He had forgotten how claustrophobia had driven him outside as much as fear.

"Nice of you to call," his mother said.

He always forgot how she used to drive him out, too. Her words were a more slippery kind of assault, sliding out of his memory more easily than his father's actual blows, sliding in between the ribs of that younger Adam when he wasn't paying attention. There was a reason why he had learned to hide alone, not with her.

"I missed you at graduation today," Adam replied evenly.

"I didn't feel welcome," she said.

"I asked you to come."

"You made it ugly."

"Wasn't me who made it ugly."

Her eyes glanced off him, most of her vanishing at the first sign of active conflict.

"What do you want, Adam?" his father asked. He was still staring at Adam's clothing, as if he thought that it might be what had changed. "I don't guess it's because you're begging to move back in, now that you're all graduated and fancy and driving your boyfriend's beemer."

"I came to see if there was any possibility of having a normal relationship with my parents before I leave for college," Adam replied.

His father's mouth worked. It was hard to tell if he was shocked by the content of Adam's statement, or just by the fact of Adam's voice at all. It was not a thing that had been heard often in this room. It was perplexing to Adam how he had regarded this as normal for so long. He remembered how the neighbours used to turn away from his bruised face; he used to think, stupidly, that they said nothing because they thought he had somehow deserved it. Now, though, he wondered how many of them had huddled on the floor in front of their sofas, or hidden in their rooms, or cried beneath the little porch in the bitter rain. He felt a sudden urge to save all these other Adams hidden in plain view, though he didn't know if they would listen to him. It struck him as a Gansey or a Blue impulse, and as he held that tiny, heroic spark in his mind, he realized that it was only because he believed that he had saved himself that he could imagine saving someone else.

"You were the one who made this impossible," his father said. "You're the one who made this ugly, just like your mother said."

He seemed petulant to Adam now, not fearsome. Everything about his body language, shoulders curled like a fern, chin tucked, indicated that he would no sooner hit Adam than he would hit his boss. The last time he had raised a hand to his son, he'd had to pull a bloody thorn out of it, and Adam could see the disbelief of that moment still registering in him. Adam was other. Even without Cabeswater's force, he could feel it glimmering coolly in his eyes, and he did nothing to disguise it. Magician.

"It was ugly way before then, Dad," Adam replied. "Do you know I can't hear out of this ear? You were talking over me in the courtroom when I said it before."

His father made a scornful noise, but Adam interrupted him. "Gansey took me to the hospital. That should've been you, Dad. I mean, it shouldn't have happened at all, but if it had really been an accident, it should have been you in the room with me."

Even as he said the words that he'd wanted to say, he couldn't believe that he was saying them. Had he ever talked back to his father and been certain he was right? And been able to look him right in the eye the entire time? He couldn't quite believe that he was not afraid: His father was not frightening unless you were already afraid.

His father blustered and put his hands in his pockets.

"I'm deaf in this ear, Dad, and that was you."

Now his father looked at the floor, and that was how Adam knew that he believed him. It was possible that was the only thing Adam had actually needed out of this meeting: his father's averted eyes. The certainty that his father knew what he had done.

His father asked, "What do you want from us?"

On the way over, Adam had considered this. What he truly wanted was to be left to his own devices. Not by his actual father, who could no longer truly intrude on Adam's life, but by the idea of his father, a more powerful thing in every way. He replied, "Every time I can't tell where someone's calling me from in a room and every time I smash my head into the side of the shower and every time I accidentally start to put my earbuds in both ears, I think about you. Do you think there can be a future when that's not the only time I think about you?"

He could tell from their faces that the answer to this was not likely to be yes anytime soon, but that was all right. He hadn't come with any expectations, so he was not disappointed.

"I reckon I don't know," his father replied finally. "You've grown up into someone I don't like very much, and I'm not afraid to say it."

"That's fair," Adam said. He didn't much care for his father, either. Gansey would've said *I appreciate your honesty*, and Adam borrowed from that memory of polite power. "I appreciate your honesty."

His father's face indicated that Adam had just illustrated his point perfectly.

His mother spoke up. "I'd like you to call. I'd like to know what you're doing."

She lifted her head, and the light through the window made a perfect square of light on her glasses. And just like that, Adam's thoughts flashed along time, his logic following the same channels his psychic sense used. He could see himself knocking, her standing on the other side of the door, not answering. He could see himself knocking, her standing around the back of the trailer, holding her breath until he was gone. He could even see himself calling, and the phone ringing as she held it in her hands. But he could also see her opening the college brochure. He could see her clipping his name out of a newspaper. Putting a photo of him in his smart jacket and nice trousers and easy smile on the fridge.

At some point she had released him, and she didn't want him back. She just wanted to see what happened.

But that was all right, too. It was something. He could do that. In fact, that was probably all he could do.

He knocked on the cabinet beside him, once, thoughtful, and then he took out the BMW keys. "I'll do that," he said.

He waited just a moment longer, giving them the opportunity to fill the space, to exceed expectation.

They did not. Adam had set the bar at precisely the height they could jump and no higher.

"I'll let myself out," he said.

He did.

On the other side of Henrietta, Gansey and Blue and Henry were just climbing out of the Pig. Henry was last out, as he had been riding in the back, and he squeezed out from behind the passenger seat as if he were being calved. He shut the door and then frowned at it.

"You have to slam it," Gansey said.

Henry shut it.

"Slam it," Gansey repeated.

Henry slammed it.

"So violent," he said.

They were here in this remote location because of Ronan. He had given them vague instructions that afternoon – apparently, they were on a scavenger hunt for Blue's graduation gift. She'd been out of school for weeks, and Ronan had implied that a gift was waiting, but he'd refused to relinquish directions to it until Gansey and Henry had also graduated. *You're meant to use it together,* he had said, ominously. They'd asked him to come – both to graduation, and on this scavenger hunt – but he replied merely that both locations were full of bad memories for him, and he'd see them on the other side.

So now they walked down a dirt drive towards a dense tree line that hid everything beyond it from their view. It was pleasantly warm. Insects made themselves cosy in the teens' shirts and around their ankles. Gansey had the sense of doing this before, but he couldn't tell if he had or not. He knew now that the feeling of time-slipping that he'd lived with for so long was not a product of his first death, but rather his second. A by-product of the bits and bobs Cabeswater had assembled to give him life again. Humans were not meant to experience all times at once, but Gansey had to do it anyway.

Blue reached over to take his hand as they walked, and they swung this knot of their fingers between them merrily. They were free, free, free. School was over and summer stretched before them. Gansey had bid for a gap year and won; Henry had already planned on one. It was all convenient, as Blue had spent months planning how to cheaply hike across the country post-graduation, destination: life. It was better with company. It was better with three. Three, Persephone had always said, was the strongest number.

Now they broached the tree line and found themselves in a massive overgrown field of the sort that was not uncommon in this part of Virginia. The furry lamb's ears was getting tall already among the grass; the thistles were still short and sneaky.

"Oh, Ronan," Gansey said, although Ronan was not there to hear it, because he had just realized where Ronan's directions had taken them.

The field was filled with cars. They were all mostly identical. They were all mostly a little strange in one way or another. They were all mostly white Mitsubishis. The grass growing up around them and the pollen clouding their windshields made the scene rather apocalyptic.

"I don't want any of these for our great American road trip," Henry said with distaste. "I don't care if it's free and I don't care if it's magical."

"Concur," said Gansey.

Blue, however, seemed unconcerned. "He said there was one here that we'd know was for us."

"You knew it was a car?" Gansey demanded. He'd been unable to get the smallest of hints from Ronan.

"I wasn't going to follow his directions without any information at all," Blue retorted.

They waded through the grass, locusts whirring up before them. Blue and Henry were intently searching, comparing the vehicles. Gansey was dawdling, feeling the summer evening fill his lungs. It was this widening gyre of his path that brought him to the graduation gift. "Guys, I found it."

It was the obvious outlier: a furiously orange old Camaro parked in the midst of all the new Mitsubishis. It was so obviously identical to the Pig that Ronan must have dreamt it.

"Ronan thinks he's so funny," Gansey said as Blue and Henry made their way to him.

Henry picked a tick off his arm and threw it into the field to suck on someone else. "He wants you guys to drive matching cars? That seems sentimental for a man without a soul."

"He told *me* that it had something I'm gonna love under the hood," Blue said. She prowled round to the front and fumbled for the hood release. Hefting it open, she began to laugh.

They all peered inside, and Gansey laughed too. Because inside the engine bay of this Camaro was *nothing*. There was no engine. No inner workings. Just empty space clear down to the grass growing by the tyres.

"The ultimate green car," Gansey said, at the same time that Henry said, "Do you think it really runs?"

Blue clapped her hands and jumped up and down; Henry snapped a picture of her doing it, but she was too cheerful to make a face at him. Skipping around to the driver's side, she got in. She was barely visible over the dash. Her smile was still enormous. Ronan was going to be sorry he'd missed it, but Gansey understood his reasons.

A second later, the engine roared to life. Or rather, the car roared to life. Who knew what was even making the sound. Blue made a ridiculous whooping sound of glee.

The year stretched out in front of them, magical and enormous and entirely unwritten.

It was marvellous.

"Do you think it ever breaks down?" Gansey shouted over the sound of the not-engine.

Henry began to laugh.

"This is going to be a great trip," he said.

Depending on where you began the story, it was about this place: the long stretch of mountain that straddled a particularly potent segment of the ley line. Months before, it had been Cabeswater, populated by dreams, blooming with magic. Now it was merely an ordinary Virginia forest, green thorns and soft sycamores and oaks and pine trees, everything slender from the effort of growing through rock.

Ronan guessed it was pretty enough, but it was no Cabeswater.

Off along one of the banks, a scrawny hooved girl crashed merrily through the undergrowth, humming and making disgusting chewing noises. Everything in the forest was interesting to her, and interesting meant tasting it. Adam said she was a lot like Ronan. Ronan was going to choose to take that as a compliment.

"Opal," he snapped, and she spat out a mouthful of mushroom. "Stop dicking around!"

The girl galloped to catch up with him, but she didn't pause when she reached him. She preferred to form a lopsided perimeter of frantic activity around his person. Anything else might give the appearance of willing obedience, and she would do a lot to avoid that.

Up ahead, Chainsaw shouted, *"Kerah!"*

She kept hollering until Ronan had caught up with her. Sure enough, she had found something out of place. He kicked through the leaves. It was a metal artefact that looked centuries old. It was the wheel off a 1973 Camaro. It matched the ancient, impossible wheel they'd found on the ley line months earlier. Back then, Ronan had taken that to mean that at some point in the future, they would wreck the Camaro in the pursuit of Glendower, and the ley line's bending of time would have sent them back in time and then forward again. All times being the same-ish on the ley line.

But it looked as if they hadn't got to that place yet: They had future adventures waiting for them on the ley line.

It was a thrilling and terrifying prospect.

"Good find, brat," he told Chainsaw. "Let's go home."

Back at the Barns, Ronan thought about all the things he liked and didn't like about Cabeswater, and what he would do differently if he was to manifest it now. What would give it more protection against a threat in the future, what would make it better able to connect with other places like Cabeswater on the line, what would make it a truer reflection of himself.

Then, holding these things in his head, he climbed up on to the roof and gazed up at the sky.

Then he closed his eyes and he began to dream.

ACKNOWLEDGEMENTS

The Raven Cycle has been in the making for over ten years, and countless people have helped me in one way or another. This section, by necessity, will be terribly inadequate.

First I must thank the knights: Tessa Gratton and Brenna Yovanoff, ever willing to do battle with my dragons. Sarah Batista-Pereira, you killed dragons I didn't even see coming. Court Stevens, thank you for handing me a new sword at the end of the day.

The glittering court: Laura Rennert, my passionate agent, and Barry Eisler, her consort. David Levithan, my editor, who gave me the best gift an author could ask for: time. Rachel Coun, Lizette Serrano, Tracy van Straaten, a witchy trio of professional seers. Becky Amsel, cacao for ever.

The family: Particularly my parents, who built me a castle of books. Also Erin, who showed me how to make armour.

The true love: Ed, I'm sorry it's always a battle. Sort of sorry. Sorry-not-sorry. Look, you knew what you were getting into when you pulled that sword out of that stone. I'm always grateful to have you by my side.

ABOUT THE AUTHOR

Maggie Stiefvater's life decisions have revolved around
her inability to be gainfully
employed. Talking to yourself,
staring into space, and coming
to work in your pyjamas
are frowned upon when
you're a waitress, calligraphy
instructor, or technical editor
(all of which she's tried),
but are highly prized traits
in novelists and artists (she's
made her living as one or the
other since she was twenty-
two). Maggie now lives a
surprisingly eccentric life in the middle of nowhere,
Virginia, with her charmingly straight-laced husband,
two kids, and multiple neurotic dogs.

L♥ve Maggie

www.maggiestiefvater.com
@mstiefvater